ONCE WITHIN A DREAM

By

S.L. Kassidy

www.desertpalmpress.com

A Desert Palm Press Trade Paperback Original

Once Within a Dream is a work of fiction. Names, characters, places, and incidents are either the product of the author's imagination or are used in a fictitious manner. Any resemblance to actual persons living or dead, business establishments, events, or locales is entirely coincidental. Internet references contained in this work are current at the time of publication, but Desert Palm Press cannot guarantee that a specific reference will continue or be maintained in any respect.

All other rights are reserved. Desert Palm Press supports copyright which enables creativity, free speech, and fairness. Thank you for buying the authorized version of this book and for following copyright laws by not using or reproducing any part of this book in any manner whatsoever, including Internet usage, without written permission from Desert Palm Press, except in the form of brief quotations embodied in critical reviews and articles. Your cooperation and respect support authors and allow Desert Palm Press to continue to publish the books you want to read.

For permission requests, write to the publisher at publisher@desertpalmpress.com or "Attention: Permissions Coordinator" at

Desert Palm Press
4804 NW Bethany Blvd, Suite I-2, #148
Portland, OR 97229
www.desertpalmpress.com

Copyright © 2025 by S.L. Kassidy

ISBN: 978-1-95421-398-2
E-Book: 978-1-95421-399-9

Editing: Raven's Eye
Formatting: Anne Battis
Cover Design: Jamani Hawkins-El

Printed in the United States of America
First Edition December 2025

Dedication

This book is dedicated to my father. There are no words to explain his impact on my life and in my writing. He instilled this desire to write in me, read my work with an enthusiasm that hyped me up enough to keep me going, and always encouraged me to continue writing. This is my first novel that he won't be able to read. But he's still keeping me going, and this work will continue, thanks to him.

Chapter One

The Stuff of Nightmares

"IT'S RAINING AGAIN." SAMAR gave a heavy sigh as she leaned against a short, black, cast-iron fence. She was soaked, despite the rain jacket and supposedly waterproof boots. Her socks were drenched. Even her hood let her down, stuck to her short hair with wetness.

A passerby might have assumed she was talking to herself or at the very least to the air. Her words were directed to the empty mausoleum in front of her. Well, to the tomb inside the mausoleum. Probably not much better.

Samar couldn't help staring at the beautiful structure every time she walked by. This little slice of home kept calling out to her in this dark, dirty, and crowded city. The sun never came out, and it rained almost all of the time in Oganja. If it wasn't raining, then it was foggy or cloudy. Oganja was depressing.

The tomb's polished white stone was the opposite of the city's gloom. Ancient, so it stood out in the modern city. Not to mention, so far from where it belonged, an ocean away, a millennium away.

The square base of the small building rose about ten feet before transforming into a triangular shape. The structure was like a pyramid with the top cut off. Small squares appeared like windows on each side of the building. A path cut through the white wall, circling the building, and led to the front door of the tomb.

The building and wall were covered with faded red markings. Scenes of a woman with a baby in her arms seemed to be floating or flying above a man, who looked up with a smile. The pictures were probably restored. The same with the many statues perched on the wall, which looked almost perfect, despite the fact the building was thousands of years old. It was as if someone had abandoned it in this wretched city not too long ago.

"I see how this place inspired you, Mom." Samar sighed. The tomb spoke of the architecture of her homeland, Asale.

No one knew why the tomb was even in the city. They just knew it already existed by the time Oganja came around. Some people refused to believe it was thousands of years old because it didn't look its age. The building seemed untouched by time. Supposedly impossible to destroy, a legend said it had survived natural disasters and horrible wars through the years.

Samar's mom spent her life trying to solve the mystery of the building's origin. Researching took her all the way across the ocean to Nuri. She learned so much about Asale's history and the many migration periods of them coming to this continent, this country. Unfortunately, she died with no answers for the tomb, only theories.

Stories in Asale, fading myths, claimed the tomb was built by Goddess Asiku, the embodiment of night. It was possibly for her mortal love, Fajiri, who was slain by her jealous husband, Usuku, the Day. A marble sarcophagus gave the only evidence it was even a tomb.

No body or human remains were in the coffin though. Plenty of people had checked over the years. Her mother was one of those people. Fine, black sand filled the sarcophagus, as if someone crushed up pure onyx. As far as the city was concerned, the tomb was merely an out-of-place, rather old, building in their home.

Samar felt a connection to the tomb. It called to her and reminded her of home, her mother, and of better times than her three years in Oganja. She often shared her thoughts with the building. She didn't have any friends, didn't desire any. She was quite out of place, much like the building. She lived in the city, but it wasn't her home. She didn't even like the city.

Samar was relocated to the city. She had lived with her mother until three years ago. That life seemed so long ago, so distant. Three years ago, she had only read about cities, never seeing one in person. Three years ago, she was able to breathe fresh air. Three years ago, she saw the sun almost every day.

"I used to have color three years ago," Samar muttered with a shake of her head. She was washed out like everyone else in Oganja. Her once rich and shining copper complexion was dull.

The rain picked up. *I should probably put a move on it*. "I swear, I don't know how these people do it," Samar mumbled.

She gripped the gate with her right hand, a sharp chill shot through her palm, then patted the iron. She bumped her fists together as a show of respect for Asale before tucking her hands back into her warm pockets. She said farewell to the tomb and walked off.

Her black combat boots smacked loudly against the drenched concrete of the sidewalk as she escaped. The streets in this area tended to be empty. The crowds gathered on the popular avenues with trendy boutiques, shows and art things, despite the rain and the time.

Samar turned the corner as she came to the end of the block and entered the large city park—Okunkun. She frequented the place, not just for work like now. She spent much of her time at the park before being forced into this job. Okunkun also called to her, but in a different way than the tomb. She scanned the dangerous area before venturing deeper inside.

Samar sighed as she circled the park once and nothing happened. She was thankful in a way, but she was also bored. *Perhaps I've made a bit of a difference.* She doubted that. Darkness, like light, was never truly diminished. One came and the other left, until the first returned.

She scanned the park again before flinging herself onto a wet park bench. Two teenage boys sat down next to her a few minutes later, and she almost laughed. *And here it is. I thought everyone was inside thanks to the rain.* Of course, the rain was far from an excuse for anyone in the city to stay inside. Nightmares loved that.

"Hey, babe, what're you doing out so late all by yourself?" the boy to her right inquired. The bent rim of a baseball cap hid his eyes. His mouth was covered by the bottom half of a painted balaclava. The clown lips were a nice touch.

Samar didn't reply, but the sacred band around her arm pulsed. The black cloth tightened around her wrist a bit. These boys had Nightmares. Then again, most of the people she ran into in the park at this time did. Oganja was infested with them.

"Looking for a little party, baby? We could all have a little party," the boy to her left suggested. A grey hood covered his head, drenched by the rain, but his face was on full display.

"Yeah, let's have a little party," Clown Mask agreed.

Samar glanced at the boys out of the corners of her blue-grey eyes. They looked like they were about fifteen or sixteen years old. They didn't appear well-built by any measure, but they were probably armed, making up for the lack of muscle. Plus, they were armed with Nightmares. Neither of them carried any brains though.

"They make you feel strong, don't they?" Samar asked.

"We are strong," Grey Hood boasted with a grin.

The boys hopped up, eyes clouded like the night sky. Samar remained silent, as both boys grabbed her by her jacket and yanked her to her feet. She didn't put up any resistance. She rolled her shoulders, then her neck. Time to work.

"We've danced like this for three years now, and none of you recognize me yet," Samar said. Nightmares supposedly had more sense than that, but she had yet to meet one that thought beyond being a parasite to humans.

They squinted at her, but no recognition registered. At least they understood her. Her first year here, everyone pretended her accent was so thick that she avoided speaking the language.

Clown Mask draped his arm around Samar's shoulders, letting his hand rest on her breast. She glanced at him and then at Grey Hood, their guns slightly tucked into their belts. *If I'm fast enough, I could be rid of the Nightmares and then deal with these idiots on their own.*

She was confident the boys would give her a reason to take them off the street tonight, even without the Nightmares. After all, they already had evil intentions, which was why the Nightmares attached to them and more than likely why they agreed to host the Nightmares. She'd never leave them alone to find another woman to party with.

"You sure you want to party with me?" Samar asked, her voice naturally low, husky.

Clown Mask wrapped around her and leered. "Let's find a good place to have some fun." He stroked her chest.

Do this fast. Get one out of the way. Samar snapped her fingers and a blessed Favor materialized in her hand with a waft of smoke. The rain soaked through the playing card-sized paper, but it would still do its job.

With as little movement as possible, Samar tried to press the Favor onto Clown Mask's forehead. He pulled back just in time. He hissed at her, yanked his mask down, and stretched his mouth an impossible amount with a mighty roar. His teeth grew into fangs for a moment.

"Oh, please, come out and play." Samar made a fist, cracking her knuckles, as the Favor morphed into her short spear—Amani. The twenty-inch blade was pure black, embedded with holy symbols, with the shaft carved from the wood of the ofo tree. A Nightmare's nightmare.

Lightning crackled from both boys and out came their Nightmares, bursting forth from their necks like sizzling pimples of pure tar. Yellow and orange energy flared from gaping maws of unadulterated blackness, with claws and glowing golden eyes to match. She held up her spear, white light glinting from the symbols, and the Nightmares roared before rushing back into the boys' bodies.

Clown Mask snickered. "Now, you've pissed us off."

"It's about to get much worse," Samar said, a promise in her voice, and rushed the pair.

Once Within a Dream

Samar slashed with her spear, going after Grey Hood to sever the Nightmare from him. He moved with the speed expected of someone hosting a Nightmare. She cut the air between them and nothing more. He smirked, pleased with his abilities. His partner fell to her side and landed a punch to her cheek, pushing her back.

They're getting stronger. Three years ago, not a single Nightmare would've been able to lay a hand on her. It didn't matter. Nightmares would return to the Abyss as long as she was around.

Samar righted her footing, as Clown Mask tried to assault her further. She dodged several other punches. Grey Hood came up from behind and kicked her legs out from underneath her. A grunt escaped her mouth as she hit the wet ground. She spun into a kick to keep them away.

The boys jumped back, but their Nightmares shot out at Samar. *Work fast.* She sliced at an arm with her spear. The Nightmare wailed as half its arm sizzled, fading into the chilled night air. The other Nightmare rushed her, and she ducked several shadowy barbs from its limb. Springing back up, she cut through that limb.

She went back at the boys, her Favor in her free hand. She tried to press it to Clown Mask's head, but he sidestepped her with his damned super speed. He pushed her off balance and the Nightmares turned, lightning blasting from their eyes. She gripped her spear and blocked as she muttered a chant.

The sacred markings on her spear blade blew white smoke, fuming with the scent of holy oil—a mix of jasmine and rose. The lightning was sucked into the symbols. She ran forward, cutting through one Nightmare. It screeched like a dying owl, dissipating in a gathering of crackling embers. Clown Mask fell back, as his Nightmare retreated into him.

Taking advantage of Clown Mask being off balance, Samar was on him and attached the Favor to his forehead. He hunched over and roared, as a yellow and orange liquid poured from his eyes, ears, nostrils, and mouth. He took a knee and, mind whirling, she turned her attention to Grey Hood.

Her boots pounded through a puddle as she bolted at Grey Hood. He leaped back to avoid her and his Nightmare shrieked at her, lightning shooting from its mouth. She took the hit with her spear, propelling forward even as the force of the lightning pushed her back.

"I'm not that easy," she said with a growl, forcing more holy oil from her spear.

The lightning dissipated and she rushed forward. Grey Hood and his Nightmare fell back as rapidly as they could. Samar flung her spear, her sacred cloth swirling behind it as it flew. She caught the Nightmare through its open mouth. The Nightmare screamed while Samar kept coming. She rushed into Grey Hood, yanking her spear back to the cloth tether. It vanished as soon as it touched her hand.

Grey Hood gasped and tried to move to the side, not realizing his speed was disturbed thanks to the pained Nightmare. He tripped over his own two feet. She wasted no time materializing another Favor in hand and tapped it to his forehead. His body shook and he screamed as yellow-orange gunk melted from every orifice in his face.

Clown Mask spit, recovered from the loss of his Nightmare. "We don't need those damn things to deal with you." He moved to grab his gun, but without a Nightmare, he was too slow.

Samar shook her head and was on Clown Mask with a speed he couldn't comprehend. She took his hand, turned him around, and banged his chest against the nearby bench. He coughed in dire agony, while she removed his gun from his belt. He groaned as she handcuffed him to the park bench. *His friend should be doing something stupid right about now.*

She aimed the gun at Grey Hood as she stepped away from the one she'd trapped. She smiled. Grey Hood aimed his gun at her, his hand steady. Had he done this before? Not in this park. Never again in this park.

"How the hell did you do that?" Grey Hood demanded. The question was too vague. What did he refer to? How easily she had taken down his friend in one swift move? Not to mention, how quickly she had turned to him and had that gun pointed at him? Or maybe how she had exorcised their Nightmares? Or even, how she successfully fought their Nightmares? Hell, saw their Nightmares? So many questions she'd never have the answer to.

"Drop your weapon or I'll have to take it from you," Samar warned him with a smile. She wanted to take it from him. He deserved it for working with that damn Nightmare.

His eyes flashed with raw anger, easily seen in the dim park lights. "Who the fuck are you?"

"Just a girl looking for a party."

Grey Hood took a deep breath, which was all the time Samar needed to disarm him. She sprang and grabbed his arm that held the gun. She forced his limb around his back and ripped his pistol from his grip. She closed another pair of handcuffs around his wrist and then pushed him to the ground. With a short reach, she handcuffed him to his friend.

"What the fuck is going on here?" both boys demanded.

"My park, fellas. You're under arrest." Samar shrugged.

"What's the charges?" Clown Mask huffed.

"Well, I don't really like you and your friend starting trouble in my park, so that's strike one. Not to mention, I don't think you two have licenses for these weapons." She placed the guns down on the far end of the bench. "You also menaced me and sexually harassed me, which I don't care about. You're cluttering up my park. I wish I could charge you with general stupidity." Allowing a Nightmare in was never a smart move. The Nightmare would consume its host until the host was nothing more than their basest desires.

"Yo, you're not a fucking cop!"

"I'm not? This badge says otherwise." Samar flashed her badge before putting it back into her pants pocket.

Technically, she wasn't a cop. She was a contracted agent with a special organization, but she had all the powers of a police officer. She was more than able and authorized to make arrests.

Samar sighed and took a seat on the park bench. Leaning back, she allowed the rain to pour onto her face. "Enjoying the rain, guys?" She hated it. She hated how constant it was.

"Fuck you."

Samar nodded, not surprised by that answer. "How'd you like hosting those Nightmares?"

"We'll get more and kick your ass!"

"I'm doubtful. I marked you. No more Nightmares for you." She sighed again. She still had rounds to make, and the rain didn't seem to be letting up.

There were also more Nightmares in her future, but she'd signed up for that. Technically, she'd signed up for this too. She was less pressured to fight Nightmares though.

She called in the arrest. Her charges were picked up. Her body camera footage was downloaded. Unfortunately, Nightmares didn't appear on film, so she didn't bother addressing that. Not like the boys would bring them up. Even if they did, most people wouldn't believe them. Most people couldn't see Nightmares until they bothered to host one.

With the boys gone, Samar still had hours left in her patrol of the park. With luck, more hoodlums would keep her entertained. There'd certainly be more Nightmares, as always in her park. They liked this area the most.

Samar was only a beat agent for a private security agency that worked with Oganja law enforcement. She patrolled the park and areas immediately outside the park. She had most goons frightened to be in the park at night, but then some were emboldened by Nightmares.

Nightmares were rampant in Oganja. They latched onto humans already planning a wrong and helped them commit that wrong with supernatural assistance. They were meant to torment humanity, as if humanity didn't torment itself enough. Of course, their existence took that into account, as Nightmares were only present to help make wrongdoing easier. The effect was addictive to humans.

Samar's thumb rubbed against her hand wrap. The blessed cloth that assisted her with fighting Nightmares, helping identify Nightmares, even though she saw them plain as day. Not the norm though. The sacred cloth made it easier to summon the one weapon she had, Amani. Samar didn't carry a gun, neither for her work nor her hobby of battling Nightmares. She made the park safe and did the best that one person could do while lacking an arsenal.

If she got into trouble, the closest agent to her was well over a minute away and that was if he ran over to her area at his top speed. So, in theory, she could be shot and dying by the time he arrived to aid her. She didn't mind the danger.

She had trained to fight Nightmares, and those skills transferred to fighting humans since Nightmares infected humans. She wanted to battle Nightmares, but she mostly did this agent job through blackmail. At least the job had good benefits. Not that she'd known what the hell that meant until this job was forced upon her.

The rain continued through the night. A few other Nightmares wandered into her path. They were attached to gang members. She was used to that. She single-handedly wiped out one gang that controlled the park when she first showed up on this beat. Every now and then, new gangs would show up, trying to take it back from her. It would never happen.

As the sun filtered through the grey clouds and made things a little lighter, morning made its way through as best it could. Samar's shift was up. She was tired and soaked down to the bone.

People entered the park, walking their dogs and having morning jogs as the rain lifted. Samar staggered out of the park, drenched like a drowned rat. Jogging over a mile back to the modern, hard-angled building of headquarters shook off some of the rainwater. She dodged through a crowd of agents coming in for work, retreating into a corner office on the sixth floor. She flung herself into a wooden chair that awaited her.

The warmth of the office was heaven-sent after a chilled night in the downpour. The soft smell of lemongrass settled her. Her body learned to accept the scent as a sign to relax.

"Tough night?" Evinia chirped from the hallway.

Samar scoffed as her half-sister stepped into view. Most people would never guess they were related, let alone sisters. Well, they shared a father, who gifted them both smoky, blue-grey eyes.

Older and taller than Samar, Evinia's wavy, dark-brown hair reached her shoulders with tips bleached blond. She wore thin, wire-framed glasses, due to being quite near-sighted. With a navy-blue sweater and form-fitting blue jeans, Evinia dressed much more "adult" than Samar. Not exactly professional, but their father never brought it up. Most importantly, she was warm and friendly, allowing people to refer to her as Vinnie or Vin. And she almost always had a smile.

"Sammie, how's your park?" Evinia was always trying to get her talking.

Evinia complained about how difficult it was to have a conversation with Samar and often expressed worry that Samar was uncomfortable around her. It wasn't a horrible assumption, as they had only met three years earlier. Samar was a quiet person, and Evinia had trouble navigating this, even now.

"I thought they were out for sexual assault, but turns out drug dealers," Samar muttered with a shrug. The officers who processed her arrest of those teen boys found several baggies of suspected illegal substances.

"Drug dealers?" Evinia's full, dark red lips twisted up. "I can't believe people are still dealing drugs in your park. They must be new to the city because I know you have those hoods all scared of you." Evinia chuckled as she walked back a few steps to where her nameplate hung from the corner of a chipped desk.

She went through all of her computer equipment, looking for something. She was a techno-geek, or at least that was what everyone called her. Samar didn't quite understand the term. All she knew was that Evinia liked computers and could work one as if she had been born with a computer in her lap. Samar was unfamiliar with most technology. She might never be comfortable with it. She could barely handle her phone.

Evinia stared at her, expecting an answer. Samar shrugged. Nightmares meant she'd never be without trouble in her park. Fiends were emboldened by Nightmares. She once tried to explain it to Evinia, who laughed it off as folklore. She thought Samar was some backwater bumpkin who believed in myths and magic.

"How are you feeling, Sammie?" Evinia asked when too much silence passed between them.

Samar shrugged once more. She was miserable, as she always was and might always be. Evinia often tried to cheer her up. It wasn't possible. It had nothing to do with Evinia. In fact, Evinia understood Samar's vast, intense, endless sorrow. Evinia had also lost her mother.

"Did you go to the tomb again?" Evinia asked her sister, eyes now on her several computer monitors. She then looked under them.

Ah. "The case for your glasses is in your pocket," Samar said. Evinia always lost track of that thing once it was out of her hands.

Evinia patted her pockets and, sure enough, pulled out her slim case. "Oh, I thought this was something else. I forgot I dropped it off already. Anyway, that doesn't answer my question. Don't dodge."

"It's right there," Samar answered. The tomb was practically part of her beat and the only worthwhile place in this accursed city.

"I know that, but it's still not healthy." A wrinkle appeared through her tawny brow. "You can't just hang around a tomb whenever you're outside, then go beat up some drug dealers or gang bangers."

"I do it all the time, Vin," Samar pointed out, not following her sister's logic. That was almost her daily routine.

Evinia blew out a breath and rubbed her forehead. "I don't mean you *can't* do it, but you shouldn't do it. You're still a teenager for goodness' sake. You're nineteen. You need to go out to a club, meet some boys, go shopping, anything. Do something. Just stop hanging outside a tomb all the time."

Samar glanced away and tapped her index fingers together. "I want to go to school, like a normal nineteen-year-old." More than beating back the infestation of Nightmares in the city, she wanted to study…and go home.

Evinia sighed. "I'm sorry he won't just let you go. He has more than enough to let you be a student. Hell, most parents would be proud to know their daughter wants to go to college after high school."

"Not your fault." Their father wouldn't give her the money for college. She wasn't allowed control of her inheritance from her mother until she was twenty-one. So, for now, she did this. At least she made a difference and earned enough money to live on her own.

"Yes, but I don't approve of his methods, and he needs to know that."

"You tell him often."

"He needs to hear it often. Who the hell refuses to send their child to college, so she can work for their company and encounter dangerous people night in and night out? Our idiot father is who."

Samar shrugged. She didn't disagree, but she was also quite done with their father. She did her best not to give him too much thought.

"You really should give the tomb a rest though. It's not healthy," Evinia said.

There was a long moment of silence before Samar decided to answer, "I like the tomb."

"What do you mean? Sammie, what can you like about a tomb? It's just a building. It's a tomb."

"I know, but it reminds me of home. It reminds me of me. It fits, but it doesn't fit," Samar explained as best she could.

"How so?"

Samar stared at her sister before letting loose a deep sigh. She leaned back in her chair and rubbed her eyes with her fists. This answer took more linguistic skill outside her native tongue than Samar could muster. Evinia had learned that tell.

She rolled over in her chair and put her hand on Samar's knee, not bothered by being close to someone soaked through and through. Samar hated how Evinia's touch warmed her, reminding her she was human.

"A tomb in a dark city like this, of course, it fits. It's a tomb, nice and morbid," Samar said.

"But it's such a beautiful building and that's why it doesn't fit, correct?" Evinia reasoned.

"Yeah, Vin."

"Still, I think it'd be better for you to stop hanging around it so much. It's a tomb, after all. What appeal can a tomb hold after a little while?" Evinia asked.

"I like it."

"I know you do, but I still think it'd be better if you stopped going to the tomb and started going out, like a teenager does. Change your shift. You don't need Dad's permission for that. Go to some clubs and do some shopping."

Samar wrinkled her nose. "I don't like shopping." The fact that most of her wardrobe was black sweatsuits was a testament to that.

Evinia sighed. "I know. I just worry about you so much. You're practically a hermit beyond this job. You've made me pull rank to get you to take a vacation, and I know you stayed inside all day for those."

"I've seen the city," Samar mumbled.

"I know. I'm the one who gave you the tour, quite a few times. You'd never leave the house if I didn't force you out shopping. Whenever you go out by yourself, you go right to the tomb. Again, it's not healthy."

"Can't admire architecture?"

"You're not admiring. Try to stay away from the tomb for a while. I don't like that you're obsessed with it," Evinia said.

"I'm not," Samar insisted.

"You visit the place at least once a night. Try to stay away from it for a couple of nights as a favor to me. Please?" Evinia poked out her lip. She looked ridiculous.

"Fine," Samar agreed with a groan.

Samar still wasn't quite accustomed to having a big sister. Evinia seemed to pride herself in the position. She often offered advice, trying her best to acclimate Samar to Oganja.

As for the comment on boys, their father didn't wish for her to even think about dating. She had little desire to go back and forth with him. Their father was a stern man on a good day. Evinia was the only one out of his three children who'd think to argue with him.

"You want to change out of your wet clothes? You have a change in your locker, right?" Evinia asked.

Samar shook her head and gnashed her teeth. "I never replaced my last pair." Evinia never reminded her. "I depend on you too much."

"Don't say that. You're my little sister. I want you to know you can depend on me. Maybe you should just go home and get some sleep, kid. You look a bit worn out."

Samar blew out a long breath. She often felt exhausted, weighed down with depression and boredom. The only time it lifted was while fighting Nightmares. She forgot her negative emotions during those moments and focused on the mission she'd accepted long ago.

"What time is it?" Samar inquired with a yawn. A weariness had seeped into her now that her sister mentioned it.

Evinia patted her knee again. "Time for you to go home and sleep. I'll handle your paperwork. You just head home and don't forget you agreed to stay away from that tomb for a few days."

Samar merely nodded and tore herself away from her chair. She yawned again and waved a lazy goodbye to her sister. She trudged out of the office and nearly bumped into Mechi. Samar had to be tired to miss such a tall and wide man. He gave her a bright smile, full of perfect teeth, and raised his hand in greeting. She ignored it and him. He wouldn't be offended, very aware she wasn't in the mood for any good mornings. She never was, not anymore. Maybe one day she'd get there again, but no time soon.

Chapter Two

An Awakening

"MECHI." EVINIA SMILED AS she looked up from her seat at her desk. She stood and embraced Mechi, as he stepped completely into the office.

She sighed against his chest, enjoying the press of his solid muscles under his plain, white shirt. It'd be soothing to stay there, but she had work to do. And not just her own.

"I just saw your creepy sister." Mechi wrapped his thick arms around Evinia's waist, prolonging their embrace, despite being at work. Their display was a little inappropriate, even in her private office.

"Don't call her creepy. She's lonely and sad." Although Evinia defended Samar, she didn't pull away from the big idiot. She had to work on how he interacted with Samar…still. He was an awesome guy, but Samar threw him. He had no idea what to do with her.

Mechi snorted. "I've seen lonely before, kitten. Samar isn't lonely. She's creepy. If she had milky skin, I'd say she's a vampire. I don't think I've ever seen her outside during the day. That's how creepy she is. If she were a vampire, she'd certainly be right at home around this town." He gave a small smile, amusing himself.

"Leave Sammie alone, you bully." Evinia stepped away from him and pinched his bicep.

"Ow!" Mechi flinched. "I'm just saying, you have to accept it eventually. It's who she is. It's not like I'm saying she's got a bone through her nose or something."

Evinia glared at him, and he threw his hands up. His dark, brown eyes flashed with regret. Being from Asale, Samar had to put up with a lot of ignorant comments like that, despite the fact the city had a large population of people of Asale descent. It was disgusting to hear what people thought of their ancestral homeland.

"I'm sorry. That was in poor taste," Mechi said.

"Glad you realize that."

"Yeah, that was gross. I'll figure out my rhythm with Samar one of these days."

"Yeah, calling her creepy and a vampire isn't the way to go. You don't know what she's been through. Her life fell apart when she was sixteen, and she still hasn't been able to piece it back together. The fact that she's standing and functioning should be admired." No one understood how strong Samar was. It was more than living after the death of her mother. It was being the one who found her mother, it was being the one who had to handle the burial, and it was being forced to leave the only home she had ever known to come across seas and live with strangers in a strange land that didn't understand her. A lesser person would've bashed their head through a wall a long time ago.

Mechi let out a long breath, rubbing his head and mussing his deep-russet waves. He was properly chastised for now. It'd stick for a few days, then they'd have to start all over again. "Are you ready to go?"

She gave him a soft smile before dropping back into her chair. "I've got some paperwork to do. Besides, I was thinking about going back to my apartment. It's been a week. I need to sleep, and my poor cat is either dead or never coming back again after such neglect."

"You and your cat," he said with a laugh.

"Don't make fun. You wouldn't dare neglect your cat, after all."

Mechi smiled, eyes twinkling. "No. After all, I love that she comes back every morning." He stepped closer and leaned down to kiss her lightly on the lips.

"I'll see you later," Evinia said as he pulled away.

His perfect teeth were on display, as his smile became a smirk. "I kind of figured you would."

"You cocky son of a bitch." She pinched his bicep again.

He laughed. "Whatever." He used his thumb and forefinger to frame his rich, bronze face. He was so damn handsome. "You know you love me no matter what. Let me go before your father comes in and hears us making plans. I swear that man would've killed me by now if he hadn't known me since I was a little kid."

"I think your indispensable skills help keep you alive."

Mechi scoffed. "Nah, sometimes I think he hates me more because I'm capable. Such a weird guy."

"I'm sure you're right," she agreed. Her father was definitely a weird guy and that was putting it nicely.

Mechi chuckled, even though they weren't joking. He kissed her again, much more passionately, as a farewell. She didn't object, enjoying the caress of his lips and tongue. It was definitely too much for work though.

They were both reluctant to leave the warmth of the other's mouth, but they had to do so very soon, and not to breathe either. They pulled away from each other when approaching footsteps echoed through the hall. Mechi darted out of the office. It was obvious who those footsteps belonged to. Her father was coming to check on his eldest child.

"Vinny," her father's voice boomed, even at a regular volume. It came from deep within his barrel chest, more than fitting for his six-and-a-half-foot frame. His strong jaw, wide shoulders, thick neck and powerful body made him an intimidating presence and the voice added to that. He was one of very few people taller than Mechi. With only a few inches difference, his massive presence towered over Mechi.

Her father's domineering presence was only helped by his jet-black, five-thousand-bukun suit with a thousand-bukun tie. The fabric was often compared to spun gold brought down from the heavens, which it might as well have been considering how rare it was. His style of dress advertised how he could afford to pay people to get rid of annoyances if he didn't want to sully his own hands, but his hard, blue-grey eyes always revealed he had no problem with sullying his hands. His eyes bore into anybody he stared down, including her.

"Hey, Daddy." Evinia flopped back down into her seat, while wondering what she had done with the case for her glasses yet again. *Didn't Sammie say where it was? What did she say again?* Trying to remember would eat at her brain until she found that case.

"Is your sister back?" her father inquired, scanning the small office.

Samar was often there and hard to miss. If he didn't see her from the door, she obviously wasn't there. Evinia kept that to herself. She wasn't in the mood for a fight. Of course, her father would give her a reason for one if he was his usual self.

"I sent her home. She was very tired," Evinia answered.

He frowned. "You shouldn't send her home when it's not your job. What about her reports? Did she report to her supervisor? I doubt it, as I'm sure she didn't have her reports to hand in."

Evinia fought the urge to roll her eyes. "She spoke to me through the night on our communication lines, and I have her body cam footage, so I can easily fill out her reports for her. It's not a big deal, and she needed to go." She shrugged. It wasn't like the forms were difficult, and Samar needed a break.

His strong jaw clenched. "You have to stop babying her, Vinny. I know you always wanted a little sister, but you got this one sixteen years too late. She's not a baby and you need to stop treating her like she is. Did you call your brother?"

Now Evinia scowled. "Explain this one to me, Daddy. Why is it I can't baby my little sister, who has been traumatized and had her life turned upside down, but I have to hold my little brother's hand through everything? He, for some reason, can't get out of bed without my help. He's seventeen years old for crying out loud. Must I seriously call him every morning to make sure he's awake and getting ready for school?" This didn't make any sense to her, and she tried not to think of why her father was this way.

"Yes," he plainly answered.

"So why is it I can't baby my little sister?" she persisted since Samar needed her much more than their brother, and their brother would agree with that.

"Because she's nineteen years old. She's not a baby anymore," he pointed out as if she didn't know that already.

"Daddy, she grew up on a mountain miles away from civilization. She'd met like four people in her entire life before us." This was an exaggeration, but Samar was very sheltered. Her entire life was spent in study, martial arts, history, languages, and several other things. This life she lived now had to be jarring, even three years later. Never mind the fact that her mother died, starting this terrible shift in her life.

"That was three years ago."

He was always on a mission to be obtuse with Samar. Evinia wouldn't accept that. Samar might not care about how he acted, but Evinia did.

"I want her to be comfortable with us. I want her to feel right," Evinia said. That was important.

Her father always acted like Samar was an undesirable, like his dalliance was her fault. She was the living embodiment of his dishonesty and lies, while he liked to present himself as a paragon of virtue. His inability to understand that his continued terrible treatment of Samar only proved he was never the man he presented himself to be boggled Evinia's mind.

"I want her to know we're her loving family despite just meeting three years ago." Evinia kept her tone soft with the hope it'd get through to her father this time. Of course, she could hit him with a sledgehammer and still never penetrate his thick skull when it came to Samar.

His nostrils flared, like he was pissed. The nerve of him. Samar didn't asked him to have an affair with her mother. It wasn't like Samar asked her mother to die and force her to live her remaining teenage years with a parent who clearly didn't want to acknowledge her existence. Samar was the innocent one here.

"Stop babying her," her father ordered again.

Evinia had received that order more times than she'd ever be able to count. She was expected to comply without an argument. This was the parenting style Siku Habeen inherited from his parents. Neither grandparent was fun, but thankfully, they were across the country.

Annoyed, Evinia would normally continue to express why she felt it was proper for her to treat Samar as she did, but she wanted to leave the office as soon as possible. She needed to avoid almost everything with her *charming* father. She'd save her arguments for the next time they got into a debate, which she was willing to bet would be soon. *Oh, maybe it'll be at a family gathering. So much fun.*

"Fine, Daddy, whatever. What can I help you with besides calling Alien?" Evinia asked. Being the oldest was quite irksome sometimes. Of course, she didn't blame her little Alien. It was their father's fault.

"You can call your brother, then you can tell Mechi if I catch him in here again, I'll strangle him with his small intestines. Oh, and when I call you today, you'd better be at home," her father stated as if his word was law. His words were barely language to her at this point.

"Yes, Daddy." Evinia sighed.

As her father left the office, Evinia made a mocking gesture with her hand and mouthed the words blah, blah, blah. Her father had radar when it came to her being with Mechi. He had once come to her apartment while she and Mechi were in a rather intimate situation and had stayed for a whole hour while Mechi hid in the bedroom. As her father was leaving, he commented it was a late hour and Mechi might want to get home before his shift at work started. Her father certainly was a jerk when he tried hard enough.

He was a control freak. Everything in his life had to go his way or there'd be hell to pay. He was especially that way with his three children. Evinia always pressed back, just enough to irk him. Then her mother died, and she developed a rather massive rebellious streak that only continued to grow.

Alvin was a different story. He did everything their father wanted. She wasn't sure if it was out of fear or out of hero worship. With luck, he'd grow out of it. He had so much potential to be something much more than their father if he'd just step out of the man's shadow. She and Mechi pointed out glimpses of that promise throughout Alvin's life, which he didn't yet acknowledge.

Then there was Samar, whose story wasn't promising at any angle. Samar tried to be indifferent to their father, but she was so scared of the man. He seemed to know and not care, as long as it got her to do what he desired, like using her skills in his security agency. He told her what to do and she did it, no fuss.

"He treats Sammie like a kid, but I'm not allowed to baby her. To hell with that." Evinia pulled up Samar's reports on a monitor and got to work. Alien, her nickname for her baby bro, was getting a chance to be responsible for himself. He had ten minutes to wake up on his own before she called and cursed him out.

Samar stumbled into her tiny, junky, cluttered, and rather filthy studio apartment. She kicked a small pile of dirty clothes out of the way. She punched the heavy bag she'd set up in the far corner. Pausing, she hit the bag a few more times out of habit. It was only a few steps to her bed after that.

She was tempted to collapse into bed, but she was soaked to the bone. Shower, then sleep. Turning around, she marched to the bathroom and started the shower. She unwrapped her sacred cloth, symbols flashing as she placed it on the sink. Holy symbols on her wrist flashed as well.

She peeled off the shirt clinging to her copper arms like a second skin. Her socks were wedded to her feet for longer than she liked. A pile of wet clothes on the floor, she hopped in the piping-hot shower.

Sighing, she pressed her hand against the tiles of the bathroom wall. She enjoyed the water for a few minutes, before scrubbing herself with the shea butter bodywash Evinia always bought her. Hanging up her washcloth, she grabbed for her shampoo. Might as well wash her hair since it got drenched like the rest of her.

Short, auburn curls were scrubbed, shampooed, and conditioned. Shower over, Samar brushed her teeth, then rewrapped her sacred cloth around her wrist. She made her way to her nightstand and donned a white, sleeveless t-shirt and black boyshorts before collapsing into bed. It was a long drop to the thin, futon mattress on a low platform. She landed on several pairs of sweatpants instead of her pillows.

"Gotta be cleaner, like Vinny says," she murmured, as she flung the pants somewhere behind her until they were all gone and her face met her pillow.

Holding her sacred wrap tight in her fist, Samar mumbled a prayer, then fell asleep without a problem. When she woke up, she checked the marks she'd made by her windows. All of those Favors were intact. She relit some incense, and wafts of jasmine smoke floated through the apartment. No chance of Nightmares creeping in to tempt her.

She ate a bowl of cold cereal for breakfast. It was late afternoon, but it was her first meal of the day. If she was *home*, breakfast would've been early in the morning, with porridge, fruit, and warm bread. She would've been eating lunch by now. She liked meat pies and sweet buns. She could find such foods around Oganja, but it wasn't the same. Which was why, three years later, they stayed on her mind.

About to add her spoon and bowl to the pile of dirty dishes in the sink, she scratched the back of her head. It'd be best for her to do the dishes before they started cultivating a new type of fungus. Afterward, she practiced her martial arts and beat up on her heavy bag for a few hours.

Samar made herself comfortable on her sofa and read an old history book from her mother's library. The sofa was higher off the floor than the furniture she was used to. It was a mark of the fixtures around Oganja and a constant reminder that she was far from home.

When she was done with reading, she had nothing. She was tempted to dress and visit the tomb. Unfortunately, she had promised Evinia she'd stay away from the tomb for at least a couple of days.

She intended to keep any promise she made to her sister. Evinia was trying to look out for her, and Samar would accept her sister's help to the best of her ability. It wasn't like anyone else cared about her. *Do I care about me?* She wasn't sure.

She'd like to prove to herself she wasn't obsessed with the tomb. She'd stay away from it for a little while. *Guess I'll start a new book.*

What happened? It was only a thought. Not sure where the thought came from, but more followed. *Why is it so quiet? Where is she?*

Kouji wasn't quite sure what any of this meant. She tried to move, but the motion didn't happen. She wasn't sure how she was aware she didn't move. She was unable to see herself. It was pitch black, but she felt herself, or something like herself. That mattered less than the deathly silence.

Once Within a Dream

Where is she? Kouji wasn't sure who "she" was. She was a voice, a friend, an ally. She was the only person to regularly remind Kouji she existed. She made Kouji feel like more than this void, more than the endless dream she was trapped in. Kouji couldn't continue to dream without that voice, without that presence. *Get up. Find her.*

Kouji strained the nothingness that was her form, anxiety scratching at unseen fibers of her being. She had to find the voice, had to make sure she was all right. *What if those Nightmares took hold of her? Then get up!*

A rumble sounded around Kouji, like stones rubbing against each other. A loud crash rang out, like an explosion, and light poured in. It hurt in the way light hurt eyes that had been closed for too long. Kouji blinked…maybe. She was able to see, but it was blurry with a bright light, and it didn't feel like her eyes.

She moved, holding up a hand that looked like a blob of black sand. *Wait, is that me?* She was a blob of black sand. *Pull yourself together, so you can find her.*

Staring at her hand, Kouji remembered her fingers and focused. Gritting teeth that existed only in her mind, she forced out digits. Then came dark, bronze limbs with golden bangles on each wrist and golden bands around her biceps.

Eyes made themselves known as the world came into focus. She ran a hand across the top of her head and black plaits fell into place down her back. Brushing sand from her cheeks, she felt flesh settle under her fingertips as her face took form. Finding her ears, she touched two small, gold-loop earrings. Ropes of beads clattered against her chest, pressing a dark-blue silk top against her chest.

She stood on numb and wobbly legs covered by familiar white, knee-length pants. Around her waist hung a sash of midnight blue adorned with a shining sun. A golden bangle wrapped around her left ankle above her bare foot.

She stared around the small room. *Why am I here?* No memories or explanations flashed through her mind, but a reason existed. She was sure of it, but her mind was cloudy. Before anything else, she needed to find the voice…*Samar. Her name is Samar.*

Stepping out of her sarcophagus, Kouji avoided the lid of her tomb, as the cold floor registered to her bare feet. She yawned and stretched. Her bones and muscles sang at the freedom to move. Being nothing hadn't sat well with any part of her. Well, now she could move.

As she scanned for an exit, she thought a statue at the far end of the small room followed her. But once she spotted the door, escape was the only thing that mattered. She marched out into the night and felt the tapping of light, warm rain. She held out her hand, catching raindrops.

"She was right," Kouji muttered with a smile. Feeling rain and knowing Samar hadn't lied made Kouji's heart light. The idea of Samar, of finally seeing her and bearing witness to this life she spoke about, made Kouji's heart thump.

"Kouji," a voice that seemed to be the wind but sounded suspiciously female to her ears said in a low voice. "Kouji," the voice floated past her once more.

Kouji ignored the voice, or the wind, whichever it happened to be. She walked off to the corner, scanning the dark and empty streets. It was quiet, but her skin prickled with a familiar buzz scratching on her nerves. *She said this place crawls with Nightmares and they make her teeth itch.*

The Nightmares were secondary. Kouji only knew what Samar told her. They were dangerous, empowered the wrong humans, and plagued this place. Kouji had faced worse—she thought—so Nightmares didn't matter.

Samar was the mission. *She said she patrols a park.* She wasn't too sure what a park was, but a noise in the distance got her attention. Her ears twitched and she jogged off in that direction. She passed metal gates and entered a wooded area with paved paths, like a garden. She came to the source of the noise. Samar was battling it out with four masked warriors and solid shadows, their Nightmares.

"I know those things," Kouji mumbled. She wasn't sure how she knew Nightmares beyond what Samar had told her. Her eyes stayed on Samar.

Kouji recognized Samar without ever having seen her before. Grunts and growls reached her ears as Samar fought. Kouji was familiar with every pitch of that voice, so the sounds were all she needed. Seeing Samar was grander than hearing her.

Samar was mesmerizing, moving with the grace of a dancer and fluidity like water, as she dispatched the Nightmares, terrifying living shadows. Her spear was an extension of her arm, and she pulled Favors from the air with the ease of a priestess. She worked through each warrior, severing their connection to their Nightmares. She focused on the warriors once they were alone.

Samar didn't use her spear on the warriors, who wielded knives and strange clubs. She disarmed them, dropped them, and chained them to a bench in uncomfortable positions. All without being touched. Kouji's breath hitched in her chest. *She's amazing.* She'd been aware of Samar's activities, but bearing witness was something so much more.

Kouji's body hummed, muscle memory echoing through her form. She'd fall in line with Samar and fight battles with her. She'd enjoy fighting a righteous war and doing something virtuous with these damned hands if she only had the chance.

Kouji went rigid as blue-grey eyes pierced through her. Kouji was frozen to the spot. *She wields such power over me.* Kouji would fall to her knees for Samar should she command it.

Samar scowled. "Who are you? You with them?" Samar nodded toward the dazed bandits cuffed to the benches.

Wow. Okay, it's her. Say words. Nothing came to mind. *I didn't think she'd be that incredible.* Kouji smiled, the expression small from insecurity. *You're better than this. How could you, of all people, be in such awe of someone that you're speechless?* There were no answers, and she was drenched in awe more than she was soaked from the rain.

"What're you doing in my park? You didn't come to cause trouble, did you? I hate that." Samar stance was guarded, ready for combat.

Speak, fool! Kouji opened her mouth, but only a cough came out. When was the last time she'd used her voice? Nothing came to mind. Was speaking an option now? For a moment, words failed her completely, even as thoughts. That was a moment too long for Samar, who was used to only encountering people seeking the wrong thing if they were in her park past midnight.

"Look, you're not causing any trouble right now, but I don't like the way you're dressed, and I don't like the looks of you. If you don't get out of my park right now and go somewhere else, I'm gonna have you taken in with this lot of scholars." Samar curled her lip.

Kouji took in the words and considered the scene she'd just witnessed. That might be the solution. She smirked and crouched down, beckoning Samar with a wave of her hand.

Samar raised a questioning auburn eyebrow. "You sure you want to do that? Not many people like to challenge me after they see me work, especially when they don't have Nightmares."

Kouji's smirk became a grin. She didn't need a Nightmare. She was a nightmare. *Now, if you might say that in response, we'd move forward.* She opened her mouth only to cough again.

"I hope you're not wasting both of our time. I have work to do," Samar said.

Kouji managed a laugh, suppressing a cough. Samar charged her and went to work right away, not holding back. Kouji's voice might've been useless, but the rest of her muscles were serviceable. She dodged lightning-fast punches with ease. It was hard to believe Samar was human.

Samar growled. "How are you doing this?"

Kouji shrugged and Samar upped her effort. Kouji continued to slip out of the way. Samar scowled and came in for a devastating punch, only for Kouji to grab her wrist. Samar moved to counter with a kick, only to have her ankle locked in Kouji's grip. Samar's frown deepened.

"Who the hell are you? No one from this city has ever been able to stop me with such ease," Samar said.

Kouji opened her mouth, but no voice emerged. Samar snarled and brought her leg down out of Kouji's hold. She recovered to the point she kicked Kouji in the chest with the same leg. Kouji fell back. *Faster and stronger than I thought. What if she's like me?* Kouji smiled again.

"Stand down," Samar ordered.

Kouji shook her head, wet braids swaying with the movement. Samar attacked again. Kouji blocked several kicks, feeling a sting in her arms from the force. Samar hit harder than anyone Kouji recalled. *Everything about her is amazing. That's why I missed her.*

"You stopped coming by," Kouji finally managed, her voice almost lost over the loud patter of the rain.

Samar paused. "What?"

Keep going. "I was worried about you."

"What?" she repeated, squinting at Kouji, as if trying to place her face.

"I'm happy you're okay. I hope you come back."

"Come back where? Who are you?"

Kouji glanced in the direction of the tomb. "I should go back to sleep before Mother gets worried, or worse." Kouji snapped her fingers and vanished in a brief whirlwind. Muscle memory was a great thing.

Samar wasn't sure what the hell just happened. She had seen people disappear before, not in Oganja though. Shamans, monks, and some of her teachers back in Asale had the ability. There was no way someone in Oganja vanished, even if they had a Nightmare.

"Maybe she used Nightmare speed," Samar muttered. Except that woman didn't have a Nightmare. Samar neither saw nor sensed one, and none alerted any of her sacred artifacts. This didn't make any sense.

Samar searched the area from where she stood, scanning for the tall woman with weird, shiny lavender eyes. She was gone. Samar turned back to her four prisoners and hoped they'd seen the woman. They were distracted, bickering with each other and passing blame for their current position.

"Did you guys just…?" Samar didn't finish the question and shook her head. She was probably overworked. She did nothing other than train and read when she wasn't working. "I need sleep," she mumbled. She hadn't slept well in the past few days, barely getting a couple of hours. She was seeing things or something. Right?

Samar's mind refused to relinquish thoughts of the young woman in the strange clothes. She was certain someone had been there, had fought her, and had stopped her as if she hadn't trained her entire life for battle. The phantom touch of hands gently gripping her wrists scratched at Samar's brain as she tried to focus on her job. The small smile played in her mind. It was rare for people to smile at her, to smile in a nice way.

She seemed to know me. She said she was worried about me. Samar was certain they'd never met. Right? Something about the woman plagued her mind. The woman bested Samar in a fight, which wasn't something she'd forget, but it was more. *It was like I knew her.*

Chapter Three

Restless

SAMAR MADE HER WAY back to the headquarters of Moonless Night Security as morning came and settled in. She flung herself into the chair that awaited her in Evinia's office. Looking around, her sister was nowhere to be found. With luck, Evinia would be back soon. She wanted to speak with Evinia before their father came by to do his morning check.

"Sammie, where's Vinny?" Mechi poked his head in the doorway.

Samar's jaw tensed. She didn't bother to glance up. "Please don't call me Sammie." The nickname was only for her sister to use. "She wasn't here when I came in." She folded her arms across her chest and stared at the floor with the hope he'd go away.

"No? That's weird." He let loose a long sigh. "Uh...so good morning, kid. How was your night?" he asked.

Why does he do this? She hated his attempts at being friendly. It was either weird or too familiar. She wasn't sure why he bothered. She was already aware of what he thought of her from back when he had the gall to assume she didn't speak the language. She refused to speak to him for the longest time thanks to that. She should try, if only for Evinia.

"Awkward," she mumbled.

"What?" He leaned down as though to hear her better.

She shook her head. "Nothing. Have you seen my father?" She might need to head out and check in with her supervisor. Anything to avoid being seen by Siku.

He chuckled. "As you can see, I'm still breathing, so no. I don't have a single clue where he is. Are you avoiding him too? Like me?"

"No," she replied in a quiet tone, focusing on her feet. She wasn't avoiding Siku, but more trying to make sure the last time she saw him was the *last* time she saw him. She had never experienced such utter disdain for her existence before him. *But it was always like that, wasn't it?*

"Well, you always keep watch for him."

She curled her lip. "Not always." He made it sound like she was scared of Siku. She fought Nightmares for a living. She didn't know fear.

"Seems like always."

"Not always," she insisted.

"Whatever, kid. It's nothing to be ashamed of. I mean, I'm avoiding him too. Nobody likes that damn judgmental stare he gives, like he's better than all of us."

She nodded. The man had a habit of staring people down like they were all lower lifeforms. How he managed to attract her mother would always be a mystery. Of course, she had no idea how or why anyone attracted anyone else. She tended to want to be left alone, especially since moving to Oganja.

Mechi let out a weird noise, like a sigh and a grunt. "He'll be here in a minute or so to do his morning check on Vinny. I wonder where she is. He comes like clockwork, and he'll make her life hell if she isn't here. Where might that little cat have gone?" Mechi clicked his teeth. "I'll be by again a little later. Try not to get into too much trouble until your sister gets back, and tell her I was here."

Samar didn't respond. Mechi didn't expect her to. This was already more conversation than they usually shared, definitely more than Samar liked.

Mechi left and Samar waited. She yawned. *I really need some sleep.* She hadn't been sleeping well since she stopped visiting the tomb four days ago.

She'd worked herself to exhaustion on her heavy bag and other exercises. When sleep still didn't come easy, she read until she fell asleep without realizing it. It sounded good in theory, but it wasn't working.

Loneliness ate at Samar, nipping at her in bigger and bigger bites with each day that passed. It gnawed at her through the quiet. It was like this when she first came to Oganja, drowning in a sea of strangers.

She thought more and more about the few people she had ever met in her life, back home. She'd loved and been loved in return by even fewer people. They were all left behind when she lost the most important person ever. She was dragged across an ocean to a foreign land that mimicked her homeland yet offered none of its kindness and warmth. This place was barely a shadow of Asale.

It was odd to witness how much culture and custom could be lost over time and distance. It was even odder and harder to comprehend how the original bit ended up being looked down on for no reason at all. *Why are they like this?* Maybe that was what happened when the sun was a memory.

"Samar," her father called into the office as he stepped in, taking her from her thoughts.

"Oh…*Dad*." She shifted in her seat. This word never sat well on her tongue and left her mouth as if she was unsure how to pronounce it. This was the title her other siblings used, so she followed suit. It never tasted right.

She had met her father a long time ago, but she had never used this word with him. She'd seen him from time to time over the years. She always tried to forget him after what seemed like a yearly visit. She used to call the man Him. Her mother would laugh. She never pressed Samar to give him a title, let alone a term of endearment. For some reason, Siku had insisted she call him Dad when she came to Oganja.

Samar's stomach rolled. She did her best to lock eyes with Siku. Would she be more comfortable around him if she had been able to refer to him as Siku rather than this false term of affection? Did it matter? Once she finally got her inheritance and was free of him, she might give it a try.

For now, Samar was uncomfortable around this man, her so-called father. It never felt right to speak with him or be in the same room with him, alone or not. The only time she ever met his eye was when he commanded it. If they were in a crowded room, she tried to hide behind people, so he would not find or see her.

Sometimes, she felt a flicker of connection to him, but it always fizzled out soon after. He was like a relative she interacted with every so often and was expected to remember, but nothing else. He treated her like the child of a friend he rarely encountered. If only she could be so lucky.

"Where's Vinny?" Siku inquired, his voice a normal volume but still with an edge her fragile ears heard.

"Dunno." Samar shrugged.

He grunted. "When are you going to start on your paperwork?"

"Dunno," she admitted, eyes still on a wall.

"Don't you think that you should hop to it? You can't depend on Vinny forever, especially to do part of your job."

Samar only nodded and shifted in her chair, needing to face away from him as much as possible while still watching part of him with the corner of her eye. *Can Vinny come back already or he leave?* She preferred the latter idea, but if Vinny came back, her presence would be more than welcomed.

Siku stared down at her, as if willing her to move. She tucked tighter into herself. The silence stretched between them, crushed her in its grip, and her stomach twisted more. She might throw up if he didn't leave soon. He had to know, his eyes were too intense not to know.

"You should start your paperwork." The suggestion was an order, like everything that came out of his mouth.

Samar nodded and, thankfully, he left. Eyes still on the floor, Evinia entered the room according to the shoes she focused on. She offered Samar a cup, causing her to look up.

"Thanks," Samar said in a small voice as she accepted the cup.

"No problem." Evinia took her seat at her desk. "It's not the blend you usually drink."

"That's fine. I have to buy that from the Asale market on Sun anyway. They're the only ones who do it like home."

Evinia nodded. "I'm glad you found so many little places around the city with authentic Asale things. You deserve a taste of home."

Samar sighed. She wanted more than a taste of home. She wanted home. She needed home like air, but she'd never have it. Home was with her mother, and her mother was gone. She'd never breathe again.

"Um, Mechi came by," Samar reported. Evinia would be glad for such news, and they needed to move on from the topic of home. She sipped the tea. It wasn't bad. The little shop at the corner tended to do a decent job.

"He's so clingy. I just saw him not too long ago," Evinia replied with a lighthearted laugh.

"Likes you," Samar said. Of course, her sister knew that.

Evinia and Mechi might end up married. They had been together longer than Samar even knew Evinia. They seemed like a happy couple, not that Samar had witnessed many of those in her young life.

A soft smiled settled on Evinia's face. "Yes, he does, and I love the attention. I was only kidding, Sammie. We've got to find you a sense of humor, then we have to snag you a boyfriend. A proper boyfriend."

Samar shook her head and squirmed in her seat. She sipped her tea again. A boyfriend? No thanks.

Evinia laughed and put her cup of coffee down. She reached over and rubbed Samar's head, massaging tight curls. Samar hunched over, ducking her head.

"One day, I'll figure out how to make you smile," Evinia said.

Samar frowned and shrugged. She never wanted to smile again. She was certain she'd never be happy again and honestly had no desire to be anyway. As much as she hated this grey city, the gloom matched her soul perfectly.

"What's wrong, Sammie? You seem down," Evinia said.

"Nothing," Samar replied. *Am I down? I'm always down.* Somehow, she felt worse than usual, like the rot inside of her had bloated, festered, and turned. It wasn't her worst, but enough to make her want to curl up and die. She might vomit.

"No, it's something." Evinia put a finger to her chin as she examined Samar. "Mechi didn't say anything to you while he was in here, did he? I know sometimes he says stupid things and might upset you, but he likes you. He's trying to get to know you, but he's an idiot and doesn't have a freaking clue what to say sometimes."

Samar shook her head. Somehow the rot became that much heavier. "He didn't say anything."

"Well, it had to be something since you look miserable. Are you okay?"

Apparently, Samar looked the way she always felt, miserable. *But why more so than usual?* Siku might've poisoned her air with his presence. "Yeah. I have paperwork to do." She was trying to be dismissive, which Evinia saw right through.

"I suppose you'll be wanting my help."

Samar only sighed and her older sister rubbed her head again, understanding the noise. It was irksome to be an adult, an academic (at least in her own mind), and have her own job, but require assistance to perform the job properly. Samar wasn't prepared for this job. She hadn't planned for it. She had been thrown into a whole new environment and abandoned by the man who put her in this situation.

With paperwork, Samar needed assistance from Evinia for several reasons. Samar spoke multiple languages, but her thoughts often took time to translate from her native tongue to this one. Typing up reports might take hours, even if she started in her native language, then let the computer translate. The translation still needed to be proofread and always needed so many changes.

"I could just do the work for you. I still have an hour left in my shift, and I never have anything to do at this hour," Evinia replied.

"He said I should do it." Samar didn't want to give Siku a reason to bark at Evinia. Plus, she needed to practice doing these damn things properly. She'd be on this job for at least two more years, after all.

"Who? Daddy?" Evinia inquired. Samar nodded and Evinia sucked her teeth. "That explains why you look more depressed than usual."

"I'm not."

"Sammie, I don't blame you for not wanting to deal with Daddy. He treats you terribly."

Samar grunted. "Whatever." She didn't care. In two years, she'd leave him behind, go back to Asale, and attend a university. Then, she could truly figure out what to do with her life.

"If it were up to Daddy, you'd be doing this work and nothing else in life. You can't always listen to Daddy, not that you do. He only thinks he knows everything. He doesn't actually know everything," Evinia said.

"Yes, I know." Oh, how she knew. "But I'm going to be here awhile. I need to learn eventually."

"No, you don't." Evinia wagged a finger in her face. "This isn't a skill you need, and I don't want to give Daddy any excuses to try to keep you at this job longer than it takes to collect your inheritance. You're not staying here a second longer than you need to."

Samar's eyes burned as she nodded. If not for Evinia, she would've gone stark, raving mad. Evinia was all she had, the only person who tried to help her adjust. She might have actually taken her own life a year into her stay if not for Evinia.

"Vinny," Samar said, needing off this topic. She had a crazy night and still wanted to speak with her sister about it. "Vinny, there was this lady in the park…"

"A lady?" Evinia echoed curiously as she pulled back up to her desk. "A lady in the park this late at night? Was she causing trouble?"

"No, she was…" Samar rubbed her head, trying to think of the right words. "Almost ethereal."

Evinia's face went soft, but in a troublesome manner. "Uh-oh. Are you trying to take my advice, Sammie?" A teasing smile was on her face. "I had no idea you went for the ladies."

Samar wasn't sure what her sister meant. "She was dressed quite oddly."

Evinia arched an eyebrow. "In what way?"

"Well, for one, she didn't have on any shoes. She had on way too much jewelry for being in my park that late. Her clothing was traditional, but ancient. She wore rows of neck beads."

Evinia's face scrunched up. "Traditional neck beads? You don't see that around here often, even with the most recent arrivals from the coast."

"Not unless there's a celebration or something. But also, the neck beads themselves didn't correspond to any celebration or clan I could think of. I've never seen the pattern or design before. The sash around her waist, I think might have been an old royal symbol, but I can't be sure."

Evinia nodded. "Yes, quite weird. You think the gangs you keep out of the park figured out you're from Asale and want to mess with you?"

"It's possible, but she had a chance to do me harm and didn't."

Evinia's mouth dropped open. She pushed her chair back to Samar. "I'm sorry, she had a chance to do what? Sammie, I've seen you literally dodge bullets. I don't know what the hell those monks in Asale taught you, but it's damn near magic. How could anyone have a chance to harm you? Did you arrest her? Can we talk to her?"

Samar blew out a breath and rubbed the back of her head. "Arrest her? I couldn't even touch her." It didn't make sense. She had always been an exceptional warrior, praised by all of her teachers. How could she not touch someone?

Evinia frowned and shook her head. "I don't understand what you're saying. You got banned from HQ's gym for beating up five people at a time. How could you not touch her?"

Samar shrugged. "I just couldn't. She was too fast. I got in a kick, but nothing impressive. She called me out, challenged me. I stepped up and I couldn't touch her. She was faster than anyone I've ever seen. My mother. The monks. Visiting warriors. Then, she said a bunch of funny stuff and disappeared."

Evinia's forehead wrinkled. "Disappeared like vanished?"

"Yes. It was quite weird," Samar replied.

"There's something more? I hear the little sliver of excitement in your voice, Sammie," Evinia said.

Samar chewed the inside of her cheek before deciding to continue. "I want…I want to see her again." The very notion, the possibility, excited her, seared its way through the sludge in her system. They needed to fight again. What Nightmare or special power helped make that woman so much faster than Samar?

"Why would you want to see such a weirdo again?"

"To fight," she answered. If they got to fight a second time, she should be able to adjust enough to touch her opponent. *Provided she doesn't do anything new and murder you where you stand.*

"Of course," Evinia nodded. "Well, you are a brawler."

"Excuse me?"

Evinia held up her hands in surrender. "Okay, not a brawler. I'm aware you consider yourself a warrior and you're out there trying to be a hero. You inherited some genes, Sammie. Your mom was probably intrigued about Daddy's military career to the same degree he had to be curious about her growing up in a warrior temple like her life was a TV show."

Samar scratched her head. "I honestly have no idea. Mom never talked about him, and I never thought about him beyond the few days he popped up. Most of the time, I forgot he existed between visits."

"Your mom really never said anything about him?"

"Nothing unless he showed up. Sometimes, years passed between visits. I don't think I saw him at all until I was six, then I don't think he showed up again until I was eight or nine. She used to tell me folktales of children being shaped like pottery. For a long time, I think I assumed she made me from clay like a pot."

Evinia laughed. "Oh, that's adorable. So I guess you don't know how your mom met Daddy, huh?"

Samar shook her head. "Never thought about it." It was probably something that plagued Evinia though. What was it about her mother that made Siku cheat on his wife at least once? *Did Mom know he was married?*

A soft smile settled on Evinia's gentle face. "Either way, they made one hell of a hero scholar. Have you ever actually lost a fight?"

"When I was younger, yes, but not recently. I couldn't even touch her," Samar said with sheer disbelief, eyes drifting to her hands. These hands had taken down groups of ten at a time. These hands had sent gaggles of Nightmares back to the Beyond. These hands had saved countless lives by beating back hordes bent on harm and destruction.

"Maybe you were simply tired, Sammie. Or it's possible you were distracted? Maybe from the way she was dressed," Evinia replied. "Don't let this eat at you."

"No, she was too fast. It was…um, it was," Samar searched her mind for the right word. " Fantastic. Yeah, she was fantastic."

"All right, I can see you're attracted to weirdoes," Evinia teased.

Samar scowled. "Not attracted. I want to fight her again. Nothing more." She might ask some questions, gain some wisdom. She could get some advice or tips from that woman.

"If you say so." Evinia shrugged. "What did she look like besides the way she dressed?"

"She had braids down her back," Samar answered. The woman's face flashed through Samar's mind, almost angelic, as if she could never harm a single soul. Her cheeks had been slightly chubby and her eyes just wide enough to be puppy-like.

"Okay, braids down her back. That's probably half the population in this city, especially in this neighborhood," Evinia commented. "What was her age? Older than you or younger?"

"Dunno. It was hard to gauge. Maybe younger. She had fat cheeks," Samar answered.

Evinia laughed. "You said it, not me. Was she taller than you?"

"Yeah."

"By much?"

Samar scratched the back of her head. *Where is Vinny going with this?* Evinia usually didn't ask such asinine questions. She eyed Samar, silently pressing her.

It took several seconds for Samar to answer. She had to visualize the height by the punches she threw. "Maybe a little taller than you or your height."

"My height?" Evinia nodded to that information. "What color were her eyes?"

"A purplish color. I'm not sure of the word for it."

Evinia blinked. "Purple? Her eyes?"

Samar nodded in confirmation. "Yeah, maybe a light purple. Why?"

"That's pretty strange. I suppose she could be wearing colored contacts. Why would anyone with a working brain want purple eyes?" Evinia wrinkled her nose. She wasn't a fan of purple.

"What's wrong with purple eyes?" Samar asked, offended for some reason. Those eyes were absolutely stunning. Evinia needed to bear witness to understand.

Evinia chuckled and threw her hands up again. Samar frowned. Evinia laughed even more. She was up to something.

"Purple eyes are a little strange, but there's certainly nothing wrong with that. It shows you were paying very close attention to her," Evinia said.

"So?" Samar asked. She failed to understand what paying attention to a person had to do with anything. She was supposed to be observant. She was a damn warrior, after all.

Evinia smiled. "You are so sweet and innocent. I'm glad that year of high school you had to do here didn't take that away from you."

"What?" Samar was utterly lost.

Evinia shook her head. "It's nothing. Let's get to your reports."

"Okay, but Vin…"

"Yeah?"

"Why'd you ask me all those questions?" Samar asked.

"Just to see something," Evinia answered with a lighthearted shrug.

"Okay, but what?"

"Nothing important, Sammie. Come on, let's do your reports so we both can get out of here. You need some sleep."

Samar nodded, even though she doubted she'd get any sleep. At least today the reason wouldn't be unknown. She'd think long and hard about her encounter in Okunkun Park.

They crowded around Evinia's desk where her central computer monitor sat. Samar paid careful attention, as Evinia filled out the reports. This work seemed so easy for Evinia.

It had taken Samar only a few months after meeting her sister to figure out how intelligent she was. Samar wished she had a fraction of her big sister's brain power. Yes, Samar had vast depths of book knowledge, but applying it in the real world or using it for problem-solving wasn't her forte.

Evinia made everything appear so easy, but whenever she let Samar take over, everything Evinia made look so simple was quite complex. Samar was always left with her chin resting in both of her hands while in total awe, which was the case when Evinia finished showing her how to do the reports…again.

"You're so good with computers."

Evinia scoffed. "First off, this is nothing. And you say that like I didn't watch you read Daddy's personal library in about a month. You could probably do what I do if you put your energy into it, and I'm sure it'd take you less time to learn compared to me."

"You're not giving yourself enough credit."

Evinia held up her index finger. "No, you're the one not giving yourself enough credit. I'm very aware of what I'm capable of. If I needed to, I'd be able to rebuild this whole system without much help. You don't realize you could do the same if you poured yourself into technology like you do with your studying. Look, you put all your energy into being a warrior. I put all mine into tech. Take some computer classes when you go to college."

"You think?" That had never occurred to Samar.

"I think you need more hobbies. You should find new interests in college. This is also why I refuse to let you get comfortable here. You're going to college, if only for the social experience. Beyond that, I know that's what your mother wanted for you."

Samar nodded. "She actually wanted me to come here to study for a year. She wanted me to have experiences." She scowled, the words leaving a bad taste in her mouth. Yes, Oganja would be more bearable if her mother were alive, but Samar still wouldn't have enjoyed this experience.

"I want that too. I want you to meet different people. Make some friends. Learn what foods you like. Enjoy some activities. Be a crazy kid for a little while. There's so much to experience, Sammie. I won't let Daddy hold you back."

Samar smiled. "Thanks."

Their moment was interrupted when Mechi stuck his head into the office. "Hey, kitty cat."

Both sisters glared at Mechi, who yelped. He gave a nervous laugh. Evinia sighed and shook her head. Samar scowled. She hated hearing his little pet names for her sister. It was weird, like she shouldn't witness these things.

"Sammie, what're you still doing here?" Mechi asked, like his voice filling the air would make things less awkward. She growled and he held his hands up. "Sorry. Samar, what are you still doing here?"

"Reports," Samar answered. Her shift was over, and she should've been home already, but it was nice to sit with Evinia.

"I thought you couldn't read," Mechi said.

"Mechi," Evinia scolded him.

"What? I'm teasing!" Mechi let loose an easygoing grin. "I know she's read a library's worth of books this week alone, more than likely."

"I've told you, time and time again, not to tease her. You're quite bad at it. Offensive even," Evinia said.

Mechi winced. "Sorry. I'm just…" He blew out a breath. "I was just wondering when we're leaving."

"Give me a second for crying out loud. I'm trying to show Sammie how to use the computer," Evinia answered.

"You're kidding me." He let loose a laugh, which earned him another glower from both sisters. "Sorry, sorry, sorry." Mechi gulped and shrank back into the doorway.

Evinia kept her eyes on him. "You done?"

"I'm just going to stand here. Promise."

Evinia turned back to Samar. "That's enough for today. You turn it off, just like I showed you."

Samar nodded and shut down Evinia's computers, even though Evinia didn't usually do that. This was practice for Samar. She was definitely computer illiterate despite several such lessons. This couldn't be as agonizing as watching Samar with her phone.

Evinia stood up and rubbed the top of her sister's head. "Call me later, kiddo. Try to stay away from that tomb and get some sleep."

"Yeah." Samar didn't see sleep in her future, but she'd try.

Samar sighed and leaned back in the chair as Evinia and Mechi left. The urge to go back to the tomb was like an itch under her skin, weighing down on her even more now that she had failed to rise to a challenge. She wasn't a weak person. She wouldn't let a building impact her emotional state. Nothing should have that sort of power over her.

Samar ripped herself from her seat and made her way home before her father popped up again. She passed by the tomb across the street. She stared at the structure for a long moment before forcing herself to continue home.

Once in her apartment, she showered and put on comfy undergarments and shorts. She tossed and turned on the futon, easing the bedspread up after only a couple hours of sleep. Strange dreams haunted her. Not nightmares, not hard memories of her mother, but flashes of the woman from the park. She felt familiar. It tore at Samar, clawed at the edges of her brain.

After her troubled sleep, Samar saw what she had done to her bed. *What's wrong with me?* She was more exhausted now than before.

She rolled to the edge of her bed and searched for her phone underneath piles of books, papers, and a few articles of clothing that were missed when she'd done laundry a couple of days ago with Evinia. She dialed her sister's number. It went to voicemail. Samar never left messages, and she didn't text. *Why does she tell me to call and never pick up?*

She got out of her bed and poured herself a bowl of cold cereal, as usual. She ate it quickly, leg bouncing as she did so. She dropped the bowl in the sink, where the dishes were piling up again. She'd do them later. She didn't have it in her to clean at the moment. In fact, she didn't have it in her to do things she enjoyed. Only one thing was on her mind.

Samar donned her usual gear of black pants and a hoodie before jogging to the tomb. She hopped the gate in front of the building and sat down on the front stairs. She watched people go by for lack of a better thing to do. Her nerves, still twitching, relaxed a bit. Something was still off.

Chapter Four

Darkness

"IT'S NOT RAINING TODAY," Samar informed the tomb. "The sun's not out though. It's never out." Her eyes traveled to the eternal grey sky. As always, cloud cover hid Oganja from the sun.

The sky over Oganja reminded Samar of a story her mother used to tell her when she was younger of a land beyond the ocean, beyond the sunlight, where the Sun dared not touch. Supposedly, Asiku—the Night—made this land for her favorite child. The Sun—Usuku—wasn't allowed on the land because he hated her child. *Is that why you liked this city, Mom? It reminded you of the old stories?*

A small smile twitched on Samar's face for a moment. "I mean, you know the sun's in the sky because you can tell it's daytime, but clouds are always in the way. These people have no idea what they're missing out on. The sun and white clouds and blue sky are amazing. They act like this grey stuff is normal. They might think it's normal."

Samar sighed and leaned against the wall of the tomb, eyes on the sky, watching slate clouds that never seemed to leave. The sun never tried to break through the drifting puffs of concrete, as if it had no interest in shining on Oganja. She shook her head. Three years without the sun, without a clear sky. She might wither and die because of the lack of natural light.

"My sister tried to teach me some basic computer things today. She does that. I think we're equally fascinated with each other's intelligence. I'm terrible with computers, even the simplest things. I never had time to use one before now, not like I need to anyway. This shocks her. I hate to think what my father would say if he knew how little I know of computers. He already thinks I'm an idiot for whatever reason. My mom would think I'm being silly for caring what he thinks, but she's the one who wanted me to connect with him or something. She left me with him, after all." Samar sighed and shrugged.

Her stomach twisted, as it tended to when she thought of her mother. It'd be nice if the tomb or whatever was inside could answer her back. She wouldn't mind answers or just hearing another voice directed toward her.

She never cared about such things before she came to Oganja. When she was with her mother, if she wanted to talk to someone, her mother was right there. She was always able to tell her mother what was on her mind. Nothing with her mother was as complex as everything was now. She needed support and guidance. But the one person she went to for that was gone, forever and always.

"My sister answers me sometimes. I'm not as open with her as she wants me to be. I'm trying, but it's hard. She likes to make sure I'm all right. I'm not all right. She gets it. She lost her mother too. I'm not sure if she was as close to her mother as I was to mine," Samar said.

Evinia wasn't as open about her mother as Samar sometimes yearned for. Evinia's silence hinted that the pain tearing Samar apart, the overwhelming absence, would never go away. For the rest of her life, this void, the dreaded twist in her gut, the impossible pinch in her soul, would always exist.

"She told me to call her today. She's worried about me, probably more than usual. No idea why. I don't think I'm in worse shape than usual."

Samar blew out a long breath and rubbed her forehead. It wasn't like she ever felt good. It was rare for her to have even decent moments. So why was Evinia more concerned now? *She might see something you don't.*

"She didn't answer her phone though. She always tells me to call, which I do. Not sure why I do since she doesn't answer her phone much. She won't answer, but I call, just in case. I feel stupid for calling. I mean, she's with Mechi. And if she's with him, why does she want me to call her? But she tells me to call and I do. It's stupid and I'm stupid for listening. I might be stupid," Samar said with a light laugh.

She tended to feel stupid at least half of the time since coming to Oganja. There were so many things she had only read about in books or glimpsed in videos. She was lost on how things worked or what was proper. She never figured out what to do with herself or how she was supposed to fit into the new world around her. Often, she didn't care.

What did anything matter with her mother gone? What did life matter if she might not go to college? What did life matter if she never made it back to Asale? Did anything matter if her father kept her in this wretched place to use her fighting skills? *He's not even aware of the damn Nightmares!*

"That might be the thing that bothers me most with him. He recognizes my skills as a warrior, but has no clue why I've been trained this way. He doesn't believe in Nightmares. Had the nerve to tell me Mom was studying simple, ignorant folklore. So arrogant, like most of these people who can't tell they're surrounded by Nightmares making their lives worse, until they, too, succumb to Nightmares and offer themselves up." Samar sucked her teeth in disgust.

People walked by and glanced at her. Some stared like she was an anomaly. Though she wasn't the one who'd give herself to a Nightmare. *Of course, you are one of the few who can see the Nightmares, so they're not quite wrong.* For all their gawking, no one stepped closer to the tomb, not to check on her nor admire the structure.

"I wonder why people don't come here, except for stupid kids who come to throw stuff. It's peaceful and beautiful. Mom liked it here. Not Oganja, but here at the tomb. She told me about this place. I never thought about it when she talked about it, but now I can't stay away." That might have been the thing calling her to this place. The tomb connected her to her mother as well as her homeland.

Of course, she didn't often think about her mother seeing this place. That thought was a blip in the many stories her mother told her. *I miss those stories. I miss you, Mom.*

"I wish I could've had such a beautiful building made for you." Samar sighed, scrubbing her face with both hands for a moment.

She'd like to build some kind of monument for her mother, no need to be grand or striking like the tomb. Only something for her to visit and to make people aware that this amazing woman once existed and contributed to the world.

"I don't have the money right now, and I think she'd like to keep things simple. That's how Mom was, real simple when it came to so much. We lived in a little house in the mountains close to the temple I learned at, and Mom translated texts into modern language."

Tears stung her eyes as Samar remembered their home. It was only a cottage but on so much land. She had been able to run and play freely as a child. Her mother indulged her, allowing her to explore whatever interested her on their property and beyond. Samar had many interests as a child. Now, she had none.

"She used to live here, you know? That's how she met Dad, but I don't think they interacted much until after he came to Asale while she was working. Some kind of gathering. I don't know. I don't think she liked him very much. He visited a few times when I was little, but I don't remember him much. She never wanted to see him. Me neither. Definitely don't want to bother with him now," Samar confessed to the tomb.

A few stray leaves blew onto her foot and got stuck on the cuffs of her pants. She brushed them away and found her mind straying to her mother and father together. It was easy to tell they disliked each other. She wasn't sure why. Her mother never explained. She also never explained what possessed the two to be together.

"When I was little, like six, after I first met him, I asked my mother about them. She said, 'Mommy made a mistake, that's all. But I'm glad you came along.' Then she hugged me and that was enough."

Now that Samar was stuck with Siku, she craved more and she'd never have it. He'd never tell her. Even if he did, he didn't hold the answer she yearned for. What was the mistake? What led up to it? What happened afterward, aside from her being born?

"Was the mistake that he was married?" Samar scratched the back of her neck. "Did I ever say anything about that? I'm Siku's middle child by another woman. I must've said something about that already. It's baffling. Sometimes, I wonder if he drove her off when he found out she planned to have me. It seems like something he'd do. I don't know the story, and he'll never tell me the truth. Unless, of course, it was Mom's fault." Samar sighed.

She understood her mother wasn't perfect. She wouldn't lie to herself about such a thing, even with her mother being dead. *But I want to stop thinking about her.* Thinking about her mom made Samar miss her, and her mother was never coming back.

"I've made it to a point where remembering my mother makes me happy, but I still miss her so much and it hurts so much. Sometimes, I just want to be miserable because she's not here. How can I ever be happy with her gone? Oganja makes it easier to be miserable." It was easier to be gloomy in her new home where fresh air, sunlight, and vast, open spaces were myths.

There were no goats or birds for her to chase, a favorite pastime when she was a child. Only a few trees were thick enough to climb, not that she had such ambition anymore. Barely more than saplings, how did the scattered trees remain alive in this place?

Her eyes strayed to her park. How did Okunkun Park even exist? The park should've been a patch of dirt. Most of the trees were bald. Leaves didn't live long, doomed in heavy storms. Flowers needed so much care and were gone in a blink.

"Speaking of the park, I wonder where that woman went. She might come back tonight for a rematch. I won't arrest her. We could talk after. She didn't seem too happy either. Maybe she knows this is a city of sorrow. What's her name? Where did she learn to move like that? If Mom saw me now, she'd think I was being too eager, but she always said being young is to get everything stupid you have to do out of the way."

She rubbed her face once more, cheeks cold. She blew on her hands as a damp chill settled in the air. It always seemed like it was the start of winter in this place, but it never quite made it to the season. It was always the start of death in Oganja.

Her hands began to freeze. They were always the first part of her body to frost over, but she never brought gloves. After a long while sitting in silence at the tomb, she checked her watch.

"I've gotta go to work. I'll be back later. Maybe I'll have a story or two," she sort of joked as she stood.

Samar clocked in for work. It was a disappointing night, mostly because the young woman in the strange clothes didn't show up. No one tempted her in the park either. There were no Nightmares. Nothing. It was empty.

Okunkun Park was clear for the first time in days. Apparently, she was extraordinary at her job. That's what Evinia liked to tell her. Samar wasn't sure what that quite meant.

Before tonight, troublemakers and their Nightmares came through the park like it was part of some highway. She wasn't sure if Okunkun already had tempting targets for those up to no good, or if the Nightmares dragged their hosts to the park. Were they in the area for her or for other reasons? No one being out tonight was strange and wormed its way into the back of her mind.

Samar stumbled into her sister's office once her shift was over. Lack of sleep threw off her equilibrium, and a lack of Nightmares boggled her mind. She collapsed into the chair that always waited for her. Evinia was absent. With luck, Evinia came around before their father did.

Samar yawned. She needed a full night's sleep sometime soon. The roughly three hours she got during the past week or so wouldn't cut it, especially when fighting Nightmares. Not being on top of her game was a good way to lose her intestines.

"Hey, sleepyhead, what're you doing yawning?" Evinia entered the room with a giant stack of loose papers in her arms.

"Tired."

"Yeah, that one's obvious. Active night…or day?" Evinia asked with a suggestive smirk.

"Hard to sleep." Samar rubbed her eyes. She understood her sister was implying something, but she wasn't sure what.

Evinia dropped the papers on a cluttered spot on her desk and put her hand on Samar's shoulder. "Why? What's wrong?" So much concern echoed in her voice.

"Nothing."

Evinia squinted, studying her. "Are you sure? You can tell me about it."

"It's nothing. It's been hard to sleep lately."

"Ah." Evinia nodded and cleared off a proper space for all of her papers. She sat in her chair and then popped back up. "Whoa, I can't do anything without coffee," she said, more to herself than Samar. She called over her shoulder. "Sammie, I can't make it through the end of my shift or keep my sanity without coffee. I'll be right back. You want some tea? It might help."

Samar chewed on the inside of her cheek. She had no desire to be left alone in the office, not at this time. If Siku came by, he'd bother her about reports or something else. Evinia offered Samar a smile.

"Come on, you. It's about time you learned how to make coffee and tea with our little machine. Then I can send you on these runs as my lackey, like a proper younger sibling," Evinia remarked.

Samar didn't argue or even react to the joke. She followed her sister out of the office. Samar didn't enjoy walking around headquarters. People had the bad habit of staring at her as if she had four heads and orange skin. She sometimes heard them referring to her as the foreigner or the weirdo. She'd heard these things in high school as well.

She didn't understand why they said such things about her. She had never done anything to them to warrant words of any kind. She barely talked to people, both now and back in high school.

Everyone always avoided Samar like she had the plague. She didn't mind to a degree, but it made her mind whirl. Did they do this to everyone from another culture? How could such a large city be so closed-minded? Was it only here and high school? In smaller environments of this vast, uncaring world?

"Samar," Evinia said.

Samar blinked. "Huh?" It was rare for Evinia to say her entire name.

"Are you paying attention? This is how you make our cheap tea since we can't always run out to the spot we love down the street."

"What stopped you tonight?"

Evinia snorted. "Daddy met me at the door and handed me all of those papers to scan and digitize ASAP. I can't figure out why, considering I read through some of them and they don't require a hurry."

"Well, he said so."

"Oh yes, that is true. Look, this isn't that complicated, which is also why the place down the street is superior."

Samar watched Evinia work. The device wasn't too complicated, involving a pod and picking a cup size. It was mostly pressing buttons. Evinia bounced on her toes as she waited for her coffee.

"Are you all right?" Samar asked.

"I really need my coffee to make it this last hour. We're both very aware I have a problem." Evinia chuckled.

Samar nodded. Evinia drank a cup of coffee every few hours while at work. Evinia often claimed she'd fall asleep at her desk without the coffee, even if she had to do logistics for an operation. Samar didn't relate. She had always been a nighthawk.

"It's crazy to me how you can drink tea late at night and pass out right after," Evinia said, as she added sugar to her coffee.

Samar shrugged. "I'm used to it, like staying up late. I used to stay up and watch the stars with my mother. It'd be nice to see a star around here."

Evinia snorted. "Good luck with the weather here. This city might as well be cursed."

Samar nodded. She wasn't sure about cursed, but it definitely had more Nightmare activity than she had ever seen in her life. Granted, most of her life had been spent on the side of a mountain, but she had visited towns before.

"So Sammie, lately, how many hours of sleep have you been getting?" Evinia asked as they made their way back to her office.

"About three," Samar answered with a shrug. She didn't require much sleep, but everyone needed more than three hours. She wasn't sure what to do about that.

"That's it? You'll be dead on your feet if you keep that up. Any reason why?"

Samar shook her head and sipped her tea. "I've been off lately, not sure why."

"Anxiety back?"

"No." She had suffered from anxiety for her first year in Oganja to the point where she needed medication. "I'm just off." She wasn't sure how else to put it.

"Well, what have you been doing with all your spare time?"

"Read, box."

Evinia sighed. "I should've known. You need to clean. I'm shocked you don't have rats with the way your apartment looks."

Samar shrugged. She was messy, and it was as simple as that. The idea of rats didn't bother her. Although she had no idea what the rats would live on. She had one half-eaten box of cereal and a tube of toothpaste in her apartment. The rats would move out a week after they moved in, unless they wanted to live off books. Samar kept that thought to herself. Evinia hated it when she found her sense of humor over something this serious.

"Sammie, I need you to start living like you care. I understand you don't plan to be here forever, and I encourage you to leave for your mental health. I also encourage you to act like you live in that apartment for the same reason. A clean living space might help you feel better," Evinia said.

"Maybe." Samar doubted it and sipped her tea.

"I'll come over and start the process, if you don't," Evinia said. It was meant as a threat and a promise. She'd come over and begin cleaning, aware Samar's manners wouldn't let her sit by and watch.

Samar shrugged. She didn't have the energy to clean. She focused on her tea and checked the time. There was nothing to do and she wanted out of this place.

"So did you see that woman again?" Evinia asked the question that must have been burning her brain.

"No."

Evinia nodded and turned to her monitors. "You sound disappointed. Did you want to?"

"I guess." Samar folded her arms across her chest.

"You guess? You either did or didn't. What's to guess about?"

"I dunno." For some reason, she didn't want to admit hoping for another encounter to Evinia.

"So did you want to see her or not?" Evinia pressed the issue.

"Yeah."

"Why?"

"To fight her." Samar made a fist. But there was something more. Something unspoken gnawed at her insides. Visiting the tomb tended to set her at ease. It lessened the feeling without settling her completely. *Something's wrong with me, more than usual.* She was off.

"Life's just a great big fight to you, huh?" Evinia smirked at her.

"You want me to have fun. It's fun." Samar was trained. She was meant to fight Nightmares and ensure they didn't hurt people. There was also a thrill in that. Fighting people was exciting, more so when it wasn't a life-and-death situation. Being able to show off skills or test skills was enjoyable.

"If you say so, kiddo. So why didn't you call me yesterday?"

"Didn't answer."

Evinia turned to glare at her. "Why don't you leave a message? I told you my phone bugs out sometimes, and it doesn't tell me I missed a call, or it doesn't ring. It won't kill you to leave a message."

"It doesn't matter. I didn't have anything to say. It's okay."

"You need contact every now and then."

"Here." Samar motioned around them.

"Here you only talk to me. That's all and that's okay."

"And outside, who do I have to talk to? Here or outside, there's only you." Samar countered.

"Look, we need to talk more outside. It'll allow us to talk about other things. I try to take you places and you never want to go, even when I suggest those Asale-friendly places with stuff you like. You only want to stay holed up in that pigsty you call an apartment. That's not healthy," Evinia explained.

"You got me that apartment." This wasn't relevant, but it was all she had.

"That I did, and I don't recall it looking that bad when I got it. I couldn't leave you with Daddy. It scares me to think of the mess you'd be now. Anxiety and PTSD would be the least of it." Evinia scowled and shook her head. "I hoped you'd make friends and chill at your place. Don't do that now though. A library threw up there and it's not fit for company."

"It doesn't matter. I don't care. It doesn't bother me." Samar shrugged off Evinia's concern.

"Nothing really bothers you, Sammie, and I don't think that's making things better. Your mom would want better for you."

Samar stared at her feet, and Evinia turned her attention to her computer. The click of the keyboard and the sip of coffee made Samar look up. There was something comforting about the sound.

Evinia glanced over at Samar, as a paper cup clattered to the floor. Samar had fallen asleep. Luckily, she'd finished her tea before dropping the cup. Evinia reached to pick up the cup, but a knock at the door got her attention. Her father stepped in. His eyes fell on Samar immediately and he frowned.

"What happened to her?" He nodded toward Samar.

"She's tired."

"Tired?" He said the word as if it was foreign or impossible.

"She hasn't been sleeping well recently." He might surprise her. Would he suddenly care about the well-being of his middle child?

He scoffed. "Maybe she needs you to rock her to sleep."

"You're being exceptionally evil this morning. Did you eat someone's children before coming in here?" Evinia teased with a smile. He was certainly being rather mean. She wouldn't be surprised if he woke poor Sammie up and told her no napping at work.

"Watch your mouth," he said with a growl.

Evinia was half-tempted to reply that Mechi watched her mouth for her. He'd miss the humor and catch all of the hostility, again. She wasn't in the mood for that fight and didn't want to risk waking Samar.

Besides, she had actual work to make it through. That was excuse enough not to talk to him. The plan was to get him out of the office as soon as possible.

"Sorry, Daddy. If you're wondering, yes, I did call Alien. He's up and should be out of the house by now," Evinia reported. Alvin was pretty responsible if left to his own devices. Not that their father would ever leave the kid to his own devices.

"Good, that's good. So where were you all day?" her father inquired, which was really none of his business.

"Daddy." Evinia huffed.

"I don't want you staying at Mechi's place."

"Daddy, I'm grown," she felt the need to point out, as she did every now and then. She took the idea of being legally independent quite seriously. It was part of the reason she had moved out of his house two months after turning eighteen. She would've been out faster, but she needed to find someplace very cheap to stay at the time.

"Stop staying at his apartment," her father commanded.

Evinia frowned. He was being more ridiculous than usual, which was quite the feat. She doubted he'd ever accept she was living her life, so there was no room for him to live it too. Might as well annoy him since he *needed* to bother her.

"If I stop staying at his place, he'll simply stay at mine. That's probably better. My apartment's superior to his." None of that was a lie, though Mechi had a problem with her cat, Dusk.

Siku growled. "Don't be smart with me, Vinny."

"Don't tell me what to do with my boyfriend, Daddy. I'm grown, and I've got the voting privileges to prove it. I'm not sixteen anymore."

"You're still my daughter, and you'll do what I say. You have a name to uphold."

Evinia snorted. "You think me partially cohabitating with my long-term boyfriend is the stain on the Habeen name?"

He scowled, probably understanding how ridiculous that had to sound coming from him. "Don't do your sister's reports for her. When your shift is over, you go straight to your own home. I'm sick of having to deal with this nonsense where you think you can do whatever you want."

He turned and left before she could respond. On his way out, he shook Samar by the shoulder. She woke with a gasp.

"Clock out. I'm not paying you to sleep," he said before disappearing out the door.

Evinia gawked in disbelief. How dare he?! She was tempted to chase him down and demand he apologize to Samar, but poor Samar looked so confused. Evinia had to stick around for her. *That was so fucking immature.* He was always like that. Of course, she was always defiant of the man, despite knowing how he'd react.

Evinia usually tried to do everything, but what he wanted her to do. It got worse when she was a teenager, but the rebellious streak had always existed.

When she was little, he wanted her to be in school plays. She made sure to only be in the science fairs. He made it a point never to go and refused to display her ribbons until her mother forced him.

In junior high, he wanted her to join a sport to supplement her training. She never went to an activity that might be mistaken for a sport. Not even chess, despite her talent at the game. She did computer club and a robotics team. He refused to buy her any items she needed for those interests.

In high school, he wanted her to achieve the best grades. She could have, but always ranked second in her class standings on purpose. It was because he never requested. He always ordered.

He wouldn't be happy until he pushed them all away. He thought he had a hold on them thanks to his successful company. It made him wealthy and gave them access to material goods, to a degree. He spoiled them at his leisure, but starved them to the same degree.

The company also allowed them to work for him, but he was wrong in thinking this gave him power and control over her. This was her first job and, once upon a time, she needed the money. He had withheld money she was supposed to inherit from her mother but eventually, she got it. She now had the experience for when she wanted to get a better job.

She stayed for Samar. Her sister needed her, especially since their father would definitely try to hold her inheritance too. Samar was too in-demand for him to let her go. Beyond being paid to patrol the most dangerous part of the city, Samar was an often-requested bodyguard for visiting celebrities or other high-profile people. Samar made him tons of money. He wouldn't let her go. She'd need to run, and Evinia would be there to make sure she did.

"Let's get you clocked out," Evinia said to Samar. "You'll sleep better in your bed than in your chair."

Samar groaned. "Doubtful, but okay."

"I'll give you a ride home."

"I can make it myself. You still have work."

"You sure? I don't mind leaving early." *Especially after what Daddy did.*

Samar waved her off. "Yeah, I'm sure. Night, Vin, I mean, morning." She yawned.

Evinia watched Samar stagger out of the building. *I hope this isn't a mistake.* Samar could take care of herself better than anyone Evinia had ever seen, physically speaking anyway. But she was in shambles right now. *At least she won't get mugged.*

Samar made it a point not to carry much cash and only had a debit card, but a robber wouldn't know that. If nothing else, they'd delay Samar from making it to her bed. Once, during her first few months in the city, a couple of idiots had tried to rob Samar at gunpoint. They ended up trying to press charges against her after a long hospital stay. Mugging her was pointless. She was broke and would leave the criminal broken. *Still, I'll call her later to make sure she made it home.*

Chapter Five

Into the Night

SAMAR PRACTICALLY FELL INTO her apartment after ramming the door open with her shoulder. The stupid thing stuck sometimes. It probably didn't help that she kicked it shut. Evinia's voice in the back of her head ensured the two deadbolts were locked.

She threw her jacket off and discarded her black shirt. She wore a sleeveless t-shirt underneath. She tossed herself onto her disheveled bed, kicking her pants off as soon as she settled. She fell asleep with ease and slept through most of the day for the first time in a long time.

She showered when she woke and threw on a black t-shirt and a hoodie with joggers. She slipped on her sneakers and went out for a ten-mile run. She came across a Nightmare, attached to a jerk trying to mug a kid in an alley.

"Bold choice to do this in my neighborhood," Samar said as she stepped into the alley.

The mugger turned, pointing a large combat knife at her. "Keep moving, you fucking bitch." His eyes flashed.

"You're a real charmer. You have a Nightmare, a huge knife, and still had to pick a child to bother." She glanced at the child. "Run."

The kid didn't need to be told twice. The mugger tried to hold onto him. Samar punched the mugger on the jaw. He crumbled, as she expected of such a coward, and the kid bolted. The Nightmare blazed out at her.

Samar couldn't move out of the way fast enough and found her back smashed into the brick wall behind her. She coughed, and Amani appeared in her hand. The Nightmare was too close to dodge her thrust and got to eat her short spear, all the way down to her elbow. With a flash of lightning, the Nightmare shrieked. Samar was on the move again.

She rushed the mugger and punched him again. He fizzled down to the wet ground. He moaned but tried to struggle to his feet. She didn't give him a chance.

"Try robbing someone without your Nightmare, you fucking bitch," Samar spat, as she tagged him with a Favor. She was so sick of these predatory morons. Even with the power of the supernatural, they still refused to pick on someone their own size.

The mugger dropped and she called it in but didn't stick around. She hobbled out of the alley. Her back would bruise. Teeth marks dotted her forearm. Thankfully, she wasn't bleeding.

That Nightmare was somehow not as strong as the ones she fought in the park. *I thought they were getting stronger.* Perhaps, she was better because she got a full night's sleep. She wasn't sure. She also didn't have the time to figure it out.

She grabbed some lunch and headed back home. She beat on her heavy bag for an hour, back throbbing as she did so. Another hot shower helped relax the muscles in her back. Her sweaty clothes were piled on the floor. She stared at the pile and shook her head.

Donning black gear practically identical to what she had just taken off, she ate her food, then put on her boots. She made her way to the tomb. She sat on the front steps and leaned against one of the pillars. Ease seeped into her bones, while a knot continued to tighten in her stomach.

"My sister and Siku got into a little thing this morning. They thought I was sleeping. He has a problem with Mechi. He's a weird guy, but she loves Mechi. She wants to marry him. It should be okay for her to sleep with him…I think anyway. I don't understand this sorta thing much."

Samar scratched her head. She tried to think of something else to discuss with the building. Mechi was on her mind. They had something in common.

"Siku uses Mechi something like he uses me. Mechi's quite the competent and accomplished warrior. If he could see Nightmares, he'd be incredible at fighting them. I'd try to train him, but he thinks my entire culture and upbringing are akin to living in the trees."

The media still portrayed Asale the way it had been about a century ago. After casting off the shackles of colonialism, Asale endured a long, ruinous civil war that left them in a bad position on the globe. People were poor, sick, and starving. But in the past fifty years, the country had developed responsible leadership and worked its way to being quite an amazing place to live. She was happy her mother saw fit to raise her there.

"Oh, I learned how to make coffee and tea today. It's a real mystery to me how Vin drinks coffee. It smells nasty. She needs to drink it to stay awake, she says. I think it tastes as bad as it smells. She bounces sometimes when she doesn't have coffee. That's a bad thing, I'm sure. I like tea. Hot chocolate is tasty too. I never had it before coming here. My mother preferred making smoothies for us because it's hot in Asale almost all of the time. Vinny used to make hot chocolate for me when I stayed at the house. She still does it sometimes when she comes by."

"I know. You told me all about it," a familiar voice said.

Samar's body tensed. She turned toward the voice. "Who's there?" She glared into the darkness.

"Hi." The young woman with the lilac eyes greeted her weakly and stepped out of the tomb's doorway. She approached Samar and sat down next to her. The subtle scent of jasmine wafted from her. It was almost distracting.

"What're you doing here?" Samar inquired.

"I sleep here. Well, I used to sleep here," the woman answered with a light laugh.

Samar scowled. "I never noticed you before."

"I slept inside, in the coffin." She pointed to the door. "You've been inside a few times when they allow people in, with your sister I think you said."

This was all correct. "How'd you know that?" *Am I being stalked? Followed? How did I not notice?* No way that'd ever happen.

"My apologies." The woman placed her hand over her heart and bowed her head slightly. "I'm Kouji, and I thought you were talking to me all of these years."

Samar's frown deepened. "What? You mean to tell me you've been here since I started coming by?" Who the hell was this woman? *If she wanted to hurt you, she could've done it during your fight or any time before that. So you might as well calm down.*

"I've been sleeping." Kouji nodded toward the doorway again. "I could hear you though. Your voice cut through the void and touched me, made me conscious to a degree." A small smile settled on her perfect face. "I woke up when you stopped coming by. I thought something happened to you, thought you abandoned me, thought you might be hurt. So many thoughts. I'm glad you're okay. I haven't been able to go back to sleep since." A small, awkward shrug. "My mother's beyond angry with me." Kouji let loose an uncomfortable laugh.

Samar shook her head, but didn't take her eyes off Kouji. "I don't understand."

"I was sleeping in the coffin," she repeated.

Kouji made it sound so simple, like it all made sense. But come on, sleeping in the coffin? *Stranger things have happened. You chase Nightmares, after all.* Nightmares didn't sleep in tombs.

"You must think I'm stupid. That coffin's made of solid marble. How were you getting in and out of that thing?" Samar inquired, catching this liar in her lie.

Kouji squinted. "That's the whole point. I wasn't supposed to leave. I was meant to stay asleep. I don't think I should've been able to hear you." She tilted her head, as if thinking about it.

"And yet you claim you did." Samar glared at her.

Kouji's brow furrowed, and she shook her head. "Let me try to explain it better. I was the black sand inside the coffin. My mother put me to sleep to save humanity."

Samar scoffed. "To save humanity?"

Kouji rubbed her forehead. "I think that's why."

"To save humanity from whom?"

"Me...maybe. I'm foggy on it right now." Kouji's eyes scanned the air, as if it had the answers. "As I said, I wasn't supposed to get up. But when you stopped visiting me, something was wrong. Or something went wrong? I'm not sure how to put it. I was aware of your absence. I missed you. I was worried about you. I thought something happened to you, and I enjoyed your company so much. I decided to look for you in case you needed help or something." Kouji nodded, more to herself, as if suddenly everything made sense.

Samar was certain her ears weren't working. "Are you serious?" Did it say gullible idiot on her forehead? There had to be a reason for Kouji telling such a farfetched lie.

"Yes, it sounds completely unbelievable, but it's the truth. I wouldn't lie to you, Samar." A small smile settled on Kouji's face.

"How the hell do you know my name?"

Kouji pursed her lips, as if confused. "You introduced yourself the first time you came by to talk. By the end, I wanted to wake up and say something back to you, to let you know you weren't alone. I just couldn't. You believe me yet?"

"No, you might just be a stalker," Samar replied, scowl still in place. Not that she understood why anyone would stalk her, especially since Kouji could've attacked her and kidnapped her. But why do all of that? Because of Nightmares? Humans worked with Nightmares all the time.

"Hmm. How can I prove this?" Kouji tapped her chin. "Yesterday, you said you didn't think your parents liked each other. Wait, it's not fair to say that because I was awake when you said that. You told me a while ago it was the day your mother died. You said you were surprised when it happened. She was so healthy, but she just fell one day and didn't move again."

Samar's chest tightened and her throat burned. Tears stung the back of her eyes. *No, no more crying. Not here. Tears won't bring her back, won't ease the heartache.* She fought the anguish down before she remembered finding her mother on the floor, motionless.

"I never told anyone..." Samar trailed off. She never told anyone about the events surrounding her mother's death, not even Evinia. Her mother was gone and that was the end of it. Details didn't matter. That was how she treated her mother's passing whenever someone had the nerve to bring it up. She was gone, end of story.

"You told me," Kouji said.

Samar continued to scowl. "I told the building." A building she thought was empty.

"So..." Kouji deflated. Her shoulders fell and her face dropped. She swallowed, loud enough for it to reach Samar's ears. She wrung her hands together. "You weren't talking to me, huh?" She whimpered. "I...I'm sorry to have bothered you."

Samar's stomach crunched in on itself. The clear hurt echoed in those words was a gut punch. Kouji might be as lonely as she was. She was trying to make a connection. *You know how that can be.*

"Is it lonely in there?" Samar asked.

"Yes," Kouji whispered. Her hands still fidgeted. Her eyes locked with Samar's and they glistened in the streetlights.

"Why didn't you wake up sooner?"

Kouji squinted, staring at the ground like it had the answers. "I couldn't. I didn't think I could, anyway. I don't think I was capable of thought for a long time."

"And why don't you go back to sleep?" Samar asked.

"I tried. It...it didn't work?" Kouji's bronze brow wrinkled. "I'm not sure. But it's amazing to be up and to be able to answer you back for once." A small smile flickered across her face, her eyes shining with joy. "If you don't want my company, I'll go back to sleep. Or I'll try to, anyway. No reason to make my mother any angrier than she is if you want to be alone and you'd rather talk to the building." Kouji gave a slight shrug as if it didn't matter. The way her fingers worked against each other said there was a right answer.

"I don't want to get you into trouble with your mother," Samar said.

Kouji waved that off. "It's okay. So I can stay with you? Keep you company?"

"Let's just sit here for a little while. I have work soon."

"I know. Security agent, right?"

"Yeah." Samar might believe this crazy story about Kouji sleeping in the tomb because Kouji knew about her mother. *It is still possible she's a stalker.* Best to keep an eye on her. At least until Samar figured out what she was about.

"I can't quite remember what a security agent is. My thoughts…" Kouji motioned around her head with both hands. "Much of my mind is jumbled, but I think you said you beat up criminals for fun and get paid for it."

"That's pretty much it." Samar shrugged.

"I'm not sure those existed when I was awake. Soldiers and guards were around, and they might beat up criminals. If city guards weren't nearby, most people had to take care of criminals themselves."

Samar nodded. Kouji made it sound like she was ancient. Her clothing suggested the same. Samar recalled seeing similar outfits in history books, now that she had a moment to think about it. Kouji wore traditional clothing that went back to the first cities and the dawn of civilization.

"Why is it you beat up criminals again? I remember it's more than being paid," Kouji said.

Samar blew out a breath. "You've heard me mention Nightmares."

Kouji nodded and rubbed her head again. "I think I should know what a Nightmare is. I could almost feel what it is."

"You saw them in the park, right?"

"I believe so, but I was more focused on you. When I caught you the other night, I wished I'd woken up sooner. I mean, I've never seen moves like that or hits that hard."

"You say that, but you dodged me easily. I've never had that happen, not even with my teachers."

"Oh, the answer's simple, but unbelievable again." Kouji scratched the top of her head, mussing her braids. "I'm not really human. Well, I am human, but I'm not. My father was human."

"Your father was human?" This was starting to sound like very familiar folklore.

Kouji shook her head. "It's a lot and muddled." She tapped the center of her forehead. "It might make sense to me later, and then I can explain it better. Didn't you talk about wanting to fight me again? I'd be happy to engage you if you want. You seem like a challenge."

Samar snorted and arched an eyebrow. "Yeah? But you dodged me so easily."

"Yeah, but like I said, I'm not technically human. You are and so's everybody else. You're knowledgeable in combat. It'd be fun to fight someone who knows what she's doing. Someone who can probably compensate for my heritage. That'd be fun."

Samar nodded. "I doubt I could. You're too fast. Plus, you can disappear."

"Well, I wouldn't disappear while I'm fighting you. I want to fight."

"You could've fought the Nightmares that night and helped."

Kouji rubbed her chin. "The Nightmares…" She nodded. "I saw shadows. They moved…they moved like smoke."

"So you can see the Nightmares?" Maybe not the full image, but something.

"I feel like I should be able to, but I didn't really see them. I was more focused on you, and they didn't catch my attention. Like I said, it was like smoke. Again…" Kouji tapped on her forehead. "I think this needs time to sort itself out. But we should still be able to spar."

Samar nodded. "Yeah, we should." It'd be marvelous to spar again. She hadn't sparred in a couple of years. She had tried with people at work, but they stopped after she beat everyone. They stopped interacting with her after that as well. She also attempted with Evinia, but Evinia couldn't keep up either, despite training her entire life in a similar fashion to Samar. "Have you been sleeping ever since I've been coming by?"

"Longer than that." Kouji scratched her cheek. "When I heard you, I became aware of the outside world again and that I was sleeping. I was conscious but so confused, except I craved your voice. I yearned to know you. I wanted to answer you because you kept coming to keep me company. You let me realize I was lonely like you. Plus, I thought there was so much for us to talk about. I was always interested in what you had to say."

"Really?" That was a first. Her mother had been the only person who was interested in what she had to say all the time. Well, and maybe some of her teachers. No one in recent years.

"I have no idea why you were the one to break through my sleep, but I enjoy everything you say. Sometimes you spark my interest so much I need to learn about stuff, and I have so many questions. I wanted to know about the mountains you come from, so I had to ask my mother."

"Your mother?" What was this part of Kouji's story?

"My mother visits me. It's hard to explain. I don't understand it, but she does. I can ask her questions. She doesn't like to answer."

"Why not?"

"Maybe fear I'll wake up. I think…" She rubbed her forehead. "I hope this'll come back to me soon, so I can answer your questions. I always listen to you go on about your job. I can't quite remember if I had a job. I listen to you talk about your father because I never knew mine, except from stories. He was nothing like yours. I was eager to learn to cook after you talked about almost burning down the kitchen."

Samar blushed and laughed a little. "I don't cook." *Anymore.*

"Or clean," Kouji added with a bright smile. "You always go on about how you wouldn't have clean clothes if it wasn't for your sister."

"You're a good listener," Samar muttered. She wasn't yet sure if that was reassuring or not. Kouji seemed very innocent and harmless, but they had fought. Kouji could do her plenty of harm if the urge overtook her.

Kouji's smile remained and her eyes sparkled. "I like hearing you talk. You do interesting things too. I mean, I had to learn to cook after you told me you nearly burned your father's kitchen to the ground."

Samar blushed again. She was quite embarrassed about how she almost set her father's huge, expensive kitchen on fire. She had been banned after that. It wasn't her fault though. The entire kitchen was way too complex.

"He was so mad at me after that," Samar mumbled.

Kouji twiddled her fingers. "And you thought he was going to hit you," she said in a low voice.

Samar swallowed. "He was so mad. He raised his hand. He caught himself, I think. I have no idea what I'd do if he ever hit me. I might take it or attack him. It'd be a decent excuse to test his skills since he thinks he's so great. He always seemed ready to hit me as hard as possible, but he always stopped himself."

Blowing out a breath, Kouji gave a slow nod. "Yeah, you said you were so relieved when Vin got you that apartment."

"She's more scared than I was that he might hit me one day. She still thinks he might. She said she had to get me out of there for her sake just as much as my own. She was a nervous wreck while I was in the house. I appreciate that she cares." One day, Evinia's love might be enough to tear her from her endless misery.

"So why did you stop coming around?" Kouji's voice dropped, low and shy.

"Vinny didn't think it was healthy for me to talk to a building. She might be happy to find out I was talking to you." She was a little pleased to discover she had been talking to someone.

"Maybe it'll make her happy. Or she might hate me," Kouji said in a low voice.

"No, you seem nice enough. She's always going on about how I should meet people. Now, I've met you, Kouji. She should be happy."

"Maybe." Kouji shrugged.

A beat of silence passed between them. Samar hated how comfortable she already was with Kouji. "May I ask you something?"

"Whatever you want."

"Why are you dressed like that?" she asked, eyes on Kouji's short pants and then at her neck beads.

Kouji's shoulders squared. "These were fine garments when I was awake." Her shoulders dropped. "From what you're wearing and what I've seen other people wearing, I don't think I'm dressed right anymore. What are those things on your feet?" She nodded to Samar's feet.

"My boots. They're shoes," she answered.

"Oh, like sandals, right?"

"Something like that." Samar gave her a nod. "Why don't you have on any shoes?"

"I didn't like them when I was awake. I always tore sandals easily."

"Okay. Why all the jewelry?" she inquired.

Kouji scratched her chin. "Hmm, I think it has to do with my status. I'm certain I was royalty, but it might have been more than that." She shook her wrists, making her bangles clang together.

"Were you wearing all of that when you went to sleep?"

"I believe I was. I can't remember too much yet. It was so long ago, and I've been dreaming for so long."

"How long?" Samar would guess thousands of years.

"No idea. I never bothered to ask my mother. I never cared until you asked me about it. I was always just pleased to see my mother when she showed up. So most questions I'd ask her tend to flee from my mind when she appears."

"You see your mother in your dreams?"

"Yes. She's not always there and then it's dark and...nothingness. It's like I'm not tethered to anything. When she is there, there's...well, there is. We can see each other and converse. Scenes come into existence, and we can interact."

Samar nodded, as if that made any sense. "What type of questions do you ask your mother?"

"Well, I ask her why it's so noisy outside a lot of the time. A frequent buzz hummed through my mind. Then, constant crashes or booms or roars. It's always blaring. Sometimes, it all hurts my head. It's mind-boggling to me how people live around here with all the noise."

Samar nodded. "I understand the feeling."

"When you started coming by, I wanted to ask her who you were, but you introduced yourself. So I didn't have to ask. I did have to ask her what language you were speaking because I was unfamiliar with it. She said you were speaking more than one after she listened to you a few times. I asked her to teach them to me, even though I never thought I'd have the chance to speak with you."

"So you speak my home language?" A bashful smile tugged at Samar's lips with hope seeping into her voice.

"*I'm pretty good*," Kouji answered in Samar's native tongue.

Samar couldn't help the gasp that escaped her. Her heart swelled. She had rarely heard her native language in three years of living in Oganja, beyond someone trying to sell her something. The sound was angelic, like water in a desert after wandering for days in draining heat. Her body tingled from the sound of the sweet words, even though not much was said.

"*Thank you for that*," Samar murmured. Her native language was spoken mostly with the tongue, and she had always mumbled when she spoke it. Her mother used to scold her when she did so, but it never changed anything.

"No, thank you," Kouji replied.

The pair sat together quietly for a moment. They sized each other up as best they could. Samar had been rather accurate when describing Kouji to her big sister. Kouji's frame had escaped her before, but she was built like a trim athlete. Kouji was like a statue made of flesh, just a work of art.

Kouji stared at Samar's hair. She put up her hand, almost like she planned to touch Samar's curls, but held off. Samar wasn't surprised by the desire. It wasn't the first time. The red tint captivated people, both here and at home.

"You fascinate me," Kouji whispered.

"Oh yeah?"

Kouji nodded. "Especially seeing you in person. Your eyes, I've never seen this color before. And you have such a distant look, like seeing to the ends of the world. Such an insane amount of loneliness and sorrow exist in your eyes, deep down into the depths."

Samar swallowed hard. What was she supposed to say to that? Sorrow didn't begin to cover it. Despair didn't scratch the surface. Would joy ever live within her again? Hell, would she ever know something beyond heartache and grief?

"I understand what you mean about your skin suffering from lack of sun. Does the sun really never come out?" Kouji's eyes went the sky.

Samar was glad Kouji plowed right on. It gave her a moment to gather herself. But she didn't know what to do with the sheer innocence and awe of discovery that poured out of those wild, lilac eyes.

"I have to go to work," Samar said with the aim of dispelling the awkwardness Kouji had brought out in her.

"Are you going to come back?" A small smile lit up Kouji's visage, as if that'd help convince Samar to return.

Samar was stunned Kouji didn't plan to follow her. "Will you be awake?"

"I will if you're going to come back."

"Well, I have to come by here when I go home," Samar answered.

Kouji nodded. "So should I wait outside for you in the morning?"

"Okay. You're not going to be cold or anything like that while you wait, are you?" she asked.

"No idea. I don't think so. I've never been cold before. I should be fine," Kouji assured her.

"You've never been cold before?" Samar was almost tempted to believe this since Kouji barely had on a shirt and didn't wear any shoes.

Kouji squinted and glanced at the sky. "Not to my knowledge."

"It's always cold around here, even in the summer. It has to be from the lack of sun." Samar didn't have a better explanation for why Oganja never warmed up. "Let me go to work. I don't want to be late. I'll see you in the morning."

Kouji's smile grew. "I'll be right out here waiting."

"Okay, bye then." Samar stood and stretched. She walked off with a sense that Kouji was watching her. A chilling breeze blew. Samar didn't think anything more of it, only still surprised Kouji didn't follow her. This was such a weird night. Somehow with no Nightmares involved.

Chapter Six

Wide Awake

"SHE'S LOVELY," SAID A voice so airy it could've been the wind singing. Mother certainly enjoyed hiding in her precious shadows and tricking the senses.

"I think so. She's going to be my friend." Kouji nodded confidently. She'd never had the pleasure of having a friend. Seeing others from a distance had always sparked a longing within her. She never understood until a precious voice cut through her sleep day after day after day.

"Can you handle a friend?"

A smile lit up Kouji's face and a strange brightness burned within her. "I'll try my best. Do you think I can?"

"I think you should go back to sleep." Mother was sort of behind her, nothing more than a shadow pulled from the wall and a ghostly hand on Kouji's shoulder. She felt almost no sensation other than a slight buzz, like the temperature had dropped. It was comforting. "But if you desire this friendship, I refuse to stand in your way. You deserve a life."

Kouji's smile grew to the point it hurt her face. "I might be able to do that now." Considering her royal parents were gone. They wouldn't stand in her way of becoming herself.

"I think you need a friend almost as bad as she does. Be kind to her, and I am sure she will be kind to you." Mother's voice was fading into the ether, like she didn't think this was the best idea.

Kouji nodded. "I'll do my best, based on her laments. Should I also help her fight Nightmares?" She wasn't quite sure what Nightmares were, even with seeing them, but a faint hum at the back of her mind made her aware they were something. She must have forgotten something she once knew. *I'm sure the memories will come back.*

"Use your judgment."

"I'll do my best." Of course, she wasn't sure she had good judgment. Yes, it was something she developed in her sleep, but would it work now that she was awake?

"Call me if you need anything."

"Yes, Mother," Kouji said.

Once Within a Dream

Mother drifted into the shadows, and Kouji knew she was gone. She'd wait for Samar in the tomb. Surely, Samar would return for her.

Kouji sat down against her coffin and stared at the wall. Samar visited her more than her mother. Only Samar's familiar, constant voice alerted her to the passage of time. Samar spoke of days. It had been so long since Kouji understood what a day was.

Samar's voice set her at ease in a way she had never felt in all her years. She itched to reply to that voice and set Samar at ease in the same way. She yearned to lighten up Samar's gloomy life.

Kouji wasn't accustomed to anyone talking to her, except her mother. Her life had been devoid of any real interactions, even when awake. She was pleased Samar had taken such an interest in her.

It was impossible to imagine her life without Samar's voice, no matter what she was saying. She'd listen to Samar complain as much as she'd listen to Samar laugh. Not that she laughed much, and even then, it was usually a dejected noise. Kouji would love to help Samar laugh more, love for Samar to sound happy, *be* happy.

"Please, don't let me mess this up," Kouji prayed, pressing her hands together. "Samar deserves to be happy, even if I don't."

She had done so many things. Most of her memories were jumbled together, but blurry images came into sharper focus with every passing second. She'd have to tell Samar and hoped Samar would continue to want to talk to her. *I suppose we'll have that discussion when all of my memories straighten themselves out.*

Samar had Kouji on her mind. She had so many questions. Hopefully, answers would come later. For now, she needed to complete her shift.

She reported for work mechanically, to the point she didn't remember doing so. As long as there were no Nightmares, she wouldn't need her mind to do her patrols.

She glanced in the direction of the tomb. Kouji had been asleep in the coffin. It was impossible to prove, but Samar believed it. Kouji might have stalked her, but she didn't see the point of the reveal if that was the case. She also didn't think a stalker would spin such a fantastic tale about sleeping in the marble casket.

"It doesn't matter. I think. It might not matter." Samar shook her head. "Kouji doesn't seem to mean any harm. If she wanted to hurt me, she had the power and ability to do so at any point." She wouldn't let it go. It'd probably never fail to blow her mind. She had never been so outclassed.

This might be something to ask her sister about. Samar wasn't sure how to explain things to avoid freaking Evinia out. Evinia would worry about her, be it for a stalker or the loneliness finally making her lose her mind. *Maybe I am losing my mind.* Insanity made much more sense than having a stalker.

"Vin," Samar called, as she stepped inside the office. It was empty.

"Huh?" Evinia poked her head out from behind her massive computer system. "Oh hey, kiddo, what's up? You look a lot better. Did you manage a full night's sleep, Sammie?"

"No, but more sleep than usual," Samar answered. She had no idea why she looked better.

"You can tell. So another boring night?"

"Yeah, a nice shoot-out or something might help keep me awake," Samar remarked. It was a shock a few Nightmares hadn't popped up to keep her busy, to keep her out of her head. They were hiding for the first time in her warrior career.

Evinia scowled and glared at her. "Don't put that out in the air. I don't want to hear my little sister was in a shoot-out ever again."

Samar rubbed her forehead. "It was a crazy first year."

"My heart could barely take it. We only just got you, and I thought we'd lose you to Okunkun Park. The gang problem was horrible. Some of the worst crimes ever happened in that park."

Samar nodded. Gang members and Nightmares had made for an awful mix. They did things to people she had never seen before and never wanted to see again. Truly the stuff of nightmares.

"You're doing a spectacular job if those gang members aren't shooting in the park anymore. When they first gave you that assignment, I was so scared for you." Evinia shook her head.

"I know," Samar muttered. She hadn't been concerned, but it was still a shock. She had already been out fighting Nightmares in Oganja since she arrived. It had been a necessary and almost pleasant distraction. Not to mention, for a long time, she didn't care if she lived or died in the fights. So she hadn't thought twice when assigned Okunkun Park.

"Then I don't want you saying you'd like a shoot-out. I don't care how bored you are. Nothing worth noting happened tonight?" Evinia asked.

"Nothing much," Samar answered in more of a mumble than usual.

Samar yearned to broach the subject of Kouji, but she didn't have a clue on how to do such a thing without sounding infatuated or easily taken advantage of or worse. Evinia might think her a full-blown lunatic. Samar didn't want to worry her sister about her mental health when Evinia already "secretly" worried about Samar's physical health. She doubted a subtle way to bring Kouji up in a conversation existed.

"Nothing again? You were very quiet on the communicator, more so than usual. At least it'll make your reports easy today," Evinia remarked with a slight laugh.

"I guess." Samar did her best not to squirm. "Um…Vin…could I ask you something?"

"Of course you can, kiddo. You can ask me anything, whenever you need to." Evinia stepped closer, patting Samar's shoulder.

"Right. Um, if someone you just met told you a really crazy story, but they had some logic-like proof to back it up, would you believe them?" Samar inquired.

Evinia arched an eyebrow, then went back to her computer. "How crazy a story? Like they were abducted by aliens? That's our brother's favorite outright lie, which I say because the kid never has any proof of any kind."

Samar waved that off. "Well, this story might be as crazy." She was also fairly certain Alvin said it as seriously as he did because his tone made it funnier. She might be able to appreciate the humor more if she ever got better acquainted with him, but he'd never let that happen. She didn't hold it against him.

Evinia squinted, studying her through her thin spectacles. "You're being extremely vague. Why are you asking this? Did someone tell you a crazy story?"

Samar rubbed the back of her neck. "It's just a question. Never mind." She shook her head. She might have to decide on her own to avoid alarming her sister, about her judgment and her sanity.

"No, no, no, no never mind. Tell me what's going on in your head. You asked that question for a reason."

Samar was saved from having to respond by Siku, of all people. She stepped fully into the office as he came up to the door. Her body reacted, needing as much distance from him as possible without running through the wall. She forced herself to keep her eyes on him rather than on the floor. Evinia glanced between Samar and their father.

"Yes, Daddy?" Evinia asked.

"Did you call your brother?" He spoke to Evinia, eyes still on Samar.

Evinia sucked her teeth. "I'd love nothing more than to do that, but my phone got unplugged and, therefore, didn't charge as intended. Apparently, I should organize this mess of wires back here a little better. I'll call him as soon as I figure out what wire is what." Evinia motioned to all the wires she had her hands tangled in.

"Call him," he ordered.

"You call him. I'm busy." She pointed to the wires again.

"Not too busy should Mechi wander by, I'm sure."

"Daddy!" Evinia shrieked.

Samar did her best not to snicker at their nonsense. Evinia glared at her, quietly calling her a traitor. Okay, fair.

"Careful, Daddy, or you'll give little Sammie some very naughty ideas," Evinia smirked with her eyes locked on Samar.

Samar grimaced as if she'd been gut-punched. She didn't need any of their father's attention on her. Siku frowned.

Samar attempted to turn invisible but was let down, not having developed such magical powers. With luck, staring at the floor and pretending a tile was the most fascinating thing to ever exist would save her from anything Siku might say or do. *Why won't he leave me alone?*

"Samar's mother would be very disappointed in her if she went around playing phone tag with some punk from this city, and I'd be very upset with her if she ever got that stupid idea." Siku spoke as if Samar wasn't in the room, which was fine by her. His disrespect was better than his attention.

"Don't want anything to soil your little angel," Evinia teased their father. The sarcasm practically dripped from her words. Siku didn't think of Samar as an angel but tried to control her life as much as he controlled his other children.

"Call your brother," he commanded in a short, angry tone.

Evinia rolled her eyes. "I will, Daddy." She gave him a smirk, knowing the expression annoyed him. She might have been trying to push him out of the room faster.

"Now," he ordered.

"Fine," Evinia conceded with a sigh. "Sammie, be a dear and toss me my cell phone."

Samar complied without a sound. She grabbed the phone off the edge of the desk from between three empty paper cups. *That's way too much coffee*. She flicked the object at her sister with ease, and Evinia caught it without a problem.

Evinia pressed a button. "Barely any battery, but let's see what happens." She called their brother.

"Yo," a groggy voice answered the phone. The room was quiet enough for them to all hear him clearly.

"Alien, are you up?" Evinia inquired. From the sound of his voice, the answer was rather obvious.

"Huh?"

"Yes, I can hear you're not up. Wake up and go to school, you little alien life-form," she teased with a smile, even though it wasn't a video call. He had to catch the smile though. Evinia's voice was *that* gentle and pleasant.

"Isn't it a holiday or something?" He let loose a long, drawn-out yawn.

"Not to my knowledge, no. So get up, get moving, and get off to school, you lazy, little slimeball," Evinia ordered in a good-natured tone.

"Can you lie and say I got up? This one time?"

"Did I not do that last week?" She cast a glance at Siku. His attention was on something in the hallway. Apparently, what was happening in the room didn't warrant his attention, now that things were being done as he desired.

"Did you?"

"I do believe I did. I did you quite a few favors last week. That one was more minor than others, and you haven't returned a favor to me yet. So, get up right now and get your lazy butt to school," she commanded.

"Yes, ma'am." He groaned. "Ya old bat."

"Hey, you brat, I'm still here," Evinia said.

"Sorry," he muttered. Evinia hung up.

When she sighed and cleared her throat, Siku glanced at her. "He's alive, up, and will be moving about shortly. My work for you is done, Daddy."

"Now, was that so difficult?" Siku asked.

Evinia gritted her teeth. "No, but it's so much more fun to annoy you this early in the morning. You should loosen up, Daddy. I mean, you're a major player for goodness' sake. Smile once and a while. Go dancing. Go smell some flowers. I hear you can walk in the park with no worries now."

"Must you try my nerves forever?" he grumbled.

Evinia winked at him. "I do believe that's why Mom had me in the first place."

Siku snorted. "I don't doubt you on that, Vinny. Samar, don't let Vinny do your reports. You do them, then go straight home. Vinny, you go straight home, too, or else. Neither of you get into any trouble either." He pointed at both of them, then left the office.

"Blah, blah, blah," Evinia muttered, making a mocking hand movement.

"Vinny, why'd you try to get me into trouble?" Samar inquired once she was certain Siku was gone.

"I was only joking. You know I'd never get you into real trouble. Besides, you laughed at me. Why'd you betray me?" Evinia countered.

"Betray you? I'd never laugh at something he said," Samar argued.

Evinia tilted her head and gave her a hard look. "You almost did."

"Sorry, Vin. I didn't think he'd say that. I got caught off guard," Samar explained.

"I didn't expect him to say that either. But let's put his nonsense behind us. We were discussing something before Daddy came in. What were we discussing?" Evinia asked with a wrinkled brow.

"Nothing important. Use your computer?" Samar pointed to the machine in question.

"Of course. Whenever you want. If you need any help, ask me. I'll be down here trying to find my damn phone cord to plug in," Evinia replied, attention going back to the many wires in her hand. "Why the hell are there so many?" She was talking to herself, or at least Samar hoped so because she didn't have an answer.

Samar opened her mouth, wanting to ask a question she couldn't quite form. Evinia lost some of the strangest things.

Samar tossed herself into Evinia's chair and began typing up her reports. She typed faster than she thought possible. *Why am I so eager?* Evinia paused and looked at her, but didn't say anything for a while.

"You seem to be in a hurry," Evinia commented as she pulled a wire away from the bundle.

"No hurry," Samar replied.

"Doesn't look that way. I've never seen you type so fast. Something planned? A date perhaps?" She gave Samar a wink.

Samar rolled her eyes. "Date." She didn't date anymore. Never again.

"Been a while since you had one of those."

Samar wrinkled her nose. "I never had one of those."

Evinia snorted. "We both know that's not true. I thought it might explain why you're rushing, but maybe not. I mean, you'd tell me if you had a date, right?"

"Yeah," Samar mumbled. She had only had a proper one of those in her life and it was at Evinia's urging. Evinia set it up and everything. Samar lasted all of ten minutes. Socializing was never her thing, and being in this city made it so much worse. One of her worst moments came from trying to be social in Oganja.

"I know you would. Look, I'll be right back. I need coffee."

"That doesn't bother you, to *need* coffee?"

"Well, I always say I could need worse things." Evinia grinned as she exited the room.

Samar shrugged her shoulders. That made some sense…maybe. She focused on her reports. Was she doing it correctly? Evinia returned and stood over her shoulder. If she did anything wrong, Evinia would inform her of the mistake.

Once she was done with her reports, Samar was ready to go. She bid her sister a hasty farewell and all but flew out of the office. She almost bowled Mechi over in her haste.

"What's the hurry? You got a goat to sacrifice?" Mechi called. She ignored him and his ignorance.

"She has to paint her face and put feathers in her head before she does that!" some other idiot added. These people were so damn stupid.

Evinia watched Samar dash out of her office. Concern bubbled in her chest. Samar was downright weird during this visit and not in her usual weirdness. She was off. She hadn't bothered to comment that Evinia went out for coffee but didn't return with coffee.

Something was up. Evinia would have to get to the bottom of whatever it was. She didn't want to chance Samar doing something that would lead to despair for her again.

"Is your father around?" Mechi asked as he stepped into the office. She thought she'd heard him in the hallway, but she was too distracted by her thoughts to be sure.

Evinia arched an eyebrow. "No. Why?"

"Well, it just looked like your weirdo sister was running away from here, and I wanted to make sure it was safe for me to be around now."

Evinia glared at him. "She's not a weirdo. Do you have to talk about her like that? You know I love my little sister."

Mechi put his hands up. "I was only teasing. I made a joke with her and everything."

"A joke?" Sighing, Evinia pushed up her glasses to rub the bridge of her nose. "Tell me you didn't say something stupid about Asale."

"It was a joke!"

"How do you not understand it's never a joke? It's not funny." She hated to have to keep going through this with him. Yes, he was trying to be friendly, but he was doing it in the worst way possible.

He puffed out his cheeks, thoroughly scolded. Hard to believe looking at him now that he had the talent and ability to take down a trained team of assailants single-handedly. "I want her to talk to me for a second. I'm trying to figure out my in with her, and this is the best I have right now. I might think she's a little more human if she'd let me take her out for a drink or whatever the hell she's into."

"I know, baby, but don't tease like that. It's not cute, and she's still having such a hard time of it. You have to figure out another way to bond with her. This isn't funny, and it's annoying to have to keep telling you this."

"Sorry, kitten." He leaned down and gave her a sweet peck. "Anyway, Sammie looked like she was running away from a fire she started."

Evinia nodded. "She was rather anxious to leave. She might be tired, but also, she was trying to tell me something. I wasn't focused enough to give her proper attention."

"Lost something again?" He grinned at her.

Evinia made a face. "It's perfectly normal to lose a charger wire among computer wires."

He snorted. "There's like five wires and they're all plugs."

"Anyway!" She gnashed her teeth at him. "Sammie was probably trying to make it home fast."

"I don't think that was it. She had that 'I'm getting the hell out of here for some better company' kind of thing." He wiggled his eyebrows.

She sighed and massaged directly above her eyebrow. "Mechi, dare I ask you to clarify your expression?" Yes, she teased Samar about dating, but she liked to think she'd have noticed if Samar was eager for such a thing.

He shrugged. "It was like she was going to meet somebody. I know about that kind of moving." He flashed her a roguish grin.

She scowled at his expression, which made him smile more. "How in the world do you figure any of that?"

"Well, your father's not around, and she was still in a hurry to get out of here. It wasn't the usual hurry that suggested she was tired, or she just wanted to leave here like usual. She wanted to go for a reason."

"Yes, she hates it here," Evinia pointed out.

"This was different. She almost ran through me and didn't even apologize."

"She probably did apologize and you didn't hear. It wouldn't be the first time."

He opened his mouth, speechless. Closing his mouth, he seemed to gather his thoughts. "She didn't bother to look at me. Hell, she might not have even realized it was me. People in the hall said stupid stuff after my joke and nothing. She didn't even turn around."

"Yes, she's learned to ignore idiots."

"Okay, but she usually at least glares at me when I joke with her. Nothing tonight. Just out the door."

"If you say so, though I'm in some agreement with you."

His face fell. "So you dragged me through that pointless interrogation and you already agree she left faster than usual? Why do you do these things to me?" Folding his arms across his chest, he let out a slight huff.

"Don't be so bitter. I'll make it up to you later, especially if you live through the day," she said.

"Your father's still around? Is he creeping around to kill me?" Mechi glanced into the hallway.

"He never stops looking for you to kill you. You've ruined his brilliant first child, after all." Her eyes rolled automatically. If Mechi wasn't good enough for her in her father's eyes, no man ever would be.

He snorted. "You being a disappointment and smart aleck certainly has nothing to do with me. After all, I love you no matter how much you rebel." He gave her a charming smile, which earned him a laugh.

"I wonder how much it bothers him to know he introduced you into my life."

"You know he told me I betrayed him when he found out we were dating."

"I don't doubt you, my love. I hope Sammie finds someone like you, so Daddy doesn't destroy her. I mean, I think he'd have gotten to me if it wasn't for you." She hadn't been in a good headspace after the death of her mother, and her father hadn't helped. Mechi made it his mission to coax her back to the land of the living. And that was before they were dating.

"You act like staying at my house saved your life." He laughed.

"I think it did." Evinia tried to think back. It was a blur, even now. "It was so much. Mom died and Samar popped up. It's hazy. Some days, I don't even remember which happened first. Alvin was unmanageable in his hatred toward Samar, and I was expected to keep us together, while Daddy acted like everything was business as usual. Yeah, he grieved, but in private where we couldn't see. I'm only aware because I caught him. I doubt Alvin has a clue his father broke down a few times, and I still don't know if it was over Mom, Samar's mother, or just having the world find out about Samar."

Mechi winced. "I don't think I ever realized how much you had on your shoulders at the time. I only wanted to help you hold it together."

"And you did. You gave me the strength to hold Samar and Alvin together. Plus, I got to see this other, sweeter side of you. The one that doesn't make racist jokes all the time."

"I'm only trying to connect with her!" Mechi threw his hands up and pretended to sob. "You love my silly, stupid jokes."

"Because I've had a lifetime becoming accustomed to you, and I understand what you mean, especially when you say something stupid. She hasn't. You can't cram a bunch of years into dumb, rather offensive jokes as your only means of communication."

He folded his arms across his chest. "You don't know that."

"You've proven it every time you try to talk to Sammie. She's not in the headspace for your bullshit, anyway, offensive jokes or not."

"Still?" He wrinkled his nose.

Evinia sighed. She was afraid Mechi might never comprehend. Her frustration went beyond his ridiculous jokes. It was out of his grasp to comprehend how Samar's entire world twisted, exploded, and vanished right before her eyes. Even Samar barely understood, and it happened to her, was *still* happening to her.

"No one would be in a good place for jokes if they're living with my father and overtly aware he doesn't want you, not just there, but in general. You know how my father is. I thought he ate her soul a long time ago, but maybe not. She needs some friends or something to help her out." It'd be a good start anyway.

Samar needed more than Evinia, she knew that much. Samar needed her culture, she needed familiarity, and more than anything, she needed warmth and understanding. Their father would sooner rip those things from her hands than provide them. He'd claim it'd make her stronger.

"I know what you mean with your father, man." Mechi shook his head. "He might as well tattoo *Daddy's little secret* on her forehead. I bet life sucked for her growing up and seeing him a whole three times a year."

"Baby, you can't make fun of my father, either," she said quite seriously. Yes, the man was screwed up and anyone who knew him well could see it, but he was still her father.

He made a twisted face. "I can't make fun of a man who wants to kill me? Amazing. After all of this, you're still Daddy's little girl." He shook his head.

She shrugged. "He's my father. Besides, I don't even want to think about how he must have treated Sammie back then. So I'd prefer if you didn't bring it up."

"All right." He blew out a breath. "No problem. I hope Sammie's okay for wherever she was going in a hurry."

Evinia nodded. "I'll have to text her sometime soon to make sure."

She was curious about what her little sister was up to. *Hopefully, she's not just rushing off to the tomb. That's not healthy.* It probably wasn't the tomb. Samar went there often and had never acted as she had that morning. She seemed anxious or eager.

It meant something. Samar was doing something she didn't want her to know anything about. Or was that what Samar was trying to tell her, and she was too distracted to follow along? *Maybe I should trust her for now. She's an adult, and she needs to sort herself out sometimes.*

Samar was slightly aware of any odd behavior. That sense kept her from running to the tomb. She was a block away when a group of five stepped into her path. She wasn't surprised by the Nightmares hovering over them, lightning of yellow and orange crackling around them. Samar rolled her shoulders. Amani appeared in her hand, pure white light glinting from the jet-black blade.

"Since when do you guys find me?" Samar wondered aloud. In all of her days of battling Nightmares, she always had to find them. This was new.

"Since you made yourself a problem," one of the Nightmares replied. This was also new. They didn't usually reveal themselves immediately and definitely didn't talk before their human hosts.

"Just when I thought all the Nightmares fled this city," Samar said.

"You should flee this city," a Nightmare hissed.

Samar smirked. "Not just yet."

The Nightmares roared at her, wide mouths black enough to swallow starlight. The humans whipped out guns. Samar was fast enough to reach them and kick the guns out of two hands. The other three didn't open fire. She was too close to their comrades.

The Nightmares didn't care about that. They piled on her, reckless on their part. It was easy to tag a couple with her spear and send the rest back with drawn-out roars. Inky spikes shot toward her, but she dodged with ease. This put too much space between her and the humans though. They fired shots.

Samar avoided the bullets, a sting to her skin as they whizzed by. Best to disarm the rest. The Nightmares, in a rush to defend their hosts, became a whirlwind with razor edges swirling around her, until she stabbed at their void with Amani. The Nightmares scattered before she caught and dispatched them, but it was coming. They only delayed the inevitable.

The humans came back with knives in hand. Samar held up her short spear, wanting to remind them she had them beaten in the blade area. They weren't put off and advanced. Bad decision. Of course, hosting Nightmares showed they were poor decision-makers anyway.

The Nightmares rushed in as well, trying to overpower her with numbers. The Nightmares realized their mistake much sooner than the humans. Using Amani, Samar was able to banish a couple of Nightmares back to the Beyond. And she was able to mark a human with a Favor, severing his connection to any Nightmares.

Still, she was swarmed. Nightmares came from a distance, trying to jab her at first, then becoming mist to choke her, as she refused them access to her body. Blades skirted her skin, but nothing too deep. She dug in her heels, holy oils wafting from Amani and searing the

Nightmares. They snarled and reared back. Samar tried to catch her breath but had no time. She'd breathe later.

Chapter Seven

Out of the Darkness

KOUJI POPPED UP AS the sound of Samar shuffling toward the tomb reached her ears and rushed out to meet her. Samar was dragging herself down the path. Kouji dashed over to support Samar with an arm around her shoulders.

"What happened? Are you all right?" *What should I do? Can I do something?* Kouji's mind spun. She should be able to help Samar, but she was unsure how. *I know I can do something.*

Samar chuckled. "You should see the other guys." She coughed, spitting blood that trickled from her forehead to her mouth.

"But you're a great warrior. How did this happen?" In all of the stories Samar told her, Kouji was unable to recall a single one that involved her being injured badly. The worst that happened was Samar had sprained her ankle one night.

"The Nightmares were tougher than I expected, and the humans used them with more efficiency than usual," Samar explained with a groan.

Kouji stared out into the misty darkness. "What do Nightmares look like?" *I feel like I should know, but I can't remember.* "I thought I saw them before, but the things I saw couldn't touch you."

Samar chuckled and made her way to the steps of the tomb. It took her longer than it should've to sit down. Kouji settled next to her. Samar's eyes focused out into the breaking dawn. Kouji did the same.

"Are they coming?" Kouji asked. She had better hearing than most and caught the usual sounds of the city.

Samar shook her head. "No, they're quiet now. It's so weird. First, they were getting stronger. Then, they got quiet. Now, they're fighting at a maddening level. I don't think I've ever faced a pack of Nightmares and their hosts before, even when they possessed the gangs."

Kouji frowned. "Any idea why?"

"Nope. I'm used to dealing with some Nightmares being strong and others being weak, like humans. They all have powers they can lean on, but this was something more." Samar rolled her shoulders. "I should go home." She groaned and climbed to her feet.

Kouji hopped up as a memory popped into her mind. She put her hand on Samar's shoulder. "You should take your time. Would you be all right with me helping?" *I can help. I know I can.*

Samar arched an eyebrow. "Help how?"

"Well, I think I can help. I've done it before, but it was a long time ago, and I'm almost certain my brain wasn't scrambled when I did it." Not to mention, she only had a flash of the memory. *Brain, I need you to figure this stuff out soon. I need to be able to be here for Samar.*

"What do you mean 'almost certain'?"

"Well, my brain's currently a mess, so I'm missing chunks of my memory, and the memories I have are incomplete. I recall being with someone...it was dark, like now..." Kouji glanced around, hoping something would jar the rest of her memory. "My hand smoked or something...wounds were healed."

Samar's face scrunched up. "Excuse me?"

"Yes, it happened. Come sit." Kouji motioned back to the stairs. *I can do this, I can do this, I can do this.*

"You can't be serious."

Kouji smiled softly. "What do you have to lose?" The question was asked in a gentle tone with the hope it'd coax Samar into listening.

Samar shrugged and sat down on the steps. "I'm not as careless as I come across."

Kouji's smile grew. "I'm aware. I've listened to enough tales of your escapades to respect you quite a bit." She put her hand on Samar's shoulder. "If I had you by my side, we would've made a pair. Of course, my father would've used us for awful works." Black smoke wafted from Kouji's touch as she spoke.

"Am I going crazy or...?" Samar didn't finish her question, but her face was a little twisted. It was hard to tell in the dark. Then, she sighed.

"How are you now?" Kouji asked as the smoke faded from her hands. She stepped away.

"What did you do?" Samar demanded, standing up to get in Kouji's face. Samar stumbled but kept her balance.

Kouji's smile remained, not fearful of Samar's puffing up. "A gift from my mother to keep me alive. My father used me and demeaned my bloodline, ready to throw me at any danger. So it was helpful I had this healing ability, for myself and anyone working with me. Do you wish for me to undo the healing?" Not that it was possible.

Samar made a fist and frowned. "No." She turned her gaze upward for a second. "This is the best I've felt, physically, in a long time."

Kouji put a little more distance between them but stayed close enough to help. Her muscles twitched when Samar wobbled slightly.

"You should take your time," Kouji commented after a long moment of silence.

"I meant to," Samar replied, bouncing on her heels. "My body feels so energized, and it's hard to control."

Kouji held up a hand. "Give it a moment. It'll pass." Her eyes went to the sky. "Does the sun seriously never come out here? I can tell it's morning, but it's like the morning before rain." It seemed impossible, but she had not seen the sun yet.

"The sun never comes out."

"My mother told me it's because the city is damned, but I didn't know she meant it."

"Damned?" Samar echoed.

"Yes, damned. You know, like cursed."

"Who'd curse this city? Not that it doesn't make sense. This place feels cursed."

"No idea." Kouji rubbed the side of her head, searching her mind for some memory. "She never told me."

"And you didn't ask."

Kouji smiled and scratched her cheek. "I forget things sometimes. Asleep too long." She stretched her arms and rolled her neck. *How long was I asleep?*

Samar nodded. "Do you want to go somewhere? We could walk around and do something. The city has to look different from when you were awake. You can experience it, what it's like now."

"I'm not sure it was a city when I was awake." Kouji twisted and turned to take in the extraordinary sight. She searched for memories and saw only a barren flatland in her mind's eye.

"All the more reason to walk around and take in the sights."

"True."

"C'mon."

Kouji nodded and stepped down to join Samar on the cracked sidewalk, and the pair silently walked off. The city was already busy with rivers of early morning people, whose combined voices seemed like a roaring noise. Kouji was equally impressed and overwhelmed, her senses flooded. She had no way of making sense of the cacophony.

"What is all of this? These buildings reach the gods." Kouji pointed ahead.

"Those are called skyscrapers for a reason."

"Yes, I understand."

"I was impressed when I first saw them as well. I had only seen buildings this tall in shows and movies."

Kouji nodded, not that she had any idea what movies were. This place was so much. It was impossible to take it all in, to figure out what was happening, what was important. If only the sun were out to brighten the experience. Despite the marvels around them, most people who passed Kouji stared at her rather than at these magnificent structures.

"Why's everyone staring?" Kouji asked, head on a swivel, as she glanced at people who gawked at her.

Samar glanced at her. "It might be your clothes. They're not normal for this place. Here, wear my jacket." Samar opened her jacket.

Kouji eyed the piece of clothing. "Um, what do you want me to do with it?"

"Just put it on." Samar took back her black jacket and demonstrated by putting Kouji's arm through one sleeve.

Kouji followed her example and slid her other arm into the other sleeve. Samar pulled the jacket up on her and straightened it out, then pulled on a tab that closed the garment, covering Kouji's neck beads.

"There, that should stop some people from staring. But these people are weird, and they might keep staring for no reason that we can figure out," Samar said.

"I can understand why you want to go home most of the time," Kouji commented. She wasn't very comfortable being watched like some stage play. Vague memories scratched at the edge of her mind, urging people to look at her and see her coming. They never did.

"I don't really care about them. I miss things this place lacks," Samar replied with a shrug.

Kouji nodded and twiddled her fingers together. "Is that what makes the place a home? Having things that this place lacks?" *Did I ever have a home to understand any of this?* She was certain the answer was no. That was unlikely to change as her memories came back.

"I guess. I never gave much thought to what makes some place a home, but that sounds right. Maybe there are just some places you're comfortable. This isn't one of those places for me," Samar answered.

"What's missing here that you would find at home?"

Samar sighed. "There's so much missing. In all honesty, even if I went home, the biggest piece will always be missing. Nothing would ever bring Mom back. No matter where I go, Mom will never be there."

"Oh," Kouji smiled. "That one I don't understand." Her mother was always with her now.

"No? Isn't everyone you ever knew gone now?" Samar asked while they continued walking. Kouji stopped paying attention to the city, favoring the conversation with Samar over the sights.

Kouji shrugged. "No one who mattered. I didn't find out about my mother until nothing mattered, and now she's always with me." *Wait, did anything ever matter?* No seemed like the right answer, but she wasn't sure yet.

"Well, that I don't understand. But what about places that allowed you to be comfortable? To be yourself?"

"No, I have no idea who I am. I've never felt comfortable anywhere, except when I was sleeping. When I was asleep, I didn't have to worry about things and didn't have to follow orders. Sometimes, I'd think too hard. Then, I wasn't even comfortable being me. I guess, I'm not even at home in my own skin sometimes." Kouji looked at her limbs. What was a body anyway? A machine to carry out tasks given to her.

Yes, her memories were scattered, but it was so much more than that. She had never felt like she was herself. An itch at the back of her mind tried to remind her what was wrong. It was like she had never been someone.

Samar gave Kouji a sidelong glance and shook her head. "That's too bad. You have to love yourself before anybody else can. My mother always said so. She said, if you don't love yourself nobody else can love you because they don't know you, because you don't know you."

Kouji let those words sink in. They should've hit in some way, but they didn't. She smiled. "Your mother never met me."

"So does someone love you without you loving you?"

Kouji tapped her chin. "Yeah, a couple of people…I think anyway." She gave Samar a full look with a self-satisfied grin. "Do you love you?" she countered.

Samar was silent for a long time, eyes on her feet. "It's a fair question. I'd like to think I do. Things are muddled right now, but I don't mind who I am."

"Not really the same as loving yourself, but still more than I can say," Kouji chirped. It was pleasant to walk around and talk.

"I guess, at the most, I like myself right now. I'd like myself more outside of this city…among other things," Samar mumbled, face tense and shoulders scrunched up. She was visibly uncomfortable.

"I don't doubt that. You don't seem to have a problem with who you are though."

"I don't." Samar swallowed and clenched her jaw. "Being surrounded by so many things I dislike preys on my mind more than I like."

Kouji nodded. "We don't have to talk about this anymore, if you don't want to."

"We don't. You hungry? When was the last time you had something to eat?"

"I'm not sure," Kouji replied with a shrug and a laugh. "It had to be a very long time ago. Black sand doesn't need to eat, after all."

"I guess you make a point. Is there anything in particular you want to eat?" Samar asked.

Kouji thought for a moment, and her tongue reminded her of the best food ever. "Do they still make koies?" Her stomach rumbled at the mention of the sweet treat.

Samar made a face. "Koies?"

"Yeah, it's like fried dough with honey or syrup on it. I used to love those things." Kouji licked her lips. If they had the talent and ability to build structures past the sky, surely, they had to make the best pastries.

Samar tapped her chin. "No, I don't think they make those around here."

Kouji couldn't help the pout that conquered her face. She'd love nothing more than to indulge in her favorite treat with Samar. "But there's so much here!"

Samar nodded. "While they might not be the same thing, I know where we can get something like you described. Have some decent tea too."

"Really?" Kouji brightened. She looked forward to this treat.

"Yeah, we can have some donuts."

Kouji's face scrunched up. "What's donuts?" She didn't recall Samar ever mentioning this sort of thing. Of course, Samar didn't often discuss food, unless it compared to something from her homeland.

"You'll like them if you like fried dough. I liked them the first time I had them."

"I look forward to it then."

Samar took Kouji to a little donut place Evinia had taken her to during their first tour around the city what felt like a lifetime ago. She hadn't had donuts before that. Now, she had experienced plenty, and this place was the best.

"It smells delightful in here," Kouji said as they stepped inside.

"Tastes better," Samar replied.

Kouji stared around the tiny café as if it was some majestic estate. Samar went to the counter and bought an assortment, so Kouji had the chance to figure out which donuts she liked or disliked. Everything was fresh, as the café had just opened, ready for their morning rush. Everything was perfect, as long as the café didn't end up too crowded.

Black tea went well with the donuts. Should they eat at the shop or go home? Her apartment was barely suitable for her, so she definitely didn't want to have company. *Evinia would scold me if I had company with the place looking the way it does.* She took a seat at a table by the window, and Kouji followed. People rushed by, starting their day.

"Sorry. I didn't ask how you take your tea." Samar slid the hot cup in front of Kouji.

Kouji smiled. "I'm sure it's fine. I haven't had proper tea in who knows how long anyway."

"Are you sure?" Samar was very particular about tea when it came to sharing it with other people. It was a huge part of her upbringing, and it was rude to serve poor tea.

"Yeah, I don't like milk much, so the tea will work."

Samar's eyebrows curled. "There's more than tea and milk."

"I don't want any wine or beer either."

Samar laughed a little. *Okay, Kouji might be as old as she says she is if she thinks those are the only drink options.* "There's more than water, milk, beer, and wine to drink."

Kouji tilted her head. "Like what?"

"Drink your tea. On our way out, I'll get you something else. If you don't like that, I'll just get you another choice until you do like one."

With a smile, Kouji nodded then turned her attention to the open box of donuts. Her finger hovered as though she couldn't decide, eyes darting from one donut to another. Samar sipped her tea and watched the process.

"That one has jelly in it," Samar said when Kouji paused over a jelly donut.

"Jelly?" Kouji's face scrunched up.

"Preserved fruit filling. You might like it. It's too sweet for me."

Kouji nodded. "They smell rather delicious."

"They taste as good as they smell. I like these coconut ones. They remind me of a food we have in Asale called puff." Samar picked up one of two with shredded coconut. "Try as many as you want."

"I'll have the same." Kouji grabbed the other coconut donut. She held it to her nose. Her eyebrows jumped a little, and she bit in. She squeaked as her eyes sparkled. "That's amazing!"

A small smile settled on Samar's face. "Best ones here."

Kouji downed the donut in two bites. *Whoa!* Samar wasn't sure she chewed. She kept her thoughts to herself, sipping her tea and savoring her own donut. Kouji surveyed the remaining donuts, hand hovering once more. It was kind of adorable.

"Just pick one and try it," Samar suggested.

"There are so many. I mean, with koies, it was either honey, syrup, or nothing at all. This is different."

"Here." Samar grabbed a chocolate-covered donut with a napkin and placed it before her companion.

Kouji dove right in and bit the chocolate donut with gusto. Her face distorted.

Oh no, she hates it. Samar's stomach twisted. Then, Kouji's eyes twinkled. It looked like something touched her soul.

"This is so damn good," Kouji declared with a delighted grin. She shoved the rest of the donut in her mouth.

"Try this one next." Samar smiled and pointed to another donut in the box.

A frosted donut with sprinkles got a similarly excited reaction. Samar sipped her tea, ignoring the people who showed up and moved around them. Her attention stayed on Kouji.

"Oh, it's all so good!" Kouji giggled.

Samar's heart thumped at the sound. She continued to point out donuts for Kouji to try, until only her least favorites were left in the box. Kouji stared down at the leftovers and reached for another donut, despite the fact that her complexion had dulled and her eyelids drooped. *She probably ate too much.* Kouji munched on the donut, anyway, then took another and another and finally the last one.

"My teeth hurt, but it was all so delicious," Kouji said, massaging the right side of her face with her hand.

Samar nodded. "Too much sugar too fast. Drink more of your tea. It might help."

Kouji nodded and went back to her tea. Samar had finished her tea several donuts ago. In fact, by the time she had finished her tea and donut, Kouji had already had six.

"I can't believe you ate eleven donuts on your own. Beyond your teeth, how are you doing?" Samar asked.

"Stuffed." Kouji smiled and patted her stomach. Despite the slightly ashen complexion muting her golden skin, she appeared quite delighted and pleased with herself. It was almost precious.

"I'll bet. You're not sick or anything, right? I remember when I ate about ten donuts my first time here, I felt sick. Are you okay?" Back then, Evinia had laughed until she realized Samar had to throw up and made a mad dash for the restroom.

"No, I'm fine." Kouji's hiccup turned into a deep groan. "Okay, stomach might be a little bothered, but I'm fine. Thanks for asking. Thanks for so many, um, what were they called again?"

"Donuts."

Kouji's face lit up. "Yeah, thank you for all the donuts. They're so tasty. So what now?" Another hiccup erupted from her throat. She downed the last of her tea.

"I'm not sure. You wanna keep walking?" Samar wasn't used to looking for an activity to share with someone. When she went outside, she usually had a purpose, like going to work.

"I don't mind."

"Can you tell me more about yourself while we walk?" Samar held the door as they exited the donut shop.

"Sure, what is it you want to know?"

"Um, how old are you?" Samar wondered if someone younger was able to defeat her. That'd be more embarrassing than barely being able to lay a finger on Kouji.

Kouji squinted and stared at the cloudy sky. "Not counting how long I've been asleep, I think I'm around eighteen, nineteen, twenty. Somewhere around there. I don't think I can be older than twenty though. I never kept track of it, as it never seemed important. Of course, many things that didn't seem important before are important now. My mother would know. I'll ask her. Anything else?"

"Do you have any hobbies?"

"No."

"None?" Even Samar had hobbies.

Kouji shook her head, but that twinkle never left her eye. It was almost unsettling, as if Kouji wasn't able to form any other facial expression. "None that I can think of. I don't really know what counts as a hobby though."

"You said you cook. That sort of counts as a hobby."

"I suppose it does, but I don't actually cook. I have a general understanding of how to, in theory, but I've never actually cooked."

Samar's face scrunched up. She didn't comprehend. "So what do you do in your spare time?"

Kouji grinned. "Cause trouble."

"Me too. Where'd you learn to fight?"

Kouji rubbed her forehead. "Been learning since birth from what I understand. My father started my training. He used to have guards and warriors crush me to rebuild me. He made me a force to be reckoned with. What about you?"

That sounded more like abuse than training, but Samar kept that thought to herself. "My mother thought it'd keep my mind busy and sharp." She wasn't sure if she should mention Nightmares. Kouji didn't seem concerned about them in the park before.

"And help you fight Nightmares, like she tried to do?" Kouji asked.

"You really heard me talking to the tomb, huh?"

There was that bright, adorable smile again. "Heard every word."

"She trained me to fight Nightmares because I had the ability to see them, plain as day, when I was a small child. She wanted me to be able to deal with them, especially if they tried to tempt me."

"Did they?"

"No, never tried to tempt me. They've only attacked me since I was a small child. It bothered my mother because she couldn't actually see them. She had holy relics to help her spot them and holy marks." Samar showed Kouji her tattoo. "But it's damn hard to fight Nightmares when you can't completely see them, especially on dark nights."

Kouji nodded. "I can only imagine. The marks don't allow you to see them completely?"

"The results vary. My mother was able to vaguely make them out, but not fully see them."

"It's probably hard on a mother not to be able to protect her child the way she wants to."

Samar shrugged. "She did her best. Nightmares never hurt me on her watch, and she had me trained by the best. My teachers always said I took to it like I was meant to fight Nightmares. Not just combat, but the reading, the research. I drank it up like my mother did." She enjoyed all of it. She was not sure why, but she did.

"You genuinely enjoyed being with her, huh?" Kouji inquired in a low voice.

"I loved being with my mother. Maybe it was because we were so similar, and I wanted to be just like her. She's really the only company I ever had and the only company I ever wanted. She was like…no, she was Goddess to me. Almost everything I used to do was my way of worshipping her. I wanted to impress her with everything that I do. That's why I have to fight you again." Samar grinned.

Kouji smiled right back. "Whenever you like. Sounds like we both live to fight."

"That's nice." Samar accidentally yawned.

Kouji arched an eyebrow. "Are you tired?"

"Just a little."

"Well, maybe you should get some sleep. I can walk you home, then go back to the tomb." Kouji offered.

"You're going to spend your whole day alone at the tomb?" That didn't sit well with Samar. Sure, Kouji had more than likely been doing that in the past, but she had been asleep.

"I don't have any other place to spend my day." Kouji shrugged.

Samar chewed on the inside of her cheek. An awful idea floated across her mind. Her sister would truly question her sanity if she knew what Samar considered. Samar questioned her own sanity. *Something has to be wrong with me.*

"You wanna…you wanna…well…you could stay at my place." In her mind, Samar heard Evinia's voice scream *Stranger danger!* Right after that, she heard Evinia urging her to make a friend.

Kouji gasped. "Are you sure?"

"Well, I'm the one that woke you up, right? It's only fair of me to offer you a place to stay for all the trouble and worry I caused, right?" This sounded hospitable and that was important in her culture.

"Are you sure?" Kouji repeated. "Is this safe for either of us?"

Samar smiled. "I'm sure. If you try anything, I promise I'll stab you. If I try anything, you know you can beat me."

Kouji chuckled. "You are correct about that. Besides, my mother would ruin me should I do anything to you. I'm rather harmless at this point in my life. Besides, it'd be rather stupid of me to try anything against the one person who means enough to wake me up from a supposed eternal sleep. I'll be on my best behavior." Kouji squared her shoulders as if that made her word binding. Somehow, it was endearing.

"All right. Come on, this way. I'm sorry in advance for how the place looks and partially smells." She shouldn't be entertaining in her squalor, but she no desire to be rid of Kouji just yet.

Kouji waved that off, and they strolled to Samar's apartment. Kouji gasped at the sight, as if she hadn't seen taller, more impressive buildings during their walk to the donut shop. The building itself was quite rundown and located in a subpar neighborhood of junky lots, abandoned buildings with boarded and broken windows, torn-up sidewalks, and busted fire hydrants.

Samar never complained about where she lived. Anything was better than living with her father, and she had to take what she could afford. She turned the key in the lock but had to kick the door in.

"Sometimes it gets jammed," she explained. "Watch your step," she cautioned her guest.

"Homes in this time are weird," Kouji muttered as she stepped inside.

"Mine certainly is. Let me give you the grand tour," Samar said with a bit of humor in her voice since she lived in a small studio space. "The kitchen." She motioned to the left where her stove and refrigerator were located. "The living room." She motioned to the right where she had a sofa. "Bedroom." She pointed to the back of the room where her bed was. "The bathroom." She pointed to the cracked door. "And the entertainment center." She pointed off to the space where her heavy bag was set up. "Or there." She motioned to her bookshelf.

"You live here by yourself, right?" Kouji asked.

"Just me and whatever's in this mess that isn't paying rent. You can throw the jacket anywhere you want. If you get hungry, I've got cereal on the counter, but that's pretty much all I've got. I don't have a TV or anything."

"Yeah, because you prefer to read when you have the time. Don't worry about me. I'm not hard to entertain. I'll be fine until you wake up," Kouji assured her.

"If you say so. I'll see you in a few hours," Samar said.

Samar disappeared into her bathroom and took a quick shower. She dressed in her usual sleeveless tee and boxers. Exiting the bathroom, she spotted Kouji at the bookshelf, going through the titles. Samar simply dropped onto her bed. She fell asleep quite easily, despite having a relative stranger in her house.

Chapter Eight

A Little Bit of Sunlight

KOUJI WATCHED SAMAR RESTING peacefully. There was something comforting about watching her breathe. *I can't possibly deserve this wonder in my life.*

"I'm glad I woke up for this, for her," Kouji mumbled. They had a connection, an intrigue. Something about Samar assured Kouji she was safe, and that was so damn important. Samar wouldn't use her, despite her fight against these Nightmares.

The Nightmares. Kouji needed to learn more about them than the little Samar had told her while she was asleep. She'd been fascinated, curious, and confused, even then. But seeing the damage these creatures had done to Samar, she required more knowledge. Of course, she needed to know more in general. She needed to better understand this world, this time.

"I won't be any type of company for her if I have to keep asking her ridiculous questions." Kouji didn't want Samar to get sick of her.

Kouji gave herself a tour of Samar's little abode, wanting to figure out how things worked or what they were. Kouji inspected everything possible, starting with a heavy, hanging sack made from red leather. It was obviously a work tool, beat-up, worn, and covered with grey patches.

Kouji searched her mind, diving through words from Samar over the years, trying to figure out what this thing was. *Oh, she practices fighting on it! Her heavy bag! Yes!* Samar would need another soon. Samar once reported bursting her first one. This bag was going the same way.

"She has such power," Kouji whispered with awe.

Kouji stepped into the tiny bathroom. She guessed the tub and basin were for washing, but was unsure where the water came from. She didn't want to touch anything to find out. She treated the kitchen the same way, but peeked into the cabinets. They were mostly empty.

In the end, Kouji settled at the bookshelves, which reached to the ceiling. The books might not help her understand this time period or this city, but she'd absorb the knowledge that mattered to Samar. That was more important than anything else.

Kouji wasn't sure where to start, so she grabbed a book at eye level. She made herself comfortable on a weird, broad chair, tucking her feet underneath her. She cracked open the book and was surprised the words made sense to her, even though she was certain she should have no knowledge of this language.

Come to think of it, I shouldn't be able to speak it either. I shouldn't be able to understand Samar. She wasn't sure why she had this ability, but she was more than pleased she did.

She began reading, immediately buried in the history of Asale. She found herself familiar with the topic through Samar's words over the years. Seeing it on the page helped cement it in her mind.

Eventually, she got to stories of the Nightmares. As she absorbed more information, it clicked into place. These were called Abominations in her time. There was something else about them. Something she couldn't quite recall yet. *I'm sure it'll come to me eventually.*

Samar woke and groaned as she sat up. She yawned and stretched her arms. The radiance of Kouji's smiling warmed her before she noticed Kouji was on the sofa, a couple of feet from the bed. She had a stack of books next to her. She noticed more than that.

"You cleaned up?" Samar asked, confused. Her apartment was spotless. How long had she been asleep?

"Yes, I thought it'd be a pleasant surprise. Is it all right?" Kouji looked around as if she had done something wrong.

"It wasn't a bad thing, I'll tell you that, but you're a guest. You shouldn't clean up," she replied. Her sister didn't even fully clean her apartment.

Kouji shrugged. "But you always say you don't clean. You say you should, yet you still don't. I figured it wouldn't be so bad if I cleaned up. I wasn't sure what to do at first, but I managed. I didn't upset you, right?" Her lilac eyes shimmered.

"No, thank you. Thank you so much," Samar answered. What else could she say? It was a sweet thing to do, but it was embarrassing. She was raised better than this.

"It was no big deal, as you say." A small smile painted Kouji's full lips, then she glanced away.

Samar's throat went dry at the expression. Her brain stopped functioning for more time than she liked. *What the hell is wrong with me?*

"So since all I have is cereal in the house, do you want to go out and grab a bite to eat?" Samar was trying to be polite, but also with the hope of being normal.

Kouji tilted her head. "What do you mean?"

"Eat some food. Come on, I'm rather hungry. Grab the jacket that you had on earlier. Wait, where did you put all the clothes that were on the floor?" She scanned the room for all of her dirty clothes.

"I noticed a basket by the heavy bag and a few of your clothes were in that. I thought that was where the dirty clothes went."

Samar glanced over at her hamper, discovering it was filled with her clothes. "Wow, thank you very much, Kouji."

There was that smile again. "No need to thank me. I put the jacket thing in there as well."

"Okay, well, for the future, the jacket you can wear more than once, even if it's wet. You hang it up in the closet, which is the door next to the front door." Samar pointed to the closet. "I've got another jacket you can wear, and I'll throw on a hoodie. I'll fish that one out later."

Kouji shrugged. Samar yanked on a t-shirt and grabbed a black hoodie. She went to the closet and found her other black, baseball jacket for Kouji.

The pair walked into the grey afternoon and went to a fast-food restaurant. These were the only types of restaurants Samar tended to go to. A few of them even sold food from her homeland. It was better to have a cheap imitation than a real restaurant trying to replicate the original and falling short.

"What sort of food do they serve here?" Kouji asked, eyes glued to the glowing menu above the cashiers.

"Street food," Samar answered.

Kouji nodded. "I didn't get to that in your books."

"You had time to read too?" *How long was I asleep?* She checked her phone to make sure it was the day she thought it was. It was her usual time to be up. How had Kouji accomplished so much in a few hours? *And what am I doing wrong where I can't do that?*

"My brain processes information faster than most."

Samar was unsure what that meant and didn't have time to inquire. It was their turn and Samar ordered since the menu made no sense to Kouji. Apparently, the words were familiar, but the meals weren't.

"Where are they preparing the meal?" Kouji asked as they stood off to the side.

Samar nodded toward the back. "Out of sight, on a grill. A lot of the things they make taste better on an open flame, but it's still enjoyable." It was almost an apology.

"I'm sure it'll be fine." Kouji smiled.

It'd be wondrous to treat Kouji to something beyond fine. Kouji was in awe of everything, so she should experience the finer things in life. Except, Samar had no clue what those were and had no way to afford them if she did. Before she could spiral down those thoughts, their orders were placed in front of them.

Kouji's lilac eyes popped open. "Wow, that is fast."

Samar shrugged. "Not really compared to other places, but I guess compared to whatever people went through when you were last awake it is quite fast, huh?" She led them to a table next to a window, thinking Kouji might appreciate the dreary view.

"Remarkably so." Kouji sat down across from Samar. "Does a god or some other deity fix the food for that to happen so fast? Magic, perhaps?"

"No, I'm almost certain a grill makes the food, and a microwave or lamp of some kind keeps it warm," Samar replied.

Kouji squinted, eyes going up in thought. "I'm still unfamiliar with many things. I know what a grill is. Food was grilled in my time. You've mentioned a microwave before, but I'm still unsure what it is."

"I have one at home. I'll show you how it works." She had plenty of instant noodles for a demonstration.

Kouji nodded and Samar slid her food over to her. Kouji tilted her head toward the aluminum bowl. Samar chuckled, reminded of when that was her. Two strangers in a strange land. She popped the top and Kouji copied her actions.

"It smells delicious," Kouji said, damn near putting her nose in her bowl.

Samar smiled. "Try it. If you want, we can spice it up a bit." She pulled several sauce packets out of the bag.

Kouji nodded and they dug into their food. Samar smiled at the way Kouji's eyes lit up. Honestly, the bowl of red rice and diced goat was better than usual. Still, she added sauce to their food. Kouji squealed at her first taste. Her eyes danced as she chewed.

"This is incredible! Food never tasted like this when I was awake," Kouji said.

Samar smiled. "It's decent. Vin always tells me to be careful though. She claims this place doesn't use real goat meat." She was almost certain Evinia was joking, but she wouldn't put it past this city to ruin a decent meal.

"Tastes real enough to me." Kouji tore off a piece of flatbread and scooped up the meat and rice, the real way to eat it.

Samar had no idea how much she needed to see that sight. The natural motion of Kouji eating with her hands, without as much as a discreet glance around, was just the right bit of home. Samar sniffled.

"Are you all right?' Kouji asked.

"Yes, I'm fine."

"You're not eating."

"Oh." Samar turned her attention to her food, using her flatbread as a scoop rather than her fork. "So, Kouji, do you have a last name?" Samar asked, then started to eat her food.

"Last name?"

"Family name? Clan name?" Samar didn't have a clan name. They were no longer common in Asale, thanks to so many periods of migration and the turbulent times of the past.

Kouji's eyes lit up in recognition. "Yes, of course, I have one of those. I'm Kouji Kataban, after my living father. Kouji Kataban Kayax." The final name was more than likely her clan name.

So many questions. Start with the simple one. "Living father?"

Kouji ate a little more of her food and sipped her drink. "Oh, well, I'm complicated when it comes to parents. I had four parents, I guess you could say. My birth father died before I was born. My birth mother, I was taken away from her. She was forbidden to see me, and I was given away right after she had me. I'm named for the family I was given to, part of their clan."

Samar nodded. "You were given away? Didn't your birth mother miss you?" She could hardly imagine someone taking her from her mother. Her mother would've torn the person apart. Samar would've killed someone for daring to try to take her from her mother. She had fought the people who had to remove her mother's body from the house until they managed to tranquilize her.

Kouji's eyes misted over. "She did, very much so."

"So what happened?"

Kouji scratched her head and stared at the ceiling, as if searching or deciding. It was possible her mind was still in shambles, but it was also possible she had no desire to discuss those matters. After all, it had to be terrible to think about being ripped from her mother.

"It's all right, Kouji. You don't have to talk about it if you don't want to."

Kouji took a deep breath. "I want to. I want to tell you everything. The same way you shared everything with me, I want to share everything with you. I want you to know everything about me, but it's still…" She waved her hand in front of her face. "Hazy."

"We've got time for that, right? I mean, it's not like you're going back to sleep today, are you?" Or so Samar hoped. She longed to share other moments with Kouji. Would she take to other bits of Asale like this poor excuse of a meal?

"No, I'm not going back to sleep today. I don't think I'll ever go back to sleep now. I guess we do have time," Kouji realized with a grin.

"Then you can tell me all about yourself later on."

"I guess so."

"So eat." Samar nodded toward the lunch bowl.

"Oh yeah." Kouji laughed, a sheepish sound, and turned her attention back to her food.

Samar couldn't help herself. She was lost in watching Kouji eat. When their eyes locked, Samar's heart skipped a beat.

"This is so delicious. You're going to eat yours, too, right?" Kouji asked.

Samar yelped. "Oh yes."

"That's twice in one day you've shown me incredible food." Kouji grinned.

"Well, consider it thanks for cleaning my apartment and listening to me whine for three years."

Kouji shook her head. "I never thought you were whining. You were reaching out. I've reached out before."

"Yeah?"

"I've yearned for connection. I'm aware of how it is to need someone to talk to. My mother says everyone needs someone to share things with. You needed to feel accepted somehow. I did want you around, even though I could never say. I was always so happy when you came by. I was glad you were there, offering me that connection."

Samar was flattered, cheeks burning. *What the hell is wrong with me? I can't be so attention-starved that one person saying a kind word to me makes me want to float away.* She had no idea why she was so elated sitting across from Kouji.

The pair sat quietly and ate their meals. They stole glances at each other every once in a while, until their food was gone. Samar noticed Kouji had a huge glob of sauce on the side of her mouth. She hesitated for a moment before reaching over and wiping the sauce away with her index finger.

"Huh?" Kouji flinched and pulled away from the contact.

Samar swallowed. Had she gone too far? Kouji's eyes were large and wild for a long moment. Apparently, she wasn't used to being touched, something Samar understood.

"Sorry about that. Sauce." Samar held up her sauce-covered finger, then cleaned her hand with a napkin.

"Oh." Kouji's laugh seemed awkward, skipping in the middle. "Thank you. I was unaware I was eating so messy."

"It's fine. You enjoyed it."

"Yes. It was delicious."

"Better than usual," Samar agreed. Maybe they got a new cook.

Kouji nodded. "So what do we do now?" Her eyes drifted outside where droplets of rain tapped against the glass.

"No idea. I've got a while before work. Do you want to go to a movie?" Samar inquired. It'd offer Kouji a little more wonder for this time period.

"A movie? What's that?"

"What's a movie?" Samar tapped her chin. "Well, it's, um, it's like…a movie. Oh, I've got it." She snapped her fingers. "A movie is like a play but on a screen."

"A play on a screen? Are you sure you have time for something like that?" Kouji inquired. "A play was a whole day's event."

"Yeah, movies aren't as long. I need to go home and get money though. I can check what's playing and stuff too. Come on. It'll kill some time for us." Samar cleared their table and waved Kouji on.

Kouji had trouble keeping up with Samar on the walk home, lost in the scenery. How had all of this come about? From the history books she'd managed to read, it might've been millennia since she was last awake. It was hard to wrap her mind around the passage of so much time. How was she supposed to explain it to Samar?

"Kouji!" Samar yanked her forward just as something sped by.

"Oh." She had nearly been run down.

"Are you okay?"

Kouji nodded. "Yes. Lost in my head for a moment. I'm sorry."

"It's fine. I'm aware this is a lot for you to take in. I can't begin to tell you how many times I was almost hit by cars, and I'm familiar with them. This city is a lot."

"It is, but you dislike it."

Samar nodded. "I do. Every second of it except for today, so far."

Kouji smiled and realized they were still holding hands. She gave a little squeeze, and Samar didn't let go. It was new and warm. Kouji never wanted to let go, but they had to upon returning to Samar's apartment.

"I think we should change your clothes," Samar said. "Oh, do you want to take a shower? Bathe?"

"Um…" Kouji would love to do that. "Yes. I haven't cleaned at all since waking up."

"And you have this dirty rain just clinging to you. Come. I'll show you how to work the shower."

Kouji nodded and followed Samar into the bathroom. Samar explained how to change the temperature of the water with the turn of a handle, which had to be magic. The water rained down from a nozzle. A bottle had cleansing liquid to put in a cloth.

"I'll find you some clean clothes for when you get out," Samar said and stepped out of the room.

Kouji studied the shower. She should be able to handle this. It didn't seem so hard. It wasn't like she hadn't bathed before.

She turned on the water and stripped out of her clothing, including her small clothes. She let piping-hot water pour down on her, relaxing her tense form. She hadn't realized she was so wound up. She had no reason to be.

Since waking up, she was having the time of her life, as far as she knew. Yes, she still had huge gaps in her mind. What she did recall was nothing like this. She'd rarely had a moment in her life when her time was her own or when her decisions were her own.

She washed her body with the cleansing liquid, scrubbing every place twice as instructed by Samar. The scent of the liquid was soothing and filled her mind with images of Samar. Her stomach fluttered, but in a pleasant way.

Kouji lost track of time but eventually got out of the shower. Water dripped from her form. She grabbed a towel and dried herself as best she could. Her braids were drenched, and the towel didn't help. She stepped out.

"I'm not sure how to dry my hair," Kouji said.

Samar gagged and hopped up. "You have to wrap the towel around yourself!"

Kouji looked down at her nude body. "Why? I'm dry, but my hair isn't. What to do about that?"

Samar stared at the floor. "Here, try these clothes on first. We'll figure out your hair after that. My hair is short enough where the towel is usually enough."

Kouji nodded, even though Samar wasn't looking at her. Nudity must be a problem in this society. Kouji accepted the clothes and went back into the bathroom. She needed her clan beads, royal sash, and jewelry. Then she put on the clothes Samar handed her.

"Are the pants meant to fit this way?" Kouji asked as she stepped out of the bathroom again. She didn't mind that the pants were well above her ankles, but that didn't seem to be how they were worn now.

Samar's eyes were on the floor, but she slowly glanced up. "Oh. You have a few inches on me. I guess it's fine if you don't mind. Do they fit around your middle?"

Kouji gave a solid nod. "Yes." They plunged on her hips but were fine otherwise.

Samar eyed her. "You can tie them if you need to. You're more slender than I am."

"It's fine. My sash is more than enough."

Samar nodded. "Last, we need to get you some shoes. I don't think they'll let you into a theater without shoes."

Kouji wasn't sure what any of that meant but let Samar work. Her feet were too big for any of Samar's boots, but she offered an old pair of something she called flip-flops. The shoes, pants, and short-sleeved shirt were all black.

"We'll take the jacket just in case," Samar said.

Kouji shrugged. "You're running this show."

"We might be in trouble then."

Kouji smiled and took Samar's hand. "I think we're fine."

Samar swallowed, but didn't say anything. She also didn't let go of Kouji's hand as they started on this adventure to the theater. Kouji wasn't sure what to expect, but she thought it'd be fine if she was with Samar.

"What type of shows do you like?" Samar asked while staring at a list of titles.

"It doesn't matter to me," Kouji answered.

"Well, we'll have to figure something out."

"What type of shows do you usually see?" Kouji asked.

"If Vin drags me out, I see whatever she wants to see. I think she takes me to movies that Mechi doesn't want to see with her. I don't really like the movies," Samar admitted. She liked spending time with Evinia though.

Kouji's eyebrows closed in. "Then we shouldn't go."

Samar shook her head. "You might like the movies, so we should check it out. I don't mind sitting through it if you like it."

Kouji gave a strong nod. "If you say so."

"Vin always tells me not to dismiss something until I've tried it at least once. She says that to torture me, most of the time, but I think she has a point. We'll check it out. If you don't like it, then we never have to go again. If you do like the show, I'll bear it for you."

"Really?" Kouji asked.

"Yeah. It's fine."

Kouji smiled, flattered by Samar's willingness to sit through something she disliked for her. She wasn't sure what to expect from these movies, but Samar was with her and that was enough.

Samar walked up to an opening in the wall, where a person gave them tickets in exchange for what Kouji assumed was money. "There were only shells and bartering when I was awake," Kouji said.

"Those still exist, but also coins, bank notes—paper money, and electronic money on cards," Samar replied. "I'll tell you more about it after the movie."

The movie wasn't as jarring as Kouji had expected. "Wait, do they want us to figure this out?" Kouji asked in a whisper.

"Yeah, this is a murder mystery, which is cool. I like trying to figure out mysteries. It's a good way to make sure my brain hasn't completely atrophied since I got here."

"Ah. I've never tried that."

"Okay, well, the movie will drop clues and hints for us to determine who killed the person in the beginning."

"Understood."

They picked their suspects and, throughout the movie, presented each other with evidence as to why their suspect was the murderer. It was fun to whisper back and forth. Kouji turned out to be correct about the who-dun-it.

"I told you it was that guy," Kouji boasted with a grin as they exited the movie theater. She took Samar's hand again.

"That was a lucky guess," Samar said, giving Kouji's hand a squeeze.

Kouji snickered. "No it wasn't. You're merely upset I was right and you were wrong, even though you pointed out he was trying much too hard to prove he was somewhere else when the murder took place."

"Yeah, but I still thought the girl did it. I mean, she wasn't heartbroken at all that her husband just died."

"That was because she was having an affair. That's rather dishonorable," Kouji commented without thinking.

"What is?"

"Having an affair."

Samar looked down, and Kouji was aware she said something wrong. Samar muttered, "Sometimes people have an excuse, I guess."

Kouji stopped and thought about it. "Yeah, I guess so," she allowed after a long moment.

Samar arched an eyebrow. "Why'd you agree?"

"Because what you said made sense. I wasn't thinking when I spoke. There are millions of excuses and thousands of reasons to do something, not that that makes it right. It only helps people to understand...sometimes," Kouji explained. *Mother wasn't dishonorable, just in a vile place with no escape.*

"It does."

"Did your mother...did your mother ever try to explain to make you understand?" Kouji asked in a near-whisper.

Samar seemed a little thrown off by the question. Wide-eyed, she stopped walking. Kouji was about to apologize, but Samar spoke. "Sorry. I'm not used to being asked about my mother, except by Vinny. It would be nice to talk about my mother. I mean, sometimes people ask, but I don't think they actually care."

"I care. I want to know everything about you, including your mother. I know she was the biggest part of your life for a long time. I understand that. My mother became a huge part of my life very late, but I have no idea what I'd do without her now. Possibly be an animal, or worse."

Samar gave her a sidelong glance. "You, an animal? I don't believe it."

Kouji smiled. "You haven't seen the real me. Or at least who my parents made me. My mother saved me. You've saved me."

"Have I?"

"You make me want things out of life. This is new for me. But I asked about your mother."

Samar stared ahead of them. "No one really tried to explain the relationship to me. I didn't really ask about it at an age when it mattered. My mother left me thinking that it was normal for my father not to live with us and only visit a few of times. I'm not sure she knew he was married."

Kouji nodded. "You've said. I don't think my father knew my mother was married. Honestly, I don't think my father knew my mother was my mother."

"I'm not following."

"Sorry. My biological father probably had no idea of my biological mother's true identity, so he definitely had no clue she was married."

Samar's eyes went large once more. "Oh. Wow."

"Yes. Similar situations." Kouji motioned between them with one hand.

Samar nodded and focused ahead again. "It wasn't until I got here that I started wondering about that stuff. My mother told me she'd made a mistake, but she was happy to have me. When I got here, I started wondering what she meant by mistake because I found I had a younger brother and an older sister. They had a different mother. I didn't understand it…I didn't understand anything."

"Do you understand now?"

Samar blew out a long breath. "I'm more confused than ever. When my mother said she made a mistake, I wanted to believe she wasn't talking about having me. She said she loved me, and she was happy I was with her. I believe that."

"What was her mistake?"

"I wish I knew. It has to do with being with my father. They're so different from each other. I don't know how they got together in the first place, and I never asked. My dad was married and maybe my mom knew. So she should've left him alone. He should've definitely left her alone. He knew he was married. It doesn't make any sense." Samar shook her head.

"Why not just ask him?" Kouji suggested.

Samar cringed. "I'm not sure I've asked that man a question in my life, and I'm not starting with something so personal. I refuse to talk to him."

"I could ask him."

"He wouldn't answer you. You're nobody to him, meaningless in his world."

Kouji nodded. "I'd give myself meaning."

Samar smirked, understanding how Kouji would do such a thing. "I know, but this is something that I have to handle on my own or not at all. This is between me and him since my mother's gone now."

"Okay, I understand." Kouji's eyes strayed the sky. "It's getting mighty dark. Do you have to go to work soon?"

Samar checked her phone. "No, I don't have work for a few more hours. Hmm…what are we going to do now? Oh, I have an idea. Do you like sports and stuff?"

Kouji's face scrunched up. "Sports?"

"Yeah, sports."

"Like chariot racing?"

"What? No. Never mind. I'll just show you, and you can decide for yourself if you like it or not."

Kouji nodded. It didn't matter to her what sports were. "As long as we're together, I'll like it."

Samar made an odd noise, then reversed their direction. With every step they took, Samar seemed just a little more reluctant to continue. Her pace got slower and slower, and she frowned as she ducked into a rather filthy alley. The scent of garbage and urine were almost overwhelming. They stopped at a high, chained-off gate. She bit the inside of her lip, staring at the fence.

"Can you get over the fence on your own?" Samar asked.

"You mean like this?" Kouji inquired. She took a few steps back for a little bit of room. She ran toward the fence and leaped, clearing the fence with inches to spare. She turned and grinned at Samar.

"Um…yeah, something like that," Samar answered with a slight laugh. "I don't think I've seen anyone jump that high except the monks who taught me." Samar scaled the fence and flipped over the side. She landed next to Kouji. "Do you have to do everything so flashy?" Samar gave a teasing smile.

With a shrug, Kouji gave a smile of her own. "You told me to get over. You didn't say how."

"Ah, you're just a showoff," she retorted in a friendly tone.

"No wonder we get along so well, since you're a showoff, too, and you know it." Kouji winked. This was such a good day.

Samar laughed a little and shook her head. "Maybe."

Kouji grabbed Samar's hand once more. Samar pulled her toward the strange sound of something rolling. When Kouji caught sight of their destination, her mouth dropped open. People moved, jumped, and flipped on small, wheeled boards.

Chapter Nine

Cloudy

WHY THE HELL DID I bring her here? Samar's chest burned as she laid eyes on the skate park. Why had she returned to a place with almost no pleasant memories? Well, it used to be a place where she felt slightly comfortable, one of the few places she liked to be in the city. She hadn't been there in a long time.

"Could I try that?" Kouji's eager question disrupted Samar's thoughts. Kouji pointed to the skating.

"It's a little dangerous for first-timers, and you don't own skates or a board," Samar replied.

"I'll be fine. Can I try?"

"Well, I'm sure someone would be generous enough to let you hold a board," Samar said. The skaters had been kind in the beginning. Maybe it'd be like that again. It wasn't like they'd remember her over two years later.

"You don't want to go over there, do you?" Kouji asked, as if she sensed Samar's hesitance.

"I'd rather not, if that's all right with you," she answered with all of the honesty she managed to muster. She pushed down the sorrow and pain. She wasn't ready to go back yet. She doubted she'd ever be ready, not after everything that happened.

"Do you want to talk about it?"

Samar sighed. "It's only Nightmares and things." This wasn't exactly a lie, but it was far from the truth.

"Did you talk about it before? Have I forgotten?" Kouji frowned.

"No, you're fine. I don't think I was visiting the tomb at the time." She had barely been able to move when everything came to a head. She had talked about it, but Kouji didn't have enough information right now to make the connection.

Kouji sighed and put an arm around Samar's shoulder. The contact soothed old wounds, old guilt, old sorrows better than Samar would've ever guessed.

"Is this something they did in your old country?" Kouji nodded toward the skaters.

"Not really. It wasn't popular, but I saw videos on my mom's laptop when I was a child and wanted to try it. My mom bought me skates and told me I had to teach myself because she liked her wheels on cars. Eventually, she made me my own little skate park at our house."

"She encouraged everything you wanted to do, huh?"

Samar nodded. "She was a wonderful mother." Tears stung Samar's eyes. Would it ever stop hurting?

Kouji pulled her close. "I'm sorry." They were quiet for a long time. "Why is this place so secluded? Usually, athletes do things for audiences."

"This is true."

Kouji looked down, focused on Samar. "Are they doing something evil?"

"No. Why'd you ask that?" she replied.

"Because no one's around. Are we doing something wrong by watching them?"

"No. What makes you think skating is wrong?"

"Because nobody's around. Whenever you do something evil, you usually don't want people who aren't involved to witness."

Samar's shoulders dropped. Kouji's assumption wouldn't have been wrong back when Samar had frequented the skate park. "I did my best to clean this place up before I left."

"Nightmares?"

"And humans just being humans."

Kouji hummed. "Is evil the nature of humans? Have I been human this whole time?"

Samar arched an eyebrow. "I don't think humans are naturally evil, but what do you mean?"

"I might be naturally evil. I'm not sure. I suppose I thought they might be doing something evil since they're alone. I was often alone when I committed evil acts. Of course, I was unaware they were evil. But I also did things I now know were evil right in front of people." Kouji seemed lost in her thoughts.

That was a lot. "They're only practicing. Some people would rather be alone when they're learning. Plus, they're not really alone since they're here to watch each other." Samar paused a moment. "I mean, I like being alone. Did you like being alone?"

Kouji didn't answer right away. "No, I didn't like being alone at all, and I didn't like what I did alone. It was just the only way I knew how to be. If you like being alone so much, why'd you have to talk to me at least once a day?"

"*Point taken*," Samar muttered in her native language.

"*I didn't mean to be so harsh,*" Kouji apologized in Jinoi, as if that gave her a better chance at receiving forgiveness. She was right.

Samar blinked. "You speak Jinoi fluently?"

Kouji rubbed her forehead. "I guess so. You used to speak Jinoi at the tomb, right?"

"I did. After a while, it got hard though. Everything about Asale began to hurt."

"I'm sorry. For that and for what I said earlier."

"It's all right," Samar mumbled. It was unfair to be upset with Kouji for making a decent point. She was angry with herself. She had depended on Kouji to keep her sane before Kouji was even awake. It wasn't that she liked to be alone, but that was the only way she knew how to be.

Samar finally released Kouji's hand because her fingers were going numb. She put her cold hands to her mouth and blew on them. It wasn't working as well as she would've liked, but it was better than letting her hands freeze.

"Here, let me," Kouji offered.

Kouji took Samar's hands and covered them with her own. *She has such warm hands.* Kouji put Samar's hands to her mouth and gently blew on them. Samar flinched a bit, not expecting the thrill that shot down her spine. Kouji locked eyes with her and ignored her nervous behavior. Samar was thankful for such a small favor. She needed the warmth. She relaxed in Kouji's grip after a few seconds.

"Thank you," Samar whispered with a small smile. More than her hands were warm.

"You feel better?" Kouji asked.

"Yeah. Nobody's ever...ever done that to me before."

"I've never done that to anyone before."

Samar's stomach felt strange. "Let's go someplace quieter," she suggested. "We'll come back here later, and you can try to skate."

Kouji nodded. "Okay."

Back to the wire gate, Kouji grabbed Samar, who yelped and clung to her in surprise. Kouji leaped over the gate with Samar in her arms, once again clearing it with space to spare. Samar was shocked and clung to Kouji for a few seconds until her feet touched the ground. She stumbled and fell against a solid frame.

Kouji was softer than she expected. Yes, there were muscles and body heat, but something was right underneath those things Samar would like to become more familiar with. She gulped and pushed herself off Kouji before they were caught in an awkward moment. Then, things did get awkward.

"Give me your money," a hoodlum demanded, standing about ten feet away.

Samar and Kouji turned to face the would-be robber. He had a gun pointed at them. Not to mention, a Nightmare poked out of his neck, chuckling.

"Bold of you to assume we have money," Samar said. This was far from her first armed robbery, but like all attempts against her before, she was broke.

Kouji tilted her head, braids swaying as she did so. "Is his weapon dangerous?"

"I'm more concerned about the Nightmare making itself known," Samar replied.

Kouji squinted. "Oh, I see the outline. Do you see more?"

"I see them plainly, like a person."

Kouji nodded. "I take the person. You take the Nightmare?"

"Okay," Samar agreed.

"Hey, I have a gun here!" He waved the gun in their direction.

Kouji vanished, almost like she faded into the darkness of nearby shadows. Samar gripped Amani in her hands, blade smoking in the presence of the hissing Nightmare. It knew what time it was.

Kouji came up behind the assailant, while Samar charged the Nightmare. Kouji grabbed the gun, and shots were fired into the dark. The assailant snarled and turned, but the Nightmare lunged at Samar.

She managed to sidestep the Nightmare, which roared and flung out a sharpened limb. Samar struck out with Amani. The Nightmare tried to catch her mid-action, creating a barb on its already pointed limb. Samar's spear went through the limb without a problem. The Nightmare screeched.

"Should we switch? I could put a Favor on the human," Samar said.

"I've got it." Kouji pressed her thumb to the gunman's forehead.

There was a bright glow. The gunman screamed as orange-yellow gunk melted out his eyes, ears, nose, and mouth. The Nightmare also screamed as it was detached from its host. Samar stabbed the confused Nightmare with Amani while gawking at Kouji's work. The Nightmare let out another screech and evaporated.

"How did you do that?" Samar demanded, as she pulled a zip tie from her pocket to cuff the gunman. She had to call this in and didn't want this idiot to hurt someone. She'd leave Kouji out of her report when she wrote it up, as she wasn't sure if Kouji legally existed. She'd certainly be hard to explain to the courts.

"Hey, what're you doing?" the gunman demanded, voice a mumbled slur. He was disoriented from losing his Nightmare.

"Stay still," Samar said, her voice sharp, as she but kept her eyes on Kouji. "How did you exorcise the Nightmare from him?"

Kouji shrugged. "I've fought against Abominations before. I had no idea this was what you meant when you said you fought Nightmares. You can fully see them?" It was like she was in awe.

"Yes, but you didn't need a Favor to exorcise it from this moron." Samar pointed at the gunman.

"Oh." Kouji looked at her hands. "Um…we might need to talk about this."

"You think?" Samar huffed. Kouji winced and Samar took a moment to collect herself. She needed to calm down. "You are such a showoff." Samar threw Kouji a smirk as she climbed to her feet.

She had Kouji step out of sight, as they waited a short time for a patrolman to come pick up the gunman. Samar gave a quick explanation and handed over the criminal's gun, then they were free to go. She waved Kouji on, so they could get back to the apartment.

Kouji gave her a shy smile. "I only did that to save time. I didn't think it'd be a big deal."

Samar rolled her eyes. "I bet you say that to all the girls."

Kouji didn't take it for the joke it was meant to be. "I didn't actually. I didn't think too much about girls. Nobles did try to marry their daughters to me, sons as well, but I was never interested. Good thing I never got married, or I'd probably miss my spouse."

That was quite a bit for Samar to process. Kouji could've been married but wasn't. She didn't seem to have a preferred gender. It wasn't unheard of in the past, but many societies had become more gendered as time marched on and social roles evolved.

"Yeah, they would've been long dead, huh?" Samar asked.

Kouji nodded. "Yup. That wouldn't be very fun."

"*No…it wouldn't,*" she muttered in Jinoi.

"You mumble in your native language a lot. I remember when I was asleep, you started out speaking more often in Jinoi. Then it was like you, I suppose, gave up? You started using this language more often."

Once Within a Dream

Samar sighed. "Beyond the fact that it hurt and reminded me of everything I lost, I stopped seeing the point. I don't talk to enough people for it to matter."

Kouji took her hand. "Your culture will always matter. It not only connects you to your mother, but to your people and your homeland. Your culture connects you to positivity and caring."

Samar's heart fluttered. "I never thought of it that way."

"You want to hear my native language?" Kouji asked.

Samar blinked. "Your native language?" It hadn't occurred to her that they weren't speaking the language Kouji had grown up with, but it made sense. Languages always changed over time, especially millennia.

"Yeah, I do have one. Do you want to hear it?"

"I'd love to."

Kouji cleared her throat and began to speak a language Samar had never heard before. It was low and rapid, almost like Kouji was singing. The sound was mellow, close to soothing, and involved much more lip movement than Jinoi. Samar was speechless when Kouji finished her monologue with a smile.

"What did you say?" Samar finally managed to ask.

"Nothing too deep. I said, 'My name is Kouji. I am a child of taboo and deceit, but also of love. My father was a demon. My mother is my light. I need someone to be my forgiveness. My salvation. I think I discovered such a thing in words caught in the rain.' That's pretty much it." Kouji shrugged.

Samar's brow furrowed. "Why would you say those things?" A gnawing in her gut made her think of Kouji's ability to handle Nightmares. She ignored the end of Kouji's statement.

"It was the first few things that came to mind. I won't lie to you. Everything I said was true. I just forgot to mention I'm also a demon."

"You're a demon?" Did Kouji mean that literally? She had never met a demon, but if Nightmares existed, anything was possible.

"Not literally, but from my actions. I am a demon. I'm sorry I didn't tell you that when we first spoke. There's so much I have to tell you. I just...I didn't want you to leave me."

"You remember or you've always known?"

"It's coming back to me more and more, but I know enough now."

Samar nodded. "It's okay. Everybody does something in life that they're not proud of and they regret. It's what you do with that knowledge that matters."

"Your mother's words?"

"Yes, she was full of advice that doesn't really help, huh?" Samar blew out a breath. "No matter though. I still take everything she ever said to heart."

"Maybe that's all mothers," Kouji offered, eyes on the dark sky.

A short chuckle escaped Samar as she led Kouji back to her building. Not ready to go inside, they climbed the stairs to the roof. The alarm for the door was broken, and it was never locked. They stepped outside and were hit by a sudden chill. Samar shivered. It was getting colder by the second.

"Cold?" Kouji asked the obvious.

"A little bit."

"Here. Take this back." Kouji stripped off the borrowed jacket and draped it over Samar's shoulders.

"You'll freeze," Samar protested.

"No, I won't. I don't get cold. Don't worry." Kouji smiled.

"We're going to talk about that."

"I assumed that's why you brought me up here."

"Yes, but let's enjoy this for a moment."

Kouji nodded and Samar wrapped her jacket around herself a little tighter. The inside of her jacket was warmer than usual. Kouji walked over to the edge of the building and looked down to the street where people were fluttering about. She took a seat on the ledge. Samar sat down next to her.

"It's rather lovely up here," Kouji said.

"Yeah, I come here to get away from it all sometimes."

Kouji gave her a sidelong glance. "Why not go home or come see me?"

Samar chuckled at the phrase *come see me*, as if she had always known she was going to Kouji.

"Up here I don't have to deal with people at all. If I go to the tomb, I still have to see these people up close. I don't even want to see them sometimes. What do you do to get away from it all?"

"I was always away from it all. I was...I don't want to say misled, but I was shut off, I guess, mentally. I didn't know right from wrong." Kouji exhaled through her nose and kicked her legs.

"Do you want to...talk about it?" she asked. *Well, that sounded lame.* She wasn't used to trying to be present for someone. *I should probably make things easier for Vinny after this.*

"I'd just scare you away if I did, but I want to answer your questions."

"You won't scare me away. How bad could it be? You're aware of almost everything about me and you still want to be friends. Hell, you know about some terrible things I did, and you still want to be my friend. I'll certainly return the favor." Samar nudged Kouji with her shoulder.

Kouji shook her head. "I don't think so."

Samar reached over and took Kouji's hand, holding tight. "You can't keep secrets from me. It's not very fair. Besides, we're friends, right? Friends tell each other stuff."

A small smile tugged at the side of Kouji's mouth. "Yes. I don't want to tell you too much yet. I don't want to frighten you, but I'll tell you everything eventually. Just not right now. Okay?"

"Tell me as much as you want right now. I can wait."

Kouji took a deep breath and held Samar's hand with both of hers. "I'm the daughter of a goddess and a human, like I said. My birth father died before I was born. I don't have the details."

Samar rubbed her chin. She might have the details. This story already sounded familiar. "Did your mother love your father?"

A soft smile formed. "I think she did. She calls me an expression of love. I wish I felt like I was."

"You don't feel that way? Because you didn't know your father?"

Kouji blew out a long breath. "There's so much. My mother was forced to give me away right after she gave birth to me. I was given to a wealthy human family...a childless family. Royals."

"Your neck beads are of a royal clan." Samar knew they looked familiar. A royal clan in Asale had almost the same colors. Were they descendants of Kouji's parents?

Kouji glanced down at her beads. "Yes. They had twisted morals, which is putting it nicely. They made sure I grew up with no concept of right and wrong, no conscience whatsoever. I did whatever they told me to do. I mean, they were my parents, and they knew how to talk to me to get me to do something. Sometimes they told me to do terrible things." Kouji growled, and the fury that tore through her angelic visage was out of place. She tucked into herself, hunching her shoulders, and ducking her head.

"Like what?" Samar asked in a small voice. Kouji seemed furious, ashamed, and scared all at the same time.

Kouji swallowed and gave a pathetic shrug. "Well...some awful things that I had no idea were as bad as they were. Let's leave it at that for the moment, okay?"

Samar nodded, though she could guess. "If that's what you want." Samar shrugged to downplay the matter since Kouji was clearly distraught. Samar had done some awful things herself. She was unsure if they were equal to Kouji's awful things, but she understood, somewhat.

"It is. I owe it to you," Kouji said with conviction.

"You don't owe me anything, but I appreciate you trying. What's your mother's name?" Samar asked to change the subject.

"My birth mother's name is Asiku."

And there it was. Samar knew this story, this folklore of the Goddess of Night, this myth of the Goddess of Darkness, the name varied depending on who told the story. The goddess loved a human, which infuriated her husband, Usuku, the Sun and God of Day, of Light. There was a child, banished to live with humans...Kouji. This made no sense. Was Kouji repeating old stories to her as a backstory?

"Are you being serious right now?" Samar asked.

Kouji smirked at her and shrugged. "How else do I disappear? How else do I not get cold? How else do I beat you in a fight?"

"I'm not so egotistical to think only a legendary demigod could beat me in a fight, but everything else stands." She meant that. "It would also explain how you expelled those Nightmares without a Favor."

Kouji's smirk became a smile. "Yes, but I still don't understand why I can't see them. I'm certain I used to be able to see them. They haunted me as a child."

Samar nodded. Part of the myth was that Usuku ripped a hole in the night, opening a void into the Beyond. He released Nightmares to punish humanity for taking in Kouji, even though some stories said he was the one who gave Kouji to the humans. Most people assumed the Nightmares mentioned in the myth were the ones that haunted people's dreams. They couldn't fathom a Nightmare being a physical thing meant to torment those who wouldn't host them.

Nightmares were sent to strangle life from the living, a breathing symbol of Asiku's rejection of Usuku. Did Kouji remember that much? *Is she aware the Sun wants her dead? More importantly, does Usuku still want her dead?*

"What's it like to have a goddess as a mother? Did you worship her when you were awake?" Samar asked. It seemed like as good a question as any.

"Yeah, I worshipped all of the gods of my kingdom back then. I had no idea she was my mother. She does make eternal sleep more entertaining than it sounds. She visits me often." Kouji's face relaxed.

"How does she do that?"

"She appears in my dreams. Sometimes she scolds me if I have what she considers a bad dream. She's a kind and gentle person, and I love spending time with her. She teases me a lot and tells me I'll take to any woman who shows me three seconds' worth of attention." She snickered.

"Oh." Samar nodded and looked away. *How many times has Kouji woken up for someone?*

Kouji laughed more. "She's only teasing when she says that. I mean, if she was telling the truth, I'd be married to about a hundred women. I do appreciate a kind smile though." Then she flashed her own kind smile. Maybe she was clueless about her expressions.

"Did your parents ever try to marry you off?"

"No, they wanted to keep me close for nefarious deeds. They didn't want to chance dividing my loyalties. I was their attack dog. They didn't want anyone else to have the power to point me at someone and use me to destroy that person. So being married was never an option for me."

Samar hummed. "Would you have wanted to be married?"

"At the time? No. I was content with my existence…I think. I'm not sure if content is the right word. I was living. It didn't bother me, and I didn't think about change, really. I just was."

Samar nodded. "I understand. I've only been existing when not in total despair."

"Any other questions?"

"How much of your memory has come back?"

Kouji stared out into the city. "I'm not sure how to answer that. Some specifics are still shadows in my mind, but other things are sharp. Sharper than I like."

"You've changed since you first fell asleep."

"I most certainly have. I never wanted company before." Kouji knocked her shoulder against Samar's and smiled. "Of course, it's probably better. I wouldn't have known how to treat a friend. I didn't have a great example of proper relationships."

"I don't think it really matters. I mean, if you figure out how you want to treat a person, then you do things the way you want to. My mother had no clue how to raise a child. I'm not saying she did the greatest job, but she did her best. She treated me how she expected someone to treat their daughter, despite not having any examples from her life. You treat people how you want and how you think they should be treated, not how you see other people treat them," Samar explained.

Kouji's mouth dropped open as her bronze forehead wrinkled. "Yeah?"

Samar nodded. "That's how you learn what type of person you are. If you treat people like crap and they don't deserve it, then you're not a good person. But if you treat people right, in a manner they deserve, then you're a decent person. Of course, things change. You changed from being not so good to being good, and it goes the other way around. That's just a basic way of looking at things."

Kouji nodded almost mindlessly. "You're very smart."

Samar snorted. "Hasn't done me any good."

"No?"

"Hasn't done me or my sister any good, actually. Hell, Mechi isn't dumb either, but we're all in the same boat with Siku detesting every move we make."

"Why?"

Samar shrugged. "No idea. Vin has everything she wants to do mapped out. That's the type of person she is. But Siku gets on her about her life. He wants to control her life."

Kouji nodded. "My parents were like that with me."

"Vinny won't let him. Sometimes, he yells at her for having no direction, whatever that means. She gives him a funny look, like she's telling him to go away with her eyes. She always says it's her life, and she knows what she's doing with it. I think she does too. Whenever she sits me down to talk about the future, she has everything for herself planned out. She tries to help me plan stuff out too."

Kouji nodded again. "Every time you talk about your sister and how much she cares about you and looks out for you, it makes me wonder what it'd be like to have one."

"I used to wonder, until I got one anyway. Vin's not so bad. Sometimes, I get on her nerves or she gets on mine, but she assures me that's normal. Other than that, it's great. Siku always tells her to stop babying me. She tells him to quit riding me. I cause many fights between them. But Vin tells me they'd fought like this long before I showed up. My brother doesn't even talk to me." She sighed.

Alvin wasn't interested in being her brother. She wasn't sure how she felt about his disinterest. It didn't hurt, but she wasn't pleased. Neither of them had much family, so Evinia liked to urge them to embrace what they had. Alvin refused and Samar didn't try to bridge the gap.

"I remember you saying as much," Kouji replied. "He thinks you represent your father's betrayal to his mother. That's not very fair to you. It's not your fault about whatever happened between your parents."

Samar shrugged. "He doesn't care. Vin says he needs someone to hate, and he likes Dad too much to hate him. Alvin's never met my mother to hate her. Besides, she's dead. So all that's left is to hate me."

"Still not fair."

"Oh, it gets worse. According to Vin, he blames me for their mother dying. I don't understand, no matter how much Vin tries to explain it to me. He thinks my existence killed her on the inside. My presence in this world made their mother sick like poison. Apparently, she died a few years after finding out about me." Samar hid her face in her hands.

There were times when Samar believed she had killed her siblings' mother. Those were the times she couldn't look her sister in the eyes or listen to her voice, because she was certain she had robbed her sister of someone beyond precious. Her existence caused a horrible cancer in Nyota Habeen.

When those thoughts invaded her mind, Samar had to escape her family for at least a day. She'd bring them nothing but agony if she stuck around. Of course, Alvin was hurt by her regardless if she was there or not.

"But it wasn't your fault. She was already sick, wasn't she? You said so."

"I have no idea when she found out about my existence, so it could've been her finding out that made her sick or made her succumb to an illness she already had. Alvin makes it seems like she died the day she found out about me. Vinny says her mother was already sick, but I don't think she knows when her mother found out," Samar answered. "She says it was her mother's time. Usually, I believe Vin. When I'm really down and out, I believe Alvin."

Kouji squeezed her hand. "It wasn't your fault. You didn't give her this cancer. You had nothing to do with it."

"No, but…" Samar's sigh was weighed down with the desolation of her soul.

Kouji patted her hand. "It wasn't your choice for her to have cancer. It wasn't your choice for her to die. It wasn't your choice to stay with your father. Hell, it wasn't even your choice to be born. Don't blame yourself for something you didn't have any hand in." Kouji caressed her cheek. "You couldn't…" She swallowed hard and her eyes shimmered. "You couldn't stop what happened."

Samar noticed how Kouji had forced out that last sentence. She offered a small smile that only made lilac eyes glisten more. Kouji was ready to burst into tears.

"What's wrong? Did I upset you?" Samar asked.

Kouji shook her head, rubbing her eyes. She took a deep breath. "It's just you're broken up about something you had nothing to do with, something you couldn't have prevented no matter what. You're a much better person than I am, and I shouldn't soil you with my company."

Samar squinted, staring hard at Kouji. "Why would you say that? You think you're a bad person, but you're trying to comfort me."

"You're hurt because your siblings' mother died. When your own mother died, you carried her with your own two hands and have a physically heavy memory of her." Kouji spoke as though it had been a noble act.

"I was out of my mind with grief." Samar had been in disbelief that she had enough strength to lift her mother's body, but she had been the one to carry her to the ambulance, after fighting with people who came to help. Somehow, she thought it'd make her remember her mother more.

"You do so much to honor her as best you can. You fast on the anniversary of her death. You light candles in her memory, play her favorite music, and pray for her. You do those things on her birthday too. None of those things would ever come to mind for me. I'd never think to honor my mother in such a way."

Samar chuckled as she processed Kouji's words. "You did these things to honor your mother. You used to worship her."

"Yeah, but I didn't know she was my mother at the time. I think the closest thing I had to a mother was a nursemaid. She watched me from when I was a baby. As I grew up, she took care of my basic needs. I think I miss her. Remembering her voice makes me both happy and sad."

"Sounds like you miss her. She died while you were awake?"
"Yes." Kouji's voice cracked.
"If it's not too painful, tell me what you did the day she died."
Kouji's gaze set out again. "I went to sleep."
Samar blinked. "You went to sleep?"
"That was the day I went to sleep. It was an easy way out. It was easier than bearing my disillusion." A tear slid down Kouji's face.
"Kouji..." Samar clutched her hand. "You don't have to talk about it if you don't want to."
Kouji swallowed. "I want to bare my soul to you, but I don't think I have a soul, and I don't want to lose you."
"I'm here for you, like you're here for me."
Kouji sniffled and wiped away her tear track. "I always knew, deep down somewhere, that almost everything I did was wrong. She told me, but I pretended I didn't understand. My pretense cost her everything."
"Who came for you?" Samar guessed this nursemaid was collateral damage.
"Assassins with Abominations—Nightmares. They mutilated her. I couldn't bear to face the situation, so I went to sleep. It hit me so hard."
"Yeah?" Some stories agreed with that, while others had different details.
"It..." Kouji trembled, and Samar wrapped her arms around Kouji's shoulders. "It made me realize what my actions had done. I had taken people from others the way she was taken from me. I couldn't deal with everything I had done. I needed an escape, or I'd go insane."
"And going to sleep was the escape? You did it to yourself?"
Kouji shook her head. "My mother offered."
"You loved this woman, huh?" Samar asked.
"She was called Orica, and I don't know how I felt about her. How can you tell if you love someone?" Kouji's face twisted.
Samar shrugged. "You just know. You were upset she died. In pain, sad."
Kouji's brow wrinkled. "I wouldn't say sad. I don't think I'd ever felt sad back then. I was...angry. It was the first time I'd ever been angry. I had no idea what to do. I mean, usually, when something that I didn't like happened I made it known with my sword. People changed what they were doing really quickly. But this was beyond my control. It was beyond my understanding. My goddess mother said I

should go to sleep, and I agreed. What else was there to do? I didn't know how to handle it, how to grieve, how to deal with it at all."

"Are you okay, now that you remember?"

Kouji shook her head and more tears came. Samar held her tighter, allowing Kouji to weep. The emotion needed to come out or Kouji would feel worse. Samar was there for her.

Chapter Ten

Nightlight

KOUJI WASN'T SURE WHAT was wrong with her, but she couldn't stop crying. She had never felt like this, like a herd of wild horses had trampled her. Samar's arms around her were the only things keeping her from dissolving into nothingness. What was this feeling?

"Samar, why can't I stop crying?" Kouji wailed.

Samar held her tighter. "It's all the emotion trying to come out. It's fine. Cry all you want."

Kouji had no choice but to listen. It was impossible to stop. She clung to Samar, fingers digging into her arms. Time stood still and the world fell away. It was like being asleep all over again, except those arms bound her together.

"No one I had ever cared about died before Orica," Kouji whispered once she finished sobbing. "Of course, I don't think I ever cared about anybody else. I wasn't even aware I cared about Orica until she was dead."

"I understand how that is. I don't think I had a real understanding of death. My mother used to tell me about death. She had taught me to read vital signs and everything. 'Just in case,' she always said. I checked hers, but assumed I was wrong. I had to be wrong."

"You did the best you could."

Samar snorted. "Took too long to call for help probably."

"They told you she was dead when she hit the ground."

"But maybe..." Samar shook her head. "It rained when they told me. I went out in the pouring rain for a coffin and shovel. All of the villagers whispered that I'd killed her. My brother even said I killed her, right to my face." An odd, nervous laugh escaped Samar.

"He's a cruel one," Kouji said. Samar hadn't spoken much about her brother, but what she said proved he was unkind.

Samar shrugged. "He's hurt, deep in his soul. He misses his mother. Whenever he sees me, he thinks about how his father betrayed his mother by being with my mother, creating me. I think he feels like Siku betrayed him, too, betrayed their family. He's not wrong."

"So he should vent on you? That's not right." Kouji was almost certain it wasn't right. She only got a moral compass after something that happened affected her. She might be wrong.

Samar gave her a small smile. "I thought you said you didn't know right from wrong."

"My mother's been schooling me since she put me to sleep. She didn't approve of what I grew into." While Kouji couldn't recall every horrible act, she was aware of the overview. She wasn't too fond of what she had been either.

"My mother always said that if someone doesn't accept you with your flaws, then they can't possibly love you. Your mother loves you, right?" Samar asked.

Kouji rubbed her forehead. "She often says she loves me. I now believe her, but it's still hard for me to understand what she means by it."

"I think you believing her is the important thing right now. It'll help you grow to understand what love is and what it means to you as you live life."

Kouji smiled a bit. "She wanted me to know right from wrong. There's a difference between accepting a person's flaws and allowing the person to be a monster. She taught me, then left it up to me to draw my own conclusions. Now that I can reflect on things, I agree with her. I didn't have the best upbringing. Didn't have the best life, now that I think about it."

Kouji wasn't quite sure how her human parents learned of her abilities, but they took advantage of her divine bloodline. She had abilities no human had. They had to have seen something in her that made them realize they could make her into a monster.

"Even with wealthy, royal parents?" Samar bumped Kouji with her shoulder.

Kouji blew out a long breath. "While I was asleep, I once heard a man screaming about money being the root of all evil. I believe him, after growing up with my parents. They were able to do so much harm to people."

Samar nodded and checked her phone. "I've got work." She sighed. "I have to go in a while. I want to stay up here and keep talking with you though."

Kouji smiled. "Someone has to fight Nightmares and keep the park safe."

"When I go to work, where will you be?" Samar asked.

Kouji shrugged. "I could wait at the tomb."

"No, it's too cold for that. You'll freeze to death."

"I told you I don't get cold. Part of being half-god. I can wait there."

Samar shook her head. "No, you're not waiting at the tomb. You can wait at my place." This sounded like an order.

Kouji was flattered that Samar was concerned for her health. It was also a little amusing. Samar didn't seem to believe a demigod wouldn't get cold.

"Are you sure?" Kouji asked.

"I'm sure. Let's head down. I have to prepare for work."

Kouji shrugged. She stood and helped Samar to her feet, even though it was unnecessary. Samar allowed it though.

Despite the fact that they held hands almost the whole time, Samar's hands were cold again. Kouji rubbed them, then tucked both their hands in one jacket pocket. Samar smiled.

"You get cold easily," Kouji commented.

"Well, we're not all lucky enough to be half-god," Samar countered.

Kouji laughed. "Oh, so you do understand."

They headed back to the apartment. "Here we are," Samar said, kicking her door open.

Kouji chuckled. "I thought you were kidding about the door being broken. If you're going to go back out, perhaps you should put on a few more layers." She wanted Samar to stay warm.

"Huh?" Samar shoved the door shut.

"Now, where did you say your jackets were?" Kouji asked, speaking more to herself than to Samar. The closet. A thicker jacket had to be inside. She opened the door to search.

"What are you doing?" Samar asked with a furrowed brow.

"Before you go to work, you should layer up. The cold gnaws through you easily. You're still used to your warmer climate at home. You don't have to bear with this nonsense weather. You don't happen to have anything warmer than that jacket, do you?"

"What are you doing?" Samar repeated. "No one's tried to dress me since I was five years old."

Kouji ignored her. She weighed a couple of other jackets. They were as light as the one Samar had loaned her. This wouldn't do. Then she found something that might work. "Why don't you wear this?" Kouji pulled out a thick, red sweater.

"No." Samar shuddered. "I wear two colors, black and blue. Nothing that can be seen from passing planes. Vin gave me that hideous thing for some holiday they celebrate here. I'm almost certain it was a so-called gag gift."

"Okay, well, why not another one of these?" Kouji pulled out a hoodie. She pursed her lips. "Do you have one with no hood?" It might be hard to double up hoodies.

"Once you put on two of them and a jacket you can barely move," Samar replied.

Kouji scowled. "You're going to end up cold if you don't put something else on. Put this one on." It might've been a request, or an order. Even Kouji wasn't too sure which. She tossed Samar the hoodie.

Samar groaned. "I'll be fine. I always go out like this."

"That doesn't make it right. You're always cold. Put it on, and it'll help keep you warm."

Kouji snickered as Samar took the hoodie and went to change into her work clothes, an outfit identical to the one she had worn all day, mumbling furiously in Jinoi. She put the extra hoodie on before donning her jacket.

"It's hard to put my arms down," Samar complained. "I hate layering. It's puffy and limits my movement and it's plain annoying."

Kouji laughed. Was this what people meant when they said something was cute? "You'll be fine. You're fast enough to take the jacket off if you need to. Besides, your kicks hurt more than your punches. You'll be warmer and that's the important thing. Be careful out there. I don't want to have to look for someone who managed to hurt you, because I'll certainly hurt them."

Samar waved that off. "Don't worry about me. I've been doing this for a while now. I can manage. I'll leave some money for you in case you get hungry or something." She dug into her pants pocket and handed over whatever bills were in her wallet. She didn't bother to count them.

Kouji accepted the money. "How much is this?"

"No idea. I only hold whatever money Vin doesn't lock away in a bank for me. Do whatever with that. If the urge to go outside overcomes you, come back here if you can't let me know."

"Okay." Kouji nodded.

"Try not to end up lost if you go out."

A smile grew on Kouji's face. "I'll do my best."

"I'll see you when I come back then."

Kouji nodded, and they stood together awkwardly for a long moment. She wanted to hug Samar. Would that be all right? They had held hands almost all day. A hug should be all right. Just as Kouji worked up the courage to go for it, Samar turned and left the apartment. *Damn.* For once in her life, too slow.

Samar was distracted as she patrolled Okunkun Park. Her eyes strayed toward the tomb. Was Kouji all right in her apartment? Was she still there? *Is she actually a demigod?* It'd explain a lot.

Could Kouji really be the daughter of Asiku? If so, according to many myths and stories, Kouji had a hand in the reason Nightmares roamed the globe. According to some stories, it was actually Kouji who brought Nightmares to the world. Kouji seemed to dispute that with saying Nightmares had come after her. Other stories indirectly blamed Kouji for unknowingly bringing the Nightmares in several different ways. It was hard to know what was true or real. The first written story was lost, as it happened ten thousand years ago.

She hoped Kouji was fine on her own. She had ramen and cold cereal in the apartment, but that was pretty much it for food. Kouji would have no idea how to get takeout.

Samar paced around her patrol area, anxiety gnawing at her bones. Anyone who dared to try anything in her park was quickly dispatched without a thought. Same with Nightmares.

Once her shift was over, she headed back to Moonless Night HQ. She wanted to get her reports out of the way and return home. With luck, Kouji wouldn't have managed to hurt herself or burn the apartment building to the ground.

Samar popped into her sister's office. Evinia wasn't around. *Fine. I should be able to do this myself.* Evinia was probably out for more of her life's blood, coffee. Samar grabbed her chair and pulled it to the desk. Working the reports on her own was more difficult than she'd assumed, but she kept at it.

"Hey, kiddo," Evinia greeted her as she stepped in with a cup.

"Hey," Samar replied. She closed her mouth too late to stop a yawn's escape.

Evinia arched an eyebrow as she sat down in her chair. "Doing your own reports? Amazing. Daddy didn't catch you as you were coming in here or something, did he?"

"No. I have to figure this out sooner or later. It's not like you'll always be here to do them. Can you check them for me when I'm done though?"

"Sure, no problem," Evinia answered.

Evinia sipped her coffee and leaned in close. She stared at the computer screen and focused on Samar typing. Samar did her best not to trip over her own fingers. Evinia grabbed Samar's arm.

Samar jumped when her sister touched her. "What?"

"You're puffier than usual. You're wearing layers, aren't you?" Evinia laughed.

Samar glanced at her. "What?"

"You have on layers of clothes. You never wear layers. You're always going on about how you can take the cold as long as you can still throw a decent punch. Finally got tired of actually freezing, though, huh?" Evinia's eyes twinkled behind her glasses.

"I can take a little cold," Samar stated. She could take the cold, but Kouji had been so insistent.

"And that's why you're wearing layers?"

"Vin!" Samar groaned. Oh, that came out as an annoyed whine. She glanced at Evinia, whose mirth made her glow. Another groan escaped Samar. Now, she'd be peppered with irksome questions.

Evinia clicked her tongue. "Testy. Why are you wearing layers if you can take the cold? Have you finally taken my advice and understand it's better to be warm than always ready to break someone's jaw with one punch?"

"Yeah, whatever." Samar scrubbed her face with both hands. Sweat dotted her forehead. *Why am I sweating? I'm not hot.* Still, she yanked out of her jacket.

Evinia's eyebrow went up and she put her coffee down. "Sammie, are you all right? I'm aware sometimes you put that wall up around yourself and won't let anyone in, but it's been a while. You don't usually have an attitude with me. Is something bothering you?"

"I'm fine. It's just…well, I'm trying to do this stupid thing and it's so hard." Samar glared at the computer screen. "I'm terrible at this and it's…" Samar paused and tried to think of a word to explain herself, but none came to mind.

"Frustrating?" Evinia offered after Samar was silent for a few seconds.

"Yeah, I'll take frustrating." Samar couldn't think of a better word. She wanted this over, so she could go home.

Evinia put her hands up. "All right, I'll leave you alone. I've got some things to look over anyway." She pulled some papers from beneath Samar's arm.

Samar continued to peck away at the computer. She finished her work as quickly as she could, then bid Evinia a hasty farewell. She practically ran out of the office and nearly mowed down Mechi as he tried to greet her in the hallway. She didn't have time for his nonsense.

Evinia watched Samar leave. Something was up. Samar was anxious—no, eager. She was distracted and hadn't noticed the cup of tea Evinia left for her. This was major.

"What's up with your nutty sister?" Mechi asked as he entered her office.

Evinia rolled her eyes. "Why are you always digging on my sister?" She pulled up to her computer monitor. Samar's reports were still on the screen. She forgot to log them when she finished.

He flashed a cute smile. "I don't mean any harm. But why's she always trying to run me over in the hallway?"

"Always?" She scoffed.

He snorted and threw his hands up. "Fine, like twice. Still, that's kinda unusual."

"It's most unusual. She was distracted, didn't drink her tea, and didn't wait for me to help with her reports. She zipped in and out of here so fast that by the time I heard her say bye, she was already down the hall. I'm shocked I didn't hear a sonic boom along with her leaving."

He chuckled. "Good thing you didn't, or she would've killed me as she went by. She was in a hurry."

"I'm sure. Her reports are a complete and utter mess. She doesn't usually make so many easy mistakes." It was like she didn't care what she wrote. She only needed to jot something down. Samar wasn't usually like that.

"When does she do reports by herself?"

"She does them on her own sometimes because it's good practice. Looking at this, I'd think she was completely illiterate."

"But…she is, isn't she? Your father said that once."

"He said that because he's an ass. She can read and write. Perhaps not as well as we can, because she's got several languages taking up space in her head. We have just this one. A four-year-old could've written these. She's much better than this. She didn't bother to even try to spell so many words correctly. She skipped so much punctuation, everything is like one big sentence. Something must be wrong for her to do this kind of work. Remind me to call her and find out if something's up."

Mechi shook his head. "We both know I won't need to remind you. You shouldn't worry about her so much."

"Someone has to. She doesn't have anyone. Not even my father cares. She didn't ask for any of this."

"You're not her mother."

Evinia scowled. "And that's the problem. Her mother's dead, and no one in the world cares anymore. How fucking alone do you think she is in this world?"

Mechi flinched and rubbed the back of his neck. "I don't actually. And…and that might be it. I keep thinking I can rib her out of loneliness, I guess. I mean, I understand she's lonely, but you saying it like that makes it seem like in her head, she's the only person left on this planet."

"I think, for her, that's how it is. When my mother died, I lost a lot. There's a void that'll never be filled. Sammie lost her whole world. She lost everything, including herself. And I don't think she's got a clue how to find anything. So, yes, I understand when you tease and taunt and bother her, you're trying to endear yourself to her in an annoying brother sort of way. But all you're really doing is reminding her that everything is gone."

The color draining from Mechi's face showed he finally got it. He had never suffered a huge loss in his life. He really only understood what it was like to lose a parent through Evinia, and even she hardly had an idea of what the hell her sister was going through.

"I've never once told her I understand, because I don't," Evinia said. "I've only tried to be a shoulder for her."

Blowing out a breath, Mechi ran his hand over his head, mussing his auburn waves. "You know, I've actually been trying to be her friend. It's starting to sink in now how it's been in bad form."

"Yes, it has. Terrible form, really." Evinia was quite pleased he finally figured it out. It was one less thing for her to stress about and one less thing to press Samar. "And you need to stop believing my father about her. He knows even less about her than you do, and I think he's purposely not trying to fathom what Sammie has lost. When my mom died, he was awkward at best. I can only imagine how he was with Sammie."

Mechi's eyes popped open. "I forgot. I forgot what an absolute ass he was then. Is he human? Have we checked?"

Evinia shrugged. She had no idea what her father's deal was, other than being the only child of her grandparents. They were broken and her father was broken.

"So are you going to stop being so awkward with Sammie?" Evinia asked.

Mechi snorted. "To tell the truth, I couldn't begin to say. I don't know how to connect with her, and I've been trying. She means a lot to you, so I want to be on good footing with her. Yeah, I've been doing it wrong, but I want to be there for her. I mean, yes, I say she's weird and all, but I want her to like me."

"You have to give her time. I know it's been three years, but we have no idea how long it might take for her."

"I guess you're right. I mean, you're trying to cuddle her, and she still wiggles away from you like a scared fish half the time. Perhaps, I should give her some space."

"I think that'd be best. I'm not sure she's ready for more people in her life. She has to figure out who she is without her mother in this world." Evinia wondered how long it would take.

Mechi frowned. "How the hell did I never understand this?"

Evinia grabbed his hand. "You've never lost anyone this close to you. You've known sadness, but you've never had a hole blown in your soul. It's a lot to wrap your mind around. Hell, Alien still doesn't understand it."

Mechi snorted. "He's a seventeen-year-old. His world revolves around him."

"This is true, and he has to figure out who he is in this world without our mom before he can figure out where Sammie fits in."

Mechi leaned down, kissing her softly. "I'm lucky to have you. I'll try to talk to Sammie like a person who isn't my friend next time. Maybe start over."

Evinia smiled. "If you do, please don't call her Sammie. You need to understand, in her culture, you have to be close to be using nicknames, and you're not close."

He yelped and Evinia considered this a victory. They finally made it to a point where Mechi comprehended how he might connect with Samar. Now, she needed to work on Alvin. More than that, she had to figure out what might be bothering Samar lately.

Samar breathed a sigh of relief when she got to her door. Kouji hadn't burned the apartment down. Small victory. She opened the door without having to kick the bottom.

"Kouji," Samar called, as she stepped into the apartment and closed the door with her foot. She didn't see her guest. "Kouji." Her stomach twisted as she walked further inside. The place was devoid of life. Her insides dropped. "I guess...I guess she left."

Samar tried to shake away the emptiness creeping in on her. They had only just met. Kouji probably had a million other things to do than wait around for her. The world moved on without her, after all.

She tore off her jacket and both hoodies, tossed all three articles of clothing onto the floor with a huff. She stomped over to her bed and paused. The blankets were neatly arranged. *So what?* Why the question was snarled in her mind, she had no idea.

She flopped down and a strange smell hit her nose. *What is that?* She pressed her face to her sheets and inhaled. Honeysuckle, but right underneath it jasmine. It punched her in the gut.

"Kouji's scent." Samar breathed in deep. "Why'd she leave?" Her voice cracked, along with something inside of her. Something that had healed was torn open and bleeding out.

"Thank you, Mother." Kouji's voice was muffled by the closed door. Then, it sounded like the door was rammed down.

Samar sat up in her bed to behold Kouji shutting the door. She blinked. This might be an illusion. There was always the possibility she was dreaming. After all, it didn't take her long to fall asleep. She might've dozed off as soon as she hit the mattress.

"Kouji?" Samar rubbed the sleep from her eyes as she rose.

"Oh, good morning, Samar." Kouji flashed a pleasant smile and held up her bounty—grocery bags. "I wasn't sure when you got home, so I went out to the...it's like a small, indoor market." She set down the bags and scanned the floor.

Samar picked up the clothes before Kouji could, then embraced her before she realized what she was doing. Kouji tensed for a moment, then hugged Samar back. Tears stung Samar's eyes, but she managed to hold them back. Kouji rested her cheek on Samar's head. The slight pressure comforted Samar.

"I thought you left," Samar whispered. Her guts twisted in a very different manner than before.

Kouji pulled back enough to look at her. "Why would I leave?"

"Why would you stay?"

That smile blossomed again. "Because I like you and like being around you. You did wake me out of a thousand-year sleep."

Samar laughed, just shy of hysterical. "Right."

"I went shopping with the money that you left. I thought…well, I thought I might chance making you breakfast."

Samar's forehead furrowed. "Make me breakfast?"

Kouji gave a cute nod. "Yes, make you breakfast. My mother helped me out so I'd buy the right things and I wouldn't spend all of your money. She was a huge help. May I make you breakfast?"

"Um…I usually don't eat breakfast when I come in. I shower and sleep." *And, yes, I should definitely shower.*

"Oh. Shower and sleep then. I'll make you breakfast when you wake up. Fair?"

Samar found herself smiling. "Sounds very fair. You know your way around the kitchen, right?" Kouji mentioned cooking. A fire wasn't something Samar wanted to deal with, and she also didn't want Kouji to cut herself.

"Trust me." Kouji's smile became a grin.

Samar laughed, which turned awkward when she realized she still had her arms around Kouji. She breathed in Kouji's scent before letting her go. Kouji smelled sweet and fresh, more than jasmine now.

The aroma reminded Samar of her nights on her mountain home when fireflies were out and fruits were ripe. And…it was good. She had stopped thinking about that mountain, as it was painful. Her mother died there. She inhaled deeply, then suddenly yelped. *Oh, crap. I just purposely sniffed her.*

"So you're going to sleep now?" Kouji didn't let go, but she sounded a little weird.

"Yeah, I guess so," Samar answered.

"Then I'll start putting all that stuff away."

"Want help?"

"No, you go ahead and do your usual routine. Take a shower and go to sleep. You've earned it, more than likely."

Samar nodded and yawned. She was worn out. She grabbed some clothes and went to shower. The hot water eased the knot out of her stomach. She stayed under the soothing stream longer than usual.

She put on a sleeveless tee, and shorts over her underwear to avoid offending her guest. Samar marched out of the bathroom to her bed. She glanced into the kitchen and noticed Kouji stocking the shelves. Samar went to sleep to the sound of brown paper bags rustling.

Kouji finished putting away groceries and made herself comfortable on the floor by a bookshelf. She grabbed a book to read but didn't glance at a word. She stared at Samar.

She had thought of making breakfast to return some of the kindness Samar showed her. Convincing her mother to help her with shopping was no easy task. Her mother hadn't been supportive at all and advised Kouji to go back to sleep with a reminder of what happened to her nursemaid.

No assassins were after Samar, and the Nightmares, well, Samar chased those. She was the bane of the Nightmares' existence. Should they try to get to Kouji through her, Samar would be able to handle them. Kouji didn't understand—or had forgotten—why Nightmares would be interested in her in the first place.

"I'll never let any harm come to you." Speaking the vow aloud ensured that the universe bore witness to her promise. She wouldn't let a single thing touch Samar, ever.

You can't keep that promise. That could've been her mind, but it sounded suspiciously like her mother. Kouji didn't care. She'd put her life on the line for Samar. They needed each other. A light in the darkness. Warmth in the cold. A moment of relief from a pit of despair.

If you're going to be there for her, you must get your mind in order. You need all of your memories to come back. You need to figure out how to live in this time without her or Mother babysitting you. Figure out who you are now that you're without restraints, without sleep, and without anything to hold you back should you feel the urge to tear through the world. This is on you now.

Kouji would give Samar her best dedication, exactly like she had for her missions long ago.

Chapter Eleven

A Sun Shower

SAMAR WOKE TO THE sound of sizzling and the smell of bacon. Yawning, she reached beneath her shirt and rubbed her grumbling belly. She threw the blanket aside and staggered to her kitchen. Kouji was there, closing the refrigerator. Kouji poured two glasses of mango juice.

"I guess you are handy around the kitchen." Samar smiled.

"I was lost for a couple of hours. My mother showed up and saved me from looking like a total idiot," Kouji admitted with a smile.

"Your mother just comes and goes, huh?" She was a little uncomfortable thinking a stranger was popping in and out of her apartment. It wasn't like she cared about the place, but it was still hers.

Kouji shrugged. "She's a goddess."

"You can come and go as you please too." Did Kouji's mother move through shadows like Kouji did?

Kouji rubbed the back of her neck, knowing exactly what Samar meant. "Yeah, kind of. It takes a lot more energy for me though. I had no idea why I had the ability until after I fell asleep. I had no idea I was half-god for most of my life."

"So many stories are about you. I can only wonder which ones are true. In some, you're quite heroic."

"I can only wonder for some of them as well, especially the heroic ones. My memories still have big blank spots." Kouji fidgeted for a moment before she grinned. "So are you ready to eat?"

Kouji didn't seem ready to discuss her life just yet, which was fine. It was too early for anything deep. Samar would much rather eat, especially if everything was as delicious as it smelled.

Kouji turned and handed Samar a plate of seasoned scrambled eggs with cheese, crispy bacon, and sweet dumplings the size of golf balls. Not quite the right size, but Samar wouldn't complain.

"And I made porridge with bananas. I used nutmeg and cinnamon." Kouji nodded to the pot.

"Oh, I'd like a bowl." Samar admired the perfect traditional breakfast. She grabbed her dining mat and spread it on the floor. Plates, bowls, and cups were arranged on the mat, along with small containers of sauces and seasonings. Kouji sat across from her like it was the most natural thing in the world to do. It felt like forever since Samar enjoyed a meal in the tradition of her homeland.

Her heart was ready to burst. She hadn't been this comfortable at a dining mat since she sat down with her mother the morning before her life changed forever. Was Kouji aware of that tragic fact? Samar was unable to recall if she'd said anything to the tomb about something so simple as having a traditional meal in the traditional manner. They smiled at each other.

"Thanks for all of this. It's been such a long time since I've had a homecooked meal," Samar said. Restaurants seldom got it right. The citizens of Oganja accepted the subpar dishes masquerading as food from Asale.

"Thank me after you try it," Kouji replied.

Samar nodded and dug into the eggs and bacon. She smiled after a few bites, savoring the taste. Kouji watched her and waited with gleaming eyes.

"This is nothing short of remarkable! I haven't had a breakfast this delectable since I started living here by myself." Samar caught herself and swallowed. "Breakfast is so delicious I forgot my manners."

"Glad I can do something right." Kouji nodded and began eating. She started with the porridge, which polite people usually ate first.

"You're amazing. The eggs are the best. I haven't had seasoned eggs in years."

"Why not? Don't they make them around here?"

"Some places, yes, but it's never right. Something's always missing, like the spices are wrong in some way or the eggs are runny. And I'd never make them for myself." She never had the strength.

"Your mom?"

"We had eggs for breakfast almost every day…" Samar's voice broke and her eyes burned. *Including that day.* The worst day of her life. She shook away the memory. "This is the first thing she ever taught me to make." Samar had tried to make this dish once since she lost her mother, but broke down before she managed to crack the eggs.

Kouji put her bowl down and laid her hand on Samar's knee. "It's okay to cry, to mourn. You told me so."

"I've been in mourning for three years." *And will be for the rest of my life.*

"But you have to let it out. It does you no good to lock it inside of you. It's not honoring your mother to destroy yourself. She wouldn't want that."

Once Within a Dream

How many times had Evinia said the same thing? So why, this time, did Samar bend? Why did she allow the tears to fall? Why did words she'd heard a million times finally locate a fissure? Whatever the reason, her internal walls shattered. Strange what a simple thing like breakfast could do.

Samar carefully put down her plate. That's where her control ended. She dropped her head into her hands and wept in a way she had never allowed herself to do. She didn't have room to think, only bawl, pouring out as much of the sorrow and grief that consumed her as possible.

Pressure around her shoulders suggested Kouji hugged her, but she didn't bother to check. All she could do was cry even harder, like her chest would cave in. Samar might collapse in on herself, and that'd be fine.

As it all came out, Samar found herself not afraid she might come apart at the seams for once. Kouji held her together. Samar felt no judgment from her. Kouji was just there.

"I'm sorry," Samar sniffled. She tried to pull herself together. Kouji didn't need to watch her weeping for the rest of the day.

"Don't be sorry. You shut down. Now, you can come back on. I am all too familiar with what that's like. That's what my whole sleep was, I think." Kouji rubbed her forehead like she could will herself to remember.

Samar wanted to ask questions, to distract herself with Kouji's life, but too much was inside of her. She cried until it was impossible to cry, and Kouji held her, even when she stopped.

"The porridge is probably cold now," Samar whispered.

Kouji burst out laughing. "It's fine. I got to taste it. It wasn't worthwhile. Too much cinnamon."

Samar chuckled. Eventually, Kouji released her and she sighed. She felt lighter now. Yes, the void remained inside her, but it throbbed a little less. *I needed that.*

"I hope the rest of the food is better than the porridge," Kouji said.

"What I tasted was delicious." Samar was pleased that Kouji was willing to move on.

They continued eating. While the eggs and bacon were perfect, Kouji was right about the porridge. Too much cinnamon in both the porridge and the sweet dumplings.

"I'll do better tomorrow," Kouji said.

"We can do it together. It might be beneficial for me to cook again," Samar replied. She could make both porridge and dumplings in many different ways.

Kouji lit up, lilac eyes twinkling. "I look forward to it. How about dinner?"

"Agreed."

A small fight flared during cleanup. Kouji didn't accept the rule that the person who cooked didn't need to wash dishes. She insisted. Samar conceded by letting her dry, but she had to impose some hospitality norms on Kouji.

☾

The afternoon was quiet, or as quiet as Kouji expected from this city. Samar practiced meditation and Kouji read. Every few minutes, a faint chime created a wave in the silence, when Samar tapped a tiny bell.

Kouji glanced at her every time the bell rang out. Samar was calm, focused, in control, and absolutely breathtaking. In her sleeveless t-shirt, her broad, copper shoulders and muscular arms made it easy to see she was built like a warrior. Raised scars and light marks dotted her upper body.

"Kouji," Samar said, eyes closed, voice calm.

Kouji yelped and looked away. "Um, yes?" Was it inappropriate to stare?

"You still owe me a fight." Samar grinned as her eyes opened.

Kouji chuckled. "I suppose I do." She put her book down.

"We should do it now."

Kouji glanced around. "Where are we going to fight?"

"Here. There's enough space since you cleaned."

Kouji wouldn't say *this* was enough space. There was barely room for them to take three steps back. But they should be able to spar without breaking anything if they were careful. It'd be a test in control as well as a sparring match.

They both stood up and made their way to the living room area. They dropped into their fighting stances. Each studied the other, not moving.

Samar's stance was unfamiliar, and Kouji had seen plenty. Not that they ever did anyone any good against her. From what she recalled about going toe-to-toe with Samar, things wouldn't change, but it might still be fun.

Kouji came in first, moving at what she was certain was average speed for a human. Samar wasted no time tapping her with light punches. Samar frowned.

"You're not trying."

"I'm trying to go at a normal speed, but you're much faster than I remember humans being." Kouji ducked a punch, and stepped back to avoid several kicks that came quickly.

Samar scoffed. "Go at your pace. It'll help me and be fun for you too. It won't be fun if you stand here and get punched all day." Well, that was certainly true.

Samar moved much quicker than Kouji had realized from their brief interaction in the park. Although not Kouji's full speed, if they kept this up, she might find herself exhausted after an hour or so. She'd love it.

"Your movements are sharper than I expected," Kouji said.

"I have to be precise, make sure I hit where I'm aiming with force," Samar replied.

"To attach the Favors?"

"Yup. Miss that mark by a fraction and the Favor won't have the correct effect." Samar sidestepped a kick that Kouji had to pull back on or put a hole in the wall. Samar pushed in closer, trying to punch her, but instead getting a hard forearm for her troubles. "You're a lot like the wind, which I expected."

Kouji grinned. "I like being able to attack when necessary but also use your force against you."

"How long have you been fighting?" Samar threw a hand strike Kouji dodged with barely any movement.

"As long as I can remember. My speed and ability to vanish into shadows help. I'm also naturally quiet in movements. What about you?"

"Since I could walk, from my understanding. My mother shared all of her habits and hobbies with me."

"That's touching. You were able to create an incredible bond. My parents exploited my talents." *I should probably tell her to the best of my ability. I just don't want to lose her yet. This is so much fun.*

"Your human parents? The royals?"

"Yes. I was used for keeping people in line."

Samar hummed, but didn't pry further. Kouji smiled a thanks, and they danced around each other. This was new. Sparring had never seemed like a dance to Kouji. A hint of danger always swirled around the activity. Someone who might go too far or test her too much.

"Okay, I think I'm…" Samar blew out a long breath, as she rested her hands on her knees, panting. Sweat poured down her face.

"Done?" Kouji was damp with perspiration and her muscles burned, but not to the extent of Samar. Sweat dripped from the ends of Kouji's braids, as she pulled air into her lungs.

"It's been over two hours non-stop. You're incredible. Do you feel tired?"

Kouji nodded. "Oh yes. My muscles ache and burn as much as any human's would." She'd push herself to keep going if Samar desired. Anything to keep Samar's full attention. She studied Kouji, learning and reading her movements, and catching on so much faster than most opponents. *She would've been an incredible warrior in my time.*

Of course, Kouji didn't mind stopping. Beyond her own exhaustion, she wanted a moment to take in the sight of a glowing Samar. She was radiant. And her damp shirt was captivating. This wasn't the first time Kouji's gaze got stuck on Samar's chest.

"That was an amazing workout." Samar lowered herself to the floor. It was a slow undertaking.

Kouji settled on the floor, sucking in air. "Yeah, it was." She did her best to catch her breath, trying to erase the images of Samar moving from her mind. *What are these thoughts?*

Samar gave her a dazed smile. "You're in great shape."

"I don't know about that. It might just be that I'm not fully human. You've got tons of energy too." Even though Kouji was part divine, Samar had managed to wear her out.

"I've never been this tired after a workout. We're both going to need showers." Samar wiped her dipping face. "I usually go running and stuff after boxing, but I don't think I'd make it down the stairs. You're incredible."

Kouji laughed, not sure what to say to the compliment. "You too."

Samar smiled and groaned as she pulled herself to her feet. She disappeared into the bathroom. Kouji collapsed onto her back as soon as the door closed. She groaned as she focused on the ceiling.

"Why did that feel so wonderful?" Kouji understood her memories were still a bit scrambled, but she couldn't recall a time when sparring was downright delightful. She couldn't recollect a time she had stared at an opponent the way she did with Samar, to admire rather than discover a weakness to exploit. She had no idea what that was about.

She had no idea what possessed her to hug Samar during breakfast. Yes, Samar needed the embrace and needed to let out that sorrow. *How did I know to hug her? I didn't want to stop hugging her.* She'd love nothing more than to hold Samar as long and as often as Samar would allow. Samar felt right in her arms.

Do I have any idea what any of this is about? Not really. Kouji just knew she wanted to be around Samar, and Samar was open to that. So life was good for once. She'd savor it.

Kouji managed to grab her book. She laid back on the floor and continued reading until the bathroom door opened. Samar stepped past her, then returned and dropped a pile of clothing onto Kouji's chest. Kouji yelped.

"For your shower. Then, we should go out and buy you some proper things, like underwear," Samar said.

"Underwear?" Kouji echoed.

"We'll talk about it later. For now, take a nice, hot shower."

Kouji put her book down and walked slowly into the bathroom, trying to remember how this worked. *What if the new knowledge is blocking out my old knowledge, and that's why my brain is still messed up?* Doubtful, but the excuse was enough to keep her from having to share what she remembered.

Samar wasn't surprised when Kouji stepped out of the bathroom with her clothes stuck to her wet body and her hair dripping wet. The shower was still new.

"Let's dry you properly, so we can start our journey outside. You need pants that fit," Samar said, glancing at Kouji's ankles.

Kouji smiled as her eyes dropped. "I don't mind. They're comfortable."

"They'll be better a proper length with modern undergarments. You'll feel even better."

Kouji looked away. "Um, you know I can't pay for any of this, right?"

"Did I not leave you with money this morning? I'm aware you can't pay, but you're my guest and I can. I want you to be comfortable. So we should get going. We can buy you some clothes and eat before I go to work."

Samar helped her towel off her hair, even though that wouldn't properly dry it. She left the bathroom to give Kouji a chance to dry herself again. She stepped out of the bathroom looking a bit better.

"It'll have to do," Samar muttered to herself. She took Kouji's by the hand and led her out of the apartment. After giving the door a firm yank to ensure it was closed, Samar locked up and they were on their merry way. Right into a drizzle of rain.

"Were you enjoying the book you were reading?" Samar had noticed Kouji reading an epic poetry book.

"Yes. I finished many of your history books and wanted something different. I'm confused though. The poems reference me and my father, but our names weren't quite right, and I think I'm referred to as male," Kouji replied.

"There are many different stories about you and your origins. Names are lost to time, like many other things. Most works refer to you as Kou. Most of the time, they agree on the gender. You're a young woman in most of the stories."

"Why am I not mentioned in history books?"

"Ten thousand years is a long time. Many works have been lost. Some information is known only because it's referenced in other pieces, so we don't know what's real or fiction. Making it worse, they make a reference like it's common knowledge, clearly something popular. The historians don't go on to explain anything because they assume readers already know."

Kouji winced. "So the books have no real accurate take of my life because so much time passed?"

"Well, did anything you came across sound accurate?"

Kouji's brow wrinkled. Samar waited patiently. She'd love confirmation for some of the stories. *Mom, you'd have loved this moment. I should have a notepad.* Not that she would forget.

"Emperor Carthrone was mentioned in a story. He was a warrior long before I was born, which I guess is why I didn't know that. By the time I became familiar with him, many people were calling for his head."

Samar nodded. "And they got what they wanted, yes?" She was fairly certain how that story ended.

Kouji winced. "Yes, they certainly did."

According to history, Kouji was the reason the emperor lost his head, but Samar didn't press her to disclose that. The death was celebrated in most works. "It must've been exciting to live during those times."

"No more than it is to live now. I like this time."

"You've barely experienced this time."

"Still, like it."

Samar arched an eyebrow. "Why?"

"Well, you're here for one." Kouji smiled.

It took a moment for the words to reach Samar's brain. Her cheeks heated even more when Kouji squeezed her hand. Samar was quiet for a long moment. Kouji sighed and pushed her wet, straggly braids from her face.

"Your hair probably should be redone," Samar said grateful for the distraction.

"Yes, but I have no servants to do it now." Kouji's bangles rang out as she ran her hand through her damp plaits.

"Most people don't have servants to do their braids anymore."

"No?"

"You should take them out. Getting your hair wet this often and not doing anything with it will just make it knot together."

"I should, but I don't want to take the time to do that and risk pulling out my hair. I'm not used to doing it myself."

Samar tilted her head. *Right, Kouji is a royal.* She probably didn't do any of life's mundane things for herself. "Do you want me to take them out for you?"

Kouji smiled. "Would you?"

"When we come back. I might have to buy a comb. I don't think I have one." Samar might've had one, but she didn't make it a point to keep track of it. "I usually brush my hair." She ran her hand across her short curls.

"Your hair is beautiful. I've also never seen red hair before."

Samar frowned. "I think it runs in my father's family." She shook that off. "Tell me more about what you read that stood out."

Kouji went through stories about her that she was certain were true. Her mother was a goddess, and Kouji was given to a king and queen as a baby. She fought Nightmares. She was used as a tool to control the population and rivals. She glossed over many of the lauded feats attributed to her.

"That's not a lot of detail." Samar led them into a clothing store that would be able to supply Kouji with everything she needed.

"Well, some of the more specific things I can't confirm yet. I feel safe assuming I never fought the sky. I also didn't die trying to stab the sun. I don't know if the sun ever tried to kill me. Oh, and I'm obviously not a male. How did that happen?"

"Your name, since it's often shortened to Kou in the stories. That's usually a name given to males, although it's unisex. In stories where they use Kouji, you're female. There are hundreds of stories, many more than in my small library. In some, you're female, even when they use the name Kou." Samar grabbed a pair of sweatpants and held them up to Kouji. They were the right length. She grabbed five pairs. *Should I get her a pair of jeans or cargoes?*

"I don't think I've ever been to the Land of the Dead like one of the stories said, but that might have to do with me going to sleep. I did fight an invading army…I think."

"Were you ten when you did it?" Samar moved onto shirts. Most stories about fighting the army claimed Kouji was ten.

Kouji tapped her chin. "I think younger."

"Impressive."

Kouji shook her head. "I was an attack dog. My parents pointed and said, 'kill,' I did what I was trained to do."

"A lot of stories tell about how you came about your fighting ability. Several mention gods or enlightened individuals teaching you." Samar was hesitant in the underwear section. She wasn't too familiar with sizing as far as underwear went. Evinia took her to a proper underwear store and had her measured the first couple of times, even though she preferred sports bras to anything else.

"No, just training with warrior teachers and brutality, I think." Kouji rubbed the back of her neck. Her eyes glazed over for a moment.

Those lilac eyes made sure Samar didn't dig into that comment. She focused on undergarments. Kouji was taller than she was, but leaner. Her breasts were larger, but not by much. Samar chose one size larger in bras and the same size in briefs. She also grabbed a bag of ankle socks.

"This seems like a lot of clothes," Kouji said.

"Not hardly. I'm sure you had more when you were first awake," Samar replied.

Kouji nodded. "I had different clothes for almost every day of the year."

"Then this isn't a lot. We need a toothbrush."

"Toothbrush?"

"To clean your teeth."

Kouji's brow wrinkled. "No more chew sticks?"

"On my day off, we can go to the Asale market. They have chew sticks. There are other markets, but I know that one best."

Kouji nodded, going along with the plan. The clothing run was done. The quick and painless experience was unexpected.

"You always said shopping was awful, but this was pleasant," Kouji said.

"It can be painful if you have to go to multiple stores. We hit one store. Now, let's go get some food and we'll work on your braids."

They picked up some fast food and made their way back to the apartment. Samar didn't know where to put the new clothes, but they could figure that out later. They needed to eat and take Kouji's braids out before they knotted.

"You sit on the floor, and I can sit on the couch. That'll make it easier to do your hair."

"Don't you want to eat first?" Kouji held up their takeout bag.

"Yeah, that'd be better, so the food doesn't get cold and I'm not in your hair with food crumbs on my hands."

Samar grabbed the dining mat again and they got comfortable. She pulled their drinks from the bag while Kouji unloaded the food. Cheeseburgers with the works and fries.

"You might like some of this modern, city food."

"Maybe getting a taste for things will help my cooking." Kouji chuckled.

Samar showed Kouji how to hold a burger. Kouji nodded and mimicked the grip. The buns were packed with a thick, beef patty, lettuce, tomatoes, pickles, onion rings, cheese, peppers, and bacon. Samar had to open her mouth wide. Kouji followed suit, but still had trouble taking her first bite. She gave a delighted yelp.

"Good?" Samar asked, happily munching.

Kouji nodded. "Yeah." She took several seconds to chew. "I liked the goat more, but this is good."

"Try the fries. Tomorrow for lunch we can try something more traditional. We'll alternate to allow you a full food exploration." She smiled. That'd take a while in a city the size of Oganja.

They shared a quiet meal. Samar found the cheeseburger tasted better than she recalled. She hadn't had one in many months.

Kouji groaned as she finished off her last seasoned, steak-cut fry. "Okay, this meal is heavier than I expected."

"Yeah, it always catches me too. Ready for the hair?"

"I might fall asleep." Kouji patted her belly.

"As long as you stay sitting up."

Kouji snickered, but they cleaned up the meal and then set themselves in position. Kouji grabbed the book she'd been reading earlier. Samar was able to find a small-toothed comb, cleaned her hands, and sat on her tiny couch. Kouji sat on the floor between her legs but much too far away.

"Come here." Samar pointed down in front of her.

"Huh?" Kouji glanced around.

"Move back."

"Um, what do you mean?"

"Move all the way back to me, so I can take your braids out."

Kouji twiddled her fingers. She looked over her shoulder, then scooted back. She gulped and seemed uncomfortable. She glanced back again, tiny sweat drops on her forehead, like she was afraid.

"Are you all right?" Samar asked.

After a quick nod, Kouji buried her nose in her book. Samar shrugged and began combing the braids out. She did her best to be gentle, especially when she came across any tangles, and there were plenty. When she was younger, she enjoyed letting her mother put her hair in braids. Taking them out wasn't her favorite part. She remembered pain from her mother jerking out knots that ran through her hair. She didn't want Kouji to experience such.

Kouji shifted and placed an arm on Samar's leg, trying to find a comfortable position. She relaxed, and silence became a blanket of comfort over them. A moment later, Kouji yelped and yanked her arm back as if she had been burned. "Sorry about that!"

"It's okay. I used to rest on my mother when she took my hair out," Samar replied.

"That's different. She was your mother. It's not appropriate to touch a woman of means without her permission, especially if you're not related to her. It's even more true that it's not all right to touch a woman's legs unless…well, never mind the unless. It's not okay."

"It's okay, Kouji. Times are different now. It was an innocent touch. Besides, I'm far from a woman of means."

"But still—" Kouji started to get up, but Samar cut in.

"Your touch was innocent, and you have permission. It's okay. Don't freak out on me." They were getting along well. She didn't want to shake things up.

Kouji nodded. "You're right. I'm sorry."

Samar chuckled and rolled her eyes. She wasn't bothered by Kouji's touch. She had on pants for crying out loud. It wasn't like Kouji tried to fondle her. That idea made her shiver for some reason she refused to dwell on.

Once Within a Dream

The quiet continued, as Samar worked on Kouji's soft hair that was obviously once well cared for. What oils were used in Kouji's time? Would they be available now? Of course, Kouji probably had no idea what was used to care for her hair. They might have to take a trip to the salon. Kouji's hair was dried out. It needed to be washed, shampooed, conditioned, and oiled. Kouji was long overdue.

"Kouji." Samar pushed some hair out of the way to tackle the other braids.

"Yeah?" Kouji didn't look up from her book.

"You need to wash your hair."

"What? But it just got all wet in the shower thing." Kouji made a circle around her hair with her index finger.

"Yeah, but that's not washing it. That's your hair getting wet in the shower. Your head needs to be washed."

Kouji's brow wrinkled. "So what do I do about that? I've never washed my hair on my own."

"I figured as much. I'll do it for you. It's not that hard."

"And you'll put the braids back in, right?"

"I should be able to. I know how to braid, but it's been a while since I've done it. I'll wash and braid your hair later though. Once I finish this, I'll have to get ready for work."

"I can wait. You have to leave for work already?" Kouji pouted.

Samar offered a small smile. "Time flies when you're having fun. Should I leave some money for you again?"

"Are you going to come in hungry again?"

"Maybe."

"Then maybe I'll cook something. I'll try to do better. Okay?"

"Sounds fair, and breakfast was fine." Samar looked forward to the meal. More than having Kouji cook for her, the idea of sitting at her dining mat with someone across from her filled her with something she couldn't quite explain. "There, I'm done."

Kouji moved away, and Samar immediately missed the contact. She clambered to her feet. Her breath hitched. Kouji had turned to face her, loose hair falling in waves around her shoulders. Her hair was crimped from the braids, almost as if that was the style she wanted. Radiant didn't cut it. Her bronze skin glowed.

"Is there something wrong?" Kouji asked.

Samar shook her head. "No, I think I just saw the sun for the first time in years." *What the hell was that?* She didn't have a clue, but the way Kouji ducked her head and offered a shy smile made it worth any awkwardness. For the first time ever, it was hard to leave for work.

Chapter Twelve

Dark Clouds

EVINIA ARCHED AN EYEBROW as Samar stumbled into her office. She was a little worse for wear, flopping down in her usual seat as if exhausted. A group of hooligans had been in the park and tried to beat her from what Evinia could tell over the comms. Samar had on layers again.

"Sammie, do you have on two hoodies and a jacket?" Evinia asked.

Samar frowned. "Makes it hard to move."

"But are you warmer than usual?"

Samar groaned. She didn't want to talk about layers. *Interesting.* Evinia wanted to interrogate Samar, but that wouldn't get Samar to open up. *Wait.* Eventually, the dam would crack, and secrets would trickle out.

"So, um, how's everything?" Samar asked.

Evinia held in a laugh. This wasn't Samar's typical awkwardness. "Fine. You?" *Where is this going? Is she going to just plow right into whatever's going on with her?*

"Um, reports?" Samar nodded toward the center monitor.

"I'll do those because I need to finish some things first. These people are actually trying to make me do some work for once. It's almost ludicrous." Evinia said this as a joke, which her little sister missed, as usual. She did need to work though.

"Okay." Samar scratched her forehead and glanced away. "Um, Vin, you still braid hair?"

"I do. Do you want your hair braided again?" One of the ways they'd bonded was by Evinia doing Samar's hair when she first showed up in Oganja. Samar's hair had been long, mostly through lack of care. Evinia had tried to make her sister's appearance somewhat decent, hoping to lift her spirits and maybe even earn her some friends. The intricate cornrows failed to give her any clout at school, but the experience helped them get to where they were today. *Worth it.*

"No, not really. Remember when you let me braid yours?" Samar asked.

Where's this going? "Yes. I don't have the time for you to braid my hair though."

Samar shook her head. "No, no, no. That's not..." She sucked her teeth and rubbed her forehead again. "Did I do a decent job then?"

Evinia stared at her sister again. Three odd questions in less than thirty seconds. At first, she chalked up the reminiscing to Samar being in a good mood, which in and of itself was weird. Her sister made it a point to be as melancholic as possible in honor of her mother. Asking whether Samar had done a good job at braiding hinted at another motive.

"Are you planning to do someone's hair?" Evinia asked.

Samar's eyes popped open. "Wha-wha-why'd you ask that?"

Well, now, things are stranger still. Had Samar gotten comfortable enough with someone to braid their hair? "Why are you so twitchy?"

Samar twisted her mouth up. "I'm not. I only wanted to talk, and you're busy, and I don't know how..." She shook her head. "Never mind. I'm being stupid. You're busy. It doesn't matter."

Evinia sighed. She wanted Samar to talk to her and tell her about her life. She wanted Samar to build a life. Something was happening, and Samar needed to get it off her chest. Samar wanted to give up whatever secret she was holding. *Don't harass her about details or reasons. Just be an ear.* Evinia gave her sister a lighthearted smile.

"Sammie, you can be a real pest when you try to be."

Samar ducked her head. "I don't mean to be."

"I'm aware." Evinia moved closer, rubbing Samar's knee. Samar peeked up at her. "Your braiding was always exceptional. Your mother taught you well. Why?"

Samar shook her head. "You're sure?"

"Yes. I dare think you're better than I am."

"No way. I'd never be able to do those designs you did in my hair."

This wasn't an argument to have with Samar, who never thought she did anything well. That had to be their father's fault. No way Samar's mother let her go through life believing she was less than stellar.

"You want to practice?" Evinia asked. "We can meet up later today. It's been far too long since we've hung out." She always had time in her schedule for Samar, but Samar always had an excuse for not going out.

"It has, but not today. I have something..." Samar glanced away and pointed behind her as if that explained anything.

This is so weird. "Are you skating again?" Being around other skaters and trying to figure herself out would explain this bizarre behavior.

Samar blinked. "What? No. Why…what?"

"Just a thought." Skating had been the only hint that Samar might recover from her mother's death. It started with a noticeable burst of happiness, like now, but didn't last long. *I hope whatever this is doesn't end the same way.*

Samar squinted as if trying to read Evinia. "I can go, right?"

"I'm not holding you hostage." Evinia smiled.

A small smile graced Samar's face, then she was gone. Evinia wasn't sure what all that was about, but she'd let Samar be happy for now. It was wonderful, especially if Samar had learned her lesson from before.

"Kouji," Samar called into her apartment. Kicking the door open hurt her knee a bit. A Nightmare had gotten the better of her leg earlier, while she patrolled the park. The damn things were stronger than they used to be, but they still weren't a match for her.

"Huh?" Kouji poked her head out of the kitchen.

"Oh, you're right there. Sorry for yelling." Samar's cheeks were on fire.

"It's okay." Kouji smiled.

"What are you making?" Samar noticed a pot on the stove above a low flame.

"It's a surprise. It's almost done. How was work?" Kouji helped Samar out of her jacket and hung it in the closet.

"The Nightmare activity has increased. I had to deal with another group of them and their hosts. They were fierce, but at least it wasn't boring."

"Are you all right?"

"No worse than most fights. A shower, food, and sleep will fix everything."

"And my hair?" Kouji pointed to her flowing hair.

"I'll get to it, promise. I'm just…" Samar sighed, shoulders slumped. "Tired. Worn down. Suddenly, there's so much pressing on me. I was excited a few minutes ago."

"What happened?"

"I'm not sure. Maybe just thinking about my night. So many Nightmares, like I'm not making a difference. Why is the problem worse now? Have I wasted my life?"

Kouji gasped. "What? No! You save people when you take down Nightmares. You're doing a massive service for people. Besides, you hate not fighting Nightmares. You think it's boring."

"Yes, and I'm left wandering an ugly park in the cold all night. I hate that as much as I hate Nightmares."

"I'm aware. I remember a time when you didn't hate the nights though."

Samar's mind went blank on what to say to that comment, despite knowing exactly what Kouji meant. *Am I like this because Vinnie asked if I was skating again?* She wished Kouji hadn't reminded her of the time when she didn't despise being out in the cold. She wished she had never said anything about that time, even to an empty building. She looked away when Kouji approached her.

"What did I say wrong?" Kouji asked in a quiet, timid voice.

"No, it's nothing."

"It's something. What?"

"Could you just not..." She couldn't phrase her request without sounding rude or fed up.

"What? You didn't mind being out there at one point. You liked it out there once, right?" The twinkle in Kouji's eyes made this so much harder. Despite the pieces of her backstory Kouji had given up, she came across as so guileless, innocent, and well-meaning.

"I did, but I don't want to talk about it. It's the past, and the past is always dead. I don't want to get into that with you." Samar growled.

"Why not?" The question was asked in a gentle whisper.

Samar glared at her guest. "It's not something to talk about with you."

"No?" Kouji tilted her head, and a flash lit her eyes. "It was something to talk about with that building though?"

"Yeah, it was."

"Fine, don't talk about it with me then."

"I didn't plan on it."

Kouji frowned at her for the first time. Samar was too upset to care. She stomped off, not that she had any place to retreat to. The bathroom was the best choice.

Samar escaped into the shower to gather herself. *Why the hell did I tell the tomb my entire life?* Kouji knew everything about her, things she'd rather Kouji not be privy to. Not yet anyway. *Why? What does it matter?*

Honestly, it didn't matter. As she said, it was the past, and the past was dead. No reason to be upset over the past. It wouldn't change anything.

Samar exited the bathroom dressed in her house clothes of dark-blue, knee-length sweat shorts and a navy-blue tank top. She smelled chicken and her stomach growled. Taking a breath, she poked her head into the kitchen. Kouji had fixed two bowls of spicy chicken stew with red rice and assorted vegetables. Her usual smile was gone, and Samar's insides knotted up.

"Here you go," Kouji muttered, as she handed her a bowl and a spoon. A kicked puppy would look less pitiful. "I wasn't sure what kind of drink you wanted."

"Kouji." Samar sighed, accepting the bowl. It burned her hand, but she ignored that. She had bigger problems.

"I'll move out of your way," Kouji mumbled, turning away.

Samar moved by Kouji's side. "Kouji, I'm sorry I got upset. I don't want to talk about that with you. I wish you didn't know about Universal."

Kouji looked at her with glistening eyes. "Why?"

That was a brilliant question. Why didn't she want Kouji to be aware of Universal? She just didn't.

"I'm not sure why, but I wish you didn't."

"Didn't you love him?" Kouji asked.

Samar sighed, but she didn't answer. She seriously had little desire to discuss Universal with Kouji. It caused a discomforting tingle down her nerves, and her stomach flipped several times. She didn't know how to explain so Kouji would understand.

"I should drop the subject, right?" Kouji asked.

"Please." Samar felt as small as her voice sounded.

"Sure…" Kouji muttered agreement, but her mouth was tense.

Samar quietly arranged the dining mat. *I hurt her feelings. But can't we just leave the past in the past?*

"I bought fruit punch. Mother assured me it's delicious but also not many fruits." Kouji's forced laugh was more off-putting than expected, considering she'd been all smiles since they met.

"I love fruit punch. I get it from a specific store, so it's mostly fruit though."

"I hope I went to that same store then." Kouji opened the refrigerator and pulled out the jug of fruit punch. She poured them each a glass and put the jug away.

Samar softened and allowed herself a small laugh when Kouji brought the drinks over. "Thank you. You're trying to spoil me, huh?" She accepted the glasses so Kouji could sit.

"I think, if you let me, I'd try. Of course, I have no idea how." Kouji smiled, too, as she sat down.

"You've cooked for me, twice." Samar stirred the stew in her bowl to release some of the heat.

Kouji nodded. "Yes, but I want to."

Samar took her first bite and hummed. "Okay, this is amazing. I can't believe you've never really cooked before. You should be a chef or something."

"Thanks, maybe I'll look into that." With a soft chuckle, Kouji dug in. "My mother helped out. I'd be lost without her."

"Am I ever going to at least see your mother?" she asked.

Kouji shrugged. "No idea. That's up to her and she hasn't brought it up. She might not be able to reveal herself to mortals without being beseeched or something. That's how it was when I was awake, anyway, I think." She rubbed the center of her forehead with her thumb. "Some stuff's still hazy."

"Does she mind you're staying here?"

"Not at all. She expects me to be on my best behavior. I wasn't sure how this would work, but I think it falls under hospitality rules."

Samar sipped her juice. It wasn't the brand she normally bought, but it was enough. The food was scrumptious and offset the juice. "How so?"

"You're looking out for a stranger, which is what you should do. But technically, your status is very well beneath mine, and I shouldn't be troubling your door. Of course, since no noble clans are around here for me to trouble, Mother would have to deal with this regardless."

"Your mother's old-fashioned, but she's existed through those times to these modern ones."

"I suppose she just holds onto some values and others she doesn't. People are like that."

"True. Values and people can change. They evolve as time goes on. Like Vinnie and Mechi. Couples didn't live together before marriage back then, right?" Samar asked.

"This is true."

"Actually, they're unconventional, even for this time. They stay together all the time. They should live together, which I suppose they somewhat do. It's not official. Vin says she goes home about once a week. They're practically married, but I don't think they want to cohabitate or make things official yet."

Kouji glanced at the window. "Do you think she's happy?"

"Who, Vin?"

"Yes."

"No doubt in my mind she's happy. She loves being in a relationship with Mechi."

"You dislike him, right?" Kouji asked.

Samar turned her mouth up as she thought about her answer. "I don't like him. He's too familiar and makes the same terrible jokes people at my high school did. I've seen him with Vinnie though. He's good with her and good to her. Vin was trying to save me after my mother died, even though her own mother was gone. Siku was awful. I watched Mechi save Vin from wilting under Siku's force."

"You never talked about that."

"I wasn't sure how to feel about it and never wanted to voice it. Mechi is good to her. I respect that because I love her. He loves her. They like taking care of each other, despite how much Siku hates it."

Kouji took a breath and let her spoon dangle from her mouth. "Are you scared of him?"

Samar let that question simmer for a moment. "I have no idea how to answer that. I've never been afraid of someone. I'm unsure of how to act around him, and I don't want to be around him. I take that as fear. I'm so off when I'm around him, like I'm wrong or an anomaly. It's like when the human race was created, I was somehow formed from whatever was left over."

Kouji reached for her hand. Samar gratefully accepted the gesture of support. She had never said those words aloud. *I'm glad I said this to her.*

"I felt that way with my mother, but I got used to her after a while," Kouji stated.

"Your mom probably wanted you and is nice. You say she helps you with things in your life and talks to you about things. She accepts you."

"Pretty much, yes," Kouji answered with a solid nod.

Samar stared into her empty bowl. When had she eaten everything? She didn't even usually eat at this time. The taste lingered on her tongue, the ghost of home. Her chin trembled for a second.

"Siku doesn't accept me. I don't think he likes me much. I'm a mistake he made. He didn't want me. I was a mistake to Mom, but she never made me feel that way. She made it seem like I was a blessing, even though I wasn't. He makes me feel ashamed for living, like I don't belong here. His eyes always seem to be begging me to die."

One of the reasons she could hardly look Siku in the face was the fact that it seemed like he was trying to will her to die. If only he'd change his expression toward her, just once. She didn't ask to be born, and she didn't understand why he hated her.

Kouji sighed and put her bowl down. "That's rather rough. Why'd he take you away from the mountains then? I don't understand why he'd take you from the place you felt at home to somewhere you detest. Why take you someplace where he'd have to explain you? Where people would see you?"

With a scoff, Samar shook her head. "I have no idea. It's possible he didn't want me to live on my own. I'd have been fine. He said he didn't want me there by myself. So he brought me here to be by myself. He's a damn smart man." She rolled her eyes.

"Why do you think he did it?"

"I doubt it was his idea. I suspect it was Evinia, but it could've been his parents. Sometimes, I think Nyota told Evinia about me."

"Why his parents?"

"To save face, have control. They couldn't leave me alone to tell tales and out him to the world, like the world cares. I mean, yes, he's rich, but he's not world-famous. More likely, Evinia might have suggested bringing me here. She always says how she doesn't want me to be alone. I have no clue who knew about me or who decided I should come to Oganja. Regardless, I'm certain this wasn't his idea."

"Do you resent your father?"

"Yes. Wouldn't you?"

"After all you've told me, I guess so. I went twenty years without knowing my mother. When I met her, I didn't resent her."

"It's different. She wanted you. He didn't want me." Samar blinked. "Wait, you're twenty? You're certain of this?"

"I meant to tell you that. I asked her. Not counting all of the time I've been sleeping. I'm twenty years old. I never realized I was so old."

"Did you ever find out how long you were asleep?"

"Over ten thousand years. I was well over the age to be married, so it really drives home that I was a mere tool for my parents. People get married later now, according to my mother. Which explains why you're not married yet. I always thought you should've been married with children when you came by my tomb. My mother finally told me that times have changed a lot, which means I'm not so old and still have time to be married."

"Of course not. You're quite young by today's standards. Not many people in the city get married at your age," Samar said.

"And without my parents, this is now an option." Kouji rolled her shoulders and eased into that familiar smile. She didn't even look twenty. She had an inexplicably angelic and adorable look, as if she were a cherub. She seemed so non-threatening, like a small child or a tiny puppy. Somehow, her hair being out from its braids made her innocent appearance more prominent.

"You wish to be married?"

"I wish to live my life in a manner I choose. Marriage is now an option, and that's what makes everything so amazing." Kouji's smile blossomed into a grin.

Samar chuckled. "Yes, options are amazing." She had stopped considering options when her mother died. She should open herself up to choices again. She could do things with her life.

As they cleaned up, Samar watched Kouji's movements. Even folding the meal mat became a work of art. Her muscles were pronounced, defined, and capable. That body could do the horrible things Kouji had hinted at. *And other, more pleasant, things.* Samar shook that thought away.

Their simple chores were done, but Kouji still had one problem. Samar hadn't mentioned her hair. She was in better spirits now than when she came in but should be able to relax. Although Kouji didn't want to bring it up, something needed to be done.

"So when are you going to do my hair?" Kouji asked.

Samar's eyes went wide. "Your hair! I meant to start that when I came in."

"It's fine. You deserve your rest if you want to sleep first."

"I should probably do it with a clear head. Make sure I have my full focus for your braids." Samar yawned.

Kouji chuckled, which turned into a yawn. "I think I'm tired as well." She hadn't slept since she woke in the tomb.

"Is it safe for you to go to sleep?"

Fair question. "It should be. The sleep I was under in the tomb was magic-induced. My mother wouldn't put me back to sleep without my permission. I should be perfectly fine. Where can I sleep? I don't mind the floor."

"There's the sofa and the floor." Samar pointed to both. "Not sure which one's better, but I'd guess the sofa. Not that it matters since you'll more than likely be uncomfortable on either. You're used to the best. I mean, being from a wealthy, royal family and all."

"I promise I've dealt with worse. I don't mind. I'll take whatever you give me."

Samar fetched a pillow from her bed and a spare blanket from the closet. Kouji stood out of the way, while Samar made up the couch like a bed. She inspected her handiwork and nodded her satisfaction. Kouji watched her perform her usual check around the apartment, making sure all of her protections were in place, then drop into her bed.

"No Nightmares should be getting in here. Have a good sleep," Samar said more into her pillow than to Kouji. She was asleep almost immediately.

Kouji stared for a while, a smile growing on her face. She had never felt like this before. A mellowness warmed her and replaced the numbness she had been only vaguely aware of.

"She worries over Nightmares feeding on others, but not the nightmares that haunt her every day. I wish I could do something for her," Kouji said to the air.

From the moment Kouji first heard Samar, all she wanted to do was reach out, touch her, hold her, and let her know everything would be all right. She couldn't imagine losing her mother at this point in her life. The thought tore a fear through her that she had no way to describe, but she could hear that pain in Samar. Battling the Nightmares hadn't been a distraction from that agony.

Kouji lay down and curled her legs on the small sofa. She drifted off happily while listening to the sound of Samar's steady breathing.

The sound of a chime woke Kouji, and Samar groaned from her bed as she sat up. "What's that?" Kouji asked with a yawn.

"My phone. I set an alarm to make sure we'd have time for your hair. We have to wash it first."

"Oh, thank you. Should we have some tea before?"

"We'll do tea after. I'll get ready to wash your hair."

"Okay." Kouji nodded. She heard small thumping noises as Samar moved around out of sight.

"Bathroom," called Samar.

Kouji wasn't sure what to expect, but being bent over the tub wasn't part of it. She tensed, and Samar rubbed the small of her back. Letting loose a long breath, Kouji relaxed.

"I know it's a vulnerable position. But I promise this will be painless."

"I…" Kouji swallowed. "I trust you." The second the words left her mouth, it was a known truth for the world. *How many people have I ever trusted? A handful, if that.*

"I'm glad."

The hot water, soap suds, and Samar's fingers felt wonderful. The experience was much shorter than Kouji expected. *Will Samar be open to doing this again?* She hoped so.

"All right." Samar draped a towel over Kouji's head and rubbed. "I have a blow dryer, so we can start braiding sooner."

Kouji had no idea what that meant, but nodded anyway. Samar held something that blew hot air onto her head and dried her hair rather quickly.

"You can do the tea now, and I'll grab what I need for your hair. We'll meet on the couch," Samar said.

By the time Kouji had brewed the tea, Samar was waiting on the sofa. Kouji sat on the floor between her legs as before. She released a contented sigh.

"My hair feels so much better than it has in a really long time."

"I bet it does. My head's never even that dirty, and you don't want to know how often I wash my hair. By the time I'm done with you, your head will feel incredible."

"My head is already fantastic."

The oil that Samar carefully rubbed in was soothing. Kouji liked the feeling of the warm, sure fingers working over her head. After a little while, she reached up and felt tight, neat braids across her scalp. Samar put something else to her head, but Kouji wasn't sure what it was.

"Okay, I'm finished." Samar led Kouji back to the bathroom and stood her in front of the looking glass.

"Sorry my mirror isn't more modern. It doesn't have the ends that open so you can see more of your head," Samar explained.

"This is fine. You work miracles." Kouji admired Samar's work. The braids were smooth and shiny. The parts made clean lines. The bright ribbons wrapped through the braids were a surprise. "I wasn't expecting the decorations."

"I wasn't sure if there was a particular way your decorations were meant to go, but those are in style in this era. I matched your bead colors."

Kouji smiled. "Thank you. My clan colors. I appreciate it. These are great. Better than great, actually. I mean, the girl who usually did my hair was nowhere near this talented."

"The girl?" Samar echoed with a raised eyebrow.

Kouji noted her reaction, but didn't say anything. She couldn't, as she had no idea why Samar reacted in that manner. It was hard to tell the emotion behind it. Was she offended? Merely confused or curious? Disgusted? Kouji took a breath. She had to talk about this with Samar. It was unfair to keep it to herself.

"A servant girl used to braid my hair. Well, no, there were a couple of girls."

"Two? Did they do anything besides braid your hair?" Samar gawked at her.

Kouji's guts quivered. "Yes, I didn't really need them for much else. Sometimes, they drew my baths for me and washed me, but it wasn't a big deal."

"I thought you had one woman for that."

Kouji winced. "I had a few slaves who dressed me, not that it was too complicated. It wasn't a big deal..." She swallowed. "Unless I made it one anyway."

Samar's face tensed. "What do you mean?"

Kouji sighed and rubbed her head. She winced and slapped her hand to her side. "Don't want to mess up my hair." She offered Samar a weak smile.

Samar took a step back. Her eyes were hard. Kouji owed Samar an explanation and more.

"I didn't know right from wrong," Kouji said, as if things were that simple. *Coward. Say it, don't excuse it.*

"Did you beat them?" Samar asked. Her voice, the tilt of her head, suggested she wanted to ask something more sinister.

Kouji took a deep breath. "No, I didn't beat them. My mother always said I wasn't cruel, only misled. They never suffered."

"What did you do?" Samar asked in a whisper.

Kouji swallowed. "I had owned a sword for as long as I can remember. My father—the king—told me to use it as often as possible. I was to use the sword whenever I felt it necessary. I grew to believe it was necessary often."

Samar took a deep breath, pressing her palms together. "You killed them?"

Kouji only sighed and hid her head in her hands. She didn't want to talk about these long-ago things. It was the past, as Samar had said before, except Kouji's past wasn't dead to her. The past haunted her like shadows at night, like her own personal Nightmare.

"I don't want to keep secrets from you. I don't want to push you away, especially since I know everything about you. You deserve to know everything about me, the good, the bad, and everything in between." Kouji took a deep breath. "But you'll probably kick me out after this and never speak to me again."

Samar stared Kouji right in the eye, not a hint of fear. "Then tell me."

"I've killed people, a lot of people," Kouji confessed with a tremble in her throat. *This is where it all ends, before anything even begins.*

"Why? And don't say because you didn't know right from wrong."

Kouji's fingers twiddled against each other, but she maintained eye contact with Samar. She owed all of this to her. "I was brought up to think killing people wasn't a bad thing. I thought killing people who irked me was as natural as exhaling after inhaling. I never thought it was much. That's why I said my victims never suffered. I just killed them as quickly as possible to get them away from me. I never thought much of it until the day I went to sleep."

"Many stories don't cover that. You were raised as a weapon."

Kouji gave a small nod. "I was because I have powers. I was useful in a way no other person could be. I have to assume they banked on me having powers. All I can remember is being surrounded by death."

"And now?"

"I never want to kill, or even hurt, another person in my life," Kouji answered with her whole heart and all of the sincerity she could muster.

"Why?" Samar's gaze bore right into Kouji, as though trying to get to the heart of the matter.

"My mother…" Kouji choked out. Her chest hurt. She was a monster and now Samar knew. The past was already hell, but having Samar aware of it was more than hell.

"It's okay," Samar tried to assure Kouji. How could she dare?

"It's not. It's not okay." Kouji shook her head. Her eyes burned, tears threatening to spill out. She kept them at bay. She didn't have the right to cry now.

"It is."

"How can you think that? You've done nothing but use your time to save lives. I've destroyed them. You know it's not okay." A dry sob escaped her.

Samar gnawed the corner of her mouth for a second. "If some of your stories are true, you saved people as well. You say you don't want to kill anymore, don't want to destroy. What do you want?"

Kouji's mouth wobbled, and her throat burned. Tears blurred her vision, but she still kept them in. She had never felt this way before. "I only…I want to stay with you, be by your side. I'll do anything. I'll even join your quest against the Nightmares. I think I'm the reason they're getting stronger."

Samar arched an eyebrow. "What do you mean?"

"They tend to come for me. Sometimes in swarms."

"None have come for you yet."

"They need to build up their power. I'm not sure why they're so interested in me. I only…I want to be near you, Samar. I want to hear your voice. I want to experience what you experience." Kouji wanted to live a life standing by Samar.

"I need a moment."

Kouji nodded as a tear finally burned its way down her cheek. "I'll start breakfast?" It was that or she'd be forced to leave, forced to return to her tomb.

Samar didn't say anything. Not an encouraging sign. But she didn't stop Kouji from going to the kitchen. Not a terrible sign. Kouji wasn't sure what to expect, but she had hope.

Chapter Thirteen

Twilight

SAMAR STOOD BY HER window, ensuring all her Nightmare precautions were in place. She listened to Kouji puttering around in the kitchen. This woman had the face of a cherub but was actually a fallen angel. A tool. *Does that excuse her actions?*

Samar had done terrible things in her life, but Kouji topped her in "very bad things." Samar doubted she was capable of killing someone. She'd never been put in a position to find out. She was capable of beating someone into a coma, and had done so, but it wasn't quite the same as killing a person.

Of course, her mother raised her with a sense of right and wrong. She taught Samar the need to respect not only human life but life in general. Everything was connected and depended on each other to sustain the world. A balance existed and must be maintained.

Nightmares upset the balance. They came from the Other World to do damage here. Their nature was to corrupt. It seemed Kouji's parents were the same. They corrupted Kouji. Unlike Nightmares, they didn't latch onto something diabolical already inside of Kouji. They purposely put that darkness inside of Kouji to use her.

Even Siku, who hated Samar, wasn't as devious as Kouji's parents. He hired Samar for her skill, but he also paid her for her time and services. He used his company and his children to do something good, even though he wasn't a good person. Kouji's parents weren't good people, and they'd molded Kouji into something as evil as they were.

The weird thing was that Samar was sharing her space with an admitted killer and wasn't afraid. Granted, she had dealt with killers, thieves, and all types of gangsters and lowlifes. Samar even had a murderer in her home before, a part of the dead past. What was going on with Kouji was different.

Despite the image of dead bodies her confession left, Kouji still seemed so utterly harmless and remorseful. Samar could see how wounded and tormented Kouji was by her past. *It probably would never cross her mind to hurt me.*

To Samar, Kouji was still the same Kouji. Samar still saw the same angelic quality, the damn near innocent appearance, only a little more tormented after revealing her past. *I might dare to sleep in the same room as her.*

The phone rang and took Samar out of her thoughts. She grabbed it from its place on her bed and answered. Of course, it was Evinia.

"Hello," Samar answered the phone in a groggy tone.

"Sammie, you're not asleep, right?" Evinia asked.

"No, I'm usually up at this time."

"I thought as much but wanted to be sure. I didn't want to disturb you, because you need your sleep."

"Well, I'm awake."

"Good. I want to talk to you."

"Talk."

"For the past couple of days, you've been acting rather strangely. You've been flying out of my office. Asking all sorts of odd questions. Smiling. What is up with that?" Evinia asked.

"No idea what you mean." Samar wasn't sure how to answer her sister's question. Had she been acting strange? She didn't think so.

"You don't know? Surely you have a reason for running out on me like you've been doing."

"No." *I'm not running out of anywhere. I just leave like always.*

"You're not in any kind of trouble, are you?" Evinia asked. "I mean, we define trouble differently, but you know what I mean. Are you in trouble?"

"No."

"Anything you want to tell me?"

"Nothing I can think of right now." She'd have to tell Evinia about Kouji eventually, but she needed a better handle on the situation first. She had no idea how long Kouji would be around, even though she seemed to be planning to stay for as long as she could. How long would that be though?

"Are you sure?"

"Uh-huh."

"Okay, I wanted to check on you. I wanted to make sure you're all right."

Samar glanced at the kitchen. "I'm fine."

"You can talk to me about anything."

"I know."

"And you know I love you, right?"

"I love you too."

"No matter what happens, we're always sisters."

"I know. It means everything to me." It was one of the few things that kept her sane for the past few years.

"It means everything to me too. I'm happy you're in my life."

"And I'm happy you're in my life. I'll see you at work."

"All right. Take care."

Samar hung the phone up without trying to say a farewell. A long sigh escaped her. She stepped closer to the kitchen, but paused. Was she ready for this?

"I'm making spicy, hard-boiled eggs, porridge, and sausage. You want dumplings again? You seemed to enjoy those," Kouji said.

"I can help." Samar stepped into the kitchen.

"You don't have to."

"Oh, like you don't have to make breakfast. Besides, I think I can do the porridge a little better."

"You got me on that one." Kouji smiled sheepishly and collected four eggs from the refrigerator. She moved like someone defeated, shoulders slumped and movements sluggish. When her back was turned, Samar heard her sniffle.

Clearly, regret was tearing her apart. Samar understood that wounded feeling all too well. She didn't want Kouji to dwell there. Regret might never go away, but dwelling on it would make the wound fester and burn. Self-hatred could lead to self-destruction. Samar wouldn't let Kouji wallow. After all, Kouji had been the distraction and the outlet that kept Samar from losing herself. Kouji saved her.

She'd been stirring the porridge as she processed her thoughts. She turned to Kouji and took a deep breath. She wrapped her arms around Kouji's waist and pressed herself to Kouji's back. Kouji inhaled sharply, then the sobbing began.

"It's all right," Samar said.

"I don't want to leave. I feel so safe with you, so right. I had no idea this type of feeling could exist. I don't want to leave." Kouji wailed.

"I'm not going anywhere. I still trust you, Kou." Samar nuzzled Kouji's shoulder blade.

"That makes one of us. I don't want to hurt you. I wouldn't be able to live with myself if I hurt you or if something happened to you because of me."

"I'm tough. I can defend myself."

"From me?"

"If need be, but I don't think there will be a need. I trust my instincts as much as I trust you." Samar meant those words.

"I don't..." Kouji shook her head and wiped her face.

"You can't beat yourself up over the past."

Kouji let loose a forced laugh. "You do it all of the time."

True. Most of the time, when Samar opened her mouth, she lamented over something from the past, things she couldn't help. "Well, that's me."

"You didn't kill a bunch of people, most of whom didn't deserve to die. I'm not sure about the official assassinations I performed, but the servants definitely didn't deserve anything I did to them. It eats at me now because I understand what it meant."

"You have morals now."

Kouji continued on as if she hadn't heard Samar. "You didn't live twenty years of pure lies and meaningless damnations. You didn't live with false emotions. You knew when you were happy, or angry, or sad. I needed years of sleep and countless visits from my mother to even begin to understand I was a monster. I cried so much once I realized what she was saying. She held me when I cried. No one had ever held me before. No one told me it was all right to cry before her."

"It's okay to cry," Samar whispered. How many times had Evinia told her that? How many times had Evinia been so damn right?

"Yeah…" Kouji eased her hands down to Samar's, right above her navel. Kouji patted tentatively, before resting her surprisingly soft hands against Samar's. Kouji caressed her hands with gentle thumbs in a circular motion. It tingled. This simple skin-on-skin contact was everything right now. "No one's ever touched me like this."

"You deserve it." Everyone deserved to feel loved. *Wait, what?* Samar didn't have time to process her own thoughts. A fresh round of Kouji's sobs echoed through the tiny kitchen. Samar held her tighter as her body shook. *This feels so good.*

"I was always treated like a monster and didn't even realize it," Kouji replied.

Who was the real monster? "You're not a monster. Your parents were supposed to love and protect you, but they used you based on what you could do for them. They hurt you as much as they used you to hurt people."

Kouji turned and cried in Samar's arms, and Samar wouldn't have it any other way. She nuzzled Kouji, taking in the subtle jasmine scent that seemed a natural part of her. Samar wanted Kouji to feel as much of her as possible, to be aware she was there in every way. After a little while, the crying stopped and Kouji's breathing evened out.

"I should go back to those eggs."

"I'll do the sweet dumplings," Samar said.

Samar let go of her guest, and they fixed afternoon breakfast together. Little conversation passed between them. Kouji should have time to collect herself.

Kouji concentrated on making sure the eggs were right. She added a little spice to the sausage. It should be fine. Samar put down the mat, and they set up breakfast. They were quiet the whole time.

"Do you have any questions?" Kouji asked as she nibbled her hard-boiled egg.

Samar sipped her porridge before answering. "I have a general understanding of you. How did your parents use your lineage to hold their power?"

"Because I'm a demigoddess, I was able to best any enemy who threatened them. You've seen I'm supernaturally fast. I can move through shadows, which is how I disappear. I'm not quite indestructible, but close to it. I've been hurt by magic, and Nightmares have been able to harm me. I've come across other…I'm not sure if they were demigods or simply magical humans, but they were able to hurt me, somewhat. Other than my lineage, what put me above them was that my parents began training me to kill from the time I could hold a weapon."

"So they could hold onto power?"

"Yes. I was an attack dog for them. Whenever something or someone came to challenge them, I was sent in to put a stop to it. That was my purpose."

"You can find a new purpose. Something you like. Something that won't make you cry."

Kouji smiled. "Thank you for that."

"Thank you for the same."

Kouji's smile grew, and her egg tasted a little better. After breakfast, they cleaned up together. Then they sparred again.

It was a great workout and a wonderful change of pace. Once upon a time, Kouji had been expected to maim or even murder her sparring partners. She told Samar that most who sparred with her anticipated death. Only a command from her parents would stop her from killing a partner.

"Now, you see things don't have to be that way. You can decide for yourself. Are you happy with sparring this way?" Samar asked.

"Of course. I'd never want to hurt you, definitely not murder you."

"I appreciate it, since I wouldn't want to be murdered."

"Should I help you fight Nightmares?"

Samar waved the question off. "I think you should take a shower. You don't have to rush to help me. You don't have to help me at all, even if Nightmares are after you. I want you to take this time to figure out what you want to do with your life. I'm not here to assign you any new tasks. From now on, your decisions are your own decisions."

Kouji grinned and nodded her appreciation. She went to take a shower, as suggested. Kouji tried to think about what she wanted to do with her life. Helping Samar in her fight against Nightmares was a no-brainer. She didn't have to start immediately though. Samar seemed fine, and the Nightmares had not yet figured out that Kouji was awake.

After her shower, Kouji grabbed a book to read while Samar went for her shower. When Samar got out, they went out for lunch. As a treat, Samar showed her the Asale market. It was busier and grander than Kouji expected. Samar always made it seem like Asale culture was a joke in Oganja, but in Kouji's time, any place would've envied this market.

"I don't understand why you don't come here more often. Is it too painful? You always make it sound like it's a mockery of your homeland, but you seem at home here," Kouji said after Samar finished haggling in her native language.

"Sometimes, it hurts. Sometimes, I run into people who are scam artists and aren't actually from Asale or who don't have a single clue about Asale. It mostly depends on what happened on the last visit that determines when I'll return." Samar took Kouji's hand. They had held hands all day, like before.

"I like it here. Would you be all right with coming more frequently? I'll learn to cook more meals from your homeland." Kouji grinned. That should help to keep Samar happy with her.

Samar smiled. "I've enjoyed this trip enough for us to come back soon. We have plenty of food though." She held up a tote bag in her other hand. "Anything else you'd like? How about some beads from Asale?" She pulled Kouji toward a vendor.

"Do you have clan colors?" Kouji asked Samar, as they looked at rows of bracelets, anklets, neck beads, and waist beads.

"I do, but my clan is mostly gone thanks to the civil war in Asale several decades ago."

"That's awful. What are your clan colors? Though very prestigious, the clan of my royal parents doesn't hold the same importance to me anymore. I don't know the clan colors of my birth father, and obviously, my birth mother doesn't have a clan."

Kouji watched Samar pick out colors for a beaded bracelet. She wondered if they were Samar's clan colors. Red, yellow, white, teal, and green. Too many colors for a clan. Green was unusual.

"What clan is this?" Kouji asked as they continued through the market.

"My clan colors."

"Green is an acceptable clan color? It was a memorial color in my time."

"Still is. As I said, most of my clan died in the civil war. It basically doesn't exist anymore, hence the green. It's in memorial."

Kouji nodded. They finished up their shopping and started making their way back to the apartment. They were delayed. Nightmares.

"They didn't even wait for night to fully set in," Samar complained, as her spear appeared in her hand. They faced down four armed men on a deserted street. Hissing Nightmares floated right above their heads.

"Just give us the money and no one has to get hurt," the biggest man said.

Samar scoffed. "We're carrying grocery bags. Did you geniuses see us coming and really assume we had money?"

"I think it's an excuse," Kouji said, as the Nightmares focused on her.

"Oh, the Nightmares should know, I never need an excuse."

Samar dropped her grocery bags and sprang into action. The Nightmares roared. Kouji put down her bag and used her speed to disarm the men. Guns were gone before Kouji had a chance to learn how they worked. Samar took care of the Nightmares, while Kouji exorcised the humans.

"Oh, you got…" Kouji pointed to Samar's shoulder. A deep gash gushed blood that soaked her hoodie.

Samar turned her head to look. "Oh, wow. I didn't even feel this."

"Let me…" Kouji healed Samar's shoulder.

"Thank you." Samar rotated her shoulder, testing it out. She nodded. Her gaze went to the street. "I don't feel like calling this in because it'd be too much to explain, but we do need to pick up the groceries and the guns."

"Don't you need to alert someone?" Kouji wasn't sure about procedure, but she was willing to follow Samar's instructions.

"I can call the local police, but we'll have to wait here, like before. If you don't mind, it's fine. But then there's a whole process, more than before since there's a group. Plus, we'd eventually have to go to court since they tried to rob us."

"I have no idea what that means."

"It's fine. Come on." Samar shifted her grocery bags, so she could take Kouji's hand.

They returned to the apartment and put the groceries away together. Samar showed Kouji her protections against Nightmares coming into the apartment. Kouji had watched Samar before without understanding. She'd never seen anything like this.

"I had no idea there were ways to stop Nightmares from coming into a space," Kouji said.

"This is one of the first things I learned about the Nightmares. My mother had to set them up back home."

"To protect you."

"And her own peace of mind. Again, she couldn't see Nightmares, so it was best to make sure they couldn't come in."

Kouji nodded. That was smart. Samar freshened up protections on the front door as well. She had to change her shirt and go to work. Kouji went back to reading. She needed to know much more about these Nightmares if they'd attack her on the street with Samar by her side. Or even worse, try to attack her while she was in Samar's apartment. She had no desire to ruin anything Samar built.

Samar had to deal with Nightmares all night. That was becoming her work routine. It was like they wandered into the park after going to the tomb. They sought out Kouji, but she was safe at Samar's apartment. The protection charms around her home kept the Nightmares away, not only from the apartment, but the building in general.

As the days passed, the pair tried many new things together. Yes, they ran into Nightmares, but so far they were able to handle things as a team. A lot of shopping happened. Cooking together was one of their favorite pastimes. Kouji fell in love with the Asale marketplace, so they went often.

Things were all well and good, except Samar didn't consider that all the new activity on her bank account might draw attention. It wouldn't have been a big deal, except the bank contacted Evinia. Samar hadn't cared about money and was quite naive in regard to banking when the account was opened. She'd used Evinia's phone number as her contact information. Now, she had to deal with a mini-inquisition from Evinia.

"I don't understand why you're spending so much money on food all of a sudden and frequenting the Asale market so often." Evinia had called from home, so no worries about Siku overhearing. Samar was at her own apartment. Kouji was in the kitchen, working on a new breakfast.

Samar winced. She had to think of a plausible explanation. She had little desire to tell her sister she needed the money to buy suitable clothing for a homeless demigoddess, who until quite recently was asleep in the tomb Evinia hated but was now living in her apartment. Evinia's head might explode. She wouldn't believe Kouji's story. Evinia didn't even believe her about the Nightmares.

"But didn't you want me to go out more?" Samar asked.

"Yes, I want you to go out and explore your culture in Oganjan form. But don't spend yourself into a hole. You have to remember to budget. You don't want to spend all your savings, do you?" Evinia countered.

Samar blinked and scratched the top of her head. "Well, no. Is it bad?" She should probably check her balance.

"It's not, but the bank was suspicious of the spike in activity and, honestly, so am I. Are you sure you're all right?"

"I am. Um, can you show me how to check? I don't want to go over any limits or overspend. I'm just…I'm trying to do what you wanted me to do. I'm trying to live a little better."

"I'll show you how next time we see each other. But why the change? What happened?" Evinia asked.

"Um…" Samar glanced into the kitchen. Why couldn't she tell her sister about Kouji? No specific details were necessary, but she should say something. Except she didn't want to deal with the questions that would follow. "It's nothing. I'm just…you know, trying."

"Well, I'm glad for it."

A pot clanged in the kitchen and Kouji yelped. "I have to go, Vinnie. See you later." She hung up before Evinia replied. She rushed to the kitchen. "Everything okay in here?"

Kouji smiled. The expression had changed over the past two weeks. There was a weight behind it now. She still looked like a cherub, but her smile had meaning.

"Sorry. Got ahead of myself and knocked the egg pan against the stove. It's fine. How was your phone call?" Kouji asked.

"Only Evinia giving me an update on my bank account. I need to watch how much money we spend to make sure I don't use more than I have."

"Oh, that makes sense." Kouji put her finger to her chin. "I still don't quite comprehend money in this time, but you do want to keep track of what you have."

"It's fine. I have enough to support us…I think." She needed to check. "But do you want to go out after breakfast and sparring?"

Kouji chirped. "Oh yes. Any ideas?"

"We can figure it out over breakfast."

"Sounds good."

Ever since getting Kouji presentable for the outside world, they searched for some means of entertainment every now and then. Their sparring sessions were their favorite thing to do, but they couldn't beat each other up all day, every day. They went to an arcade, but neither of them had a clue how to play any of the games. Another day, they went to an art museum. Even though they knew little about art, it was certainly more their speed. They visited a street festival by accident, wandering into it on their way from the Asale market. They went to a couple of history museums and even did a little riverboat cruise that Evinia swore years ago that Samar would like. Evinia was right.

They explored several restaurants as well. Kouji deserved a taste of the world and such a thing was possible in a city like Oganja. After tasting seaweed noodles, Kouji tried to make them herself. She wasn't successful, but the experience proved she craved food and attractions from around the world. And, of course, reading helped her discover more about the world.

"You sure you got this?" Samar asked about the breakfast. It was a first for Kouji, trying to make a traditional Asale breakfast sandwich.

Kouji waved her away. "Just set up the dining mat. I like to think I've proven I can do this."

Samar snorted. "So far, whenever you're trying something new, you have proven you don't have this."

Kouji laughed. "Give me a break. I'm new here."

Samar chuckled as well, but she set up the dining mat. She also checked the Nightmare charms, just in case. They had done their job well over the past few weeks. She and Kouji encountered Nightmares every time they went outside, but none came into the apartment. Samar refreshed some of the charms.

"Do you think you'd want a protection mark?" Samar asked Kouji.

"What would it do?" Kouji countered.

"It'd help you see the Nightmares better." Despite Kouji's mind being rather clear at this point, Nightmares still seemed more like shadows to her than the massive black clouds they tended to be.

"That'd be helpful."

"It also tends to slow them down a little when they come at you. Of course, you're so fast, it probably doesn't matter."

"If I can see them better that'd be great, but I'm not sure if the mark would stay. You have a tattoo, right?"

"I do."

"I'm not sure if a tattoo would stay on my skin. Just like I can heal you, I can heal myself. Sometimes, it's just a thing I do, no thought necessary."

Samar nodded. "Maybe it's something you can ask your mother."

"I suppose. If she shows up." Kouji's mother hadn't been around in over a week. "I wanted to ask her about all of these myths and stories I've been reading about us. I can't believe how many adventures I never went on."

"It would've been hard to fit those adventures in only twenty years of life."

"It's funny. Most stories are right about my age." Almost all the stories about Kouji had her living until she was twenty. The stories killed her off, had her vanish into thin air, or even welcomed into the Other World. Not a single one guessed she had gone to sleep for thousands of years.

"While you didn't do what a lot of the myths describe, the accurate stories cover your actions throughout your life, right?" Samar asked.

"It's amazing how they do. They justify my actions in different ways, or paint me as protecting my parents' kingdom. Of course, if you write a hundred stories, a few of them have to be correct, right?"

"I have no idea. You still won't confirm if you were ripped from your mother because her husband, the Sun, was angry with her."

"Well, that one I don't know. Mother only ever says I was taken from her and purposely corrupted. She hasn't been around for me to ask about the stories that include her."

Samar nodded. They'd had this conversation several times already. Samar wanted to know if all the gods existed. Kouji could only confirm Asiku's existence. Samar still hadn't met Kouji's mother.

After breakfast, they sparred and showered. They settled on the couch. They sat close together, both needing to see Samar's phone to figure out what to do with their day. Kouji had her chin on Samar's shoulder as she scrolled.

"Oh, these gardens. Can we do this? They look lovely," Kouji said. "I never appreciated the gardens back at my home."

Samar hummed. "It might be nice. My mountain home didn't have much variety in plant life or wildlife really."

"It'll be delightful. Not likely to run into Nightmares there."

Samar scoffed and turned her head to look at Kouji. She paused, gazing into those lilac eyes. They seemed to get deeper every time she looked at them. They were just as incredible as Kouji.

"Um…I think we both know Nightmares will find us, regardless. And that's fine. We can banish the Nightmares back to the Beyond and make sure the person can't host any other Nightmares. Win-win," Samar said.

Kouji smiled, highlighting how close her mouth was to Samar's. "You're right."

The Oganja Botanical Garden was quite the sight. They held hands, as always. Samar even took pictures. She never used to do that with her phone. There was nothing worth remembering before now.

Someone offered to take a picture of them together, which they accepted. Kouji wrapped her arms around Samar's waist and Samar rested her head on Kouji's shoulder.

"You make a cute couple," the woman commented, taking their picture a few times.

Samar blinked and Kouji yelped. Before either of them could muster a denial, the woman took off with Samar's phone. They shook their heads and gave chase. She was easy to catch.

"No Nightmare?" Kouji asked, as Samar snatched her phone back.

"Some people are merely awful. Nightmares look for them, but they can still be awful without any help." Samar held down the thief.

The police were nearby, so they waited. A couple of agents for Moonless Night Security were there too. Samar didn't think much of their presence and didn't bother to interact with her coworkers. It wasn't like she knew them.

Evinia was more than aware something was up with her little sister, but still had no clue what. Samar had been acting strangely for a few weeks. Her bank statements revealed she was going out more and spending more.

Plus, rumors had popped up. Other agents had seen Samar standing close to some woman, like she'd made a friend. Evinia needed to get to the bottom of this to make sure Samar wasn't marching toward trouble, or already in trouble.

Of course, there was also the fact that Samar was visibly happy. She smiled more. She conversed more openly with Evinia, though nothing about her life. She talked more about her patrols and how busy Okunkun Park was again.

The park was back to the state it was in when Samar first arrived. The difference was that Samar seemed to be having problems coping with it. At least she hadn't mentioned Nightmares. It was weird to have her rather intelligent sister bringing up fairy tales as if they were real.

Evinia gasped as Samar dropped into her chair at the office. "Sammie, what happened?" Evinia rushed over to her sister to inspect her face. Samar had a huge black eye, and her bottom lip was split open.

Samar waved her off. "It's fine. More embarrassing than anything else."

"Embarrassing how? Do you need a partner? I didn't realize the park had gotten that dangerous."

"No, I fell and busted my lip during my last fight."

"It's wild. You had three different incidents tonight. That's the most in a long time."

Samar blew out a breath and nodded. Their conversation was cut short when their father stepped through the doorway. He grunted, as if signaling they should stop talking. Evinia rolled her eyes, while Samar curled into herself a bit.

"I hear you're having trouble with your assignments," he said to Samar.

Samar frowned and shot him a glare. "If you think someone else can do a better job, let them."

Oh, wow. Daddy flinched. It was only for a moment, then he gathered himself and stared down at Samar. She didn't back down like she usually would.

"Who do you think you're talking to? You think you're the only one capable of patrolling the park? I've got dozens of agents like you."

Samar glanced at him, but didn't engage, almost daring him to follow through. He didn't have the manpower. Before Samar was assigned to Okunkun, at least three Moonless Night agents patrolled each shift, and they barely made a dent in the criminal activity. Most requested a transfer after a month or so. Until recently, Samar had made the place damn near safe enough to be out at midnight. Unheard of in this city.

"This attitude is coming from you." He pointed to Evinia.

She scoffed. "I hope so. I've been trying to rub off on her like this for three years now."

Of course, he scowled. "Call your brother."

"Did it already. He's up, getting ready for school, and sick of me calling him every morning."

Their father grunted and left. He'd sucked enough air from the room, apparently. Evinia chuckled, then turned to Samar, who had the nerve to look away. Evinia leaned over enough to pop her on the knee. Samar yelped and locked eyes with her.

"Sammie, you've been acting quite peculiar lately," Evinia said.

Samar blinked, like she didn't understand. "Pe—what now?" This was part of her peculiar act. If Evinia made a comment or asked a question, suddenly she lost command of the language.

"Peculiar. Strange. Odd. Not like yourself," Evinia said to elaborate.

"Really?" Samar shrugged, as if she had no idea what Evinia meant. She pulled her chair up to Evinia's desk to do her reports. Funny enough, she had enough command of the language to do that.

Evinia pursed her lips. "Yes, really. For example, whenever you do your reports on your own, they come out rather sloppy. We both know that you read and write a lot better than what your work shows. Your reports look like they're written by a fifth grader, even though you're a scholar."

"I thought it was always bad. Fifth grade seems generous," Samar replied.

"No, they were getting better until you fell off, rushing to get them done. You're not spending time at the tomb or something, are you?"

"I haven't been by the tomb in weeks."

Evinia paused. She hadn't expected that. The tomb was Samar's second home. It wasn't healthy, but it was part of her routine. How could she quit it cold turkey? Why would she just let that go?

"That's great, but then what is with you? I try to talk to you, but you're always running out of here. I call you and you're always sleeping."

"You call right after you get out of work. Of course, I'm sleeping. I don't wake up until late in the afternoon."

"I am aware of when I call you. Not only those times. I'm checking on you then, but when I call you during waking hours, you're distracted, and I always hear noise in the background."

Samar shrugged. "I'm moving about the place. I have things to do, like anyone else."

That was true, but there was still something. "You're being dismissive. You're always trying to get out of here in a hurry, even more than before. What have you been getting into?"

"Nothing."

"It doesn't seem that way. Are you sure you're all right?" Evinia asked. She was worried about Samar. There was only one other time she had acted so oddly, and it hadn't ended well. Evinia didn't want to go through that again. She didn't want Samar to go through that again.

"I promise, I'm fine. I'm just…trying, you know? I'm finally trying," Samar replied.

"Why now?" She had begged Samar for years to go out and experience life. What happened to finally make her do that?

Samar shrugged. "If not now, when?"

Evinia frowned. Samar was hiding something. She could take care of herself physically, but emotionally, not so much. Something was going on, and Samar was intent on keeping it from Evinia. It wouldn't do.

Samar popped up from her seat. "Check this for me, please. See you tomorrow."

Samar left the office before Evinia had a chance to reply. She was speechless anyway. Samar ditching her and avoiding her questions was starting to grate on Evinia's nerves.

Chapter Fourteen

Sun Rays Through the Clouds

KOUJI WAITED FOR SAMAR to return from work. They had a routine at this point. While Samar didn't like a meal when she came in, a snack was appreciated. This was especially true after a healing session. Healing sessions were needed daily. The Nightmares always managed to touch Samar, but she never seemed worried about them and never asked Kouji to come to work with her. Kouji wouldn't include herself unless asked. She didn't want to risk offending Samar, daring to imply Samar couldn't handle her own work.

Sweet dumplings with tea was a light meal, a greeting from Kouji's time that had apparently survived to Samar's. Kouji had everything laid out on the dining mat.

Samar should be home by now. Did something happen? Should I have gone out with her? The Nightmares were stronger than ever. Samar was only human, while the Nightmares were from the Other World. They had supernatural powers and chilling desires. If given the chance to wield their powers correctly, Nightmares and their hosts would be able to do significant harm or even end Samar.

She has to be okay. There's so much I want to say to her, do with her! Kouji wanted to discuss their trip to the botanical gardens and more. Samar needed to be okay.

The loud bang of the door got her attention. She looked up as Samar stepped through the door. She had a bag in her hand, as she shouldered the door shut. She looked at Kouji and smiled.

Kouji knew her face matched her brightening spirit, as she absorbed that beautiful expression aimed solely at her. "Good morning."

"Good morning," Samar replied and locked the door.

"You're late. I worried."

Samar's smile grew, as she held up the bag in her arms. From the shape, it held a big box. "I wanted to buy you a gift. It smells lovely in here." She said this every time she came into the apartment and caught the scent of their early morning treat.

"I made sweet dumplings today." Kouji motioned to the meal mat on the floor. "What's the gift?" She rushed to Samar's side to ease her jacket off her shoulders. Samar allowed it, as she always did.

"It's a surprise."

"For me?" Kouji hung the jacket up in the closet.

"Yes, for you. So don't peek or use any superpowers. You have to wait until I show you." Samar wagged her finger at Kouji.

"Fine," she agreed, even though she was quite curious. Not to mention, she didn't have any powers that'd allow her to see into the bag. She'd have to wait.

"I can heal you. After that, we can have the snack. And, um, I'd like to ask you something."

"What?" Samar peeled off her black hoodie and her sweatshirt. She was left in her sleeveless t-shirt. She slid her pants off.

Kouji didn't reply, gaze glued to Samar's form. Sparring with Samar every day had awakened something that she had never considered might exist. Fighting alongside her whenever Nightmares popped up while they were out didn't help. They really needed to talk.

"Kouji," Samar said.

Kouji shook away her stupor. "Hmm?"

"Are you going to heal me? My eye is throbbing."

"Of course!" Kouji rushed to Samar's side and wasted no time healing her wrecked eye and busted lip. "I can't imagine you going into a store with your face looking like this."

Samar chuckled. "I turned some heads, but I had to pick up this gift. It'll help me open a dialogue with you."

"You don't need a gift to talk to me."

Samar's eyes sparkled. "Well, we can't all offer sweet dumplings."

Kouji laughed. "Lift your shirt."

Samar obeyed. Her abdomen was painted with bruises. Kouji frowned. How dare anyone mar this perfect form? *I should start going out with her. They're hunting me, after all.*

"Don't forget my thigh. I took a direct hit there. Bastards were fast and numerous tonight."

"I'll never let you be in pain if I can help it," Kouji replied in a soft tone.

"I know."

This response made Kouji lock eyes with Samar, who smiled at her once more. Kouji grinned back and healed the last of Samar's bruises. Part of her was disappointed. She liked the excuse to touch Samar like this, experiencing soft skin but hard muscle under her sensitive fingertips.

"Thank you. I feel so much better," Samar said.

"I aim to please." Kouji meant that when it came to Samar.

Once Within a Dream

Samar's face was bright. "You always do." She left the gift by her side while they sat down for their snack. Kouji was torn between looking at Samar and the box. Samar sipped her tea. "So what do you want to talk about?" Samar popped a dumpling into her mouth. She hummed and her eyes twinkled once more.

Her expression was a high compliment that fortified Kouji's pride. Samar delighted in her cooking. Samar liked her. They had been exploring the city together for weeks, enjoying each other's company and holding hands all the way through.

"I've been thinking...since our trip to the botanical gardens, when the thief called us a couple," Kouji started.

Samar nodded. "It was a wonderful picture, despite her running off with my phone."

"Agreed. We do look close in the picture."

"I like to think we are close." Samar looked her in the eye, suddenly unsteady. "Right?"

"I hope so." Kouji took a deep breath, heart in her throat. How should she approach this question? She had never thought of anything like this before. "I was wondering, how does courting go in this time?"

Samar's brow furrowed. She sipped her tea. "Um, I'm not too sure."

"You've been courted before, right?" Kouji asked. This was a forbidden conversation. The couple of times she tried to bring it up, Samar dodged the subject, even though she claimed the past was the past. Nothing would change it.

Kouji was unsure why Samar didn't want to talk about someone she once claimed to love. Samar used to ramble about Universal, when Kouji was asleep in the tomb. She had to admit, at least to herself, she'd been jealous of Universal. Samar had no idea Kouji existed then. *Would I have woken up if she had stopped coming by?* Kouji was thankful Samar had still visited the tomb daily, even though she had Universal.

Samar shoved a couple more sweet dumplings in her mouth, likely to avoid responding. Kouji waited. *She cannot chew forever.*

"You don't want to talk about that, do you?" Kouji asked, as Samar popped more dumplings.

"It wasn't courting," Samar replied in a short tone.

Kouji tilted her head as her brow wrinkled. "Then what was it?" From what she could recall, Samar claimed to love Universal. She had sounded dreamy when recounting kisses and touches. *I want kisses and touches.* How would those things feel?

"I'm not sure."

"You loved him, right?"

Samar sucked her teeth. "What do you care?"

Kouji opened her mouth, but closed it again without uttering a word. She wasn't ready to admit she was jealous, possibly envious of a person she had never met. *I did something wrong here. She's upset.*

"I'm sorry I upset you. I was only curious." Kouji focused on her tea, tucking into herself and hoping the visible surrender would help Samar relax.

Samar sighed and reached over, rubbing Kouji's knee. "No, I'm sorry. I don't want to upset you. You know that. I wanted to come in and enjoy our snack time, give you your gift, and even take your hair out, so we can do new braids when I wake up."

"Why does this upset you so much?"

With a huff, Samar rubbed the top of her head, mussing her short curls. "No clue. It's not something I want to discuss with you. Universal and I...I don't think we were courting. We didn't have the time to be courting in the traditional sense. Not that he would've done such a thing. Why do you want to know about courting, anyway?"

Kouji shook her head. "Never mind. It doesn't matter." She'd leave it alone for now. "So when do I get my surprise?" She ate a couple of the dumplings. Only a few were left. She'd leave those for Samar. The tea was enough for her.

Samar ate one more dumpling. "Once we're done. Please, eat more. You made these delicious things and you didn't even eat many."

Kouji smiled. "Thank you."

"No, thank you. For being here, for making my days so much brighter." Samar smiled as she grabbed Kouji's hand and held on.

Kouji's heart thumped. What had she done to deserve this? *And why am I trying to ruin things by talking about courting?* It was clear Samar didn't care about courting. Soon the food was gone and their teacups were empty.

"Okay, you can open it now." Samar pushed the bag toward Kouji.

Kouji yanked the bag toward herself and pulled out the box. She tilted her head. The words on the box said it was a pair of in-line skates. She had seen these somewhere before.

"Hey, these are those things from the place you took me to when I first woke up." Kouji earned an amused look from Samar.

"Yeah, those are skates. So when we go back, you don't have to bum stuff off people. Although, I think you should start with a skateboard. I skate, and I'll show you how to use these. We'll have fun, I hope."

"Really?" Hope bubbled up throughout Kouji and her eyes watered.

"Yeah."

Kouji hopped up. "Let's go out now!"

Samar chuckled. "How about sleep first? I've had a long night."

"Oh, right. Sorry. I got excited and ahead of myself."

"Yes, that's obvious. Come on, let's clean up."

They put their dishes in the sink, and Samar went to take a shower. Kouji washed their few dishes before she sat down with her skates. She had no idea how to work the things, but she was eager to learn. Skating was once Samar's passion. Kouji wanted to understand why.

"I didn't think you'd like the skates more than me." Samar stepped out of the bathroom wearing a sports bra and short shorts.

Kouji tilted her head. "What do you mean?"

"You're hugging them to your chest. You've never hugged me like that."

That sounded like an invitation Kouji wouldn't pass up. She pushed the skates out of her way and popped up, rushing to hug Samar. Samar yelped, but returned the hug. *Oh, wow.* Why had they not done this before? Was this warmth seeping into her? She needed more of this as soon as possible and all the time.

Kouji never wanted to let go of Samar. *She knows all my sins and still accepts me. She still wants me around, not to use me or my abilities.* The press of Samar's body was warm and firm. She felt right in Kouji's arms. It was like they fit together.

Samar sniffled and the moment broke. They released each other, but stared into each other's eyes. Kouji had an urge she couldn't quite identify.

"Would you lay down with me for a little while?" Samar asked.

Kouji blinked, not expecting the question. "Yes, of course." She had never been happier that she kept the apartment clean, so there was space on the bed for her.

They settled on the bed, facing each other. Samar put her hand on Kouji's bare arm, warming it. Samar was the only person who ever warmed Kouji. She'd give up her divine powers for more time like this.

"I think I stood up to Siku today," Samar said.

"Did you?" Kouji asked, only to show she was paying attention. Sometimes, Samar needed to talk out her actions, like she was speaking to the tomb once again. That was fine. Kouji was more than pleased to listen.

"Yes. It wasn't much, but it was something. That's why I got you a present. You gave me the strength to say something to Siku. You give me strength, more than the tomb ever did."

Kouji chuckled and tapped her index fingers together. "Believe it or not, sometimes I think you'd have been better off if I stayed asleep. You could've continued to offload your thoughts to the tomb."

Samar gently squeezed Kouji's bicep. "This is so much better than talking to the tomb. Thank you for being here."

Kouji grinned. "Thank you for having me here. You didn't have to believe any of my crazy stories, but you did. Plus, you haven't asked anything of me, just letting me find my footing."

"I know what it's like, so I'd never ask anything of you while you're trying to figure things out. You deserve to have a life."

"Thank you."

"You can sleep here if you want," Samar said.

"I'd like that."

"Me, too." Samar eased closer, so they were touching.

Kouji sighed. "I feel so safe with you…"

Samar didn't respond. She had fallen asleep that quickly. Usually, she had so much energy after being healed. Something emotional was probably weighing her down. Samar had managed to speak up to her father. That was huge. *My questions can wait.*

Samar woke to the smell of breakfast, which she was used to at this point. Kouji got better and better in the kitchen with every meal she made. Samar's task was to set up the dining mat and check the charms that kept Nightmares out.

Samar sat down and surveyed the meal. "Oh god, this looks so amazing." Her stomach growled.

"What have I told you about calling me god?" Kouji winked.

Samar gave a weak laugh. "You're trying to be a smart aleck."

"I'm testing it out."

"It doesn't work. Try something else."

Kouji snickered. "I have time to figure it out."

After breakfast, they sparred, as was their norm. Living with Kouji for this short time had been quite a test in Samar's self-control.

Once Within a Dream

Watching Kouji move around the kitchen was already tempting, but fighting against her was something else. Samar felt more than a physical attraction. This was more than she could figure out, and it wasn't appropriate. They were friends.

Being friends was what made things grow. Samar was emotionally attached to Kouji. She was most comfortable with Kouji, perhaps more so than with Evinia. Kouji would never judge her. Kouji might push her to do something, but would stand there with her the whole time. Samar never wanted Kouji to leave.

This would explain some of her odd behavior to herself. Samar found herself having to touch Kouji, who was always open to it. Even last night, lying in the bed with her. Samar wanted Kouji close, within arm's reach. And she slept so well last night.

"Hey, focus!" Kouji tapped her on the shoulder.

Samar shook her head. "Sorry. Lost in my thoughts." She stepped back to reset her stance. If this was an actual fight, she would've been in serious trouble.

Kouji ticked up an eyebrow for a quick second. "Anything you want to share?"

"No, nothing." In fact, she should probably forget about all of the touching she yearned to do with Kouji. Kouji allowed it, but she wasn't used to contact. It was possible Samar was taking advantage of Kouji being touch-starved.

Samar found herself on her back, and all thoughts of touching vanished. Kouji was looking at her. It was annoying that Kouji had learned to roll her eyes.

Samar blew out a huff. "Okay, sorry. I promise not to get lost in my head again."

Kouji stared deep into her eyes. "Please, if you want to talk about anything, you know you can with me."

"As you'd say, not yet. Let's finish this sparring session. We can clean up, make lunch, then go to the skate park. You can break in your new skates."

Kouji gasped, but her eyes twinkled. "So soon?"

"Yes."

Their sparring went on for almost two hours. They had separate showers, then got some reading in. Kouji made lunch, while Samar took the skates out of the box. She wanted to be able to leave as soon as they were done eating. She also had to find her own skates, not that she planned on skating much, if at all.

It had been a while since Samar last used her skates. They were buried in the back of her closet, collecting dust. She cleaned them off, then showed Kouji how to put them on. Kouji followed her lead. Samar grabbed their shoes, just in case. They were ready for Kouji to get worked over a little bit.

Kouji was unable to stand in the skates at first. Once she balanced herself enough to stand up, she couldn't move and remain upright. Samar helped Kouji practice moving at a slow pace until Samar had to go off to work. The next few days were spent teaching Kouji how to move in her skates.

"Can we go back to that place now?" Kouji asked. The paved lot they were in was the perfect place to practice skating when they weren't being bothered by hooligans and their Nightmares.

"Oh, you want to fall in front of a bunch of people, huh?"

"I'm aware of what I'm doing a little bit now, right?" It was a bit of a stretch.

"A little bit, yes. Enough not to kill yourself on a skating ramp, at least I don't think so. If you want to risk it, who am I to stop you?" Experience was the best teacher.

"I'll be fine. I only need to do it a couple of times," Kouji argued.

"And what've you been doing all the time we've been out here? Not doing it a couple of times?"

"Come on. Let's go, please." Kouji grinned and pressed her hands together.

Samar sighed and nodded. She unlaced her skates and motioned for Kouji to do the same. They hooked their skates over their shoulders, put their sneakers back on, and started toward the skate park. They hopped the gate with ease. Samar scoped out the few skaters and decided to stay out of sight while Kouji went to embarrass herself. Samar stood by a cement column, hidden by the pillar's shadow, but close enough to take in whatever happened to Kouji.

"Hey, who's the new chick?" a blond young man called out when he noticed Kouji. No one answered him, so he went over to her. "Sup, dude. You new around here?" he asked with a smile. That smile was familiar. Those warm, hazel eyes. Koko.

"Yeah," Kouji answered with her own smile.

"That's cool. You come to do some skating an' crap?"

Kouji's brow furrowed with adorable confusion. She was probably processing the words. She wasn't used to interacting with people on her own. "Came to try."

Koko nodded. "You must not be too good, huh?" Rude. Samar wanted to go shake him, but he was harmless so far, and these skaters tended to be playful-rude. Although, it'd probably be funny to shake him with such luxurious, wavy, blond hair.

"I just started a few days ago. My friend's been helping me learn."

"Where's this friend?" Koko scanned around, probably looking for another unfamiliar face or at least someone to claim the "new chick."

"She stayed behind. So is it all right if I skate?"

"Ain't none of us gonna stop ya, dude," Koko answered with a bright smile.

Kouji nodded and put her skates on. She focused on the few other in-line skaters as they worked the outer ramp and rail. Something must've made her confident, and she went for it.

She tumbled down the ramp, as expected. But she got back up and tried again. She kept trying until she managed to make it down the ramp. The skaters were impressed with the new chick's efforts and cheered her on. They got louder on each new attempt, as Kouji showed vast improvement. *She really does process information faster than humans.*

"Dude, I thought you said you ain't know how to skate," Koko said, as Kouji returned to the top of the ramp.

"I really don't have any idea what I'm doing yet. I was just doing what I saw the others do." Kouji motioned to the other skaters with one hand.

Koko laughed. "Dude, you're pretty damn observant."

"I guess, but I've also been practicing for a few days before coming here." Kouji shrugged.

"Hey, Koko, who's your friend?" a girl inquired. Three other girls came up behind her. They all focused their attention on Kouji.

"I don't know her. She's new from what I can tell, but she did say something about a friend teaching her," Koko replied, even though the girls weren't paying him any mind.

The girls were in Kouji's face, asking too many questions to keep up with. Kouji backed up a step, but didn't really have anywhere to go. The touching started once it was clear Kouji wouldn't escape.

"Hey!" Samar barked, when the four girls rubbed up against *her* Kouji. She didn't bother to correct that very possessive thought.

Samar marched over, drawing Kouji's attention as well as the other girls. Kouji offered a nervous smile and jumped away from her new fan club. She opened her mouth as though she was about to say something, but Koko beat her to it.

"Whoa! It's the Spring-heeled Sam!" Koko squealed before Samar had the chance to tell the girls off for touching Kouji.

"It is Sam!" With a gasp, Brody rushed over, almost falling on his skates. At least Brody looked the same, except for facial hair on his pointed chin.

"Sam, dude, what the hell are ya doing back here?" Koko asked with a wide smile. "I mean, it's been a long while, dude." Brody nodded along and grinned.

"I came to grab my friend," Samar replied, fighting the urge to flinch away from the pair.

"Who?" Koko inquired.

"Her." Samar nodded toward Kouji.

"This dude?" Koko pointed at Kouji with both hands. "Dude, you always know the best dudes!" He grinned at Samar, who couldn't muster the same happiness. She doubted anyone with half a brain could be as gleeful as Koko. *How can he still be so joyful after everything that happened?*

Samar sighed, shaking her head. "Koko, almost two years later, and you still talk like an idiot." While she meant those words, a fond smile fought its way onto her face.

"Dude, you know me." Koko pressed his hands to his chest against his t-shirt full of designer holes. "I like being an idiot. So what's with this dude? You're doing this dude now, dude?" Now, why would he ask that?

Samar folded her arms across her chest. She glanced at Kouji, whose face was twisted and confounded. *Thank the gods for small favors.*

"First off, stop saying dude so damn much." Samar scowled. "It still gives me a headache. Second off, I'm not doing anything with her. People can just be friends. Third off, that's none of your business anyway."

"Whoa, Spring-heel, retract the claws, dude. I was only saying it's cool that ya ass finally got over damn Universal. That took like forever and a damn day, dude, and it's cool to see you back."

"Koko, I'll give you a whole two seconds to get out my face before we both regret it," Samar warned him.

"Hey, Sam-dude, you know you ain't gonna hurt me. If you was, you woulda done that, like two days after ya met me, dude. Nobody hurts me, though, dude. I'm way too loveable." Koko snickered and stuck his tongue out, showing off a stud. He wasn't wrong. Brody gave two thumbs up behind him.

Sucking her teeth, Samar folded her arms across her chest. "You're annoying is what you are."

Koko winked. "That, too, dude. Look, you needed to get over that damn loser anyway."

A fire shot through Samar. "What?" she demanded as if Koko had offended her.

"I can call the dude a damn loser because that's what he was. Dude, you're not a loser and this dude, from what I can see, ain't no loser either. In fact, from the way she skates, I can say this dude is damn cool." Koko patted Kouji on the shoulder briefly.

"Universal was not a loser!" Samar shouted. Kouji yelped, but Koko didn't budge. Brody flinched though.

Koko scoffed. "Dude, I knew that dude way longer than you. Had to grow up with that bastard, in fact. He was a total, fucking loser. They shoulda named his ass 'fuck up.'"

"How can you talk about your own dead brother like that?" Samar glared Koko down, even though he was taller than she was.

Koko shrugged and tapped his chin with his index finger. "Mostly because I sorta sever the family bonds when motherfuckers start taking actual shots at me and have the fucking cops harassing me."

"He was your brother and he's dead." Those bonds had to mean something.

"It's about time you figured that out!" Koko threw his hands up. "You was wandering around here like it was a damn shame he was gone. That dude was the king of assholes. Just because he's dead doesn't change the way the dude lived. It don't change the way he tried to pull you into crap, and it don't change what he did at all. It don't change how he almost got us both killed more than once, how he shot actual bullets at us. No idea who this dude is, but I'll bet my damn left arm she's better for anybody than Universal was. Unless you forgot, my damn dead brother almost fucked you over...more than once!"

Samar's frown deepened. "Kouji, let's get outta here." She waved Kouji over to her. A burning, boiling sensation rushed through her stomach and conquered her chest. She wouldn't listen to any more of this nonsense.

"Sam, dude, don't run away again. We friends here," Koko said.

"C'mon, Kou," Samar said and Kouji skated over to her. The pair turned to leave, which caused the rather cheerful Koko to frown.

"Sam, dude, come on," Koko called, but Samar didn't stop. "Fine. Yo, Kouji dude, you make sure to bring Spring-heel back here! She needs the practice!"

☾

Kouji wasn't sure what had just happened, but she made sure to keep up with Samar as best she could on the skates. Well, until she fell. That got Samar to stop and wait. Kouji picked herself up. No reason to still be wearing the skates. They were at the fence that separated the skate park from the street beyond the alleyway anyway.

"So that's was Universal's brother." Kouji took off her skates to hop over the fence.

Samar waited for her on the other side. She didn't respond to the observation in any way. *Okay, she's angry. But why?* When she was talking to the tomb, Samar had always expressed a fondness for Universal's brother. What changed?

"Are you going to ignore me now?" Kouji asked.

Samar sighed. "No, but I don't want to talk about Universal or his stupid brother right now." She folded her arms across her chest.

"Are you ever going to talk about them?" Kouji jumped over the gate, and they continued on their way.

"Probably not."

"Oh." She needed to change the subject and hopefully get Samar out of her funk. "So how'd you like my skating? Was I okay?" Kouji forced a smile.

Samar rubbed her hands together. She seemed to be processing her thoughts. Kouji's stomach twisted. What if Samar was still snippy? *Maybe I should just be quiet.*

"Yes, you were decent. For a beginner." Samar's voice was nonchalant. A hint that Kouji was better than adequate and Samar had been watching closer than she wanted to admit.

"Could you do better?" Kouji countered with a teasing smile.

"Yes, I could. The only thing I found in this city was the skating. Well, the only good thing." Her face was still tense.

Kouji grabbed Samar's hand. "Are you sure you don't want to talk about it yet?" she asked in a quiet voice.

"I'm sure. Just drop it, please," Samar replied, her voice soft now.

"It's dropped to the ground, and I'm walking away from it as we speak," Kouji remarked with a grin. "I have no idea where my brain is for me to dare bringing that up again."

"It's not where mine is."

Kouji blinked. "What do you mean by that?" She didn't understand, but it seemed like it was something important. Something she should comprehend.

Samar squeaked. "Nothing!"

Kouji arched an eyebrow and regarded Samar for a long moment. *Don't press. She's upset already.* "If you say so. So what are we going to do now?"

"Get out of the rain," Samar suggested as a light drizzle quickly transformed into a storm.

"Good idea," Kouji replied. "And I just had one of my own good ideas." She hoped it'd go over well. Kouji lifted Samar into her arms without warning and bolted off in the direction of Samar's apartment. By the time they came to the apartment door, Samar had a vice grip around Kouji's neck. She'd pressed herself into Kouji's chest, and Kouji never wanted her to leave.

Samar's eyes were almost bugged out, and her fingers dug hard into Kouji's shoulders. Samar's face said it all. She didn't want to do that again.

"Never do that again, even with a warning," Samar whispered.

"What? Why? We didn't end up wet," Kouji replied.

"It was too fast, much too fast."

"Understood." Kouji put Samar down, making a mental note of her sigh of relief. *Remember to ask before taking such liberties.* "I'm sorry. I just assumed you wouldn't want to get wet."

"You're right, but that was still too fast for me. You have to remember, I'm still human."

Kouji winced. "Right."

Samar shoved the door open and stepped inside. She waited for Kouji to enter, then shut the door. Kouji noticed Samar staring at the floor. No wait, she was staring, mouth open, at the bottom of Kouji's pants.

The pants weren't only soaked almost up to the knees, but the cuffs were worn off. Kouji could feel the floorboards under her feet. At least the rain kept her sneakers from catching on fire.

"You messed up your pants," Samar said.

"Sorry. Shoes too. What should I do?"

"The pants you can still wear. Hang them up over the shower. If the rain stops, we'll go out for new sneakers. You have your slides, so you don't have to go barefoot. Of course, now I see why you went barefoot."

"No sandal could contain me when I really needed to move."

Kouji took off her sneakers and set them down by the closet. She'd dispose of them after she handled her pants. She set her skates down next to her sneakers, then lifted her pant legs up to her knees to avoid wetting the floor on her way to the bathroom.

When she exited the bathroom, her skates and sneakers were gone. Samar probably took care of them. She had become tidier lately.

"I was going to make tea to warm up," Samar called from the kitchen.

"Sounds perfect," Kouji replied. "What if I made a cake? We could eat it later, after dinner."

Samar smiled. "Sounds more than perfect."

Chapter Fifteen

Drizzle

SINCE IT WAS RAINING, Samar and Kouji were stuck inside, which was fine. They cooked, and while the food was on, Kouji went to take a shower. What was left to do for the rest of the afternoon? A knock at the door took Samar from her thoughts.

"What the?" Samar muttered as she turned to the door. "Yes?" She didn't mean to sound unsure as she called through the door, but she rarely got visitors. She rubbed her fingertips together, ready to materialize Amani if some Nightmare-hosting idiot had gotten so bold and managed to make it past her protections at the building entrance.

"Sammie, open the door," Evinia ordered.

"Vin?" Samar yanked the door open to let her sister in. *What possessed Vinny to come here?*

Evinia frowned as she eyed the door jamb. "I thought you were going to have that door fixed." She stepped inside the apartment, dripping water onto the dark wood floor. She wasn't drenched, thanks to the umbrella folded in her hand.

"I planned on it, but it seemed stupid. Having a trick door might throw off robbers or..." She shook away the word Nightmares from the tip of her tongue. She had gotten too used to talking about Nightmares openly with Kouji. "Not that burglars would get much if they did break in here. What's up?" Samar closed the door. She prayed to whoever was listening that Kouji stayed in the bathroom. *Oh, what if Vin stays?* Samar didn't want to have that discussion yet.

"I was on my way home, and I've been a little worried about you."

"On your way home?" This visit wasn't on the route to either Mechi's or Evinia's. There had to be another explanation.

"Yes, I was going home. It's been known to happen. I thought I'd check in on you."

Samar's brow wrinkled. "Why? I'm fine." *Please, don't look around.* Not many signs of someone else living with her dotted the apartment, but the fact that the place was clean would make Evinia suspicious.

"So you say." Evinia glanced around. *Oh, great. Questions are coming.* "But what's going on really?"

"Nothing, like always. So I guess this solves your mystery, huh?" A nervous laugh escaped Samar.

Evinia stared her dead in the eye, face stern. "Come on, Sammie, tell me."

"I'm okay. I promise." Samar held her hands up in surrender.

Evinia gave a heavy sigh. "I'm quite worried about you, kiddo. You've been acting so strange lately." She placed a hand on Samar's shoulder.

Samar snorted. "You should be more worried about you. You're the one that has to go back out in that rain." It was a proper thunderstorm outside.

"I'm also the one with a car. Sammie, it's not right for you to be here all by yourself all day, first of all—"

Samar held up a hand to stop her. "Trust me, Vin, that's not a problem. You worry way too much." It took all of her self-control not to glance at the bathroom door. She needed her sister to leave the apartment until she could come up with a brilliant, semi-legitimate reason for why she was suddenly living with someone.

"I have to worry about you, Sammie. I mean, it's not like Daddy gives a damn."

"I've always gotten along without him. I don't want to be a problem for you though. I'm glad you care enough to worry, Vin, but I don't want you to worry so much about me. I'm okay. Do I have to do a little dance to make you believe me?" Samar offered a small smile, hoping it would put her sister at ease.

Evinia studied her harder. "No, if you did a little dance, I'd only worry more because I'd know for a fact something is wrong. You don't have to hole yourself in here like you're ashamed to exist."

"I'm not. I'm getting better. I even went outside earlier."

Evinia's eyes went huge. "You did?" Her voice oozed with disbelief.

"Yeah, I went skating without causing any trouble." Samar did her best to give her a reassuring smile. Evinia would be pleased with her for doing something with her time, even if it was skating. And nothing terrible, dangerous, or unlawful happened.

Evinia's eyebrows jumped to the top of her head. "You're serious?"

Samar gave a rapid nod. "Very. So I'll be all right, Vin. I promise. Like I said, I don't want you to worry so much about me. I'm trying to live my life, like you want me to."

Evinia's face softened and her eyes sparkled a bit. "All right. I'll try not to worry, but it feels like you're not telling me something. I'm not used to that."

That was true enough. Yes, Samar held some things back from Evinia, but it was learned behavior. She used to tell Evinia everything, including her battles against Nightmares. Evinia hadn't believed her and liked to think she cornered Samar with questions to prove her wrong about them. The questioning doubt wasn't pleasant to deal with. Samar shared everything until Evinia pressed her with questions she had no desire to answer.

"Everything is fine. I tell you everything that's important." This was true. Sometimes, she had to work her way up to it. She'd tell Evinia about Kouji as soon as she could put this insanity into words.

A small smile graced Evinia's face. "I know."

"So I'll see you later?"

"Are you kicking me out?" Evinia teased with a grin and a twinkle in her blue-grey eyes.

"No! Of course not." Samar fought down a wince. She defended herself too forcefully. It was like she had the words *big liar* printed all over her face. *Am I sweating?*

Evinia arched an eyebrow. "You're still acting quite weird."

"I'm not. It's in your mind because you're worried." Samar made a conscious attempt not to break a sweat, though she was certain she failed.

"I doubt that." Evinia shook her head. "Are you sure you're okay?"

This one Samar could answer with confidence. "Yes. I'm healing now, like you want for me."

"I do want that for you." Evinia squeezed Samar's hand.

Samar ducked her head and gave a shy smile. "I'm doing my best. Once things fall into place, you'll see. No need to be concerned."

"If you say so."

"Don't you think you should go home before work starts?" Samar suggested.

Evinia chuckled. "Why don't you tell me to get the hell out already?"

Samar yelped. "I don't mean it like that!" Evinia should relax while she had the chance. Work was annoying for her, too, after all.

Evinia grinned. "You're right. Don't think this is over though, missy, not by a long shot. We still have plenty to talk about." She wagged her finger in Samar's face for a moment.

"Yes, ma'am." Samar would have to tell Evinia something. Her big sister would either worry herself sick or find out what the heck was going on without asking Samar anything anymore.

"Goodbye." Evinia kissed her on the cheek.

Samar almost had to rip her door out of the wall to open it. Evinia shook her head and laughed, as she crossed the threshold. Samar scrunched up her face sheepishly and shrugged.

"You should have that door fixed."

"I like it this way. See you in a little while." Samar finally breathed, relieved to watch her sister disappear down the stairs at the end of the hall. She shut the door and sighed. Her heart began to dislodge from her throat and settle back where it belonged. She remembered her guest.

"Kouji? Kouji, are you okay?" No answer. Samar went to the bathroom to check on Kouji. She knocked and called again. Still no response. She knocked louder.

"Kouji? Kouji, you okay?" She waited for a response that didn't come. "Kou, I'm coming in, okay? You hear me? I'm coming in."

Samar rushed into the bathroom and discovered Kouji in the bathtub. She was wrapped in the shower curtain, struggling to no avail to free herself. Samar had to laugh, even though the ripped curtain would need to be replaced.

Kouji squirming around the tub was too much for Samar. Once she managed to stop giggling, she peeled Kouji out of the curtain. Kouji gasped for air once her head was free. So dramatic, just like a god.

"Thank you so much," Kouji said between deep breaths.

"Do I want to know how you did this?"

"I got distracted and slipped. I feel like such an idiot." Kouji shook her head.

"You're not an idiot. Where are your clothes?" She noticed Kouji was in her underwear. Did she fall while getting dressed?

"There." Kouji pointed toward the sink, as she climbed out of the tub.

"Now, how'd they end up there?"

"I don't even know. They could've flown out of my hands while I was trying to keep my balance."

"You're just trying to kill yourself in the bathroom, huh?" Samar threw her a teasing grin and shook her head. "What distracted you?"

Kouji gave a somewhat pitiful smile. "Doing too many things at once, thinking about skating."

"Skating?" Was Kouji thinking about her exchange with Koko? Thinking about Universal?

Kouji nodded. "I can't wait to improve. It was fun, like you said."

Yes, it was fun. Long ago, before Universal ruined it. Maybe it could be fun again. Samar retrieved the clothes and handed them over. It registered to her brain that she stood before a nearly naked Kouji. Should she look? *No! Respect her like you'd want someone to respect you.*

Samar picked up the shower curtain and tried to put it back on the rod. It gave her something to do, even though a new one was necessary. The hooks had ripped through each of the holes.

From the corner of her eye, she saw Kouji getting dressed, but nothing graphic. Samar directed her out of the bathroom with a stern point to the door and a playful stomp of her foot. Kouji chuckled and marched out like a scolded child.

"On rainy days like this, you always talked about sipping tea and reading. Shall we do that?" Kouji asked.

"I was thinking we might try something different. We can eat, then watch a show. I haven't introduced you to the television yet."

"Oh, okay. I know you've talked about these things before."

"Yes. They're like short movies that we can watch at home. You'll like it." Samar was confident Kouji would like the shows as well as she'd liked the movie. Plus, there was a chance of cuddling on the sofa.

They retreated to the kitchen to prepare lunch. Their joint efforts produced a delicious peanut butter chicken stew with vegetable fried rice and banana chips.

"We definitely work best as a team." Kouji finished the last bite with a satisfied grin.

"I like how we work together, but I'm also quite happy with what you do in the kitchen on your own."

The compliment earned Samar a beaming grin from Kouji. They cleaned up lunch, Kouji cleared away her makeshift bed, and Samar grabbed her rarely used laptop. They sat shoulder to shoulder on the sofa, as Samar found a documentary. After a few minutes, Samar's hopes became reality. They were hugged up on the couch. *I could get used to this.*

And then, time was up. Samar had to get to work. She peeled herself away from their embrace, and could've sworn she heard Kouji whine.

"Don't kill yourself while I'm at work," Samar said with a lopsided grin.

"I'll try my best not to," Kouji replied with a chuckle. Samar shook her head, and they shared a hug that warmed Samar more than her layered clothing did as she trotted off to work.

Evinia winced as if the sounds coming over the comms were in her office. She checked in with Samar every night. Lately, it was rough. Samar had her hands full. Okunkun Park had taken a turn for the worse, and Evinia didn't understand why. She feared something might happen to Samar if the trend continued.

"Evinia," a deep voice boomed from the doorway.

"Daddy, you actually made time for me." Evinia had called him. She needed to make him aware of what was happening in Okunkun Park. He needed to provide Samar with backup or a partner. Something.

He sucked his teeth. "You want something?"

Evinia got up and shut the office door. This would get loud. But she needed Siku Habeen to act like he gave a damn about his middle child. Samar didn't ask for any of this, and someone had to stand up for her.

"Okunkun Park. Has the city put in a request for more security?" Evinia asked. This was her opening because if the city asked, it meant more money for Siku, and she wouldn't have to beg him to help Samar.

"No."

"It's been sounding rough over there the past couple of weeks."

He frowned. "Why do you know how it *sounds* in the park?"

She scowled right back. Mirroring his ridiculous expression was useless. The man was plenty of things, but self-aware wasn't one of them. Self-righteous to a fault though.

"I check in with my sister throughout the night because I'm concerned about her."

"I've told you to stop babying her."

Evinia bit back a snarl. "It's not babying her to care. She needs help. Something's happening in that park."

"The city hasn't mentioned any uptick of incidents, and she hasn't said anything."

"Of course, she hasn't. She doesn't say anything to you, ever. You have to open your eyes to what she's going through."

"She's doing her job."

"She's drowning, like she's been drowning for three damn years, and you just close your eyes to it. She needs help." Evinia had often said these words her father and expected her urging would probably go the way it always did. Her words would fall on deaf ears.

"You need to find a better hobby. Crying over Samar doesn't suit you."

A light knock at the door stopped Evinia from snapping at her father. She glanced at the time. That had to be Samar.

"Hold on, kiddo," Evinia called as she turned her attention back to Siku. She glared at her father from behind her glasses.

"Sure," Samar answered.

"You see how she comes to you as soon as she's done with her patrol. This is the babying. She's here to be coddled."

"She's here to complete the rest of her work. She works her ass off for you. Why won't you do something for her?"

He glowered at her. "Haven't I done everything for her? I pulled her from the jungle when she was alone. I gave her a roof over her head, a top-tier education, food to eat, and a premium job other people with better qualifications would kill for. She's gotten enough from me."

"You're her father! You should never say something like that!" Evinia wanted to tear her hair out. This man couldn't be so uncaring and indifferent about Samar's well-being.

"This isn't any of your business, Vinny. She might be your sister, but she's my daughter."

"Then treat her that way."

"When you have a daughter, you tell me how to treat one of my children."

Evinia didn't know what the hell that had to do with anything, and he didn't stick around to explain. He yanked open the door Samar was standing behind. Samar didn't jump. *Good for her.*

"Dad," Samar said with a grunt, as he loomed over her.

"Samar." He growled like she had been the one to piss him off. Of course, that wasn't far off. It seemed like her existence pissed him off.

Samar ignored his tone. As he walked off, Samar came into the office and flopped down into her chair. Evinia glanced at her. With a gasp, she rushed to her sister. It only took one step in the small office.

"Sammie, what the hell happened?" Evinia wanted to touch Samar's face, but was too scared to do so. Her nose had to be broken. Her eyebrow was split open, with blood oozing down the side of her face. *How the hell did Daddy see this and keep going?!* She wanted to punch him in the face.

Samar shrugged. "Difficult night. I think an arms deal or something happening."

"In the park?" Evinia shrieked. An arms deal in Okunkun Park wasn't unheard of years ago, but not now. Not with Samar there.

"Yes. Very weird. You and Siku were arguing."

Evinia waved that off. "Never mind that. We should take you to the hospital or at the least to the infirmary." Moonless Night had an amazing infirmary with an on-call doctor and several nurses.

Samar scoffed and shook her head. "I'll be fine. I should do my reports." She nodded toward the computer.

"I've got those for you. We have to talk." Evinia was determined to get to the bottom of things.

"About?"

"You."

"What about me?"

"You can't be serious with that question while your face is dripping with blood." Evinia gave her a deadpan expression. Surely, Samar didn't think she could continue the innocent act much longer.

Samar sighed. "You have a point."

"What's been up with you lately? Tell me what's going on. Your apartment was clean, and you had a little makeshift bed on the couch. And there were cheap sneakers by your closet. You don't wear cheap sneakers. What's going on?"

"Nothing. My place can't be clean?"

"No," Evinia answered the obvious. In all of the time Samar had that apartment, she had never cleaned it.

"You make a fair point." Samar knew what a slob she was. She gnawed the corner of her mouth, then winced. Evinia noticed a small cut lurked at the edge of her lip. Samar's shoulders dropped with a sigh. "Okay. You remember Universal, right?"

"That bastard, yeah." Evinia snarled.

It was difficult to forget someone who was the very definition of a jackass. He got Samar jammed up in so many different ways, including almost getting her killed. If he wasn't dead, Evinia would've killed him after learning he once took shots at her sister.

"Wait, you met somebody?" Evinia's brain finally caught up with the question.

Samar rocked her head from side to side. "Maybe?"

"How do you 'maybe' meet someone?"

"No, I met her, but it's not quite the same thing." Samar fumbled with her words.

Evinia arched an eyebrow. "Her?"

"Yeah, her."

"You never mentioned being attracted to women." Just when she thought she knew everything about her little sister, surprise!

Samar shrugged. "Never mentioned being attracted to men either. You sort of assumed."

"You got me there. Is this a cultural thing or you?"

"Me. I'm not attracted to anybody. Universal was an anomaly until now."

"Well, you're only nineteen and you hated high school, so there wasn't much opportunity for you to find out if you're attracted to anybody."

"I have eyes. I can see people. I'm still not attracted to them."

"Fair enough. Please, tell me she's not like Universal."

"No, not really. They're kind of different, but sort of the same." Samar's face twitched awkwardly, like she hardly knew what she was talking about.

"In what ways? Is she a drug dealer or user?"

"No."

"Does she treat you like some little toy?"

"No."

"Did she almost get you arrested?"

"No."

"Did she almost get you killed?"

"No."

"Have you had to seriously fight her at any point in time?"

"No."

"Then how the hell are she and Universal anywhere near similar?" Whoever this girl was, she sounded a million times better than Samar's first dip into the dating pool.

Samar glanced away, agony showing on her face. "Universal was all right at first."

"You know what, at first he came across all right, but as you two went on, he was messed up. He had some deep-seated issues, and it was obvious he was going to end up in jail or dead." And how right she was about that.

"Vin." Samar sighed.

"I'm sorry, Sammie, but that's the truth. I'm also glad it was him and not you. He played with too many lives, and I didn't like that he played with yours too."

Samar stared at the ceiling. "Well, he can't do it anymore."

"I know." Evinia smiled, trying to lighten the mood. "Tell me about your lady."

Knowing the secret was dating and not something wrong with Samar was somewhat of a relief, but Evinia remained concerned. Evinia had seen the type of person her sister was attracted to. The problems that came with Universal were too much to even think about without getting a headache. Evinia didn't want her little sister going through more trouble like he brought along.

"You'd never believe me about this girl. Besides, we're not really together. She's a friend who camps out on my couch."

Evinia rolled her eyes. "Too late to sell me that. You like her. I can see it in your eyes. So that's why you've been acting so odd. That's why you've been all smiles lately. You've been running out of here to go back to your girlfriend." Evinia gave a little laugh. Samar's disposition put this mystery girl ahead of Universal as well. She was certain when Samar was with Universal she didn't care if she lived or died. That didn't seem to be the case now.

"She's not my girlfriend. She's only a friend."

"Yeah, Universal was only a friend all the way until he died."

"Look, Kouji is my friend."

"Oh, Kouji. That's her name?" Evinia smirked. That was too easy.

Samar groaned, palming her face. "And you all claim I'm smart. Yes, her name's Kouji."

"Where was she when I came to see you?"

"The bathroom."

"Hiding?" Evinia was certainly amused.

"Cleaning up. We got caught in the rain." Under her breath, Samar said, "And having a fight with my shower curtain."

Evinia's face scrunched. She'd ignore the shower curtain bit for now. "I'll believe that one for the moment. So what's Miss Kouji's last name? What does she do? How'd you meet her? When do I meet her?"

Samar groaned and slid down in her seat. "What questions are these?"

"Sammie, don't play coy with me. I was the first person you told about Universal. I'm sure I'm the first person you've mentioned this Kouji girl to. Now, tell me about her."

Samar sucked her teeth and eyed the ceiling. "I don't want to."

Evinia put her hand on Samar's shoulder. "Why not? I'm here for you."

"This is just embarrassing."

Evinia understood that. "At least tell me her last name."

"I should head home. Don't want to be late for our snack." Samar stood up.

"Snack? Please, tell me that's not a code word."

Samar pursed her lips and squinted. "Kouji cooks a snack for me for when I come in since I don't usually like to eat a heavy meal until I wake up."

Evinia's mouth dropped open. *That's so sweet!* "You went out and got you a lady who cooks for you?"

"She's good."

Evinia gasped. "That's why I smelled food in your apartment!"

"Well, we cooked that together."

Hold it together! It was hard. Evinia wanted to squeal and bounce around. Samar's story was cute and wholesome. "Well, that's lovely. I take it she cleans, too, unless you're head-over-heels in love with her to the point that she's got you straightening up." Evinia didn't try to hide a small, amused smile.

Samar sucked her teeth. "Don't be dumb, Vin." Samar had vowed never to fall in love again, not after the mistake that was Universal. That bastard did so much damage.

"You're not fooling me, Sammie. So what's lover girl's last name?"

"Kouji Kataban," Samar answered, then she charged out of the office. Evinia let her go. The conversation went better than she had imagined.

Something clicked in Evinia's mind, and she spoke her thoughts out loud. "That name sounds familiar." She couldn't recall why…yet.

Her sister's last venture into romance had been a huge disaster. With luck, this second relationship would be better. It wasn't difficult to top the first one. Evinia would keep an eye on them, just in case.

Kouji swore under her breath. Samar would be home any second and the apartment was full of smoke. She opened the kitchen window.

"Kou!" Samar opened the door, voice alarmed.

"Ignore the smoke. I've got everything under control!" Kouji assured Samar with a laugh, as she rushed out of the kitchen and opened the other two windows.

"What happened?"

"I left the pies in the oven for a little too long. I put everything on, then went to try to fix the thing in the bathroom. I'm not sure what happened, but I came back out as soon as I smelled the smoke."

"You didn't burn it, did you? I was looking forward to your pies." Samar grinned.

Kouji waved that off. "I think it's still edible. Something leaked into the oven or something. Let's check it out." Kouji went back into the kitchen.

Samar was a step behind her. Kouji had to brush away more smoke, then pulled the pies out. They seemed all right. She inspected the side and sucked her teeth.

"What happened?" Samar asked.

"I must've broken the pie pan or something. The filling poured out of the bottom. I'll have to clean the oven, but the pies look good. Hopefully, they don't taste like smoke."

Samar sighed. Kouji knew she was looking forward to the pies. Samar appreciated everything she did around the apartment. Kouji had learned the term used for her role was housewife. She was content with the role, so far.

"Maybe still taste it to see if the smoke infiltrated the flavor," Samar suggested.

Kouji chuckled. "Fine, but after that I have to heal your face. You have to be in so much pain."

Samar rolled her eyes. "I've been through worse in training. Packs of Nightmares come through the park now. I think they're coming from your tomb or going to your tomb."

"They're looking for me?"

Samar shrugged. "They don't seem to know where to find you, so that's good. I don't think we have to worry about it, but I always put up protections against Nightmares anyway."

Kouji nodded. She pulled out a knife from the rack and cut a small slice. It looked good, though it smelled a bit like smoke. She took a tiny bite and licked her lips. She caught Samar's gaze drifting to her lips and wasn't sure what to think. Samar was probably just fascinated with the treat, wanting to make sure it was edible. A wicked smile curled onto Kouji's lips.

"You've got to try this." Kouji held the slice she'd bitten to Samar's mouth.

Samar swallowed hard enough for Kouji to see her throat move, then opened her mouth for the slice. Kouji eased it right past her lips.

Samar hummed with a satisfied grin. "It's perfect."

"Not quite, but better than I expected," Kouji replied.

"No, it's amazing."

"I'll cut us a couple of slices, and we'll have some ice cream with it. But first, let me heal your face."

Samar didn't argue. Kouji's hand smoked and she healed Samar, as she did every night. The growing threats Samar faced were worrisome. Kouji didn't want Samar to suffer the same fate as Orica. Those Nightmares were hunting her, not Samar. She should be the one to stop them.

"Hey, what's going on?" Samar asked, putting her hand to Kouji's cheek.

"I hate that you're being hurt by creatures who want me," Kouji replied.

"I was fighting Nightmares long before you showed up. None of this is your fault. It's been my decision for a long time. Don't hold it in your heart at all."

"I could help you."

"Unless you can end the Nightmares passing into this world, then you can't help."

"I could ask my mother."

"I'm sure if your mother could stop the Nightmares, she would've done so a long time ago. If the stories are true, this is a punishment for humanity tempting her and her giving in to that temptation. It's not your fault, but it's also not her fault or humans' fault. It's on Usuku to stop this."

Kouji glanced away, wanting to argue, but nothing came to mind. She eased Samar's jacket from her shoulders and hung it in the closet, while Samar stripped down to her sleeveless tee. Samar put the clothes in the hamper.

Samar went for the usual dining mat, while Kouji fixed their pie and ice cream and poured some lemonade. She had gotten a taste for lemonade from a fast-food restaurant they frequented. Thankfully, Samar liked it too. Kouji would drink it all the time if allowed.

They ate in silence, which wasn't uncommon. It was easy to appreciate Samar's presence without conversation just as much as with. The lack of conversation did leave Kouji's mind to wander.

I have to be virtuous in some manner for my restraint. Kouji wanted to scoop Samar up in her arms, kiss her softly, and never let her go. The feeling grew and ached with every passing moment. She'd happily live this life with Samar forever. She'd go out and fight Nightmares with Samar to keep her safe. Hell, she'd go fight the damned Sun to protect Samar from this life that might actually kill her.

I have to talk to my mother. This has to stop. If it came down to Kouji having to challenge Usuku himself, she would. The conviction settled in her mind.

When the meal was over, Samar took her shower before getting into bed. She invited Kouji to sleep next to her again. This might be a great habit to start. She wouldn't let Nightmares or even the King of the Gods take this from her.

Chapter Sixteen

Rest

A LOUD THUNDERCLAP ECHOED through the apartment and woke Samar out of her sleep. With a gasp, her eyes shot open. Immediately, she looked to the windows, making sure no one with a Nightmare had attempted to enter. Her gaze went to the front door, waiting to see if someone tried to enter. Nothing. All was calm except for the storm outside.

She settled back on her pillow and took in the peaceful face inches from her own. Kouji was asleep beside her, her mouth partially open. She was beautiful, as always. The soothing patter of the rain seemed to be keeping Kouji asleep. Not to mention, she liked to say she was safe with Samar. She could afford to sleep through thunder that sounded like it broke the sky.

A light smile curled on Samar's face. She wouldn't mind sleeping next to this lovely face for the rest of her life. Her fallen angel.

Her thoughts drifted back to Kouji tasting the pie earlier. Kouji had looked incredibly sexy, a devilish twinkle in her eyes, as if she was fully aware of what she did to Samar. It was bold, if Kouji meant it the way it came across.

Beyond those simple things, the domestic role Kouji worked herself into was adorable. Everything about Kouji was attractive. Kouji could fight as well as Samar, even better. Her hunger for knowledge impressed Samar, and she treasured the times they just sat and read together.

A month of living with someone she was attracted to was a test, but with everything Kouji gave her, Samar was fine with their situation. Sometimes, during their sparring, she wanted to tackle Kouji and kiss her senseless. So far, the new sensation was easy to avoid. She didn't want to push Kouji away.

Kouji didn't seem interested in having a romantic partner when she was first awoken, and it didn't seem like her attitude had changed. Samar wouldn't embarrass herself or make Kouji uncomfortable.

She's so sexy and adorable, but I'll be content to share space with her. This is perfect. Samar closed her eyes, drifting back to sleep. *I wish you could've met her, Mom. You'd love her.*

"Samar..." Kouji muttered.

The sound of her name woke Samar. Kouji kicked the blankets off herself. Was she talking in her sleep? Lilac eyes fluttered open.

"Are you all right, Kou?" Samar whispered. In the dark, she could just make out the fullness of Kouji's lips, and she fought down the urge to kiss them.

Kouji blinked several times, glancing around the room. "Yes. I'm still getting used to sleeping under blankets."

"Hmmm." Samar didn't know what else to say.

"Why are you awake?" Kouji's tone was quiet, as if the fact that they woke up suddenly meant they had to keep their volume down.

"You missed the earsplitting thunder strike."

"Oh." Kouji popped her head up and looked through the window. "It's pouring. I hope it stops soon. I want to go out after breakfast."

"We can still go out. We should find something indoors to do. We can call for a ride to get there, so we don't end up drenched. Or we can always public transportation. I think you'd like the subway."

"No idea what that is."

Samar chuckled. The howling wind cut through the apartment's shoddy walls and she shivered.

"Are you cold?" Kouji asked in a soft tone.

"Always," Samar replied.

Kouji jumped up and walked over to the windows, making sure they were shut. She shrugged after seeing they were all secure. She turned her attention back to the bed, which made Samar smile.

"They're all closed. I'm not sure what's happening." Kouji scratched her head.

"Yes, they are. This place is poorly constructed, and air comes in through every crack. Come, lay back down."

Kouji obeyed but shifted the second she lay down. Samar wondered why until Kouji spread her own blanket over Samar.

"No, Kou, you don't have to." Samar tried to push the cover off.

"It's fine. I only use it for comfort, and it's not comforting for me right now. You can use it."

"I could put on another shirt or a hoodie." Samar pushed the cover away.

"Or you could take this." Kouji fixed the blanket around her shoulders. "Don't be stubborn."

"What if you want it back?"

"Don't worry. I mean, I've been sleeping in a marble coffin for thousands of years. Do you think sleeping without a blanket will bother me? Take this to warm you up." Kouji smoothed the blanket over her.

"Kou," she whined. *What the hell?* She never whined!

Kouji hit her with that warm smile. "It's fine. You're warm now, and I know how to get comfortable so I can go back to sleep."

"Really?" Samar was quite skeptical.

"Yes." Kouji moved closer and snaked an arm around Samar's waist.

They weren't touching, but Samar could feel Kouji's body heat. It wasn't too much. In fact, it was perfect. She'd have no problem dozing off with Kouji wrapped around her.

"Is this all right?" Kouji asked.

"Perfect." Samar sighed. "You're so warm," she whispered.

"My mother said, on the day I was born, my body stole all the warmth from her beautiful night. She, of course, took the warmth back. Then, she decided to take a star from her sky for me to have. Now, I'm never too cold or too hot. She said it's the honest truth," Kouji reported in a very soft tone.

"Gods do stuff like that," Samar replied with a little yawn.

"Yeah, and humans do stuff like sleep. Let's go to sleep," Kouji suggested.

Samar nodded and closed her eyes, taking a moment to revel in the calming press of Kouji against her back. Kouji's body heat was like a star that had been perfectly made for Samar on such a cold day. If only she wasn't so entangled in her blanket, she'd be able to feel Kouji's breasts against her back and her arm around her waist. She pressed herself into Kouji as much as possible and fell asleep.

Kouji woke up, still wrapped around Samar, and found she'd nuzzled into Samar's neck. This was the best sleep she had ever had. Kouji struggled to comprehend the ease within her. *But I want more.*

Her mother had warned her against such in her dreams, but it was impossible to listen. Her mother had also told her it was impossible for her to call off Usuku, so Kouji should consider going back to sleep. That wasn't an option. She wanted nothing more than to stay by Samar's side.

She yearned to crawl under the two blankets and curl against Samar with nothing between them. Absolutely nothing. *No. Stop thinking like that.* She didn't want to disrespect Samar, even in her own mind. *But is it really disrespectful when she obviously wants to be close to me too?* Samar looked at peace for the first time.

Kouji wanted to press kisses to Samar's face and have Samar smile from the attention. She wasn't sure if such a thing would be welcomed. *I need to get up before I give in.*

Making sure not to wake Samar, Kouji eased her way out of bed. She went to the kitchen to see what she could make for breakfast. Something simple would do. Everything didn't always need to be top tier, especially when she didn't have the ingredients to make things happen.

Porridge was on. Spicy eggs with cherry tomatoes. Spicy sausage. To make it complete, there should be some sweet bread, which would take a little more effort. As she worked, arms wrap around her waist and she purred. She welcomed the embrace, with Samar's chin on her shoulder.

"Someone's in a good mood," Kouji noted.

"Repaying the reason I had an amazing sleep. Thank you," Samar replied.

"For what?"

"For keeping me warm. Will you do that every day I'm cold?"

"Only if you want me to."

"And if I want you to do it every day?"

A laugh was the only response Kouji could manage. Her brain refused to formulate a proper reply. Samar didn't press for more.

Kouji would gladly sleep next to Samar every single day for the rest of her life. She might do whatever Samar wanted her to do, within reason anyway. She craved Samar's happiness.

Did I ever have thoughts like this before? She had never cared about men or women in any sense. People existed to do the things she demanded. If they didn't, she'd be rid of them. She'd never want to be rid of Samar.

She was never attracted to a particular person like she was with Samar. *This feeling has been growing since before I woke up.* She was attached to Samar to the point where she never wanted to leave her.

Kouji shook her thoughts from her head and finished with breakfast while Samar brewed their tea. They sat quietly on their mat, as usual, but for some reason, there was tension between them. The silence weighed heavily, as though trying to squeeze conversation from them.

"When I met Universal, he almost ran me over with his car," Samar said out of the blue.

"I remember you complaining about almost getting killed." Kouji frowned. She didn't want to talk about that man, but she did at the same time. He ruined a great thing. He had Samar in his life and tossed her away for power. Kouji would never.

"Hell, that could've been a lot of times."

Kouji gave a small smile. "That's true."

"I thought I loved him."

I know. I heard you. "You don't think that anymore?" Kouji asked.

Samar's brow furrowed, pursing her full lips. "I don't think I had it in me to love him. I accepted his flaws, like my mother said you do when you love a person. The only thing is, she never explained what the limit was or how other feelings should be there."

Kouji nodded. "Mothers don't always give out the full advice, hmm?"

"It doesn't seem so. Maybe she didn't think there was a limit to how many or how big a flaw you should ignore. I should've tried to stop him from doing things I knew were wrong. Instead, I let him drag me into all types of messes." Samar shook her head.

Kouji tilted her head. "Didn't you think it was fun at the time?" *Is she having fun with me? More fun than she had with Universal? Better fun?*

Samar sucked her teeth. "I was stupid at the time, plain and simple. I did the dumbest things. Things my mother would've punished me for until my brain started working again. I'm not sure why I did those things."

"I know how that is," Kouji replied.

"I guess I need to face the fact that the first person in this stupid city to make me feel wanted was a jerk, but it's hard to admit. It only shows my judgment is the worst, and I'm capable of doing some of the stupidest things to fit in. That's why I stopped going by the skate park. I wanted to forget I did those things, forget I ever associated with most of those people."

"Koko included?" Kouji asked. "I remember you speaking fondly of him, but you didn't seem too fond of him when we ran into him at the skate park."

Samar waved those words off. "Ah, Koko's annoying, but a decent guy. He only wants to skate. I wasn't ready to see him though."

"Why not?"

"I buried what happened with Universal, buried what I did with him. Seeing Koko forces me to face those mistakes."

"And you're talking them out with me?"

Samar smiled. "If not you, then who?"

Kouji sat up straighter. Okay, she was more than an empty tomb for Samar to dump her burdens on. This was good. She wanted to carry all of Samar's burdens with her.

"This is a good thing, then?" Kouji asked.

"I hope so."

Kouji nodded. "All right, so Koko is okay, but no one else?"

"I did stupid things with other people I met there. I don't like thinking about it. I used to beat people up with them. I didn't know why they were fighting half the time, but I used to go and bust ass with them because they accepted me. I wasn't even smart enough to realize they were bad news or that they were using me for my skills."

Kouji sighed. "They hosted Nightmares?"

"Yes, and no matter what, I will always fight Nightmares. They weren't too happy with me doing that, but the damage was done. My damage was done. That's part of why I don't mind being alone now. It's safer that way."

"It seemed like you just needed to grow up a little and accept your new surroundings."

"I'm ready to move on though," Samar said in a low voice.

Kouji nodded as if she understood, but she wasn't a hundred percent sure what was happening. Samar was ready to move past the pain Universal caused her and the guilt she carried around. Kouji dared to hope she meant more. Perhaps, Samar was ready to love again.

"It always seemed like that's what people wanted from you," Kouji commented.

"Yeah, most people saw Universal for what he was. Thanks to him, Vin doesn't trust me to make friends, even though she wants me to."

"It'll be all right."

"I still think she'd like you," Samar said with a small smile.

With a tilt of her head, Kouji arched an eyebrow. "Why?"

"Simple, you're not Universal. Kou, you're a good person. You cook, you clean, you get me to go outside, and you treat me as a person who matters and not like a tool you can use. That's why I haven't kicked you out yet." Samar chuckled.

"And here I thought my winning smile was keeping me here." Kouji flashed her best smile.

"It helps. I promise." Samar briefly touched Kouji's arm.

Kouji's smile grew. Samar was opening up to her even more. She related to most of what Samar had said and wanted to find a way to connect with her. "I'll never judge you for your actions with Universal. After all, I allowed my parents to turn me into a monster."

"It's not quite the same. You didn't know any better, because you were raised into that. I knew better. It wasn't until he hosted a damn Nightmare that I admitted I was doing the wrong thing. I needed something *that* extreme."

"I needed Orica to die before my eyes, killed by the assassins and Nightmares that were after me. We both needed huge shocks to our systems to jolt us into action. We're still working our way out of the mire. Slowly, but surely."

Samar reached out, and Kouji gripped her hand tight. When Samar tugged, it took Kouji a moment to understand. She got up and sat down next to Samar, who leaned in and wrapped an arm around Kouji's waist with a sigh.

Kouji froze for a moment, as a strange, soothing feeling washed over her. This was amazing! She laid her cheek in Samar's short hair. The simple scent of her vanilla shampoo was relaxing. They ate breakfast like that. Best breakfast ever.

Then, they sparred for a couple of hours, showered, and went out. They saw a movie and had lunch at a restaurant. Perfect.

Samar was on a mellow high during her patrol, even though Nightmares would ruin it the first chance they got. Still, she enjoyed the feeling while it lasted. Spending the day with Kouji was satisfying. The gentle contact they had throughout the day made her skin itch for more at night. She yearned for each touch, no matter how innocent. Samar feared she might go crazy if she didn't touch or feel Kouji again soon. *I might be addicted.*

Wanting such simple things was ridiculous. She had never craved company in such a way, and she was driven to distraction. Might explain how she ended up surrounded.

"You really don't learn, huh?" Samar put her hand out and her short spear appeared in her grip.

"Give us the Abomination!" The Nightmare's words sounded like a hiss. It loomed over a man wearing a fancy jogging suit. If he was willing to host a Nightmare, he was probably looking to do more than a late-night jog.

"The Abomination?" Samar had no idea what the Nightmare was talking about. It didn't matter. She didn't negotiate with Nightmares.

"The thing from the tomb," another Nightmare chimed in. Its open mouth revealed a void that might swallow her whole. A small, young woman hosted the gaping mouth. She was likely running a scam. Pretending to need help would lure people into isolated areas of Okunkun, where the pair could rob them at gunpoint. The crime was popular before Samar cleaned up the park.

"How about I put this thing in your neck?" Samar held up Amani. White smoke fumed from the holy symbols on the blade.

Six Nightmares roared at her. Samar stood her ground, unafraid. They converged on her and her training took over. Larger groups weren't the problem they liked to think they were. Samar always found a chance to place a Favor on someone, purge the host, then dispatch the Nightmare.

Of course, that didn't mean she'd leave unscathed. This time, she ended up sliced across her chest and leg. Usually, she'd wait until she was home and let Kouji heal her, but she was leaking. Bad. She went to the medical office in Moonless Night Headquarters.

Stitched, bandaged, and refusing pain meds, Samar made her way to Evinia's office for some help keeping up with her finances. She was supporting another person now.

"Vin," Samar called as she entered her sister's office. Her voice was weaker than she liked.

Evinia was typing on her keyboard, eyes focused on her monitor. Samar took a seat and waited for Evinia to finish up. It'd give her time to gather herself.

Samar's leg bounced, anxiety dancing on her nerves. She wanted to go home and be with Kouji, but she reined in the desire. She had some control. There were important matters to take care of first.

"Hey, Sammie," Evinia said in an absent tone, eyes still on her work.

"Reports," Samar reminded Evinia.

"One second."

"Do them for me?" Samar's torso throbbed. She wouldn't be able to focus on the reports.

"I suppose so. I should start charging you for this." Evinia looked up long enough to wink.

"You kinda got all my money, anyway." Samar shrugged.

"I don't have your money. I only keep up with your accounts because you never bother. Good thing one of us does, or you'd never pay rent."

Samar nodded. "I should get better with that."

Evinia arched an eyebrow and glanced at her sideways. "Yeah?"

"I should be more responsible and ready to learn how to live in this city. I should at least learn how to check my bank account. I mean, I trust you, but I'm ready to see things now, as well."

Evinia's eyes sparkled behind her glasses. "Very good. I've never had plans to rob my little sister. I'll show you how to use the app again when I'm done with this. Why am I doing your reports? So you can run back to your cook, while I have to watch my poor baby ducking Daddy?" She threw on an exaggerated pout.

Samar rolled her eyes. "Ha, ha, ha. I'm sure you were listening over the comms when I got jumped, yet again."

"I have to assume it sounded worse than it was since you're sitting here, but it still seemed bad. You went to the medics, right?"

"I did."

"Very good. I didn't even have to nag you. I'm glad. And you want to check your bank account. Look at you growing up." Evinia rubbed Samar's knee.

Samar sucked her teeth. "Cut it out."

"What's got you curious about your money anyway?"

"I spent the money I had around the house and I've been using my card more often," Samar replied.

Evinia tilted her head. "Yeah? On what?"

"Food, I guess." Samar shrugged. Not to mention, Kouji's skates and her clothes. Of course, Kouji would happily walk around in her neck beads and short pants until the end of the world. Then, there were groceries, dining out, and activities.

"Food? Well, I guess for two people now…" Evinia's smirk made it obvious she was aware that money went to more than food. Had she checked Samar's card activity? Well, if she did and disapproved, she hadn't said anything. "Are you comfortable with spending money on your little chef?"

"Yeah," Samar muttered. *Please, don't ask any more questions.*

"Your little chef must be into the expensive ingredients."

"Maybe. Her food is delicious."

Evinia snapped her fingers. "That reminds me. I learned something amusing about your little chef. I knew the name sounded familiar. Didn't you read folktales about someone with the same name?"

Samar blinked. "I didn't think you listened."

"I did, but it wasn't until I looked up the name that I recalled you talking about those things."

"You looked up the name?" Samar forgot Evinia could track down almost anybody with nothing more than their first name. *I opened myself up to this one.* Of course Evinia tried to dig up information on Kouji. She probably didn't understand why she only found old stories.

"Kouji Kataban. I saw all of those myths and stories you studied. I found a little slice of history, but it's so ancient, no one's sure if Kouji Kataban actually existed."

"Tell me about what you found." Samar leaned forward. She had put her hands on hundreds of stories about Kouji, a passion for her since she learned to read. Her mother's library was filled with ancient history, folktales, and religious works.

Samar was eager to hear what Evinia found online. She'd love to just hear someone talking about those things again. These conversations had died with her mother.

"Why?" Evinia asked with a teasing smirk. "This is your life's work."

"Most of my life's work was done reading in a library. Some books were too old for me to touch. Maybe you found something on the internet I've never heard of because it was in a book that was forbidden to me." She hadn't learned any solid historical facts about Kouji and assumed those records were lost. Perhaps, she was wrong.

"You'd figure she'd know this one and talk about it. She's named for the legend, after all. Or maybe the historical figure. Not that I see the point in naming a child after this particular legend."

"Why do you say that?" It was a very common practice in Asale culture to name children after famous figures or important people. Kouji had great feats to her story, despite the ending.

"Kouji's more infamous, really." Evinia tapped her chin.

"Are you going to tell me about it or not?"

Evinia chuckled. "Don't get all huffy. Since you're into history and folklore, you probably know Kouji Kataban was an assassin. A couple of accounts tell how Kouji Kataban assassinated Emperor Carthrone so her father could annex the territory that'd eventually become Asale.

She somehow managed to enter the palace and assassinate the emperor in front of party guests. No one saw her coming or going."

"This I never read. I know about the assassination, but no details. How'd you come across this information?"

Evinia waved the question off. "I take it with a grain of salt. It was pieced together from a bunch of fragmented sources on a website that almost admitted the original language those pieces were in is somewhat of a mystery."

Samar nodded. "Now that I do know. Makes research a struggle. What happened next or even before? Is that the entire legend of these fragments?" What else might be written that she had missed out on? The idea made her itch a little.

"No, she moved so quickly no one could prove it was her, and that's what started the legend."

"How so?" Samar managed to keep the excitement out of her voice, but a buzz traveled down her spine. How she had missed these sorts of discussions.

"Kouji was an emotionless assassin with the ability to move through shadows and haunt nightmares. People claimed to dream of her before they died. I found a sentence claiming she killed someone in his dreams. So many assassin stories. Her victims didn't have time to gasp. Most of them deserved it. Everyone feared her and said she was a demon. Swords couldn't cut her. Arrows went through her. She was supposedly born without a conscience, born numb. Ice ran through her veins. Nothing in the world held any value to her, but her actions extended the kingdom and made people wealthy," Evinia explained.

Samar was posed to disagree. Kouji was sweet to the point she seemed innocent, despite the fact that she'd admitted to being a murderer in her past. She was far from a demon. She had a conscience and regret. Sorrow showed in her lilac eyes when she talked about the past. Though she smiled outwardly, it seemed she wept on the inside. Samar had been crying on the inside ever since she lost her mother. The only thing that stopped the tears was talking to the tomb, the only thing she trusted in the whole forsaken city.

"That's not really a lot of information. I was hoping for new things."

Evinia shrugged. "It was mostly fragments and I'm paraphrasing, as well as filling in the blanks. The information is all bits and pieces of old books, pottery fragments, and translations of translations. I'm sure you've read the epic poem about Kouji though."

"I've read many epic poems about her. They were written in the classical period over two thousand years removed from the times they talk about. She's painted more as warrior than assassin. Later poems and plays make her more tragic, but always a legend."

Evinia nodded. "A poem I found was so eventful and colorful. I wish they'd taught it in school. It has everything you need in a story."

"Which one did you read?"

"*The Dawn of Midnight.*"

Samar nodded. "That one is excellent. A true classic." It was one of the first she had ever read. She practically knew it by heart.

"Yes, I didn't appreciate it when you first came here and were so eager to discuss it."

Samar had learned, early on, to shut up about her studies and interests. No one wanted to hear. "You had a lot going on."

"I did, but now I've read it. It paints such a vivid picture of Day and Night and how Usuku was arrogant over how the humans loved him above Asiku. His superiority boastings drove her to the arms of a human who did love her in ways the Day never could. I didn't expect an ancient epic poem to tell a beautiful love story. Not to mention understand and lay out the nuances of how relationships can grow to become toxic like Usuku and Asiku."

"*Dawn of Midnight* has more details than other epics, but that doesn't mean it's right."

"Well, it's mythology and folklore. There's no actual right."

Samar sighed. She'd had this discussion with Evinia before. The stories were more than mythology and folklore. "There's still a living religion attached to it."

Evinia made a meaningless hand gesture. "But Kouji isn't connected to the religion, so again, mythology and folklore."

Samar shrugged. "The living religion has roots in the origin story, but continue. I'm glad you're interested now." Sharing history with Vin made her feel a little less alone. She wasn't sure why.

"I remember you talking about Nightmares when you first came. The poem gets into the origins of Nightmares. Asiku felt underappreciated by humans and gods. She left the Other World to come to ours. During this time, it was always daytime, and humans seemed pleased by this. The situation incensed Asiku."

Samar nodded. "Yes."

"She met a simple carpenter, who was extra pissed over the sun never setting. He wasn't able to sleep, and it began to ruin his work.

Not to mention, food was harder to get because constant sunlight ruined the crops. He was the first to pray for the Night to return. Asiku appeared to him, and they started a conversation. Then she was always with him."

"There's a cute story that focuses on just them. Asiku pretends to be human. My mother used to read it to me as a bedtime story."

A small smile settled on Evinia's face. "I might look it up for more. The poem gives it good focus to set the stage, but I wouldn't mind a deeper look. Anyway, thanks to the carpenter's appreciation, Asiku brought back the night and humans learned to appreciate it. Of course, Usuku was outraged by humans now thinking the night was as equally important as the day. Making matters worse, he found out Asiku had married her carpenter and refused to return to the Other World."

"Yes, and the story gets sad."

"It does." Evinia's expression dropped for a moment. "Her divine husband wasn't happy being replaced by a lowly human. One can only imagine the shame. His rage mounted when he found out the meager human had impregnated Asiku. He killed her human husband, reducing the man to mere ashes which blew away in the wind. He demanded Asiku return to the Other World, but she went into hiding. Three days after she gave birth to her baby, her husband found her. The King of the Other World snatched the baby from her, leaving little Kouji with humans of questionable morals. He lied to Asiku to get her back to the Other World."

"Day refused to yield to Night, but Night also refused to yield to Day."

Evinia nodded. "I figured they were going for something like that. But they have to sync up. Each needs the other to exist."

"But Usuku wasn't done."

"Oh no, he wasn't. The other gods weren't happy with the way Usuku resolved things, but they begged their queen to stay. The Other World was off balance with her absence. Usuku decided to make everything fear and hate the night."

"Unleashing Nightmares onto the world."

"You always made it sound like Nightmares were physical things, but the poem makes it seem like they're the things that disturb our dreams. They make us not want to sleep, meaning we're wasting our night and harming ourselves."

Samar sighed. "Two things can be true. Usuku wanted to show that, when given the chance, humans would consume each other.

Asiku thought her human husband understood her and cared more than Usuku. He wanted to prove her wrong."

"The more I read, the more I was sorry I never sat down and had a conversation with you about these things. These aren't just your interests, but it's also your religion and culture. It's a huge part of you." Evinia squeezed Samar's thigh.

"You got there just because I'm friends with a person named Kouji?" She should've been happy for the leap, but it was such a leap, she couldn't help her curiosity.

Evinia scoffed. "As an intellectual, you have to know it's sometimes the smallest thing that leads to the biggest realization. I want you to be aware, I don't reject those things with you. You can talk to me about them."

Samar twisted her mouth up. "When I tried to talk to you about Nightmares before, you said I was being superstitious." It hurt. She expected words like that from any other person in Oganja, but not her sister.

Evinia offered her a sorrowful smile and rubbed her knee again. "I'm sorry. I was being ignorant at the time. I want to know more about this. Is naming a child Kouji popular in Asale? I've never met a Kouji here."

"You've met a Kou, I'm sure. That name is popular and comes from Kouji. I'm not sure why the ji was dropped over time. So what did you think once the poem actually shifted to discuss Kouji?"

Evinia blew out a breath. "It was a lot."

"If you think so, you should try reading the other poems and stories. Kouji has been through it all."

"Yet never comes across as a hero, I read."

"Well, hard to be a hero if you have no emotions. One of the main things you're supposed to take from the story is a parent's responsibility for their child's well-being. Children will become what you give them."

"Yes, and Kouji's parents gave her nothing and exploited her divine powers. She was raised with no morality, as though it were unnecessary, and she was used to assassinate humans. There were a lot of adventures, but in the end, Kouji was still a stone-cold murderer. It's said she sometimes smiled as she worked, but that was the most emotion she ever showed. The poem goes into great depth about the horrific deeds and the carnage Kouji left behind with a smile on her face."

"Usuku used Kouji as proof of how humans had fallen, while Asiku lamented what her child had been turned into."

"She had reason. According to the story, Kouji's adoptive parents were pure evil. Usuku left Kouji with them on purpose. Kouji obeyed them without question though."

"As children were expected to do."

"The poem makes it sound like Kouji wanted to believe her parents were just, but knew in her heart, this wasn't the case."

"The heart recognizes love, people who care for you, and those who don't." Another lesson that was meant to be learned from the poem. *Trust your heart.*

Evinia nodded. "Kouji expected her parents to love her as parents are meant to love and care for children. I think it's funny because the poem makes a point of making us understand dark and night aren't bad things but then always describes Kouji in such a negative way. The same with the parents."

"It might be to let us understand that both night and day have good and bad aspects. In the beginning, we got to see the good things that Day gave us, but then it became too much. Night isn't what we expect, but then Kouji becomes what we do expect of Darkness."

Evinia grinned. "This is cool to discuss with you. Kouji's illusion of her parents was shattered when assassins entered their palace. To avoid their own deaths, her parents pretended to be commoners and gave up Kouji's servant as her mother. The assassins murdered her."

"Oh, you didn't read the version of this that's worse."

"There's a worse one?"

"Before the assassins come, Kouji's parents get into a big argument over a money issue. In a rage, her father struck her mother with the closest thing at hand, which unfortunately, was a marble statue about a foot long. Kouji saw him kill her and couldn't comprehend what that meant. Spouses are meant to protect each other. Then the assassins show up, so Kouji gets a crash course in how murder is wrong and hurts tons of people, all in one night."

"Damn."

"Yeah, it's supposed to let us know that no matter how awful we've become, we can break out of it and become good people…or that'd be the theme if we had the ending of the poem. It's speculated Kouji learns her lesson in the end."

Evinia sucked her teeth. "I hate that so many of these poems don't have endings. In that poem, does Kouji also happen to suffer a psychotic break, killing not only the assassins, but everyone in the palace?"

"The breakdown happens in a few versions of the story, but not all. Depends on how much action the author is going for," Samar answered with a laugh.

"This author obviously wanted it all. Servants, guests, even pets weren't spared, including Kouji's own pet monkey. It says Kouji set the palace on fire, then sat down in the flames only to find she didn't feel the heat and didn't burn. She screamed to the heavens to let her die. She invoked the patron goddess of the palace — Asiku. What are the odds?" Evinia chuckled.

Samar laughed as well. "Fair if you're telling an exciting story. Being beseeched allowed Asiku to finally meet the daughter she hadn't seen since she was three days old. The gods are meant to answer our prayers if we're in true need. If they don't come, it means you're meant to carry yourself, and the obstacle can be overcome if you put in enough effort. Sometimes the gods test your support system to let you know if you've surrounded yourself with good and proper people."

"Well, it's clear Kouji didn't have a good or proper support system. Asiku came. Kouji wept on the goddess, begging for her nightmare to end. Asiku refused to give in to Kouji's request, saying Kouji would have to earn her place in the Other World. She laid Kouji to rest in a land the Sun was never allowed to touch, which sounds like Asiku killed Kouji to me. Supposedly, Kouji will rise to commit some grand act that allows her to go to the Other World." Evinia's brow wrinkled. "Does this mean anyone who is part divine goes to the Other World rather than the Afterlife?"

"It depends. It's like some demigods have abilities and others just happen to be very clever or lucky."

"Kouji was neither."

Samar nodded. "It just depends."

"I was confused by the ending. What's the meaning? It seems like Asiku actually killed Kouji, like she wanted."

"No. It's about how you can be redeemed, if you actually have remorse and patience."

"The end of the poem, or where the poem cuts off anyway, was weird. Asiku demanded Usuku remove Nightmares from Earth since Kouji was gone. Usuku refused. Then, Asiku curses the Other World, promising Kouji would spark the change when she redeemed herself. Spark what change?"

Samar rubbed her hands together. "There's a lot of theories about what that means. I go with the idea that it means you have to be the change you're looking for, but also as a parent, you have the responsibility to teach your child the changes you want to see in the world. I'm really surprised you read all of this."

Evinia shook her head. "You know how I am with information once I let it take hold. I'll do some more reading. I'm intrigued. Is your Kouji anything like the Kouji from the stories and poems?"

Samar smiled. "My Kouji is kind, warm, and loving. She likes to cuddle and cook."

"And you said you cook together?"

"Sometimes."

"I do that with Mechi. I enjoy it. I also enjoyed this." Evinia motioned between the two of them. "I'm going to make it a point to do this more with you, but not here. We have to hang out more outside of work."

Samar smiled. "I'd love to discuss this and more with you. Hell, might even convert you."

Evinia chuckled. "I doubt it, but you can try. Go home and enjoy your hot meal and company. You deserve it."

Samar grinned, elation popping through her veins. She hugged Evinia before rushing out of the office. Evinia yelped, then laughed.

Chapter Seventeen

Good Night

KOUJI CHECKED THE TIME. Samar should be home any second. The idea made her giddy. Samar's presence made her giddy. The idea being able to make Samar happy made her giddy. And the big snack Kouji prepared would definitely make Samar happy. Kouji was sure of it.

"Kou," Samar called as she entered the apartment.

"Right on time." Kouji stepped out of the kitchen to greet Samar face to face.

Samar's brow wrinkled as she shoved the door closed. "For what?"

"To die of food poisoning with me. I made fried fish balls."

Samar's face didn't change. "And?"

With a grin, Kouji wiggled her eyebrows. "I made it all by myself. My mother didn't help. I'm scared to try it alone."

"You're such a coward." Samar laughed.

"There are worse things to be. Let's eat, then pray." Kouji returned to the kitchen to fix their servings.

"I think we're supposed to pray, then eat." Samar hung her jacket in the closet and peeled off her pullovers. Freed from layers of clothing, she reached into a long stretch.

Kouji had to tear her eyes away from Samar, trying to focus on putting food into small bowls. Something about the way Samar moved called to her, and her gaze drifted right back.

Samar tossed her two hoodies in the hamper. She made a show of inhaling the food's aroma.

"Does it smell good?" Kouji chuckled.

"You have to be joking about the food poisoning and prayer because it smells perfect. I haven't had these in so long. Fried fish balls are the perfect way to end this night."

"With some healing too." Kouji motioned to the torn and bloody shirt.

Samar glanced down at herself. "Oh yes. Nightmares have gotten a bit tough as of late."

Kouji scowled. What if Nightmares continued to grow in power until it was impossible for Samar to fight them? That wouldn't do. She wouldn't allow Nightmares to take Samar from her.

"I'm so hungry." Samar groaned as she rushed off to get the dining mat.

"We can eat. Let me heal you."

Samar nodded. The healing session was quick, so they could focus on the food. Kouji had gathered the sauces and tea that tended to go with this meal, but Samar surveyed the food as if something was wrong.

"Did I mess up to the point you can see it?" Kouji asked.

"No, but in my culture, this is served in a communal bowl. You pluck out the ones you want to eat."

Kouji nodded. "Oh. I'm used to everything being served individually. Is the tea right with this?"

A bright smile lit up Samar's face. "Tea is right with anything."

Relieved, Kouji waited while Samar picked up one crunchy fish ball. She examined it with a twist of her wrist, then popped it in her mouth. Kouji was fascinated. She craved Samar's thoughts on her cooking, but she was also drawn to the way Samar's mouth moved. *I want to know what those lips taste like.*

"How is it?" Kouji asked, only to get her mind off Samar's mouth. Her insides flipped and fluttered.

Samar eyes sparkled in a way that she probably wouldn't believe. "It melted in my mouth. It's the perfect balance of crunchy outside and soft inside. You seasoned the potatoes just right. I've never had fish balls this delicious. You're an incredible cook."

Kouji straightened up, spine perfect and shoulders squared. "I'm getting better. I like it. Make sure you try the sauces too."

Samar nodded and dipped fish ball in the red sauce. Kouji watched how carefully she chewed, savoring the flavor. Her tongue darted out to get a little dot of sauce at the corner of her mouth, and Kouji swallowed hard. Would she be able to taste her cooking if she touched those wonderous lips with her own? She unconsciously licked her own bottom lip.

"Are you going to eat or just stare at me? You see you don't need to pray after all," Samar said with an arched eyebrow.

A sheepish laugh escaped Kouji. "Oh yeah." She was more than able to both eat and stare. It was a habit at this point. Still, her cheeks burned from a blush.

Kouji quickly covered a first fish ball in hot sauce and popped it in her mouth. Delicious, not quite how she remembered them, but better still. The company probably made it so. She didn't take her eyes off Samar. She liked to watch Samar, regardless of what Samar did.

Watching Samar was her favorite pastime, beating out cooking by a wide berth.

"Um, Kou," Samar trailed off, dipping a fish ball in black sauce without saying more.

"Yeah?" Kouji briefly ducked her head. She thought she'd been caught staring again, but silence followed. She could see Samar was troubled. Her eyebrows were scrunched up, her face pinched. Something was wrong. "Is it the food? Did it make you sick? I shouldn't have done this on my own. I'm so sorry!"

Panic gripped Kouji. She had no idea what to do. She looked for a spot to put her food down. It didn't register just to put it in front of her.

Samar held up a hand. "It's not the food," she assured Kouji with a small smile. "It's touching you worry about me so much though."

Kouji frowned. "Of course, I worry about you. I care about you. If not the food, then what?" She searched Samar's face, trying to figure out what she might've done to bother her.

A wobbly smile settled on Samar's face. "You're the only friend I have. I mean, there's Koko and his special band of trauma-ward morons. I can't really talk to them, if you noticed. They weren't so bad when I skated, but that's all they care about. They're not really my friends, not like you are…"

Kouji nodded. "I'm aware of that. You already said this when I was sleeping. You told me about how they made fun of your accent. You said only Universal would listen…" She bit back a frown. *What a fool. He had a gem and tossed her away for wretched power he was all too aware she wouldn't let him have, power she warned him against.*

Samar smiled and reached over, touching Kouji's bare knee. "Yes, but I was wrong. You listened to every word, way better than Universal, even when I was whining or so hurt that I wanted to cry. I only…I only wish you'd open up to me like I did to you."

Kouji tilted her head. "I have opened up to you. You know more about me than anyone, save my mother. And you have to remember, you opened up to the tomb."

Samar pouted and looked away. "*I guess…*" she mumbled in Jinoi.

Kouji frowned. Samar was upset and this wouldn't do, not while they shared a space and had tasty food in front of them. She'd tell Samar anything she wanted to know.

Once Within a Dream

"What do...what do you want to know?" Kouji asked with a tremble in her voice. She wasn't sure what she had left, but whatever it was, what if it sent Samar away?

Samar offered her a small smile. "Tell me how you feel."

"About what?"

"About everything."

Kouji wasn't quite sure she followed. "Well, let's see...I feel very close to my mother. I like her a lot. I like you a lot. I like dreaming about things that don't involve fire. I'm not really a big fan of fire anymore. I understand it has its place, but I'd like it to stay out of my dreams..."

"Because you burned your house down and waited to die?"

"Well, yes, but don't forget, I first killed my father and anyone else around. I think I killed a messenger mid-sentence." Kouji tapped her chin. "It's still a blur. It's like I was in a trance that day, so I might've killed more people, aside from the ones I mentioned."

Samar nodded. "Why did you call on your mother to rip your soul from your body?" Her voice was gentle, kind.

Kouji blew out a long breath. "I *felt* for the first time, and I didn't like what I felt. Pain. Disgust. Pure agony. I couldn't understand it at all, and I thought I'd go mad if I had to keep feeling like I did. I begged the goddess of the Dark because she's also in charge of the damned. She was the only goddess with the power to do what I wanted. It was out of everyone else's hands."

"Was it seeing your adoptive mother get killed that made you feel as you did?" Samar asked.

"I think feeling happened in stages. I saw my father murder my mother and came to understand they weren't who they were supposed to be. I witnessed Orica's murder. It was so much. Too much."

"You loved your parents?"

Kouji rubbed her forehead. "They were parents. I had to at least like them, right? Something inside of me wanted to like them. I think you'd disagree, huh?"

"Yeah," she answered with a stiff laugh. "You don't care that they used you and raised you like they did?"

With a sigh, Kouji shrugged. "You can only expect so much from wicked people."

"I'll take your word on that. Should I have limited expectations of you?" she asked with a teasing smile and a little pinch to Kouji's thigh.

Kouji chuckled. "If you should, I'll have to go back to sleep because it means I haven't changed. I want to believe I've changed. I want to change. It's tough realizing your every mistake. It's even tougher trying to correct those mistakes or wondering if they can be corrected."

"I still trust you." Samar rubbed Kouji's knee.

Kouji's eyes drifted to the hand on her knee before returning to Samar's face. "Do you?"

"What's not to trust?" Samar posed with a shrug and smile.

"Well, I'm going to start with my crazy story," Kouji replied with an awkward shrug. She was warmed by the trust Samar had in her. This was going well, especially considering who she was. Life had never been this amazing.

"Your cooking makes up for any lie you might ever tell me."

Kouji laughed. "It's not that good."

Samar shrugged. "It's getting better every day. I'm glad you're not upset that I asked."

"I'm not sure you could do much to upset me, except push me away. If you want to know about me, I'll tell you. I know everything about you, so it's only fair for you to know about me. Feelings are harder for me because of my upbringing, but I'll do my best to share them with you. The telling may hurt both of us."

"I'll do my best to continue to share with you as well."

"What brought on the question?"

Samar ate another fish ball. "My sister. Evinia read one of the epic poems about you."

Kouji nodded and ate her own fish ball. "It's still odd to find out there's writing about me."

"Volumes. My sister found it interesting. She couldn't figure out why it wasn't more popular. Of course, it's popular in Asale. She thought it was unusual that your name is the same as the legendary warrior in the poem. She's unaware you're very popular in Asale and in surrounding countries. Your name's popular in those places. She talked about that legend and how everybody thought you were a demon. She got to see that you're in history books for killing the emperor. On your father's orders?"

Kouji shrugged. "Yeah."

"Why?"

"My father and the emperor never really got along. I think my father always coveted the emperor's land. Then, the emperor tried to seduce my mother. She told my father, who told me maybe it was time for a new emperor. I didn't care much about the man, about most men. My parents wanted him gone, so I made that happen. It all seemed so simple at the time."

"Is life still simple?"

"No, not at all." But she'd rather sort out emotions and memories with Samar than return to that simple life.

"Why not?"

Blowing out a breath, Kouji ran her hand through her braids. "Well, thinking for myself is quite new. Then, there's the fact that I'm feeling stuff again. I'm not sure how to deal with it, but I definitely don't want to run from it."

"What are you feeling?" she asked in a quiet tone.

Kouji twiddled her fingers together. "I'm unsure how to describe it. I've never felt this way before. I do like it though."

Samar nodded, but her brow wrinkled, as if she didn't know what Kouji meant. Kouji wasn't quite sure what she meant. *Does Samar feel the same way or even close to the things I feel?* She never wanted to leave. She wanted to stay by Samar's side for the rest of her life.

Kouji dared to hope their little routine would go on for all eternity, changing more slowly than evolution allowed. They might always be friends. She didn't care if she had to stress over emotions for the rest of her life. She only wanted to always be with Samar. *You should say that. She wants to know how you feel.*

How do I put this into words? What am I actually feeling? It is wholly pleasant and welcomed. Is this love? Kouji knew of love in the abstract sense, mostly thanks to stories. She loved her goddess mother. She'd go as far as saying she loved Samar. Was she in love though? She had no idea.

She was also aware of lust, at least in the abstract sense. She had never felt it before and didn't understand it in the slightest. But something buzzed just under her skin that made her want to touch Samar, kiss Samar, and all the more.

Could the closeness and the buzzy need to touch coexist? Did she have to pick one? She could hardly differentiate between the two. Was it love or lust that made her want to touch, kiss, and hold Samar? How did people understand what was going on with them internally? She was so lost.

"Do you like the fish balls?" Kouji asked, unsure of what else to say.

"They're great," Samar replied.

Kouji nodded and ate another. *Now what?* "Oh, I bought cookies today, when I went to the store."

"What kind?" Samar asked.

"I remember you saying chocolate chip are the best kind. I thought we'd share those whenever you want. Plus, I want to try hot chocolate with you. What do you think?"

Samar smiled. "Sounds perfect. We should do that and watch something for a little while. I'm going to go take a shower. Did you take a shower today?"

"Yes, I did, before you came in. I also took the liberty of cleaning your bathroom." Bathing hadn't been a daily thing in Kouji's earlier existence. She was getting into the habit now.

"Thank you so much. You're such a darling." Samar blinked and shook her head, turning her focus back to the remaining fish balls. She rushed off to the bathroom right after. Kouji wasn't sure what just happened, but she shook it off.

Samar groaned in the safety of the bathroom. The word darling couldn't have possibly left her mouth. It simply wasn't possible.

"What's going on with me?" Samar asked the air. She knew the answer all too well. The problem was that she wasn't sure if Kouji felt the same and refused to risk things if she didn't. *Which is why I want to know about her feelings.*

Samar shook the thought away. It didn't matter. Kouji was probably still processing her previous life. She didn't need Samar trying to make things harder with complicated emotions.

"Do not add to her troubles. Enjoy her as you have her. You understand life is short and can end at any given time. Be happy with what you have," Samar told herself.

She allowed the hot water to wash away her heavy emotions and focused on gratitude. She had someone who cooked for her, who cleaned her bathroom, and who was glad to tour the city with her. They read together, talked, and practiced their martial arts together. This was so much more than enough.

Proof waited when she got out of the shower. Kouji sat, smiling, on the sofa, with hot chocolate and cookies on the coffee table. Samar grabbed her laptop and sat down.

"So many sweets before bed," Samar sighed and shook her head.

Kouji grinned. "It's okay to be bad every now and then."

"True."

Kouji giggled and grabbed her cup of hot chocolate. She downed a massive gulp, apparently forgetting the hot part. The steam puffing up from the cup had to be a clue. Kouji coughed and held her throat. *So, she can feel hot.*

"I can't believe you did that." Samar reached out, caressing Kouji's cheek.

Kouji let out a long breath. "I didn't think it'd be that hot." She wheezed and tried to draw in another deep breath.

"You're the one who made it," Samar pointed out with a chuckle.

Kouji shook her head, coughing once again. She wiped away a tear. "I must look so silly."

"I promise, you're fine. You look fine." Samar meant that.

"I'd believe you if you weren't laughing. I almost died and you think it's funny." Kouji threw on an exaggerated pout, poking out her lip.

Samar laughed harder. "Where in the world did you learn that expression?"

Kouji shrugged and Samar chuckled more. She sipped her chocolate and Kouji got past her "near-death experience." Kouji loved chocolate chip cookies almost as much as Samar did, and they ate all of the cookies in one sitting.

"That was amazing." Kouji wiped a crumb from her lips.

"And funny." Samar smirked.

Kouji twisted her mouth as if offended, and Samar patted her knee as an apology. Suddenly, Samar yawned.

"I should go to bed."

"I'm sure you're tired. It had to take a lot out of you to laugh at my near-death experience."

Samar laughed more and tried to help clean up, but Kouji stopped her with a glare. Samar held her hands up in surrender.

"Bed, now." Kouji tilted her chin to the bed.

"I can help. It's nothing to take dishes to the sink."

"So you can let me do it. Go to bed."

Samar didn't put up a fight. She slid into bed, trying to get comfortable. She heard Kouji puttering around the apartment, and running water in the sink meant she was washing the dishes. After a couple of minutes, the lights went out and it was quiet.

Something was off. Samar should've been able to fall asleep in the quiet, but it still wouldn't come. This wasn't normal. She sat up and saw Kouji tilt her head to the side.

"Had a dream about my near-death experience and want to laugh about it more?" Kouji asked from her space on the couch. A hint of a pout was on her face.

Samar rolled her eyes but got an idea. "Kou," she said with a yawn.

"What?"

"Stop being a baby. Come here."

"What?"

"Come here. I'm cold."

The pout vanished from Kouji's face, and her eyebrows shot up. Samar laid back down, knowing Kouji would take her up on the invitation. She closed her eyes as Kouji slid into bed.

They had taken to sharing the bed a few days ago. It was awkward initially because Samar was unsure how to get Kouji to wrap around her when she was cold. Cold was a flimsy excuse, but they went with it every time.

With Kouji pressed against her back and an arm draped around Samar's waist, she ran her fingers across Kouji's hand. Samar gasped when Kouji sighed and nuzzled her face into Samar's neck.

"Sorry," Kouji mumbled, but she didn't move. "I couldn't resist."

"It's okay. I like it when you're this close."

"Yeah?"

"Yes."

"Good, because I like the way you smell. It's like fresh water and crisp air. So pure," Kouji whispered.

"I'm not…I like how you smell too. Jasmine reminds me of home."

"I had a little clue. That first week you kept smelling me."

Samar stiffened. "You knew? How embarrassing!"

"I noticed. I was glad you were so interested in me." Kouji tightened her hold around Samar's waist.

"Yeah?"

"I'm interested in you too," Kouji told her with a yawn.

"Oh…" Samar muttered with a yawn of her own. She wanted Kouji to talk about how she felt earlier, not now. Samar prepared to say something, but Kouji's breathing went to a steady, calm pace. Kouji was asleep. It was always a surprise at how quickly and easily Kouji fell asleep.

Samar relaxed, as she always did with Kouji so close. She listened to Kouji breathing for a few minutes, feeling Kouji's heart beating against her back. This would be a soothing habit if they continued to share a bed.

Over the past few days, they'd enjoyed the touching that came along with sharing a bed, but none of the touches got too personal. They were hyper-aware that neither of them was accustomed to being touched, so they tried not to overdo it. They had no desire to mess things up in any way. Neither was used to being content and they wanted the feeling to last.

Mom, I wish you got to meet her. You'd like Kouji. That simple thought made it easy to go to sleep, at ease and relaxed.

Samar slept only a couple of hours before waking again. She looked around, on high alert. Had something forced her from her sleep? Nothing noticeable. No Nightmares. No one was trying to force their way in. Hell, there wasn't even a breeze to knock something over.

Why did I wake up now? She checked her watch. It wasn't even noon, way too early. She groaned in a low tone to avoid disturbing Kouji. *Why the hell did I jolt out of sleep like that? Hope I can get back to sleep easily.* She yawned and settled back into her pillow, then became alert again.

Oh. She glanced at her chest and saw Kouji's hand had wandered from its usual spot at her waist. The strong hand now cupped Samar's small breast. She held in a chuckle. *So she's a little naughty in her sleep.*

As if on cue, Kouji flexed her hand. *More than a little naughty.* Kouji was still asleep, but her hand seemed quite aware of what she wanted as she gave Samar's breast a gentle squeeze. The tingle was almost unbearable.

Thankfully, her small yelp of surprise didn't wake Kouji. Samar certainly didn't mind the sweet attention from the demigod. *I'd like her to try something like that when she's conscious.*

Samar covered Kouji's hand with her own, partially to let Kouji know the touch was all right if she woke up. And hopefully, to keep that hand from moving away.

The intimate touch made Samar yearn for so much more. Was it wrong to desire more? She didn't think so, especially since Kouji seemed to want the same, at least subconsciously. Samar reminded herself it was enough for now and fell back to sleep with little problem.

Kouji woke first, as she tended to do. She was ready to start her day and put together a worthwhile breakfast, but something was amiss. There was a wonderful softness pressed into her palm, much different from Samar's taut muscles. *What is going on here?* She gulped as she peeked over Samar's shoulder.

A rush of negative emotions flooded Kouji. How dare she take advantage of Samar's trust? What type of woman was she to grope someone in their sleep? To touch someone in such a manner without their permission? This sort of behavior was cheap and demeaning. Samar was a treasure. *I do not have the right to touch her like this without her consent.*

For all those thoughts, Kouji didn't move her hand. She liked the way Samar's breast felt against her palm, even with the t-shirt between them. And she couldn't move her hand without waking Samar, whose tight grip held Kouji's hand in place. *Did she cover my hand unconsciously, or does she seriously not want me to move my hand?* She hoped it was the latter, but she'd never be sure.

Kouji's was certain her heart would break her ribs and escape her chest with how heavy it pounded. What was she supposed to do? She couldn't yank her hand away. She didn't want to shock Samar out of sleep, only to have to explain why. But it wouldn't be right to leave her hand be.

"Samar," Kouji whispered in her ear with the hope that Samar would let go of her without fully waking up.

"Hmm..." was Samar's only response.

"Samar," Kouji whispered again.

Samar made a small noise that sounded like a purr and it vibrated through Kouji. She hated to admit her desire to hear Samar make the noise again. This brought back her confusion on love and lust. Kouji liked Samar as an individual, as her friend. She always wanted to make Samar happy. Samar made her happy by paying her attention and accepting her for who she was. Samar took her as a whole, flaws and all. If only she could leave things at that, at the level of two friends, then Kouji believed she wouldn't feel so bad.

The lust Kouji was aware existed inside of her made her feel terrible. Could she both love someone and lust after them? Samar had said it was wrong when she learned that her father had lusted after many women. Was it impossible to love and lust for only one person?

That train of thought was thrown off completely, as Samar turned around and faced her. Kouji's breath hitched with fear. What if Samar had noticed?

Kouji breathed a sigh of relief. Samar was still sleeping. Kouji tried to figure out how to separate from Samar without waking her. Sleeping Samar had other ideas. She snuggled her head under Kouji's chin and rubbed her face against Kouji's neck. Her pulse racing, Kouji shuddered from the contact. While they had shared the bed a number of times, they had never faced each other in their sleep. At least the new position solved one problem. Her hand was no longer on Samar's breast. Good thing.

Not the best though. Kouji's hand was now on Samar's lower back and getting lower by the second without any command from her brain. *What the hell is happening? Stop doing this, you idiot.*

Kouji found herself too curious to cease, dying to know what it'd be like to press Samar to her and cling to her. Certain, her hand continued its journey of its own accord and eventually rested on Samar's rump. She noticed how fleshy the area was and wanted to learn more. Kouji was ready to explore before Samar moaned a little. Kouji was sure her heart stopped. Samar pressed herself closer and quietly groaned Kouji's name. Kouji gulped.

"By the great gods that came before me, what am I supposed to do now?" Kouji wondered aloud.

Her hand seemed to have an idea of what she should be doing, but Kouji didn't think it was a good idea. All thought went out the window when Samar brushed her lips against Kouji's neck. A warm sensation spread through Kouji's body. *I'd better wake her up before something else happens.* She shook Samar very gently until she stirred and her eyes fluttered open. She stared at Kouji for a long moment with a dreamy smile. In that moment, Kouji allowed herself to imagine Samar meant the expression, meant this cuddling, and meant to bring Kouji this feeling.

Chapter Eighteen

Sweet Dreams

SAMAR WAS FOGGY. WHY did Kouji wake her? *Wait, can she see into my dreams? Her mother is the Goddess of Night and gave Kouji god-like powers, so it's possible.* She hoped it wasn't true. Kouji didn't need to see what was happening in Samar's mind, and Samar didn't want to explain those images. She took a moment to gather herself.

"It's time to wake up already?" she asked with a yawn.

Kouji stammered, her mouth making sounds, but not words. "Actually…um…it's not…but… um…"

Was witnessing Samar's dream why Kouji was so tongue-tied? *Oh no, I stole her innocence, and not in a way for us to enjoy.* Samar tried to play it cool and not make things more awkward. "But what?" she inquired in a sleepy tone, still yawning.

"I…um…wanted to talk to you?" Kouji offered with an uneasy shrug.

Samar gulped and took a breath to keep her voice steady. "About what? Can it wait?" She tried to steel herself for questions about her dream.

"I guess it could."

Samar breathed a sigh of relief. Kouji's abilities must not include seeing into dreams if talking about it could wait. "Then why didn't it?" she asked with calculated innocence.

"No idea?" Kouji answered with a stiff shrug.

Samar's brow furrowed. How was the product of an immoral family such a terrible liar? Apparently, lying was harder than killing people, at least for this assassin with the face of an angel. But did that mean Kouji knew what Samar had been dreaming about? Her brain was too foggy to figure it out. She needed to go back to sleep.

"Huh? You're being silly." Samar was already practically asleep again. She settled back into Kouji, who tensed up. That got Samar's attention. "Am I making you uncomfortable?"

"No."

Samar scowled. "You're lying. You want me to move?"

"Closer to me, if possible," Kouji mumbled under her breath.

Samar definitely wasn't meant to hear that comment, but how could she not? Kouji's lips were almost touching her ear. She held in a gasp, which was fortuitous as Kouji continued talking.

"No, you're all right where you are," Kouji said.

"Then why are you acting like this?"

"Um…" Kouji obviously didn't want to say what was on her mind. She took a deep breath. "Samar…" she said Samar's name with such reverence.

"Yeah?" Samar answered through a yawn. She'd love to circle back to Kouji holding her closer. They might make it through this. She had to be patient, but she was exhausted. *I'm going to fall asleep.* Questions would have to wait.

Kouji shook her head. "Never mind. Go back to sleep. We'll talk about it later."

"Okay." Samar wouldn't have been able to stay awake for more anyway. She snuggled her face into Kouji's neck without a thought and draped her arm around Kouji's torso. Kouji let out a sweet sigh, as Samar made herself extremely comfortable and sleep took over.

Kouji was ready to melt. Samar had consciously pressed against her, cuddling face to face. Kouji took a moment to adjust, wrapping her arms around Samar in a way that was comfortable for both of them. She stared at Samar in the dark for a long time, appreciating the sight of peace. Samar deserved peace. Kouji wanted to be her peace. *Is it possible for me to be anyone's peace after what I did?* From the way Samar snuggled into her, she was certain Samar believed in her. *I should believe in myself the way she does.*

Kouji wanted to be everything Samar believed her to be, to be this good person Samar thought she had inside of her. She pulled Samar closer. The press of Samar's body reminded her of where her hand had been earlier. *A good person wouldn't have groped her.*

Would a good person want to touch Samar as much as she wanted to? Kouji craved Samar's skin. This was lust. She wasn't sure if lust was appropriate. She'd revere Samar, if allowed, even if she never gained permission to touch.

Her gaze drifted from Samar's entire face to focus on her partially open mouth. What would it be like to kiss her? Kouji had seen kissing, of course, but had never shared a kiss with anyone. She'd never had a desire to do so until now. Honestly, she'd never had the urge to touch another person like she wanted to touch Samar. She'd never wanted someone like she wanted Samar.

She had no idea how to be intimate with anyone and had no real idea how intercourse worked, but she understood that she longed for such intimacy with Samar. She had seen pictures in bathhouses, painted on the walls and tiled in mosaics. She never understood why the images were there, but she always assumed it had something to do with nudity. What if the images were a guide? *Weird to be in a bathhouse, but they might be helpful.*

Helpful how? *You leave Samar alone. She's too virtuous for you.* Samar should be worshipped, not defiled. *Intimacy isn't the same as defiled, nor is intercourse.* That she understood, but for someone like her to touch Samar would be tainting Samar.

Yet her eyes fell to Samar's lips once more. Would she be able to reach Samar's mouth with her own without waking her? She was so tempted to try but held off. She kissed Samar's forehead instead. This simple act was beyond lovely. So much so, Kouji did it again. *I could be content with this.*

Kouji told herself to be content with the simple kiss, but her heart cried out for more. *What am I meant to do?* Everything seemed so complicated.

"I should've asked my mother about this when I started feeling this way about you," Kouji whispered to Samar's sleeping form. "I should've talked to you, but it seems embarrassing. I should already have a hold on such things. What am I supposed to do? Can I have you? Do you want me? And if you do, then what do I do from there?"

Samar shifted in her sleep and lifted her head slightly. Her mouth was suddenly within range, and Kouji's heart thumped hard against her ribs. Temptation was thick in the air. Should she try again? Samar would never know, and Kouji's mind would be at ease with the knowledge of how those lips felt and tasted. Would it be so wrong? Samar would never know and that way would never be angry with her.

Kouji cradled Samar with a gentleness she never knew she possessed, as if Samar was made of glass and Kouji refused to shatter her. Kouji caressed her bare arm lightly and kissed the side of her head. Samar purred in her sleep and cuddled in closer. The action brought a smile to Kouji's face and a comfort she never knew existed.

No, I'll never take anything from her. Kouji would treasure Samar like the precious gem she was, despite the fact she had no clue about how to do that. She'd do her best and die trying to be everything Samar deserved.

"Hmm..." Samar nuzzled Kouji's neck. Maybe she liked the little attention Kouji gave her arm. Samar let out a small sigh and somehow relaxed more.

"Like that, huh? Well, let's try something else," Kouji mused.

Kouji drifted her hand to Samar's stomach. The soft cotton of Samar's tank top was wonderful against her fingers. She resisted the urge to roll the t-shirt between her fingers and touch flesh. Samar softly whimpered in her sleep and wiggled against Kouji's hand.

"Hmm...Kou..." Samar mewed and managed to snuggle closer.

"Amazing. Is she dreaming about me? Is she dreaming about me...touching her?" Kouji wondered. Based on the way Samar said her name and moved with her touch, the idea didn't seem farfetched. Kouji's skin tingled.

She let her fingers creep to the edge of Samar's shirt. She was about to lift the hem, just enough to caress Samar's bare belly. She stopped herself, again, but added a little more pressure to her touch above the t-shirt. She hoped it'd still be comforting, but more noticeable.

Samar moaned and twitched more. She pushed against Kouji's hand, then against her body, as if chasing Kouji's touch. She kissed Kouji's neck and squeezed Kouji in her sleep. *Incredible.*

It was such a shock. The next moan was much louder than before, but it was Kouji. She bit her lip, as if that'd make the sound disappear. Too little, too late. Samar's eyes fluttered open.

"What the?" Samar muttered and locked eyes with Kouji.

Kouji swallowed hard and yanked her hand away. She wasn't sure how to explain any of this. "Uh...I was just trying to make sure you had a pleasant sleep."

Samar's brow furrowed. "What do you mean?"

Kouji's gaze drifted down to her hand. Samar's remained on her face. *Oh, right.* Samar's sight probably hadn't adjusted to the dark to see where Kouji had her hand. She gave a slight press.

"Um...is this okay?" Kouji asked. It seemed okay a moment ago.

Samar's breath caught. "Oh, Kou."

Kouji wasn't sure what that answer meant and shame flooded her entire being. "I'm sorry."

Samar shook her head. "No, don't be. It's okay."

"How?" Kouji asked. None of this should be all right. "I know better."

Samar let loose a low sigh. "I don't think you do."

Kouji's eyebrows knitted close. "No, I do. We've gone over this. I've learned, or I'm learning. Either way, I know better."

Samar offered a small smile. "This wasn't something wrong. I enjoy your touch. I welcome it every time it comes." She took Kouji's hand and placed it back on her abdomen. She rubbed the top of Kouji's hand with hers.

Kouji blinked. "I...um...what?" Her brain didn't comprehend what was happening. She had been wrong for stealing touches while Samar slept, right? Even if Samar was practically in her skin, right?

"I want you to touch me," Samar answered.

Kouji's brain refused to accept these words. "You want me to what?" She must've heard wrong. There was no way Samar would allow her this honor, no way Samar would allow her to defile her perfect form with her soiled presence.

Samar locked eyes with her. "Please, touch me."

"Are you sure?"

"I've wanted you to for a while now."

Again, Kouji was certain her brain was misinterpreting the words coming out of Samar's mouth. Why would Samar want her in such a manner? "But..." Kouji wasn't even sure how to object, and she had no real desire to. She wanted to touch Samar and now she had permission. Something was still wrong though. Her guts twisted.

In an ideal situation, they'd be married, spouses. That was how things were done, right? This bond was announced, blessed by the gods, witnessed by loved ones, and the precursor to creating their own family with children who were the embodiment of these feelings they had for each other. *I want all of that.* It had never been something she concerned herself with, even when Samar lamented to the tomb over her parents and how they had never built such a life together. *Does she want that kind of life with me?*

The honorable thing would be to get married. The thought filled Kouji with sweet, thick emotion. She wanted to do the proper thing for Samar and for herself. She wanted them to have something pure and good after all that life had thrown at them.

"Do you...do you not...?" Samar swallowed hard.

"Of course!" Kouji popped up, needing to stare into Samar's eyes, needing her to see the depths of emotion, affection, and everything else she felt.

"Then what?" Samar's fingers danced across Kouji's hand. The simple touch made Kouji's brain go fuzzy in the best way.

Once Within a Dream

"We're not supposed to do things like this?" It came out as a question. Kouji couldn't focus enough to make it a statement. Besides, they had done many things they technically shouldn't do, according to their places in society. It was a weak argument at best.

"Like what?" Samar brought Kouji's hand to her lips. She gave a gentle kiss to the top of Kouji's hand, then kept watching Kouji's face as she placed a sweet kiss to her palm.

Breathing was impossible. All of Kouji's air was caught in her chest. Her lungs refused to do their job. The slightest movement could change the world, as if the world hadn't just changed forever.

Samar didn't mean that gesture the way Kouji interpreted it, right? The ancient gesture would mean nothing today, nothing to a modern woman like Samar. *But she's a student of history.*

"You mean that?" Kouji asked, voice quivering. She dared to hope.

Samar looked into her eyes and let her see the depth of her sincerity. "I want you to understand, trust, and believe I'm serious. This is the happiest I've been in a long time. I don't want you to leave. I want to wake up next to you, sleep next to you, and touch you whenever possible. I'm confident I'm not going to change my mind, but we don't have to run off and elope right now."

Kouji sniffled. "I want to do right by you. I'm not sure I can."

"I'm sure you have already, but I understand what you mean. I worry over the same things. I want to do right by you. I have to think I'm doing something right because you've stayed."

"I've never felt like this about anyone other than you. I want to do everything with you, for you. I just want you to feel as special as you are."

Samar smiled. "I want you to feel that way too."

"I'm aware marriage isn't the same now as it was when I was first awake, but..."

"Kou, I understand. It means something to you based on your status and your culture. I respect that. But I also think we might make it."

"I don't want to force your hand."

"Oh, Kou. You're not." Samar sat up enough to press her forehead to Kouji's. "I want to do all of this and more with you for the rest of my life. You gave me my life back. You gave me a reason to exist beyond destroying Nightmares. I just ask that with time you'll accept my promise."

Kouji nodded. They definitely shouldn't rush into marriage, but it seemed Samar was ready. Hell, Samar proposed, but she would give Kouji the chance to process, to accept the weight of it later. Kouji was allowed the chance to consider her own decision to the proposal. The very idea jumbled Kouji's mind.

"I want to honor you properly. You deserve the right thing. More importantly, you deserve more than me," Kouji said.

"Except, I just want you, Kouji." Samar leaned in closer, their lips almost touching. Kouji yearned to bridge the gap.

Kouji whimpered. Samar dipped her head, rubbing her cheek against Kouji's. This intimate contact was too much. Kouji pulled away, but Samar grabbed her and held her close. Kouji froze.

"You want me too, Kouji," Samar whispered against her ear.

Kouji shivered. "Uh-huh." She gave a mindless nod. She wasn't sure how she managed that.

Samar smiled. "Have at you then." She went in for a kiss, and Kouji's brain fizzled out.

Samar's lips were soft, warm, and perfect. She was the tastiest treat in all of creation. Kouji's eyes drifted shut, as she returned the kiss as best her inexperience allowed. She didn't have much practice at showing affection in general and almost nothing when it came to romance.

Kouji's stomach flipped. What if she wasn't good enough for Samar in terms of romance? When Samar pulled away, Kouji's entire spirit dropped from disappointment.

"Samar…" Kouji whispered.

"Hmm?"

"Marry me," she breathed out the request.

Samar chuckled. "I already proposed. Your asking is both too late and too soon. I don't want to get married immediately."

Kouji's face burned. "Right."

"Are you all right with giving me what I do want right now?" Samar asked.

Was that all right? Kouji swallowed. She had no idea. She had no clue about the standards or propriety for moments like these. People waited, right?

"Um…I'm not sure what to do here," Kouji admitted. "I'm not sure what's proper. I know that people behave like married couples without being married."

"Kouji, you do what you're comfortable with. If you want to go back to sleep, we can. If you want to trade kisses until you're sick of it, we can. If you want to give yourself to me, I'm more than happy to be here for you. Like everything else in your life, I'm leaving it up to you. But understand and believe, I'll be here regardless. It's not shameful to me to be with you, to want you. It's not shameful to love."

Kouji blinked. She had followed society's rules before and allowed blindness to ruin her. Now wasn't the time to be weighed down by tradition. Samar chose her. Samar protected her and let her be herself. That's what someone does for the person they love.

"You're right, as always. While I don't want you to take back the proposal, we should live our lives how we want to and do the things that feel right to us," Kouji said.

"Exactly." Samar smiled once more.

"It feels right to kiss you. I wouldn't mind giving myself to you as well. I just… I don't have the first clue about any of this. I was never romantically involved."

Samar's smile grew. "Let's start with a kiss."

There was no time to reply. Kouji squeaked, but returned the attention as best she could. The simple press of their lips was everything Kouji imagined. Kissing Samar was warmth seeping into her blood and electricity buzzing under her skin in the best ways.

"May I touch you?" Samar's lips were close enough for Kouji to feel them forming the words. Samar's breath tickled her face, giving her new life.

"You can do anything you want to me," Kouji replied and meant every word.

Samar chuckled. "I'll do my best not to abuse that power."

Did she want Samar to keep that promise? Not wanting to think too hard, Kouji went in for another kiss. Samar was right there with her. Kouji jumped and broke the kiss.

When did Samar put her hand there? The caress to her side tingled. Kouji chuckled. "Sorry. I'm new to this."

"I'm aware. We can take our time. Everything is at our pace."

They kissed throughout the afternoon, drowning out the noises of the city. Kouji focused on the wonderful blessing before her, Samar and all of her affections. Samar saw her worthy enough to kiss her palm, a promise marriage, down the line, at their pace. Samar, who awakened her and allowed her to live life. This was more than she'd ever dare ask for.

A question echoed through Kouji's mind, as she drifted off to sleep. *Is this wise?* It sounded like her mother.

Going in to work giddy wasn't the best approach, but impossible to avoid. Samar had spent the entire day making out with Kouji. Kissing someone had never felt so right. She wanted to go back home, back to her routine, with kisses now added. Kouji had been so enthusiastic. The affection came through loud and clear. Kissing Universal was never like this, even when Samar thought she was in love.

What a fool she'd been. Evinia tried to tell her how toxic he was. Hell, his own brother, Koko, tried to tell her. Only now, with Kouji in her life, could she see how awful her life had been with Universal. Beyond the fact that the dumbass hosted a Nightmare.

She'd never felt cherished when she was with Universal, not even important. She didn't realize he was using her until he hosted the Nightmare, and that only made her feel stupid. She never wanted to think about Universal again, not while she had Kouji in her life.

Ruffians came out of the bushes in Okunkun Park. She grinned, as their Nightmares hovered above them, and Amani appeared in her hand. She was more than ready to take down some Nightmares. She'd never been this energized before.

When she marched into Moonless Night Security headquarters, Samar was untouched for the first time in a long time. She tossed herself into her usual chair. Evinia was focused on her computer monitor but handed Samar a cup of tea.

"Sounded like you had a busy night," Evinia said without looking at her.

"Yeah, just like it's been the past few weeks." Samar sipped her tea. She resisted the urge to request Evinia do her reports so she could run home. She needed to act normal, be cool, or Evinia would hammer her with questions about why she was acting so weird.

Evinia glanced at her. "You look better than you have in the past few weeks. Back at the top of your game?"

"Not sure." Emotionally, Samar was in a different place. She wasn't sure how long that'd last. The fights would eventually return to being tough.

"I'm going to hold out hope. Your reports will be easy if you want me to do them."

Yes! Samar cleared her throat to make sure she didn't sound too excited. "If you don't mind."

"No, it's easy when I don't have to add your injuries. If you could go back to being untouchable, it'd be great on my nerves."

Samar sighed. "Sorry." She never liked being a pain to Evinia. This was also why she had to keep Kouji a bit of a secret. Evinia would worry about her, especially after everything that happened with Universal.

Evinia turned around, only to rub Samar's knee. "You know what I mean. I'm not trying to pressure you. I just don't want you to get hurt."

"I know. This is all out of love. I understand that."

Evinia smiled. "It is. This is also why you can't let Daddy rope you into doing this any longer than you need to. Take your inheritance and become a scholar. I expect to be reading a history book from you in five years."

Samar snorted. "I could probably write one now."

"There's an idea. Consider writing about the folklore you enjoy so much. You need more hobbies anyway. Now, go home and get some sleep. Maybe it's good sleep that keeps you invincible."

"I was sleeping well before." They both knew that wasn't true.

Evinia sighed. "You're right. I just want you to be back at the top of your game because I worry."

Samar gave her a small smile. "I appreciate it. I'll do my best to always come back to you. I don't want to hurt you or worry you."

"I know. You can't help it though. You're my little sister. It's my job to worry about you."

Samar nodded. "I understand that." And that was another reason for her to hide the extent of her relationship with Kouji...for now. Evinia would worry out of her mind if she found out Samar had proposed. Evinia would think they hadn't known each other long enough. She also wouldn't understand the significance of a palm kiss, and Samar didn't want Evinia questioning the validity of her culture right now.

"Be careful then. We have to make up for meeting late in life."

Samar smiled. "You're really worried, huh?" It wasn't like Evinia to talk like this. It had to be from seeing Samar worked over so many nights recently. "I'm fine. You see how fast I bounce back, right?"

"True. I've held off asking about that."

"You wouldn't believe me if I told you." That was a fact.

"I don't even care, as long as you stay alive."

Samar nodded and took her leave, needing to escape before Siku showed up. He might be able to bring her mood down.

She ran home. Kouji met her at the door and had to be in the same thralls of withdrawal as Samar. No words passed between them. They kissed as if it were the only thing that mattered in the world. Samar's back was pressed against the door. She combed her fingers through Kouji's braids. Kouji's hands clutched her hips.

"I missed you so much," Kouji whispered against her lips.

"Me too. The night couldn't end fast enough." Samar's cheeks were burning. She ducked her head. "I was scared you might change your mind while I was out."

Kouji chuckled. "I had the same fear. I thought for sure you'd come to your senses."

"My senses begged me to rush home, so I could have more of your amazing kisses and we could eat together. I look forward to this moment every morning, even without the kisses."

"Really?" Kouji's mouth twitched, ready to smile.

"Yes. I enjoy sitting with you. I love your company, Kou. I want to be around you."

"Same. So…" Kouji glanced at the kitchen. "I realize I never formally accepted your proposal. I don't know if it's still acceptable to do that through a meal, but I made tarts."

Samar leaned in for another, brief kiss. "In my culture, yes, food is an acceptable way to answer a proposal. I like what you made."

Kouji puffed up, shoulders squared and chin tilted. Samar had to kiss her again. Kouji returned the kiss to the point of distraction. The tarts were cold by the time they got to them. They were still delicious though. This was worth the rush home. Samar had no doubt she'd enjoy living like this every day, if possible.

Chapter Nineteen

Losing Sleep

KOUJI WAS UNSURE HOW she had gone her entire life without Samar's romantic affection. She doubted she could last longer than the workday without Samar's kisses. But there was more.

Samar was a very giving partner. Every morning, when she came home from work, she brought a surprise for Kouji. Nothing over the top—candy, books, beaded jewelry, and all sorts of decorations for her hair. Kouji had been different—special—her entire life, but now she felt it. Samar treated her like she was precious, not just privileged.

Beyond the little gifts, simple gestures went a long way with Kouji. Whenever Samar redid Kouji's plaits, she added some flare with intricate designs, ribbons, colored strings, and golden loops.

The kisses were the best gift of all. Every morning, when they lay down for sleep, plenty were exchanged. Samar held Kouji in her sleep like she'd never let her go. Kouji felt cherished, and she tried to hold Samar the same way. Concentrating on that helped keep Kouji awake, which was exactly what she wanted.

Kouji refused to sleep. Her mother kept showing up in her dreams, questioning her about her engagement. Her mother didn't approve for a couple of reasons. The Nightmares would target Samar that much harder once they realized her importance to Kouji. Kouji brought the subject up to Samar, who wasn't bothered in the slightest. She seemed to like an excuse for more Nightmares to come after her. Samar wasn't afraid.

Kouji's mother also believed the engagement was too fast. Kouji and Samar barely knew each other, according to her mother. Never mind the fact that if Kouji had been treated as a normal princess when she was first awake, she could've easily been married off to someone she had never met. She'd known Samar for three years, based on how long Samar had been talking to the tomb. Theirs was a long engagement. Her mother wasn't happy with that argument.

"You can't escape this conversation, Kouji," the wind whispered. It wasn't really the wind.

Kouji grunted. "There's no conversation to be had."

The wind whipped outside, but Kouji wasn't sure if that was her mother or the stirring of a storm. A loud thunderclap rattled the window, and Kouji jumped. The movement was enough to wake Samar. She sat up, ready for war. Her short spear appeared in hand.

"It's okay. It's okay." Kouji wrapped her arms around Samar.

Samar blinked and glanced at the window. "Oh, it's a storm."

"Hasn't started raining yet."

"What are you doing awake?" Samar made a noise and settled back down, pressed against Kouji. She glanced up. "You're tense."

Kouji sighed. "I haven't been sleeping well."

Samar sat up, making eye contact. "Why not? Why didn't you say anything?"

"I didn't want to trouble you…"

"Kou…" Samar rubbed Kouji's side with gentle fingers. "Your troubles are my troubles. We're supposed to be here for each other. That's what my proposal meant. I assumed you'd share your joys and sorrows with me when you agreed."

Kouji's heart swelled, and she wept. What had she done to deserve Samar? She had never had someone so completely present for her.

"You saying stuff like this, being like this, is why I didn't want to say anything. You're so good to me. I don't want to be a bother."

"Bother me anytime. Bother me with everything. I want to know you the way you know me. Your hopes, your fears, your dreams, and everything in between."

Kouji swallowed. "My dreams?" She didn't mean it the way Kouji thought, but it still was on point.

"Yes, your dreams." Samar gave her a soft peck on the lips.

"My dreams lately have been a mess. My mother is against our union."

Samar blinked and pulled back a little. "She is? Is it…did I do something?" Her voice cracked.

"No, no, no." Kouji cupped Samar's face with both hands. "You didn't do anything. She's worried about you, about the Nightmares targeting you."

Samar scoffed. "We've talked about this."

"Yes, we did. She just worries."

Shaking her head, Samar gave Kouji another sweet kiss. "I'd fight Nightmares, regardless. They'd come after me, regardless. And I won't let Nightmares stand in the way of living my life or stand in the way of you living your life or us living together."

With every word, Kouji fell deeper in love with Samar. "Us living together?"

Samar smiled. "I proposed and you accepted. That's a promise of a life together, yes?"

Kouji gave a small nod. "I want a life with you so much."

"Then, we can have that." Samar leaned in, kissing Kouji in a manner that promised so much.

Kouji was very comfortable with kissing Samar now, having had lots of practice. She wrapped her arms around Samar, pulling her closer as Samar slid her tongue into Kouji's mouth. The first time this happened, Kouji had been confused and jumped, but now she relaxed and responded. Her tongue caressed Samar's and they melted against each other.

They lost themselves in the kisses, and Samar adjusted her body against Kouji's. Kouji helped move Samar as well, wanting to make sure she was comfortable. As they shifted, Samar's thigh fell between Kouji's legs bringing a shot of pleasure. She moaned…loud enough to be heard over the thunder. Samar pulled away.

"Sorry?" Samar asked, unsure.

Kouji shook her head. "No, um…it felt good. Really good."

"You want me to do it again?"

The suggestion caused Kouji's throat to close a little. "Um…yes…"

Samar grinned and rocked into Kouji. The moment Samar's thigh made contact, Kouji moaned once more as delight shot through all of her veins. *What the hell is this?* How could anything feel so marvelous?

"You like it? Want more?" Samar asked.

Kouji nodded. "Yes, please."

Samar smiled, then kissed her again and continued to rock against her. The pressure was even better this time, and Kouji arched into it. Samar pulled away, making Kouji whimper.

"You really want this?" Samar asked.

"Yes! Now, kiss me and make me feel good." Kouji grinned.

"Oh, you almost asked nicely."

"My pretty smile wasn't nice enough?"

"You win." Samar kissed her again, lying on Kouji with what had to be her full weight. It was glorious.

Samar caressed Kouji's bare arms and pressed her thigh with purpose. It took all of Kouji's wits to keep kissing Samar and not lose herself to the pleasure playing out between her legs that built and built. Kouji feared she might explode, but in the best way possible.

She broke their kiss, needing to turn her head to let loose a deep moan. Samar continued moving, kissing her cheeks and her neck. All of that added to the intensity already happening.

"You like that?" Samar whispered into her ear.

"Uh-huh." Kouji couldn't manage more than that.

"Then, just let go. Let it happen."

Kouji had no idea what Samar meant, but it didn't matter. Samar's hands were suddenly on her hips, guiding her, grinding her. Kouji closed her eyes, losing herself in the feel of it all. Out of nowhere, the explosion happened. Colors burst behind her eyelids like magnificent fireworks, as pleasure flared throughout her body. Every nerve flashed like light dancing through her.

"Kou, are you all right?" Samar's voice sounded so far away, but she was so close.

"Um…" Kouji wasn't sure how to make words.

Samar snickered. "That good, huh? First time?"

First time at what? What the hell was that? Was there a way to experience it again? She had so many questions, but words were a memory.

Samar kissed her cheek. "Tell me when you're okay."

Kouji swallowed, clearing her throat enough to make words. "Wha-what happened?"

"I think you just had your first orgasm."

Kouji blinked. "Does it…is it always so overwhelming?"

"Not to my knowledge, but we can keep trying to see." Samar smiled.

It took Kouji a long moment to understand what she meant. "Yes, let's keep trying."

"You sure?"

"I want you now more than ever, Samar. I want to make you feel that good. I want to share every part of me with you and enjoy every part of you as well."

Samar smiled. "I want that too."

"Guide me?" *May that not be too much to ask.* "I'm a fast learner."

Samar gave her a gentle kiss as rain pattered softly outside. "You can take as long as you want. You know that."

Kouji nodded. One of the things she loved about Samar was how Samar encouraged her to go at her own pace. She was allowed to discover herself.

Samar sat up, needing to look at Kouji more directly. This was a big moment. She didn't want to ruin it for Kouji. Such a huge responsibility.

"Do you want me to talk you through what we can do, so you know and can decide?" Samar asked.

Kouji sat up. "Is that what you wanted your first time?"

Samar winced. "Please, don't." She didn't want to think about her first time. She didn't want to think about herself with someone else.

"I'm jealous, you know?" Kouji caressed her cheek, touching her with near awe. "Jealous he had you and didn't even understand what a gift you were."

"You're the gift to me. My treasure. I want you to be as comfortable as possible. I might not be as experienced as Universal was when he was with me, but I know more than you and want to make sure you're all right with anything that happens."

"I'm fine as long as it's you, but I think an explanation will help later on, if I try to initiate intimacy."

Samar chuckled. "You initiate it all the time. You're the one holding my hand, hugging me, and making sure I'm warm. Those things are just as intimate as what I'm about to do to you." Those things meant more to her than every single time she had sex with Universal.

"I'm going to initiate it now because I'm going to kiss you."

"Threaten me with a good time why don't you?" Samar grinned.

Kouji came in slow, as if giving Samar a chance to retreat. She met Kouji head-on, lips first. The kiss started out with a simple press of their mouths but grew more passionate, as their kisses had a habit of doing. After a few seconds, their tongues met and glided against each other with a darling caress.

Samar stepped it up, palming Kouji's breast through her sleep shirt. Kouji moaned into her mouth, but didn't pull away. Samar took that as permission to continue, so she kneaded the plump weight in her hand. Kouji mimicked her, and Samar moaned into the touch.

"Was that all right?" Kouji asked in a breath.

"I should be asking you that. However I touch you, it's fine for you to do the same to me. Now, would you like to try this without shirts on?" Samar proposed.

She heard Kouji's breath catch. "Yes, let's do that. Maybe…nothing at all."

"Fair enough."

They kissed and worked their way out of their shirts. They eased apart again, eager to see what they'd uncovered. Samar stared in awe, the sparse light from outside just right to admire Kouji's full breasts with small, dark nipples.

"I'm going to kiss your chest," Samar stated as if it was a pure fact.

Kouji swallowed. "I think I'd like that."

Samar leaned in, dotting Kouji's breasts and collarbones with wet kisses. Kouji squirmed, making small cooing sounds. Samar paused, palming one breast and stroking the pert nipple with her thumb.

"Too much?" Thunder crashed outside, but Samar barely registered the background noise.

"I wasn't..." Kouji blew out a breath. "It feels so amazing. I wasn't...didn't expect..."

Samar smiled. "May I continue?"

"Please."

"I'm going to use my mouth as well."

Kouji nodded, and Samar placed a soft kiss on her lips before turning her attention back to Kouji's magnificent bosom. She wrapped her lips around a plump nipple, and Kouji keened and shivered. She ran her hands through Samar's hair, encouraging her onward. Samar hardly needed the motivation, but the attention made her purr.

"Sam...Samar..." Kouji's voice trembled as badly as her body.

"More?" Samar hummed.

"There's more?"

"You might want to get out of your shorts and underwear."

Kouji nodded. "It's...um...damp there..."

Pride buzzed through Samar. She'd made Kouji wet. "As it should be. You're enjoying this, right?"

"Yes."

"That makes doing even more possible."

Kouji fell over herself to get out of her sleep shorts and underwear. Samar managed to keep a straight face. She didn't want Kouji to feel embarrassed or self-conscious over her desire. Samar eased herself out of the rest of her clothes so they were both nude.

"Should I touch you?" Kouji asked, eyes roaming Samar's body.

"Whenever you want to. I'm going to do a lot of touching now, mostly between your legs." Samar grinned. She had never done this with a woman, but she had touched herself enough to know what she liked and would use that knowledge. Kouji nodded her assent, and more kisses were shared between them. Their vocal appreciation drowned out the rain.

Samar kneaded Kouji's breasts, and Kouji tried to mirror her actions on Samar. The attempt was clumsy but still perfect. Each caress of her fingertips left traces of bliss floating across Samar's skin, down into her blood, and humming in her soul.

She managed to coax Kouji onto her back without needing to say a word, and her kisses drifted along with her hands. She stroked Kouji's muscled thighs, enjoying the might that lay right under her hands. This demigod, this magical being, was at her mercy due to the power of her affection.

"My fingers are going to go between your legs, okay?" Samar kept her voice low and soothing.

"Yes, please. I ache there," Kouji admitted.

"I'll take care of you," Samar promised. She meant that in every way possible.

"I trust you will."

Samar eased her hand to Kouji's desire. Kouji moaned at a slight touch and her hips jumped. Samar craved more of those sounds and was more than eager to give Kouji everything she desired. She wasted no time stroking Kouji's clit. Kouji rocked into her touch, moved with her fingers, and continued with those beautiful moans.

Samar sucked Kouji's nipple into her mouth, and it was like she pressed a button. Kouji clutched her shoulders with enough strength to bruise and shuddered with a high-pitched wail. Samar pulled back to watch Kouji melt into the mattress.

"Done?" Samar asked as Kouji's eyes drifted shut.

"There's more?" Kouji countered.

"If you can handle it, I wouldn't mind going down on you. I've never done it before, with a woman anyway, but I want to with you." She'd love to see Kouji's reaction to her mouth, but this was more than enough to sustain her for now. Not to mention, she'd love to taste Kouji. She suspected it was something she might end up becoming addicted to.

"If you want to, I'm willing to try. It'll give me one more thing to try on you." Kouji smiled.

Samar kissed a trail down Kouji's abs and settled herself between Kouji's legs. Kouji moved to accommodate her and propped her head up to observe. Samar didn't mind, tracing the lines of Kouji's abdomen with her tongue before going lower. She focused on Kouji's dripping core. She dove in with more desire than she thought she was capable of.

The taste was as sweet as expected. Kouji always smelled sweet, and she tasted as delicious as a ripe peach. She arched into Samar's face, screaming her pleasure for all to hear. Hell, the neighbors might hear her over the storm. Samar worked to get that reaction, licking every drop of Kouji.

Kouji rocked against Samar's feasting mouth. Samar ran her hands up and down Kouji's torso. Every now and then, her fingers strayed across Kouji's nipples, and she pinched. Each time, Kouji bucked harder into her mouth and cried out loud enough to match any thunder.

Samar sucked on Kouji's clit, and Kouji howled as her legs snapped around Samar's head. Samar didn't stop, despite the pressure on her skull. She worked until Kouji collapsed onto her pillow.

"No more," Kouji begged, breathless, body trembling as if she was cold.

Samar chuckled and moved to rest against Kouji's side. "Really? Thought you'd be willing to go all day."

"Three times…takes a lot out of you…" Kouji panted.

"I'll take this reaction as a compliment." Samar would be walking with her chin in the air for the rest of the day. She gave Kouji exactly what she deserved.

Kouji blew out a long breath. "You should. I've never felt so amazing before. I had no idea that was possible."

Samar tilted her head. "You really never even touched yourself?"

Kouji shook her head. "Never had the urge. I never would've imagined it would feel like that."

"Well, it's actually different when you do it with someone else. At least, in my limited experience."

Kouji turned onto her side, looking Samar in the eye. "May I touch you now? I'd love to make you feel like that."

"I accept." When Kouji came in for a kiss, Samar slowed it down, silently letting Kouji know she didn't have to rush. Kouji seemed to understand, and they kissed like they had all the time in the world.

Samar settled onto her back, and Kouji floated kisses all over her body. Kouji's braids tickled and teased her skin, as Kouji left a burning, wet trail of pleasure across her torso.

"Your skin tastes amazing. I'm going to try to taste the rest of you the way you did me." Kouji grinned.

"Please, do." Samar looked forward to whatever Kouji tried.

Kouji's drifted low, and she dove right into Samar, no warning, no hesitation. With her full mouth, she devoured Samar like she was a complete meal. Samar howled as pleasure rushed through her, flooding every bit of her within seconds. She was about to overflow before it really began.

"Oh, keep doing that," Samar urged, as Kouji ran the flat of her tongue through her.

Kouji didn't respond, but she followed directions. Samar threaded her fingers through Kouji's braids, being careful of the jewelry woven into the braids. Samar's pleasure soared, rocketing through her, and she exploded within minutes.

Samar lost control and pumped her hips into Kouji's questing mouth. Kouji didn't relent. One climax bled into the other. The world went black with only ecstasy existing, engulfing Samar. *Is this what it's like when you really like the person? Love the person?* She had no idea, but this was better than any time she had been with Universal. With Universal, it had always been like an activity to get out of the way or kill time, not intimate or connecting.

"You okay?" Kouji's voice broke through the cloud of ecstasy.

"Perfect." Samar sighed.

"You taste delicious. I want to do more to you."

Samar shook her head. "Not now. I'm wiped out." Twice was enough for her, especially since they could do it again later.

Kouji grinned and settled against her side. The press of their bare skin was heaven. Samar wrapped her arms around Kouji to ensure she wouldn't move. Kouji sighed.

"Sleep?" Samar suggested.

"If I get to sleep in your arms, yes. If I get to wake up in your arms, yes. If I get to experience you once more when we wake up, yes," Kouji answered.

Samar doubted she had ever fallen asleep as easily as she did this time. Certainly not since coming to this city, and especially not with a storm raging outside. Soon they were both asleep.

Kouji woke with a start, heart pounding in her chest. She sat up, gasping for air. Samar sat up with her, holding her tight as she got herself together.

"Are you all right?" Samar asked.

Kouji rubbed her forehead. "I'm not sure."

"Did you have a bad dream?"

Kouji searched her mind. "I'm not sure. It's been so long since I couldn't remember a dream."

"Was your mother in the dream?"

"No…" Kouji squinted as she tried to grasp what had happened. "Your father was."

"Excuse me?" Samar's voice was loud.

Kouji ran her fingers through her braids, pushing the thin plaits out of her face. "I didn't see his face, but I knew he was your father, Siku. He was angry with me."

"That sounds about right."

Kouji shook her head. "He reminded me that I have to speak with him."

Samar seemed to choke on the air she was trying to breathe. "You have to what?" She gawked at Kouji as if she had gone mad.

"I have to speak with your father."

"No," Samar replied, her voice firm. Her gaze hardened.

Kouji was all too aware of how Samar felt about her father. Samar wasn't angry with Kouji's decision, but afraid. Siku intimidated Samar. Siku tried to frighten Samar away from associating with people point-blank, mostly to keep people from finding out about her.

Kouji wasn't sure how Siku would react to finding out they were together, living together, and engaged. He might not mind, since Kouji didn't know anything about the man that mattered. Not to mention, it wasn't like Siku had any actual care or concern for Samar.

"I have to speak with him," Kouji insisted.

"No, Kou. I'm not supposed to…" Samar clutched her bicep. "Look, Siku won't take meeting you well. He'll try to hurt you. He doesn't want me to be happy."

"I won't be hurt. I just want to do things right. I have to request permission from your parents to marry you. I wish I could ask your mother, but that's not possible."

"Kou, this isn't ten thousand years ago. You don't have to ask him anything. You don't have to request anything from him. I'm in charge of my own life, not him."

"I'd like to at least tell him. It'll make me feel better. Don't worry. I just need to be able to tell myself I'm doing this the right way." Speaking to Siku would set Kouji at ease. Samar deserved Kouji doing her best and trying to do things in the proper manner, even if it was outdated.

Samar frowned. "If that's the case, I should talk to your mother, since I'm the one who proposed."

"Technically, we should both speak to each other's parents to get their approval for the marriage, but my mother has already made her disapproval well-known to me."

Samar's frown deepened. "Still? Why does she not approve? She knows I can fight the Nightmares. What else is there?"

Kouji winced. "It's not you. You know that. She thinks highly of you. She honest and truly fears that marrying me will put you in danger."

Samar blew out a long breath. "Listen to me. I've been in danger since I've been able to see the damn Nightmares. I was in danger since being born to my mother because she fought the damn things. This would be my life with or without you. I'd prefer with you. Tell your mother that."

Kouji nodded. "I know. You've made that clear, and I've said it to her. She understands, but she still worries. This is also why I need to speak with your father. I need to make my intentions clear."

"Kou, please."

Kouji gave her a soft kiss. "It'll be okay. Trust me."

"I don't want him to be angry and hurt you. I don't want him to take you from me. Please." Samar wrapped her arms around Kouji and held her like she never planned to let go.

Kouji held her right back, but scoffed. "No one can take me from you. I'm ignoring my mother's warning to be with you. Besides, if he does get angry and comes at me, how fast am I? I'll just move. He won't take me from you. I'll always be here with you. It'll be okay." She kissed Samar's forehead.

"He won't like this, or you."

"Don't worry," Kouji whispered and kissed her again.

"He will try to ruin you, ruin us."

"Don't worry."

Each time Samar protested, Kouji tried to assure her everything would be all right. Each reassurance came with a kiss. Each kiss was more passionate than the last, and they ended up right back where they started before this realization and conversation began.

They melted against each other like two burning candles much too close. Samar was burned out by the end, and went back to sleep. Kouji fought to stay awake.

"I want to do the right thing for you," Kouji whispered to the napping Samar. She placed a gentle kiss on Samar's cheek. "Everything will be okay."

Well, as okay as she could make it. She might never be able to sway her mother. She might never be able to shake the Nightmares. There was no way for her to contact or confront Usuku to stop his revenge. She had to do this one proper thing.

So she took a quick shower, brushed her teeth, tied her hair back, and dressed in outside clothes. She put on her neck beads over the black t-shirt she wore. They made her feel complete, and she needed every inch of herself to do what was necessary.

"I have to do the right thing for once in my sorry life. She's worth that much." Kouji gave Samar one last look and left the apartment. A chilling breeze blew as soon as she hit the hall. Kouji sucked her teeth. "Not now, Mother. Now is certainly not the time."

The wind died down, but Kouji doubted her mother was gone. She wanted Kouji to stay safe, go back to sleep, and stay alive. But how was that living? Being with Samar was living.

Kouji ventured outside into the cold. At least it wasn't raining anymore. She soon realized she had no idea where to go. She was lost. Samar's job had to be located somewhere around the park. They had gone by the park before…maybe? She'd figure it out.

A loud buzz cut through Samar's mind and sleep, waking her up. She groaned and rolled over in a dazed stupor. She groped the floor for her phone and retrieved the annoying device.

"Hello?" she said in a scratchy tone.

"Sammie, where in the heavens are you?" Evinia inquired.

"What do you mean?" Samar rubbed her eye with her free hand.

"Your shift started."

"My shift?" Samar echoed. What the hell was Evinia going on about? Then it dawned on her what her sister meant. "Oh, my shift!" She glanced out the window to see it was dark. "Siku's going to kill me!"

"Yes, Daddy's calling for your head already. I tried to tell him this was the first time you ever missed a day, but he's going crazy. He's got Alien out looking for you, like the boy doesn't need to be asleep at this hour. Alien's not very happy about it, of course. So what's the deal?

Even though I can guess, since you're living with someone now," Evinia commented in an amused tone.

Samar groaned, hating Evinia's accurate assumption. How could she sleep the day away? *Because you were comfortable, relaxed, and at peace for one of the few times in your life since coming to this place.*

"I'll be there in twenty minutes," Samar assured her big sister.

"Hurry. Every second you're not here, Daddy's thinking of ways to punish you for being so irresponsible, as he put it. He's not sure whether to think you're dead in an alley somewhere or if you're just being a teenager and doing whatever you want. Or should I say *whoever* you want?" Evinia teased.

"Vin, if you keep talking, I can't leave," Samar pointed out.

"That's true. See you in twenty."

Samar ended the call. Sighing, she ran her hand through her hair and glanced to her side. She was alone in bed. Not the best way to wake up after a day of sex and sleep, but Kouji might've tried to start her usual day, unsure of how to react after so much intimacy.

There was no water running, so Kouji wasn't in the shower. Did she go to the store to buy some food? No, it was way too late for that sort of thing. *No way Kouji actually went to speak with Siku.* Deep down, Samar knew that was exactly what Kouji went to do.

"Damn it!" Samar charged out of bed and took what she believed to be the quickest shower in the history of showering. Should she worry more about Kouji finding Siku or the hordes of Nightmares that now roamed Okunkun Park finding Kouji? *Kouji should definitely worry about me finding her.*

Chapter Twenty

Darkness Falls

SAMAR STORMED OUT OF her apartment, still pulling on her jacket, only to discover it was raining. Not a surprise, but a problem that'd make things a little more dangerous. No matter. She had been through worse. She took the shortest route to her job, which was also the most dangerous.

She had to hop a few fences, high with barbed wire. Her hands caught a few nicks, but nothing that stopped her. She had to outrun dogs in a couple of yards she ducked through. The wet ground made this a trick, but she managed. She slid into Moonless Night HQ, scanning for any sigh of Kouji. Nothing caught her eye. She ran to Evinia's office.

"Vin, have you seen a dark-skinned young woman with purple eyes about so tall?" Samar held her hand a few inches above her head and tried to catch her breath. The panic and fury bound her chest in a tight, icy grip.

"Um…no." Evinia turned from her computer and jumped in her seat. "You look like a drowned cat!"

Samar pointed behind her, in the direction of outside. "It's pouring rain, like it does every other day around here."

Evinia nodded. "Must've started not too long ago. Why are you looking for a dark-skinned young woman with purple eyes?"

Samar sighed in relief until she registered the follow-up question. She only allowed the panic in her mind to reach her face for a few seconds, but Evinia noticed. Samar went rigid, which didn't help.

"No reason," Samar tried to assure Evinia.

Evinia snorted. "So you're looking for a dark-skinned young woman with purple eyes for no reason at all, and that's why you asked me about her?"

"Exactly."

"And that makes how much sense to you, Sammie?" Evinia leaned forward, elbow on her desk and chin in her hand.

Samar was saved from answering that question but unfortunately moved into a much more awkward situation. Their little brother came into view. Samar would have preferred Vin's inquisition to whatever verbal torture her brother had for her. He was the spitting image of their father, although in a shorter, sleeker form.

Alvin wore dark joggers with a hoodie, much like Samar. He was also drenched. He frowned, marching over to within a few feet of her.

"Dad, here she is!" Alvin pointed to Samar. He curled his lip as he regarded her and tried to strike her down with a glare. "Sammie, next time you end up lost, do us all a big favor and stay that way." He even sounded like their father.

"Alien!" Evinia shot out of her chair.

Alvin sucked his teeth. "What? Like you weren't thinking the same thing? Nobody cares about her."

"Al." Evinia growled, as she came to stand in front of him.

Alvin sucked his teeth and threw up his muscular arms. "What-the-hell-ever, man. I just wasted an hour of my life looking for her."

"God forbid somebody check her apartment," Evinia remarked.

Alvin curled his lip. "Who really gives a crap?" He stared Samar down, making sure she saw in his gaze that he couldn't care less about what happened to her.

Mechi strolled up, surveying the scene. "What the hell is the Alien yelling about?" His eyes searched Evinia, as if checking on her.

No one got the chance to answer Mechi's question because Siku strolled over. Mechi flinched, like he wanted to bolt for the nearest exit, but stood his ground. Samar related to that. She stood her ground as well. She wouldn't let this man run her off anymore.

"Al, you said that Samar's over here?" Siku leveled a hard glare at Samar with cold, blue-grey eyes. It was like he was trying to destroy her insides with his rigid will. His disdain was almost tangible.

Samar took a breath and steeled her nerves. She didn't need to fear this man. So he might not care for her. He wouldn't break her like he hoped. She wouldn't give him the satisfaction. Not now. She had things to live for.

"Here she is, Dad," Alvin said, with hatred in his blue-grey eyes.

"I can see that, Al. Good work on finding her," Siku replied, as if Alvin actually did something.

"Are you mad? He didn't find her. She wasn't lost to begin with. Neither of you bothered to call her or check her apartment before assuming she was dead in an alley somewhere." Evinia huffed.

Siku ignored Evinia, as if she had said nothing at all. "Samar, where the hell have you been?" His tone was unforgiving. Not too long ago, she would've shrunk into herself from the sound, but not now.

Alvin snickered, expecting Samar to recoil, which was one of his favorite things. He enjoyed when Siku spoke to Samar as if she didn't matter. Alvin thought Siku made Samar aware of how unwanted she was in their family whenever he talked to her. *If I'm so unwanted, why will this man not leave me the hell alone?*

"Answer me." Siku growled, glaring at Samar in a way that would've made her wither right before his eyes a few months ago.

Alvin made a face at Samar, as if trying to goad her into responding to Siku. She tuned him out, which wasn't that difficult. He once had the nerve to ask her why she hadn't done them all a favor and killed herself years ago. He didn't believe anyone would miss her. That was when she knew he'd never say anything worth listening to. She didn't need to take the abuse.

"What's to answer? I was home," Samar said, stating the obvious.

Siku folded his arms across his chest. "Watch your tone with me. Why were you still at home? You were meant to be here. Are you too stupid to tell time?" His tone was as harsh as his words.

Samar gulped, but resisted the urge to curl into herself. She wouldn't give this man the power to make her cower again. *Take his words and keep your head high.*

"Daddy!" Evinia barked, stepping closer to glower at Siku.

Siku ignored her, staring at Samar and doing his best to crush her soul. Her guts quivered, but she kept her strong stance. *Mom, what the hell did you see in this man?*

Siku advanced on Samar, loomed over her. She stood her ground, waiting for her father to strike her, as she always did. A glint in his eye always betrayed his true desires. He craved to cross that line, but held off. If only he would, then she'd finally be done with him, and he'd have to drop the facade. He'd have to stop pretending to have her best interests at heart. If he actually struck her, he'd go away, and they'd be done with each other. They'd be free.

"Daddy, you will not talk to her that way."

Siku finally took notice of Evinia. "Stay out of it, Vinny. This isn't any of your business. Samar, why are you late?" he pressed with an angry growl in his throat.

Samar's nerves trembled under her skin and her stomach flipped, but she didn't back down. His gaze burned her muscles and clawed at her insides. *Don't be scared. Don't be scared. Don't be scared.*

Intellectually, Samar was more than aware Siku couldn't hurt her, even if he hit her. Sure, it might pain her physically, but nothing beyond that. This man honestly meant nothing to her, so why did he have such power to frighten her? She had been through hell and back with Nightmares lately and never felt like this before. Perhaps, if she remained silent long enough, he'd leave her alone, go away, and end this torture.

Instead, Siku puffed up more and somehow took up all of the space around them. His presence oppressed her, punished her. Her very spirit quivered, like he emitted an energy that could shatter every bit of her.

"Why are you late?" His voice was somehow more severe, squeezing her.

"She's probably too dumb to figure out how to answer that," Alvin muttered, eyes sparkling with amusement over Samar's torment.

Siku didn't spare his son a glance. "Don't act like you don't understand. You might be stupid, but you know how to speak."

Evinia grabbed Siku by his wrist. "Daddy, don't say that to her!" Her voice trembled as she pleaded with him, like she too was afraid. She knew they were at a tipping point.

Evinia had witnessed plenty of insults from Siku directed at Samar over the past three years. Samar was certain Evinia took them worse than she did. This time he didn't bother trying to disguise his disgust. Something about Siku seemed different.

The words didn't bother Samar. Nothing he said was true. Sure, it should hurt that her father demeaned her, but he was nothing to her. He became less than nothing to her. He wanted her to be ashamed of herself because he was ashamed of her, but he was the one who should be ashamed of himself.

"I don't have time for this." Samar needed to find Kouji before some Nightmares did. Sure, Kouji had the skill to handle the largest pack of Nightmares, but Samar didn't want her to. Kouji deserved peace.

Samar turned to leave, but Siku grabbed her by her bicep. He gripped her as if she were a criminal. With a growl, she eyed him as if he were the same and shifted her stance.

"Where the hell do you think you're going?" Siku demanded.

Samar's knees wobbled, like they might buckle. *No, hold it together. You're not wrong. He's wrong. Don't fear him. You stare down Nightmares for a living. Stare him down like you would any other wicked creature.*

He might've read her mind. He squeezed her arm, letting her understand his strength. It hurt to the point she hissed, a wince tearing through her face. His eyes blazed and he leaned down, getting closer to her face. Weirdly enough, he smelled like lemongrass, like Evinia, but that didn't stop her heart from pounding against her ribs.

Siku had to know he was finally having the effect he wanted on Samar. He clutched her a little tighter. She was unable to fight down a whimper. This was worse than facing any Nightmare, any horde of Nightmares.

"Daddy, you're hurting her." Evinia gripped Siku's sleeve, as if trying to tear his arm away.

"Where were you?" he asked Samar one more time.

"She was living her life," Kouji's voice answered from down the hallway.

Everyone turned around, not only Samar's family, but agents pretending to have business in the hall only to witness Siku tell off Samar. Kouji appeared unbothered by all of the attention. Samar tried to rip herself away from Siku's grip, but he had her. *I never would've guessed he's this strong.* It would've been something to admire if he didn't use his strength to be a bully.

"Leave now," Samar called to Kouji. *Please leave and save us both the wrath of Siku Habeen.*

Kouji didn't show any signs of hearing her. She stood still, apparently taking in the scene. Everyone else stared at Kouji. This was too much. Samar grunted as she tried to tear away from Siku, only for him to hold her with more power.

"Who's that?" Mechi asked Evinia, nodding to Kouji.

Evinia chuckled. "My guess is she's a woman with purple eyes who stands about my height, and I'm willing to bet she cooks."

Evinia tilted her head as she studied Kouji. Vin looked pleased. Samar would be proud, if only she wasn't locked in a battle of wills with damn Siku. He managed to look more upset than before. He flexed his hand, crushing her wrist.

"Samar, who the hell is that?" Siku demanded.

"Kouji, leave," Samar commanded and begged at the same time. Kouji stared at her, as if considering her words, her pleas.

Kouji had a hell of a time finding this building, but she was pleased when she recalled the name of the company. People had pointed her in the right direction. It was the only place her mind came up with to find Samar's father. She hadn't expected to come into the ugly and angry scene she found.

She hadn't expected Samar would be at work already and realized how much time she'd wasted wandering the city instead of asking for directions. Now she was witnessing Samar's father manhandle her. The man was as much of an ass as Samar described, not that Kouji ever doubted her word.

Kouji held Samar's gaze. "You know I can't leave. It'll be all right."

"It won't." Samar's eyes were wet.

"Who the hell is this, Samar?" Siku demanded. That rough voice was no way to talk to his daughter.

"I'm the reason Samar was late," Kouji replied.

"And who are you?" The glint in his gaze indicated he was on the brink of snapping.

"She's nobody! Kou, go!" Samar ordered, fear etched in her voice.

Kouji had never heard Samar be afraid. This warrior had faced down swarms of Nightmares and their hosts, but her own father scared her. Samar was aware of Kouji's powers and still thought her father had the upper hand. Fear was irrational.

Why was Samar frightened for her? Did she forget Kouji was half god? She slid through shadows. She moved faster than light. She banished Nightmares with a touch. She was more than able to take care of Siku.

Kouji laughed and stepped closer. Samar's eyes widened and she tugged at her arm, trying to free herself from Siku's grasp. Kouji stopped only when she was feet away from the family.

"Kou, stop. He'll hurt you." Tears welled in Samar's eyes as her gaze begged Kouji to listen.

This spoke volumes about what type of father and what type of man Siku Habeen was. Samar was almost hysterical. How was Siku unable to comprehend how awful he was?

Kouji held up a hand. "No, he won't. You are aware of that." Kouji fixed her gaze on Siku. "Sir, my name's Kouji Kataban. I've been out searching for you tonight. I only need to talk to you this one time, and you'll probably never have to see me again."

Siku scowled. "And what do you want from me?"

Kouji flashed a huge, lopsided grin, unable to help the joy inside of her as she thought of why she needed to see this man. "Sir, I am so in love with your daughter. She asked me to marry her, and I accepted. I wanted to inform you."

"Wait, what?" Kouji noticed a tall man with reddish-brown hair, probably Mechi. He stood close to the only other woman in the group.

She must be Evinia. Mechi appeared ready to pounce to defend Evinia. Odd. Samar always described him as being afraid of Siku.

Evinia straightened, her face twisted. "Yes, what?"

"Well, this just got better. Apparently, Samar and this total stranger are in love and getting married. Dad..." A young man, who had to be Alvin, turned to Siku with devilish delight in his eyes.

"Sammie, how long has it been?" Evinia's eyebrows curled. She looked concerned.

Siku growled and yanked Samar to him. "Do you want to explain any of this?" He glared at Evinia. "And what the hell do you know about it, Vinny?"

Evinia shrugged. "I know if she cooks as well as Sammie claims she does, I might go to the other side." She winked at Kouji.

Alvin had the nerve to cringe. "That's gross, Vin." He looked at Kouji. "Being with Samar is gross too."

"Samar, what the hell is going on?" Siku demanded.

Kouji stepped closer. "What's going on is that you're hurting your daughter and demeaning her in front of everyone she works with. In front of her own siblings." She motioned to Evinia and Alvin. "This is why her brother doesn't respect her. You don't respect her."

"Who the hell do you think you are talking to me like that? You think you can come here and take advantage of my idiot, backwoods daughter. She doesn't even have any money, you fool," Siku said.

"I don't care about money, you fool," Kouji replied.

"Excuse you?" Siku glowered at Kouji, then shifted to Samar. "You will disassociate yourself from this little bastard."

Samar flinched. "I won't." Her voice was strong now, like all of her fear and worry had vanished.

"You ditzy, little hick. You don't even understand you're being taken advantage of, just like with that awful boy you used to run around with," Siku snapped.

"You can call me all the names you want. I won't leave Kouji. I love Kouji, and I did propose. We might never get married, but I promised her forever because we make each other better." Samar's voice was stronger now.

"Sammie," Evinia interrupted. "I am all for you standing up for yourself, and I think you need to make more friends, but are you sure about marriage? How long have you known Kouji? Three months tops? That's fast. I mean, yes, we have different cultures, but this is fast, regardless."

"I know this is right," Samar stated.

Evinia's brow furrowed. "How can you be sure? You've known this kid for a few months. This is no time to be thinking about marriage."

"These have been the best three months. I've healed so much, thanks to Kouji," Samar replied.

"Three months?" Siku bellowed, interjecting himself back into this little conversation.

"Daddy, calm down." Evinia waved her hand at him.

"I will not calm down!" Siku's voice roared and his face reddened beneath his dark complexion. Alvin snickered, despite the fact it looked like Siku was about to pop a blood vessel in his head.

"Daddy," Evinia said again.

Siku turned to Kouji and put his finger in her face. "You listen here. If you ever touch Samar, I'll make you regret it. Now, you leave her be. Get out of my business and never bother my daughter again."

Kouji tilted her head. She stared at Siku's finger. "Touch? You mean like this?" Kouji wrapped her arms around Samar's waist and freed her from Siku's grip with ease. Kouji leaned down to kiss Samar's cheek.

Mechi winced. "Oh, wow, she's dead."

Alvin rubbed his hands together. "Honest and truly. This should be good."

Siku puffed up, almost like he literally got taller in front of them. Kouji wasn't sure what to make of this. He put his hand on Kouji's shoulder, clutching her tight enough for her to wince. He was a powerhouse. Impressive.

"Sir, I'm not sure why you have this reaction. You belittle Samar as if you don't care about her. You treat her as if she doesn't matter. Are you merely a bully, and she's your favorite target?" Kouji asked. She'd love to understand this man if only for Samar's peace of mind.

"Kouji!" Samar gasped, concern in her wide eyes.

"Listen to Samar, little scam artist. You don't want to test me." Siku strengthened his grip on her shoulder.

Kouji swallowed hard from the pressure, but she didn't buckle. She wouldn't bend for this man. She'd free Samar from his poisonous hold. She'd help Samar live her life.

Siku's eyes darkened. He pressed harder. Kouji flinched and her knees wobbled, but she refused to go down. Samar grabbed onto her, holding her close and giving her strength. Kouji managed to straighten herself out.

"And you wonder why I never proposed," Mechi said to Evinia under his breath, but loud enough for all of them to hear.

"Who said I wonder?" Evinia replied. "Daddy's obviously psychotic if he's going to beat up a kid who wants to make Samar happy."

Siku scowled. "I am far from psychotic. I'm protecting Samar from herself. This kid's clearly trying to scam her."

"Sir, that is far from the truth. I understand you disapprove of me being with your daughter. I'm hardly worthy of her, but you should learn to respect your daughter's decisions. I mean, she is an adult and really none of your concern, considering your attitude toward her."

"Who the hell do you think you're talking to?" Siku bellowed.

"Maybe you should cool down, Daddy. You're coming across as unhinged in front of everyone." Evinia motioned to the employees milling about, pretending they were busy. Kouji was very familiar with people trying to act like they were not listening.

"Yes, you should let Samar make her own decisions," Mechi chimed in.

Siku glared at him. "You don't have the right to tell me how to raise my daughter! She doesn't have a damn clue about how to make proper decisions, especially in this city."

Kouji leveled a hard look at Siku. There were so many words that needed to be said. "You haven't raised your daughter, sir. Perhaps, you should've left her on her little mountain, where she wouldn't have to consider such decisions in this city."

"You don't know what happened," Siku said.

Kouji continued, as if Siku had not spoken. "Instead, you had the brilliant idea of bringing her to a city she hates and that hates her in return. You ignore her for the most part because you're too ashamed to take responsibility for her. You hate her because you hate your own behavior. Then, when you're sick of being ashamed of yourself, you take it out on her to make her feel just as bad as you do that she's alive. You shouldn't beat her down because you think you made a mistake or because you don't want her. And just because you don't love her doesn't mean someone else can't."

"Shut up!" Siku burst into Kouji's space. He was fast, possibly faster than Samar, which was incredible considering his size.

Samar flinched, pressing herself closer to Kouji. But she also put herself between Kouji and Siku. Despite all this abuse, despite her fear of Siku, Samar still wanted to protect her. She was such an amazing person.

Siku raised his hand, as if he planned to punch Kouji, but Samar was still there. She trembled against Kouji, fully aware Siku might strike her, even to get to someone else. Likely, the only thing staying his hand was all of the prying eyes.

"Daddy." Evinia didn't move. It was like she knew how far gone he was. Siku was damn near foaming at the mouth.

Kouji kept her eyes locked on Siku. "You're obviously not a man who likes to hear the truth, sir. I can keep going though. You know you made her cry so many times and you don't even care." She'd never forget Samar standing outside the tomb, blaming her tears on the cold, or the rain, or stress. "You hurt her so much. You insult her often, making her feel like a creature unworthy of proper affection, or merely a mistake who has no right to be alive. If you didn't want her, why did you take her from her home?"

Siku's face twitched. "It's none of your business."

"What do you even care if I marry her or not? Is it only because you won't have someone to take out all your frustrations on?"

Kouji never liked to hear when Samar came to the tomb and spoke about her father. She never had anything good to report. Kouji always wondered how a father could do such a thing as to make his daughter feel like she was wrong for existing. Samar had no say in the matter. She didn't ask to be born. Kouji's father might not have been the most moral person on the planet, but the man never made her feel worthless. Her father never bullied her like Samar's father did her.

"You have no place to judge me," Siku snarled.

"Someone has to," Kouji insisted.

"You can't tell me how I feel about my own daughter," Siku said.

"No, but I can tell you how she thinks you feel and how right she probably is. You never did one good thing for her in her whole life. You never said a kind word to her and never smiled at her, not even when she was little. She learned to never be happy around you because you'd always make her feel stupid for that. You always regarded her with hatred in your eyes. You hated that you were responsible for her. Then you brought her to this city, and despite how many times you told her she was stupid and uneducated, you didn't bother to enroll her in school until Evinia pressed the issue. You left her in her room in your house like she was some ogre that you didn't want people to know about. You treated her like a troll, but you're the troll."

"What do you know about it? Who the hell do you think you are?" Siku barked.

"I'm the person she cries to when she knows she can't go to you. I'm the person who gives her affection she knows she'll never get from you. I'm the person who understands and accepts her because she'll never get understanding from you."

Siku visibly trembled with fury. His offspring, even Samar, gawked. His subordinates were the same. It was like Kouji was juggling a bomb right in front of them. She wouldn't care if Siku exploded.

Samar clutched Kouji's arm. "We should probably go."

"I won't let him run us off."

Samar shook her head. There was something else. Kouji followed her eyes, taking in how she watched her father. No, she looked just beyond Siku. There was a sort of shadow right behind him.

Samar wanted to rub her eyes, but dared not blink or look away. Her eyes had to be wrong. No way was this real. Above Siku's head was the dense blackness of a Nightmare. It groaned right above him, requesting that he host it.

"Take me in, and we'll show that little Abomination who the real troll is," the Nightmare hissed, focused on Kouji.

Samar had never seen a Nightmare inside Moonless Night Security. She had put up protections, but she had also come across others. She was never sure where they came from, but they made sure the headquarters remained free of that particular trouble.

The surreal situation got stranger. Siku growled and turned to the Nightmare. "You'll never get anything from me. I don't know how the hell you got in here, but you'll want to leave or you'll regret it. So be on your way." He spoke directly to the Nightmare. He saw them!

Samar's mouth dropped open. "You can see Nightmares! You hear them!" That'd explain why her mother was fascinated with this complete and utter jackass. Siku had made it a point to make Samar feel foolish if she mentioned Nightmares, yet he shared her ability. *This is probably where I got it from!*

Siku's nostrils flared. "I can ignore them just as well."

Mechi tilted his head. "Nightmares? Is that what you call the shadows?" He pointed behind Siku.

Samar blinked. "You see them too?" How the hell had she missed that? Oh, right, Mechi never had a serious conversation with her, and she made it a point not to be around him whenever she could help it.

"I've seen shadows with people, but you sound like you see it as a solid thing." Mechi might see Nightmares in the same way Kouji saw them. Aware of them, but not quite certain of the shape.

"It is a solid thing, and it's trying to get Siku to host it," Samar said.

"Host it?" Mechi echoed, brow furrowed.

"If you host me, you could actually take on the Abomination, keep it from taking your daughter," the Nightmare hissed.

"I don't need you to make that happen," Siku replied. "How the hell did you make it past the holy icons?"

And he knew about the symbols! Who the hell was this man? Samar's brain spun, trying to make sense of any of it. Words died on her tongue and her mind sputtered out.

The Nightmare laughed. "Maybe they need a touch-up, or maybe they've been overpowered. We never had a reason to come here, but now the Abomination is here. Host me and we can destroy it together."

"You think I'm so weak-willed I'd need your help to destroy anything?" Siku sucked his teeth and turned up his nose. Wow, he not only resisted the Nightmare, he insulted it. As horrible as he was, he didn't give into Nightmares. His pride was his salvation.

"What is happening?" Evinia, obviously, didn't see the Nightmare.

"A hostile takeover!" the Nightmare declared.

They were surrounded by coworkers. A dozen Moonless Night agents now hosted damn Nightmares. The holy icons had definitely been overpowered, thanks to the sheer number of Nightmares.

"Kouji, let's do this!" Samar held out her hand and Amani appeared in her grip. She shoved it into the Nightmare right behind Siku. It roared as smoke poured from her short spear.

"Samar, what the hell is going on?" Evinia asked again.

"These are Nightmares, and they need to be banished, like I've been telling you." It didn't matter. Evinia couldn't see them. But Mechi and Siku saw them, and that was too much information for her brain. She needed to put some work in.

Kouji turned around, taking care of the Nightmares at their back and the bastards who agreed to host them. She pressed her hand to the forehead of a close agent, excising the Nightmare from him. The

Nightmare screeched when Samar stabbed it. There'd be no chance to seek out another host.

There were too many people. It might be too easy for the Nightmares. If enough people agreed to host Nightmares, they could easily swarm Kouji and Samar.

Strangely enough, they weren't alone in their battle though. Siku fought off agents with Mechi at his side. And…Alvin. He focused above his opponent. Alvin could see them too. What the hell?

Chapter Twenty-One

Nighttime

SAMAR WAS LOSING FAITH in herself, Kouji, and her family's ability to emerge unscathed from this situation. In addition to the agents who hosted Nightmares, people from outside poured into headquarters. While Samar's family could see and fight back, they didn't have the ability to exterminate the Nightmares or purify the hosts. Samar had to do something.

"Mechi, give me your arm," Samar ordered.

"I kinda need it right now!" Mechi replied, as he punched a coworker away from him.

Samar spun over to him. She yanked his arm in mid-punch and shoved Amani against his forearm. She had never done this before, only heard of it, but she hoped to the Other World it would work.

"What the hell?" Mechi hissed, as Amani burned his flesh.

"You should be able to banish the Nightmares now. Just punch the dark clouds you see," Samar explained.

Mechi glanced down at Amani's holy symbols seared into his arm. The weapon's spiritual energy should be embedded in his arm now. It was a temporary solution if it worked, but it might help them get out of this madness.

Mechi turned back to the brawl and gasped. "Oh, shit! Is that what these things actually look like?" He pointed at a Nightmare hovering right above him. "I thought just the dark shadow thing was enough!"

Mechi punched at the Nightmare. The symbols on his arm smoked and the Nightmare snarled. It managed to knock Mechi off his feet before it disappeared with a shriek. The man hosting the Nightmare bent over, going through all of the usual issues of someone separated from his Nightmare.

"Ew! Is that gunk supposed to come out of them like that?" Mechi backed away from the orange goo oozing out of his coworker's mouth, nose, and eyes.

"Focus on banishing them rather than how horrifying they are or what happens when they're parted from their hosts." Samar grabbed her brother. "You can see them, right?" She needed to be sure. Using Amani on him wouldn't work unless he saw them.

"The horde of screaming monsters, yeah. The hell? Are they here for you? Here because of you?" Alvin demanded with a frown. Of course, he'd think this was somehow her fault.

"I'm not as important as you want to think I am. They're here for humans. Now, hold still." Samar shoved Alvin's sleeve up his arm and pressed Amani to his skin. His arm wasn't as big or thick as Mechi's. Amani covered his entire arm.

"Ah!" Alvin hollered in agony, as the short spear empowered his arm. "What the hell?" He glared at her, as if they had time for his attitude.

"Punch the damn Nightmares!" Samar shoved him away. She scanned the melee for Evinia, not surprised to find her beating back the crowd. This would be tough. Evinia couldn't see the Nightmares, and probably still didn't believe in them still. "Vinny," she called.

"Kinda busy, Sammie. A lot is going on here with people clearly losing their damn minds." Evinia shoved her foot into a coworker's chest. Everyone was probably surprised Evinia was as strong as she was. They were used to seeing her behind a desk, but Siku Habeen had made sure his children had more than enough skill to hold their own if someone picked a fight with them.

"Just stay close to me. I'm going to hand you tags and you have to stick them on their foreheads. Directly at the center." Samar wasn't sure if this would work either. In order for the fetish to work, Evinia would need to have some kind of spiritual power, which meant she needed to believe in something virtuous. It didn't have to be Samar's gods or religion, but it had to be a sort of righteousness. *It should be fine. Vinny's the best person I know.*

"Tags for what? How will that help?" Evinia asked with a grunt, as she blocked several punches.

"Just trust me. Forehead, now." Samar made a Favor appear in her hand and passed it to Evinia, who went right for the sweet spot.

Evinia nailed it, and the Favor did its work. Evinia stood still, probably stunned. It was probably worse for her than Mechi because the Nightmares were invisible to her. All she saw was goo pouring out of someone's face for no reason.

Someone flying in and punching Evinia right on the chin brought her back to the brawl. Samar passed her another Favor, but this system wouldn't work. She didn't have hands to spare, as more and more people came in. They'd be overwhelmed soon enough.

"Give us the Abomination and we'll go!" the Nightmares roared.

"You'll go regardless." Siku pulled a knife from his sock. Familiar smoke poured off its blade. He had a holy weapon? What the hell?! *Who is this man?!*

Samar didn't stop to watch Siku take out Nightmares. She had to figure out how to protect her sister. She glanced down at her wrist. The holy cloth connected to Amani. *It could work.*

"Vinny!" Samar called her sister again, ducking closer to her.

"Passing another thing?" Evinia eased close to Samar.

"No." Samar unwrapped her holy cloth and yanked it from Amani's hilt. "Use this to make your own Favors. You only have to believe in the righteousness of ridding people of Nightmares."

"I only have to what?" Evinia sucked her teeth. "Never mind. Explain the whole thing when this is over."

They had to hope it would be over. More and more people spilled in, hosting their own Nightmares, howling for the Abomination. There was no escape.

They fought and fought. She and Kouji exorcised Nightmares and dispatched them. Evinia handled freeing people from their Nightmares, while Mechi and Alvin took out the Nightmares. Siku was a machine, banishing Nightmares back to the Beyond as if he was born to do it. But there were too many.

Kouji was devastated. This was all her fault. Thanks to these Nightmares coming for her, Samar's family was overwhelmed, cut, bruised, and bloody. Kouji had brought Samar nothing but misery. So, yes, maybe it was a mistake to accept her proposal.

A chilled wind rushed through the corridor, tearing Kouji away from her thoughts. Everyone shivered from the arctic breeze. Kouji looked around.

"Mother?"

"I told you to call me if you need anything, and you only call me to help you cook or shop. I feel ignored." Her voice was gentle and low.

"Just to check my sanity, we all heard that, right?" Mechi scanned the area, while making sure to keep sight of the enemies around them.

"It's only Kouji's mother," Samar replied.

She'd never had the pleasure of meeting Mother, who shied away from humans and didn't want to encourage Kouji's romance.

"I swear, Kouji, all you had to do was call me as soon as this mess began," the ethereal voice said.

Kouji's mother appeared in a beam of moonlight. She was dressed all in stylish black, silky clothing, and wafting much like thick smoke. Kouji liked to think herself tall, but her mother towered over her by at least a foot.

She was a ghostly pale woman with skin the color of the full moon and sharp, lilac-colored eyes that twinkled like the stars. She was slender with long, raven hair in small braids that flowed freely down her back and appeared as smoky like her clothes. She smiled and hugged Kouji with one arm. She kissed Kouji on the cheek, ignoring the fact that all eyes, including the Nightmares, were on her.

"I'm sorry, Mother," Kouji apologized. "I merely want to prove I can handle myself. I don't want you to worry. I want to show I can take care of Samar like she does me."

Her mother waved that off. "It's quite all right. You're grown, after all. I'm aware you like to handle your problems without help from your mother. Besides, I'm the one who is truly sorry because I have to interrupt all of this." She snapped her fingers and everything paused, except for Samar and her family.

"What do you mean?" Kouji's heart sank. It couldn't be a good thing for her mother to reveal herself to so many humans.

"I have some rather dreadful news," she replied.

Kouji shook her head, knowing what was coming already. "No, Mother, I can't," she argued with a trembling voice, her insides doing the same.

"You have to," her mother said. "It's the only way to stop this." She twirled her finger, referring to the army of Nightmares and hosts around them.

Kouji held out her hands, shaking her head. "No, I don't. I won't. I don't want to leave Samar, Mother. I want a chance to live my life with her."

Samar paused, short spear in the maw of a Nightmare. "Leave me?" She turned to face them.

"Don't make me leave her, Mother." Kouji rushed to Samar so quickly no one noticed her move. She pressed Samar close to her body, never wanting to let her go. "I can't leave her, Mother."

Mother's expression was so soft, but sorrowful, saying more than her words would ever dare. "I only want what's best for you, my dearest child. I don't want you to be unhappy. I want you to live your life. You have so much to give, and you do your best with Samar. I see that. I know you love her—" Kouji cut her off.

Kouji's chin wobbled, as tears threatened to pour from her eyes. "Then why do you want me to leave her?" This was the end of the world.

"Usuku isn't happy you're awake. More, stronger Nightmares have passed into this world and are seeking you out. They're hunting you now as they did when you were first awake. Eventually, they'll make this look like a game, and the slaughter that originally sent you to sleep will look like broken toys. The gods fear Nightmares will consume all of the humans. They want you to go back to sleep before Usuku destroys the world hunting you."

Kouji swallowed hard. "Would he?" If all of the humans were gone, if the world was destroyed, gods, including Usuku, would lose the one thing that kept them alive, attention from the mortal realm. Belief and consideration from mortals fed the gods' existence. No mortals, no gods.

"It seems to be the case. It doesn't help that he hates the idea of not being able to touch this city," Mother replied.

"So he'll destroy us all?" Kouji asked with wide eyes.

Mother sighed. "Sometimes, the gods aren't rational. Often, actually."

"But Mother, Samar needs me," Kouji said.

Samar clutched Kouji tight, like she'd never let go. "Yes, I truly do," she insisted. Samar bowed, pressing her hands together. "Forgive me, Great Goddess. I am not worthy of your daughter, but we make each other better."

Mother smiled. "I am very aware that you do. You've made Kouji happier than anything in existence, including me. You've helped her come to grips with actions even I couldn't get through. But Kouji made a vow long ago, and she has to keep it. You both are quite aware of that."

Samar took a deep breath. "This isn't fair."

Mother gave her a sorrowful look. "Life is like that, unfortunately. You know how important someone's word is."

"It's a currency," Samar muttered.

Kouji's word meant everything, not only for her, but for her mother, and also her love right now. If she didn't keep her word, she'd taint Samar, who didn't deserve that.

"What do you expect me to do, Mother? Leave her and go back to that cold, empty existence in that stupid box?" Kouji demanded with tears burning her cheeks. She held Samar tight, as if telling Mother, she'd have to pry Samar from her cold, dead hands.

Mother sighed. "I expect you to live." She motioned around them to paused humans and Nightmares. "Is this meant to be your life?"

Kouji sniffled. "I'd take this life if it meant being with Samar."

Samar nodded. "I already promised to fight every Nightmare I encounter, and I'd do it twice as hard for Kouji."

"I know you would, but Kouji has not yet redeemed herself." Mother rubbed her forehead, frustrated with them. Her eyes cut into Kouji. "You don't wish to know what awaits you in death, despite the madness that grappled with your brain when you sinned. You'd still be under my supervision, as I am Goddess of the Dead. I cannot show you any particular mercy just because you're my child, and you didn't know any better most of the time. There's still the matter of the one time you did know, and that was, after all, the worst you have done. So you will go back to sleep unless you're willing to be separated from Samar, even in death," Mother ordered in a stern tone.

Kouji sucked her teeth. "And how will I redeem myself asleep? How will the Nightmares stop with me asleep? Nightmares still roamed the world when I was asleep before." Sure, they hadn't destroyed every human, but they were still around.

Mother put her hands on her hips. "I see you want to be difficult. Tell me this, Kouji, what use are you to her if you are dead?"

Kouji sighed, head dropped, chin almost on her chest. Mother had a point. "I am useless dead," she conceded.

"Nothing gets passed her," Evinia muttered.

Kouji reached out, taking her mother's hand. "I don't want to go back to sleep, Mother. I don't want to leave Samar. We'll both be so lonely."

Mother gave a small smile. "I think, thanks to you, she'll have a better chance with some people." She made a show of looking at Evinia and Mechi. Yes, after this, Evinia and Mechi would probably be open to talking to Samar about her religion and her fight against Nightmares.

Samar's father jumped into the conversation, even though it didn't really concern him. "If you're this girl's mother, it's best you keep her away from my daughter."

Mother turned to Siku with a curious tilt of her head. "Excuse you, but who are you to command me? I own the night."

"I'm Samar's father, and I won't let some little con artist take advantage of her," Siku declared.

Mother chuckled. "Take advantage of her? You make it sound like my godling has harmed your daughter, when Kouji saved her from drowning in a sea of misery you created, drowning in your shame, not allowed to grieve, for it would take her down faster."

Siku snarled. "No one stopped her from grieving! Your daughter lied to her, scammed her."

"Kouji wouldn't have a clue how to begin scamming someone. Oddly enough, this is a very honest child, like your three." Mother glanced at Evinia and Alvin. "It's amazing the job you did here with your wife when you were honest and true. Is that why you hold anger toward Samar? You realize you lost yourself when you betrayed Nyota? You remember the pain from her loyalty, as she stood by you when she found out? You remember how your soul ripped in two when she stayed, and you loved her all the more realizing how you'd ruined the best thing you ever had?"

Siku flinched. "You don't know me."

Mother fluttered closer to Siku, staring down into his eyes. "Oh, but I do. I've heard the tales, and I've seen the sights once Kouji became heartsick for your child. I know everything about you as I gaze into your eyes, and you hope like hell you're somehow worthy of everything around you. You could've been, you know? You could've earned the love and respect of your brilliant children, if you didn't think ruling by fear was the better parenting tactic. But how could you not think that? You were raised in fear, and you think you did well for yourself, so obviously they will too."

"I have done well for myself."

"Have you?" Mother's eyes fell on Samar, Evinia, and Alvin. "I think all three of them would argue otherwise for different reasons. I'm all too aware of what it's like to fail as a parent, but I also know, with some children, it's never too late to set things right. Instead of focusing your anger on my little godling, consider saving that energy for honest conversations with your own children."

"I've prepared them well for life," Siku said, chin in the air.

Mother laughed. "You've prepared them for trust issues. They'll do well in spite of you. Every single one of them. You did well out of fear of failure. They'll run laps around you, if only to rub your face in their greatness. But knowing you, you'll take credit for it anyway."

"How dare you and your damn daughter assume you know a damn thing about me? At least I'm not some con artist who lies to people to take advantage of them." Siku pointed to Kouji, so there was no confusion about whom he meant.

Samar stepped forward, hand raised. "Siku, you have to realize who you're addressing. This is the Goddess Asiku. You have to show her respect. Surely, you know that."

He scowled even more. "You can't possibly be this stupid. Your mother had so many degrees and you're standing here believing some random liar is a goddess?"

Samar's brow furrowed. "Um…she's stopped time." She motioned to the frozen Nightmares and their hosts. "Unless you think you did this." Siku didn't respond.

Mother sighed and rubbed her forehead. "Humans, I swear. The only one who ever made any sense to me is gone. I won't see my daughter suffer the same fate as her father." She turned back to Kouji. "Kouji, you are to go back to sleep. Usuku is getting impatient with me trying to stall for you."

"So?" Kouji asked.

"He has threatened you, which means he has also threatened me," she explained.

"What will he do?"

"I have no desire to find out, considering he unleashed Nightmares on the world last time and now this. I'm already troubled by how much of your life he has cost you. He knows, if he manages to destroy you before you've redeemed yourself, only pain and suffering await you in the Land of the Dead. That'd ruin me for the rest of eternity, sweet child." Mother caressed her cheek with an impossibly soft hand.

"Surely, I cannot mean so much to you," Kouji argued. She only wanted to stay and be with Samar.

"You mean more than you can ever know."

"You have dozens of other children." Mother was one of the original life forms of the universe. She had hundreds of offspring. *Why is she so focused on me?*

"I do. But you are the one memory of him…" Mother whimpered. "I cannot let his legacy be ripped apart any more than it has. He was a tender, wonderful moment in my life, and Usuku couldn't even stand to let me have that."

"Why can't you reason with the Day? You are the Night. You can do it," Kouji pled, tears prickling her eyes. Was not the whole point of her story that Day and Night understood they were equals? They were both needed? They could stand on the same level?

"On most things, yes. On this, not so much. I have given humanity tools to fight Nightmares, but Usuku will never stop hunting you and tormenting them, making sure they fear the night."

Kouji sighed. "I do not understand the gods."

Mother laughed. "We're not meant for you to understand any more than an ant understands you. But know I love you, and I want to keep you safe. I want you to be able to live."

"There is no life without Samar, not now, and not ten thousand years from now."

Mother sighed. "I know and I understand better than most, my child. But all you do is leave yourself a target, making her a target, fighting Nightmares until you die. And that's if you're lucky."

That hit Kouji in the gut. She couldn't be responsible for Samar's death. She had already had her hand in the death of too many innocents. She wouldn't be able to live with herself if Usuku harmed Samar to get to her.

Kouji let loose a long breath, shoulders dropping. She turned to Samar with all of the despair in the world weighing her down. Samar shattered right before her eyes.

"Don't…" Samar whispered.

Kouji took Samar around the waist. "I have to. I don't want this life for you."

"This is already my life."

"No. Your life is in books, scholarly pursuits, and maybe saving some souls on the side. You're more than a hunter of Nightmares, Samar. You deserve the life your mother wanted for you."

Samar clung to her. "She'd love to know you found me. You saved me. She'd love to know I had someone to take care of me, to make sure I was all right, and to share my interests with me."

"But she wouldn't want you to die by Nightmares, or something worse. In fact, hasn't she been protecting you from Nightmares your entire life?" Kouji refused to undo all of Samar's mother's work.

"She didn't want me to be alone…" Samar whispered.

"You won't be. You'll leave this place. You'll go to school. You'll meet people who understand your wonderful mind and your holy actions. I promise you, it'll get better. You'll be great with or without me. You know where I'll be, my love." Kouji kissed her, needing Samar to experience everything that was within her, everything Samar gave her. She needed to give it all back and more. She needed Samar to understand how truly amazing she was.

Samar kissed her back, pouring love into her. Fortified by Samar's love, Kouji would keep her word and do right by humanity, despite the fact that her insides were torn apart. It took all of her willpower to stay on her feet.

When Kouji pulled away, she saw the universe in Samar's eyes, every happiness and sorrow to ever exist. She saw all of her dreams in those eyes and felt all of her desires against her fingertips. Surely, this would sustain her through thousands of years of sleep.

"Underneath it all, you've learned to care, not just about me, but about yourself and others. You could be someone great if allowed to stay awake." Samar's gaze drifted to Mother.

Mother gave her a sad smile. "I agree with you, my child. Unfortunately, sometimes, we have to make the hard choices."

"Even gods?" Samar asked.

Mother chuckled. "Even gods. There's more to this world than you, or even I will ever know. Usuku won't stop. If the Nightmares don't do his will, he'll conjure creatures capable of greater horrors."

"You'd think the Day would have better things to do," Samar muttered.

Mother shrugged. "Gods can multitask…and hold grudges. We're very good at holding grudges. I mean, you saw that in how Kouji came to be created. Humanity shunned me, and I did the same back. I have humiliated the Day, so he shall return the favor in some way. Now, please." She motioned to the door.

Kouji swallowed as she caressed Samar's cheek. "We may not understand, but we know what must be done. You've helped teach me righteousness. I must do this for us all. I need you to live your life. I need you to live."

Tears streamed down Samar's face, but she nodded. "Never forget, you saved me."

"We saved each other. And no matter how long I'm asleep, I'll never forget what you did for me. I'll never forget how you make me feel. I'll love and cherish you long after the sun has died," Kouji vowed. Her emotions would outlast the Day by eons.

Mother stepped over and put her hand on Samar's shoulder. "I want you to know, I never once disapproved of you. I've always held you in high regard, even before you met and loved my daughter. Your mother was devoted to my teachings and brought you into my fold.

You pass out my Favors and cure mankind. I have always recognized the greatness in your line. I would've enjoyed having you as my daughter."

Samar's mouth moved, but no words came out for a long time. "I do my best to honor those of the past."

Mother smiled. "I'd never ask more of you. Forgive me for hurting you like this. You have the strength to survive. Besides, you have more to live for now than ever before." She glanced over at Samar's family. "Someone has to train that lot to properly fight Nightmares, now that they know what they're looking at."

Samar nodded. "I'll do my best."

"That's all any of us can do." Mother kissed Samar's forehead, leaving a tiny black dot on Samar's skin, then stood to her proper height and turned to Kouji. "It's time to go."

In a mist of blackness, Samar faded from Kouji's eyes, but she'd never fade from Kouji's heart and mind.

Samar couldn't stop herself from reaching out and trying to grab the smoke that took Kouji from her life, leaving a void in her soul. She wanted to yank Kouji back. She wanted nothing more than to hold her.

"I can't!" Samar took off, right for the door. She wouldn't survive another loss. She needed Kouji to make it through life.

"Sammie!" Evinia called out, but Samar had no plans to stop. She had no idea what she'd do, but she had to get back to Kouji.

Evinia's footsteps pounded behind her, but Samar still ran full speed. She made it to the tomb in record time, Nightmares on her back. They halted as soon as she crossed the threshold of the tomb.

The door was open. Kouji and Goddess Asiku were in plain sight. This was wrong, but then again, so was Kouji going to back to sleep. Nothing good had come from Kouji sleeping for ten thousand years. She didn't get to live, and Nightmares roamed the entire planet, ruining people more so than people ruined themselves. Samar rushed inside.

"Excuse me, I just…I can't leave it like this!" Samar threw her arms out as her chest heaved and her insides trembled. Kouji and Goddess Asiku turned to her. "I've only just met Kouji. She's not in my imagination in this building. She's here, real, flesh and blood."

The goddess smiled at her. Samar should already feel beyond blessed. The goddess favored her, kissed her, even blessed her to be with Kouji if it were possible. She should be smote for daring to interfere, to ask for more, but how could she not?

"Does it really have to end this way?" Samar asked, eyes darting between mother and daughter.

Kouji gave her a half smile, chin shaking. "It does. We have to keep people as safe as we can."

"But has this worked? Nightmares still plague people. I'll still be alone."

"That's the beauty now. You're not alone. You know where I am. You have your sister. I can't put you at risk, and neither of us can put others at risk. You're not built that way."

Samar was unable to argue that. She was in the business of saving people as best she could. At least, keeping them from hosting Nightmares and allowing them to harm others.

"I'm sorry, Samar. I was only a dream," Kouji said.

Samar sighed, body in full revolt, every nerve ready to rip out of her. "Then, what am I to you?"

Kouji grinned, like everything would be all right. "The reason I woke up."

"Like when my mother left, I'll be lost without you. What am I meant to do without you by my side?" Samar asked.

"You don't need me, Samar. You have more than you're willing to recognize right now. Mother already pointed it out. Besides, I'm still here. You can come talk to me anytime, and you know I can hear."

"But you can't respond. You can't spend time with me. We can't spar, or go skating, or cook, or read together. This isn't the same. You made my apartment feel like a home. I was always rushing to get there. I always want it to be like that. I want to feel how I feel when I get home and smell food cooking all the time. I want you there to keep me warm when it's cold. I want you there to drag me outside and go skating. I just want you with me."

Kouji smiled once more. "It was such fun. I'll miss all of that, but I can't put you or anyone else in danger. You taught me to protect people. I'll honor you in this act."

Samar ground her teeth, biting back a sob. "Of lying down and never getting up again? Going to sleep the first time didn't solve anything. When will it ever be safe for you to wake up?"

Kouji shook her head. "I have no idea." She glanced at her mother for guidance.

"I wish I knew," Goddess Asiku said. "You know I'll come for you, eventually."

"It was already ten thousand years, my Goddess. When does Kouji get this life we all wish for her?" Samar had the nerve to ask. *Someone* had to ask. Kouji had a habit of following her mother, probably on faith, on instinct, and on culture.

"I wish I knew." Goddess Asiku's eyes were wet.

"That's not an answer," Samar stated.

"I'm aware. But at least you can still visit her as you once did. Now, say your goodbyes. I can't hold off Nightmares forever without destroying the fabric of this world," Goddess Asiku said.

Samar turned back to Kouji, planting quick kisses to Kouji's lips. That bright smile remained, but lilac eyes were full of unbearable sorrow. It cut somewhere past Samar's soul. This was like attending Kouji's funeral, complete with a coffin and the Goddess of Death standing by.

"Ready?" Goddess Asiku asked.

"I doubt I'll be getting any more ready than I am now. Watch over Samar for me, Mother. Try to keep away anyone that means to harm her," Kouji requested.

The goddess nodded. "The night shall be her guardian. Every shadow on the land will defend her. Every spirit will protect her," she promised.

Kouji sighed and smiled. She squared her shoulders and stood tall. "Then I can sleep without any worries." This was decided. There was no way to change Kouji's mind or her mother's. Kouji had accepted her fate.

"Goodnight, Kou," Samar whispered.

Kouji gave one last sigh and gave Samar one last kiss before stepping over to her coffin. Kouji stared at the marble box, then turned back to Samar. She reached out and yanked Samar to her.

"Never forget I love you."

"You also never forget I love you," Samar replied.

"All right, you two," Goddess Asiku said.

"Dream of me," Samar requested of Kouji.

"Always." Kouji eased the marble slab off her resting place. Stepping into the coffin, she sighed. Goddess Asiku took a deep breath. They both closed their eyes and Goddess Asiku waved her hand in the direction of her daughter.

Kouji gritted her teeth, bracing herself for whatever was to come. As the goddess chanted, Kouji's body cracked and shifted to the color of coal. She became black sand that fell into a pile in her coffin.

It was over.

Chapter Twenty-Two

Midnight

"WHOA," SAMAR HEARD ALVIN from the doorway of the tomb, but he sounded a million miles away.

Samar was a million miles away, no longer of this world, consumed by sorrow and fury. Why? Why was she left to mourn again? Why! "Kou..." Her insides ground against themselves, like glass shards shredding her from the inside out.

Several minutes passed before Samar turned. Her family, including her father, stood right outside the gate. They stared at her as if she'd turned to dust right along with Kouji. Samar would never give Siku such satisfaction. Taking a deep breath, she did her best to shake it off and pull herself together. She needed to keep going, to live life for herself and for Kouji. Samar wipe tears from her face.

"So, Sammie, was that actually Kouji Kataban of the legends?" Evinia glanced between Samar and the closed coffin.

Samar's heart thumped, squeezing hard on itself. "Yes, that was Kouji." She looked back at Goddess Asiku. "Will she ever wake up?"

"One day, when she's ready," the goddess promised, but this didn't instill Samar with confidence. "But do not wait for her. Live your life, as she would want. Live for her. Live for your mother. Live a life they'd both be proud of."

Samar swallowed around a lump in her throat. "I'm not sure I know how." She had drifted through life without her mother. Could she handle another loss?

Goddess Asiku smiled at her, eyes sparkling, like she knew Samar better than Samar knew herself. "You do, my dear. Despite what your father says, he knows you're extraordinary. You know it too. You have merely forgotten under these grey skies and cold rains."

"Will that change one day?"

Goddess Asiku glanced at the tomb. "I think it will have to. While I am the Night, I understand the need for both. We need balance after chaos to continue to exist."

"And does the Day not understand the same?"

"Of course. But do we always do the right thing only because we understand it's right?"

"Even the gods?"

She shrugged. "Even the gods."

Samar nodded, even though she didn't fully understand. The gods weren't as perfect as humans liked to believe. It'd take her a while to reconcile her faith with reality.

"You should return to your family. You have things to do. Kouji will be back. Don't doubt it. She woke up before because she worried for you. Now, she'll miss you and be worried. I have no illusions that she will rest peacefully. She won't sleep long without you," Goddess Asiku said.

"Didn't you say it was dangerous for her to wake up?"

"It is, so I have to work fast. She'll want to prove herself to you, prove she can protect you. She'll want to face Usuku and settle things, as she tried to do once before."

Samar's eyes shot up and she stared at the goddess. "She tried what?" Why in the world would Kouji try to challenge the King of the Gods? Insanity.

Goddess Asiku held up her hand. "I did not allow it. But now, I have to do something. Keep your head up until Kouji's impatience shines through. Until then, I'll listen for your prayers." Goddess Asiku vanished in a swirl of darkness. A hint of jasmine lingered, followed by a whiff of lemongrass.

Samar was alone. But not really. She put her hands on the cold marble of the tomb. *Kou…* Her insides quivered and picked themselves apart. She took a deep breath, trying to pause the grief for now.

Her attention went back to the doorway, where they all gawked at her.

"Sammie…" Evinia's soft whisper reached Samar.

Samar moved without a thought and fell into Evinia's arms. Evinia held her tight. Hell, held her together as she bawled. Evinia cooed something in her ear, but her brain refused to make sense of it. The only thing that mattered was Kouji was gone.

Evinia desired nothing more than to take Samar home. She was shocked Samar didn't break away and run home. It wasn't like it was far. But Samar clung to Evinia and Evinia held her, keeping her upright as best she could.

"We need to get back to HQ and see what that mess looks like," Siku said.

"You think those shadow monsters are still there?" Mechi inquired.

Siku frowned. "If they are, we'll handle them. If they're not, some people need to be fired after all this nonsense."

"But weren't they possessed or whatever?" Alvin asked.

"No. They welcomed those Nightmares, hoping the damned things would help them achieve whatever darkness they had in their hearts."

"What do you mean? What do you know about those things?" Evinia pressed her father.

"I know enough. Now, back to base. We'll debrief in my office."

Evinia glanced at her sister. "Maybe Sammie should go home." She watched her father turn and leave.

Despite everything that happened, his feelings for Samar hadn't changed. Incredible. Evinia followed, trying to hold up Samar's dead weight. Surprised when her load lightened, she glanced over to find Mechi at Samar's other side. Evinia gave him a grateful smile.

They made it back and found Moonless Night Headquarters much more orderly than they'd expected. People were even tidying up. Apparently satisfied, Siku kept moving. They took the elevator to the top floor and walked the long hallway to the executive office. The scent of jasmine wafting through the air contrasted with the black furniture and dark walls.

Evinia and Mechi set Samar down on the leather couch, then settled beside her. Evinia wrapped her arm around Samar's shoulders and pulled close. Samar had calmed down enough to stop crying, but she shivered as if freezing. The office was silent.

Suddenly, Samar laughed. The sound was borderline unhinged. "That's why she liked you." Samar was still laughing like she'd heard the punch line of a great joke.

"What?" Evinia asked.

Samar swung her head in Siku's direction. "Of course, that's what she saw in you! You can fucking see them!" Her laughter was now truly hysterical. "You can see them, and you never even warned your son? You never checked to see if he could see them, if they might be tormenting him?" She focused on Alvin.

Siku snarled. "He's fine."

"Fine? Alvin, how long have you seen them?" Samar turned back to Siku. "Because if he's been seeing them as long as I have, he's not fine. And I know what the hell I'm looking at! I can only imagine what hell he's been through!"

Alvin blinked and ducked his head, suddenly shy. "It's been fine."

Samar shook her head. "They used to wake you out of your sleep, didn't they? Whisper to you? They promised you things, but something always told you they were dangerous, right? Something that unnerved you, crawled under your skin, and scratched at you? The way they moved, morphed, even smelled bothered you. And you thought you were being haunted? Then maybe even hunted?

"My mother started teaching me as soon as I mentioned the things that tormented me at night, but they still left their mark. I remember. And I hate to think what kind of trauma Alvin has lived with, having to deal with those things on his own for his entire life."

Alvin swallowed and his voice shook. "Ye-yeah."

"Did you ever teach him the prayers or at least spray rose water for him?" Samar climbed to her feet.

Siku frowned. "Lower your voice."

"No! Just no! You knew about these things. You knew what I was dealing with in the park. You knew. You assigned me to Okunkun Park because of the Nightmare activity. You're a worse terror than the Nightmares." Samar huffed and dropped back down to the sofa.

"What are you even talking about?" Evinia finally asked. She seemed to be the only one who couldn't see, or comprehend, whatever the hell they were so upset about.

Samar shook her head, scrubbing her face. "The Nightmares. I told you when I first got here. I hunt Nightmares. You thought I was just being crazy, or superstitious, or whatever. But I bet Alvin used to run to you about the shadows in his room."

Evinia nodded. "He did. It lasted for years."

Alvin sniffed, folding his arms across his chest. "I used to go to Mom. Dad started sending me back to my room when I was about six."

Samar shook her head. "I can't believe it. How could you do this to him?" She glared at Siku as if he were the worst person imaginable. "He was a little kid. You were supposed to help him, protect him."

Siku growled and pounded on his chest with his fist. "He was fine, just like I was! You think you're the only one who grew up seeing those things! I dealt with it and so did he!"

"What the hell kind of way is that to think?" Samar glowered at him with a burning intensity. "Mom would've given everything to be able to see those damn things to protect me from them!"

"Instead she had you fighting them!"

"Of course, she had me fighting them. They were tormenting me! Like they've been tormenting Alvin." Samar turned to their brother. "Look, I'm more than aware of how you feel about me, but I'll show you how to stop the damn Nightmares from bothering you. You can choose to fight them to help others if you want, but you at least need to be aware of how to keep them away from you."

Alvin only nodded. He scrubbed his face with his hands, but it did nothing for the worry lines under his eyes. Maybe Evinia was lucky not to be able to see whatever the hell they were talking about.

"Mechi, I'll show you too," Samar said.

Mechi chuckled and bumped his shoulder against her. "To hell with that. You'll show me everything. I've always wondered what the hell those things were. I thought my eyesight was messed up, but no doctor ever wanted to give me glasses. Parents thought I was out of my mind, and I learned to stop talking about them. Do they possess people?"

"No, people agree to host Nightmares. Nightmares seek out people with dark desires and promise them the power to commit those acts. Most people agree. Unless the Nightmare is exorcised from the person, it'll feed off its host until the host is nothing more than their desires and they'll do anything to get what they want. They're here to corrupt humans, but not in the way we want to believe. We're already capable of the things we do with Nightmares, but they give us the opportunity to take things to the extreme," Samar explained.

Mechi nodded. "So we're surrounded by people who would've killed us for power?"

"Yup," Samar answered as it if were so simple.

"Damn. Explains why they're getting fired." Mechi sucked his teeth. "Do you have any idea why we can see them?"

Samar shrugged. "Nope. Only some people can fully see them. Some people can vaguely see them. And some people can't see them at all. There are ways to help enhance your sight, and your ability to fight them." She held out her arm, displaying her tattoos. "I can fully see them, but the marks help protect me when the Nightmares use their powers."

Evinia took Samar's hand. "Is this why...is this why you've been getting so beaten up lately?"

Samar nodded. "They were in overdrive, trying to find Kouji."

"From the epic poem?" Evinia asked to be sure. This was so insane.

"Yes," Samar confirmed.

Evinia sighed. "That makes as much sense as everything else tonight. I need a drink." She turned to their father. "Daddy, unless you have something important to add here, I think we're all going to leave."

Siku puffed up. "Excuse me? You were not dismissed yet."

Evinia stood. "All the same, it's been a long night." She needed to get her siblings to safety, and safety meant away from their father. Samar could explain all of this in the comfort of Evinia's apartment. "Sammie, you're staying with me tonight."

Samar didn't argue. Siku barked at them as they left, but they had to go. Evinia was exhausted. She could only imagine how the others felt. She loaded her siblings into her car and told Mechi to meet her at her place. They arrived at the same time.

Evinia's condo was modern, decked out in dark blues and whites. Dusk rushed out to greet them, rubbing against all of their legs. They all gave the large, black cat attention with head and back rubs, and Evinia poured them all some whiskey. Yes, including her underaged brother.

Alvin sipped and winced. "I can't believe he never…" He shook his head. "Why would he do this to us?"

Evinia sighed. "You heard him. That's how he was raised. Let's consider moving forward rather than back. Sammie said she'll help you. Is that enough for now?"

Alvin took another sip. "I guess it'll have to do. It just…it feels like a betrayal for him to know and not do anything. I used to be so freaked out."

Evinia chuckled. "You act like I wasn't there. You crawled into my bed until you were ten. After that, I had to make up a little bed for you on the floor." He'd slept on her floor most nights until she moved out. She reached out and grabbed Samar's hand. "I'm sorry for doubting you. I can only imagine how much more isolated this made you feel. But I'm here for you. For anything." *Shit, Sammie just lost her fiancée along with all of this other madness.*

"I'm aware." Samar downed her drink in one gulp. Well, this was bad.

"We're here for you, Samar, like you're here for us." Mechi clapped her on the shoulder.

Samar only nodded. Once they finished their drinks, everyone agreed it was time for bed. Samar walked around the apartment, carving something near the windows with that short spear that appeared in her hand. This really was a lot. They'd have to talk more tomorrow.

Time moved on, as it tended to do. Samar kept working, shocked she wasn't fired when her father "cleansed" the office. She didn't ask questions, didn't make assumptions. She ignored him now. He didn't exist as far as she was concerned.

Beyond working, her days were spent teaching. Evinia, Mechi, and Alvin were good students. Samar contacted her former teachers for guidance on teaching her family, including Mechi, about Nightmares. She hadn't reached out to them since her mother's death, and they were glad to hear from her. Knowing she'd been missed gave her some joy. She'd do better with them.

She asked for contacts they might have in Oganja to get her family proper protection tattoos and marks to help them against Nightmares. Her old teachers provided a short list of trusted people for her to get in touch with. She did so immediately.

Through the teaching and learning, the family began to enjoy spending time together. Evinia threw herself into the scholarly pursuits of Nightmares. She also made it a point to cook one meal with Samar every day.

"You don't have to do this, you know?" Samar said, as they moved around each other in the kitchen.

"Of course I don't. But it's about time for me to learn more about your culture and to teach you about mine."

"Yeah, I'm kind of curious about the stuff you do."

"I'll be more than happy to show you. I'm sorry I didn't make proper time for you before."

"It's fine. You have your life and your own problems. You were there for me more than anyone else."

"And I'll still be here for you, always and forever. You can pour your heart out to me if you need to."

"I've always known this."

They finished their meal, a mashup of their different cultures. Evinia ate at the dining mat for the first time. She had tons of questions as to why they ate on the floor rather than at a table. And also "why eat with your hands?" Samar was more than happy to answer every question.

Things improved with Alvin. He took to his Nightmare training with vigor, which was expected. Siku had made sure both Alvin and Evinia were masters of martial arts before their double digits. Weird he didn't do anything about their spiritual training.

Alvin had a million inquiries about Nightmares, and she did her best to answer them. She also recommended tons of books. He borrowed from her bookshelves and made sure to return each one just as he got it.

Little by little, Alvin used the Nightmares to open up about his mother. He doubted Nyota could see them, but she seemed to understand what he was seeing more than Siku. Nyota comforted him when Siku allowed it and assured him he could see those things because he was meant to protect people. He thought it meant he'd protect people like Siku did, working at Moonless Night Security.

"Do you think she meant I'd protect people like you've been doing?" Alvin was sitting in Samar's living room with a book in his lap.

"Maybe." She shrugged. "I have no idea what Nyota knew about Nightmares. I only know her through Evinia's stories, and Evinia wasn't aware of Nightmares. She didn't believe me when I told her."

"I suppose. I wish I knew what this was back then, so I could ask her."

"I'm sorry. I know how that is. From fighting Nightmares here and from meeting Kouji, I have tons of questions for my mother."

Alvin sighed and glanced away. "Yeah, I'm sorry."

They were quiet, but it was something. He had stopped insulting her, stopped wishing her untimely death. They might be all right one day, or so Evinia said. Samar began to believe her.

Things seemed to be all right with Mechi as well. The way he threw himself into their training reminded Samar of training when she was a small child. He was happier than Alvin to finally make sense of the shadows he'd seen his entire life and never understood. They frightened him when he was younger. When he came to realize not everyone saw them, he assumed they couldn't harm him. How wrong he was.

"They never really bothered me," Mechi said, as he traced the symbols on his wrist. He had gone all in with holy tattoos on both wrists, his left forearm, his right bicep, and one he planned for his chest. It was fine. The more tattoos, the more he could focus his energy on stopping Nightmares and keeping them at bay.

"That's weird. Can you hear them?" Samar asked, as they made their way through Asale market. Her insides twisted with every step, remembering Kouji. But they needed to come through to buy books.

"They sound like whispers to me, but I can't really understand them. Do they speak Jinoi?"

"No. They speak whatever language they need to for the human to understand. I'm impressed with you."

He gave her a sidelong glance. "Why?"

"I've heard theories that if you can't understand them, they can't corrupt you. I've never met anyone like that though. I guess you are special."

"That's what my girlfriend says," he replied with a laugh.

"I guess I can see what she sees in you."

"We should probably go pick her up from the bookstore. Without supervision, she'll have bought all the books by now. Why did we agree to leave her there?" Mechi scratched his head.

"Because we had other books to gather, and we didn't want to stand there for the better part of two hours with her." Samar thought her mother was bad, but Evinia might have spent a month's pay on books without them to stop her.

"Yeah, she's dove into this with enthusiasm, huh?"

"Says the guy who just got his fifth holy tattoo in less than two weeks."

Mechi chuckled. "You got me. I'm really into this, and it's been fun learning from you. I like protecting people. It's one of the things that I learned from Siku. It keeps me around, even though he's an asshole."

"Was he always this way to you?"

Mechi shook his head. "No. He used to be real good to me. Treated me like a son. I liked it since my own father was often away."

"Doing what?" Samar didn't know much about Mechi's family.

"Military. He's great when he's here, and he's great to talk to over the computer, but I needed the physical presence Siku offered. He was good until he noticed how my affection changed for Evinia. I didn't even act on my feelings until Nyota…" A soft smile settled on his face. "She told me to take care of Evinia, to make sure Siku doesn't crush her."

"They always clashed?"

"Yeah. I think he didn't exactly know how to raise her. He really is the product of his own parents. Nyota experienced them enough to understand what Siku lived. I didn't understand what she meant until he turned on me."

"Do you…do you hate him now?" Samar never would've thought to ask Mechi such a personal question before.

Mechi tapped his chin. "I don't really hate him. I think I'm more annoyed. Like he can't see the forest for the trees, or some metaphor I don't get. He can't see the world or people in any other way than his. Having met his parents, I kinda understand. They controlled him, so now he tries to control the world. You see a bit of it in Evinia. Only she handles it better and can turn it off. He can't."

"That makes sense."

"Do you hate him?"

Samar sighed. "I am not a perfect human being, despite almost being a monk."

He laughed. "For about a year, I assumed you were a monk."

"Yes, you were terrible for a long time. Only now do I understand why my sister sees fit to date you."

Mechi continued to laugh, but he clutched his chest over his heart. "Ouch."

"I hated that man for a long time. In my culture…our parents are revered. You hear it in how I talk about my mother."

Mechi nodded. "Yeah, she's definitely holy to you."

"She earned that. He's supposed to do things to earn that status in my eyes, and he never did. Then, coming here and seeing how he treats Evinia and even Alvin…he's not worthy of being a parent. But he is and I hate that. I hate that he had the nerve to have kids but has no idea how to be a parent."

"Makes sense, I guess."

"You think you might be a parent?"

Mechi yelped. "You don't just get to ask that!"

"Welcome to how I felt every time you said something stupid to me."

"I was an idiot. I was trying to get to know you in a very dumb way, and I'm sorry about that. Thanks for looking past it and giving me a chance."

Samar shrugged. "It's nice to have others who can see, who want to hunt. It doesn't hurt you're my sister's partner. And unlike the gods, I don't hold grudges."

A grin smeared across his face. "You sure you're not a monk?"

Samar chuckled and they made it to their last shop, then had to double back to the first bookstore, where Evinia was somehow still looking at books. She had a pile on the counter. The cashier met their eyes, like he remembered they'd brought Evinia in.

"We're keeping her. She's one of us now," the cashier joked.

"Sorry. She's not from Asale. The people will never go for that," Samar replied.

The cashier laughed. "I'll adopt her into my clan. We need more people. She knows all of the books in here and can summarize them."

"Yes, she's a genius, which is why we have to take her back." Samar shrugged.

Mechi paid for Evinia's mountain of books. They practically had to drag Evinia out of the store, so they could return to Samar's apartment. She and Evinia started cooking, while Mechi read a philosophy book that explored the concept of who might accept Nightmares and why and the trouble those decisions could cause.

"How are you doing, Sammie?" Evinia separated ingredients on the counter.

Samar took a deep breath. "I'm better than I expected." *But still awful.* Having her siblings and Mechi around was a good distraction most of the time, but she remained raw, hollow.

"I'm sorry this is how things worked out for you, but what if this was for the best?"

Samar inhaled sharply and glared at her sister. "How could this be for the best? You think Kouji was like the stories? A monster?"

Evinia held up her hands. "I didn't say that. I know there's something more to her than the stories from the way she went back to sleep to keep you safe. But maybe it's for the best because you've already been through so much. You've had your life blown apart once before. If... if the Day succeeded with destroying Kouji in the worst manner possible, I worry you might not survive that."

All strength drained from Samar instantly. It was a miracle she didn't fall over, but she leaned on the counter to remain standing. "I'm not sure I'm surviving this. I'm only distracted. When at least one of you is around, I can put all of my focus on you. When I'm out fighting Nightmares, I can focus on them. In quiet times, when it's just me, I crumble. I feel her everywhere. Then I realize she's not here, and all the feeling leaves and I'm empty. I'm empty." A sob escaped her.

Wonderful things happened around Samar, and she couldn't even appreciate them. Her relationships with her family had improved. She went out more because of those improved relationships. She had a life of some kind. It meant nothing to her. She was nothing.

Evinia wrapped her in a tight hug. "Let it out. Let it all out, and slowly good things will trickle back in."

Samar wasn't sure that was true. Yes, her world had imploded when her mother died, and she was now piecing it back together. Life was different, a little misshapen, but reforming. Maybe things would get better if she could only wait that long.

Samar stood outside the tomb, hands clutching the iron gate. She came to the tomb every night, just like before. Except now, her voice abandoned her. She couldn't tell Kouji about her life. How could she? Not when Kouji wasn't allowed to have a life.

She opened her mouth, but couldn't bring herself to say those words either. Kouji would hear her. She didn't want to be seen as wallowing. Kouji made this sacrifice to protect her, to protect humanity. It wouldn't be fair for Kouji to listen to Samar being miserable.

The silence fit with the emptiness inside of her. Even her words had deserted her. They only came when she needed to put on a show for her family. *Is it a show?*

No, it wasn't a show. She enjoyed being around her family. She was less alone in the world and in less danger. People cared about her. She should be happy. Kouji wanted her to live. Samar dishonored her love by not even trying to find fulfillment.

I have no idea how to live like this. It was draining, which explained why she was empty. She didn't know what to do. Was this something time would cure? Would she wake up one day and not think of Kouji? What kind of person would she be if this were the case?

The wind rustled, blowing leaves off the ground. Samar felt a hand on her shoulder. Asiku never failed to join her when she visited the tomb. Asiku let Samar stand in a long silence every time. She had to have some insight though. She wasn't just a goddess. Asiku was *the* goddess.

"I feel I owe you an apology, dear Samar," Asiku said. "I see your misery, just as I see Kouji's. I had no intention of making either of you feel this way."

Samar didn't blame the goddess. Hell, she didn't even blame Usuku. Misery seemed to be her natural state of being now, and Kouji had practically been born cursed. What hope could they have?

With a sigh, Samar pushed off the gate and started toward the park. "Nothing can be done."

Asiku gave her a curious look. "Of course, there is something to be done. There's always something to be done. Stagnation leads to nothingness."

"Is that not what we all came from, nothingness?"

Asiku shook her head. "Chaos comes from nothingness. We cannot exist in nothingness, no more than we can exist in chaos."

"Chaos is subjective."

"Not true, my dear. I don't expect you to understand this one. But something can be done. For you, that something is to continue living, even if it's only moment by moment. You have to put one foot in front of the other until you can walk without consciously thinking about it."

"And what is Kouji meant to do while I put one foot in front of the other? Sleep?"

"Process. Kouji's had a lot happen to her in the past few months. She fell in love and accepted a proposal. She found a purpose in life. She needs to process everything."

Samar could see the truth in Asiku's words. Kouji had woken up ten thousand years into the future and began building a life in this new time. She had done so much in such a short amount of time, and she had only gone with the whirlwind rather than gathering herself.

"And what are you meant to do?" Samar asked the goddess.

Asiku sighed, but she smiled. "Take care of the two of you and work toward a brighter future for you both."

"Are you doing that?" The question was probably disrespectful, but as she told Mechi, she wasn't a monk. Not to mention, Asiku snatched Kouji from her.

Asiku didn't lose her smile. "Of course. I would never leave the burden on you two. You have enough to worry about."

"Then, what's your plan?"

Asiku shook her head. "Nothing for your mortal mind to ponder. You barely understand the grudge. You won't be able to comprehend the solution."

Samar grunted but accepted those words. She didn't understand any of this. Asiku was the best equipped to fix this, but would she? She hadn't fixed Kouji's situation for ten thousand years. Why would that change now? Samar shook away those thoughts, as Asiku vanished into the darkness.

"Hold strong, my dear. I'll do my part," Asiku whispered through the wind. Samar had little choice. She put one foot in front of the other.

Chapter Twenty-Three

Waking Dream

KOUJI SAT IN A VOID, surrounded by darkness. She was nothing, so why not be in nothing?

"This isn't healthy," Asiku said, as she sat beside Kouji. "Especially the thoughts you're having."

"It's better than the usual dreams I have." Kouji tended to dream of being in an eternal free fall. Whenever Asiku appeared, it was nice to have company to fall with, but it was still maddening. Being asleep was maddening.

"I suppose."

"And all of it is better than dreaming of Samar." She missed Samar every moment and pain rippled through her. She'd never heal from these wounds. "I had a dream about her recently, a memory. I was holding her as she settled in for sleep. She was so warm and real…then I was falling. I ended up in this void. I keep dreaming about her." Kouji shook her head.

"I'm aware. That's why I visit you so little, to give you those moments."

"That's all I have of her."

"She visits, but she's quiet."

That wasn't helpful. "It'd be sweet to at least hear her voice." It'd make this hell a little more bearable.

"She has no idea what to say. She doesn't want to upset you, so she won't tell you any good news or any bad news. She's stuck."

That made some sense. Kouji gave her mother a sidelong glance. "Her sister actually came to visit me. I'm not sure what time it was, but she spoke a little before saying she had to go to work. She asked me what I did to her little sister because she had never seen Sammie so lost. She was drowning before, almost purposeless, but now she's something Evinia couldn't even explain."

"She's trying her best, but she misses you."

"Evinia's not sure if she wants me to wake up again." It was a surprise when Evinia properly introduced herself outside the tomb, only a couple of days after Kouji went to sleep. Evinia had plenty to say, most of which a mother wouldn't want to hear about her child. "She says I have to have some good in me because I made Samar happy enough to propose. She also says Samar has questionable taste when it comes to relationships."

Asiku smiled a little. "You once agreed."

Kouji shrugged. "It's still true to an extent. Evinia feels sorry for me. She's thrown herself into researching my past and says my parents didn't have a right to ruin me like they did and that Usuku was unfair for punishing me for something I had no control over."

"She's not wrong."

"Evinia can't support her little sister being with someone like me because of the many crimes I committed." Kouji agreed, but it hurt to hear. She wasn't worthy of Samar. "She admitted she's scared for Samar, whether I wake up or not."

"And?" Asiku seemed to know Kouji was going somewhere with this conversation.

"Evinia didn't have a chance to know me like Samar did. I want to prove her wrong. I want to show her that I want the best for Samar and would take care of Samar. I want her sister to see, to believe."

Her mother sighed. "And to do that, you'll wake up."

"I can't stay here forever, Mother." Kouji stared off into the darkness. "I'm scared she'll forget me. If you didn't tell me she comes to the tomb, I wouldn't have a clue." Kouji was already going out of her mind. Those first few days when she didn't know Samar was out there, she dry-heaved often, body—not even real—sick with worry and loneliness.

"She's heartbroken."

Kouji shook her head. "That's why I need to get up. I had such a scary dream the other day."

"What happened?"

"I never woke up. Samar faded from my mind. Usuku never forgave us, so I never woke up." The idea of forgetting Samar frightened her more than anything. Samar was the first person, outside of her mother, to care for her, not just her talents. She'd rather face Usuku and all the other gods than have Samar gone from her mind.

Asiku held up a hand. "You don't worry about Usuku. He's my burden to bear, not yours."

"Yet I'm a target."

"Because he's short-sighted at the best of times. He seems to think that punishing humanity for all eternity over a moment in time is fine, but he's not always like that."

"It doesn't seem that way."

"The Day can be fickle." Asiku shrugged, as if that made any sense or made things better.

Kouji scowled. "What does that even mean?"

"It means sometimes Usuku is irrational. You see it with the day. Sometimes, the day starts out beautiful and falls apart before noon for no reason at all."

"I suppose. Will you please talk to him? I'll wake up. I cannot be forgotten by Samar, Mother. I won't be a footnote in her life as I have been with history."

Asiku hugged Kouji tight. "I'd never let that happen. I will attend your wedding."

Kouji smiled. Her mother was trying hard to comfort her. "I'm not sure if we'll have a wedding, but I'd like you to attend."

Asiku blinked and her face lit up, eyes sparkling like the stars. "I have an idea. I have to go to the Other World."

"Might I come with you?" Kouji asked.

"I'm not sure if you can."

"I have supernatural abilities. Shouldn't that be enough?"

"That's adorable. You think being the daughter of a goddess gives you free rein to move between the realms? There's no guarantee you'd survive the journey. The Other World might decide to keep you. I'm going to face Usuku. He'll likely be angry with me and would have the opportunity to destroy you."

"Would you be able to protect me?"

"I don't know. The Other World doesn't have set rules, only the whims of the gods."

"I don't want you to go alone. If something happens, I want to be aware of it." Kouji would go insane if her mother crossed over and never returned.

Asiku sighed. "I'm opposed to this idea, but you deserve this for all you've suffered, especially being haunted and hunted by Nightmares. We'll have to wake you up. It's important to keep the physical form and spiritual form in the same realm, just in case."

Kouji held back her questions lest her mother change her mind. The void of the tomb changed. An endless darkness surrounded Kouji, waiting to choke the life out of her. Had Asiku left her behind? A sudden jolt followed that moment of doubt. She gasped, sat upright, and banged her head on the lid of her coffin. Kouji grimaced, rubbing her sore head. She eased the top off her resting place. Asiku waited for her, as she freed herself from the casket.

"Well, I suppose we should be off," Asiku said with a shaky voice. Her mother waved her hand, and a shadow enveloped them.

Kouji didn't have time to comprehend what was happening. When their feet touched solid ground, Kouji's mind whirled, dizzy from her first teleportation experience. She shook her head, trying to clear her brain. Her mother glanced down at her and pressed a soft hand to the small of her back. Asiku smiled, as if she found Kouji's discomfort adorable. Kouji tried to glare, but her head continued to swim.

"Is this limbo?" Kouji asked. They were surrounded by nothing but darkness. They could still be in her dream for all she knew. The Other World wasn't supposed to be an endless night, but many different environments.

"This is whatever the divine imagination wishes it to be. This is the land of the gods, something of a border between the physical world and the Other World. It is like a toy to them. You should be safe here since you have divine blood. The king should be here soon." Asiku tilted her head to the side as if listening for something.

"Asiku!" a voice bellowed.

Asiku blew out a breath and shook her head. "He is never late," she muttered.

Kouji frowned at the tone Usuku used to holler her mother's name. Such disrespect and fury, like Usuku already knew. Even so, Usuku still shouldn't call for her mother, the queen, in such a manner.

A blaze of white light turned into fire and formed a tall and broad man. His skin was almost jet black, with a neat mustache and beard. Spots of blond and orange-red hair sprinkled his dark, braided mane and coordinated perfectly with a yellow suit and white vest, and an orange cloth draped over his shoulder with a red wave design that flowed like a golden river. Kouji couldn't help thinking of Samar's macaroni and cheese.

"Usuku, my king," Asiku greeted him with a tight, cold smile.

Usuku's golden gaze burned. "What is the meaning of this?" He pointed at Kouji with an arm that was probably bigger than her whole body.

Asiku sighed. "My king, my child wished an audience with you. We both know it's easiest where I'm meant to live. As you can see, Kouji, I live in eternal darkness."

Usuku wasn't amused. "Should I enlighten you once again, my foolish wife? Like I had to do so many thousands of years ago?"

Asiku waved him off, as if the words meant nothing. "No, my dear husband, I enjoy my night. You simply want me to admit you are better than I."

Usuku folded his arms across his chest. He was well aware he wasn't superior, but Usuku wished it to be true. His desire was more important than the truth, or at least that seemed to be Asiku's gamble. Kouji wasn't sure that'd work. Usuku was unmoved.

"This matter was settled long ago," Usuku said, voice a deep growl.

"Was it, my dear? You unleashed Nightmares into the world and had them hunt my child. You always attempt to make it seem this is because I debased our union by loving a human, putting a human on your level."

Usuku rolled his golden eyes. "We all know you did."

"You're insulted by my being with a human."

A low rumble shook the air around Usuku. "Do you still not get it? It was more than you taking the human as a lover. You dared to love him more than me. You're meant to be my equal."

"You assume me lesser, then get upset that I didn't act as an equal?" Asiku arched an eyebrow.

Usuku circled Asiku. His halo dimmed the closer he got to her, and the dark smoke wafting from her thinned. He rubbed his eyes, looking worn, frustrated.

"What is this?" Usuku motioned to Kouji once more.

"This whole matter is unfair to my child. She's missing out on her life because you're upset with her existence, which doesn't even make any sense. You pretend this is the only child I've had with someone else. She isn't even my first mortal child, yet you've taken this to an extreme."

"It's not about who she is. It's about what she represents."

Asiku snorted and shook her head. "I'm aware. You think she represents this grand love affair I had with humanity. Yet it was all well and good when humanity worshipped the sky you flew through."

"You willingly laid with a human over me, declared to love him more. When have I ever disgraced you in such a way?" Usuku demanded.

Kouji began to understand. This was personal for Usuku and he made it personal for Asiku. Humans chose the Day, he didn't choose them. But Asiku chose a human over Usuku.

"When you took it upon yourself to agree with the humans," Asiku answered.

"We were arguing! They took up with me. They made my argument. What was I meant to do? Apologize for everything I was already saying?" Usuku thrust out his massive arms.

Asiku curled her full lip, pressing a hand to her chest. "Oh, so I was the only one out of line?"

"You refuse to admit you were out of line at all."

Asiku ground her teeth. "You've been with humans, had children with humans. I've never taken it personally."

"Because it never is." He pointed at her. "We both knew that, until that damned argument. You know it was different, and you refuse to admit it. You think I've held onto this rage for all these millennia out of pure spite?"

"Yes."

Usuku flinched. "Okay, maybe some."

That was unexpected.

"You loved Fajiri in ways you never loved me." Usuku's gaze screamed betrayal.

Asiku shrugged. "He was different from you. Our relationship was different. That's how relationships work."

A literal fire burned in Usuku's eyes for a long moment. "So you admit you loved him? Still love him?"

Asiku regarded Usuku as if he were out of his mind. "Yes. That's not the point. Why do you pretend you didn't humiliate me? You didn't defend my equality to the humans, even when you saw how much I was needed. You never told the humans I was just as important. You never once told me I was equally important. The humans had to learn on their own. But you also had to learn how important I was, and you still don't want to admit that. If none of this happened, you'd still fancy yourself my better." The snarling face wasn't how Kouji knew her mother, who gestured angrily at Usuku.

Usuku was silent, gaze turning to Kouji. This was a private matter, but Kouji stood witness. She wasn't sure how Usuku would take the intrusion.

"What do you want of me, Asiku? I can never stop the Nightmares."

Well, that wasn't encouraging.

"Again, look at your reaction. When the humans picked you, I didn't unleash Day-mares to plague humanity forever and always."

"You stole the night from them," Usuku pointed out.

Asiku sucked her teeth. "To let them appreciate it and remind you that we are equals. There's a balance to maintain. What balance do the Nightmares bring, beyond making humans fear the night that much more?"

Usuku rolled his eyes. "Did you not offer ways to combat them?"

"Because they shouldn't have to be afraid of the dark."

Usuku scoffed. "Oh, but humans have a choice with Nightmares. You didn't give them a choice when you took away the night. You punished all of them, when only some of them chose me."

Asiku squared her shoulders. "So you merely want me to admit I was wrong as well?"

"I want you to admit you made things personal."

"As did you, and you took innocent lives. My husband did nothing wrong but appreciate me in ways you didn't, and you stole him from his daughter."

Usuku scowled at Kouji like she was a lower life form, which wasn't wrong. Still, it spoke volumes about how he placed himself above a girl who had never tried to harm him. In fact, Kouji had worshipped him for a great deal of her life. He was King of the Gods, after all.

"So, you want me to admit I took things too far?" Usuku asked.

Asiku's eyebrow went up again. "Did you not?"

Usuku grumbled. Kouji was uncomfortable with this whole thing. It was like watching her parents argue. Not far off. At least they seemed to be making progress. She doubted this was what her mother planned when they first showed up. She hoped Asiku didn't lose sight of their goal.

"Um...have you two never talked about this?" Kouji looked back and forth between the gods.

They both answered at the same time, claiming neither ever listened. Apparently, they gave up after a while. This seemed quite human. Maybe it was a product of interacting with others.

"Usuku," Asiku sighed the name. "Kouji deserves a life as much as anyone else. She shouldn't pay for your feelings toward me or even the slight against you my marriage to Fajiri caused. I won't apologize for loving him, but it's unfair of you to force me to pay penance for that. Perhaps you never loved another the way I loved him, but you have loved others."

Usuku pursed his lips. "I don't understand how you could love him like that. You're my equal. We...we usually at least understand each other."

Asiku ran her hand through her wafting hair. "We do, but every now and then, we might do something that puzzles even the other. Such is life. I don't understand why you went after humanity so harshly by unleashing Nightmares upon them, ruining the night in ways it wasn't meant to be. Even if it was personal, you should've just gone after Fajiri and Kouji. You did so much more."

"What if you both atone to each other?" Kouji suggested, holding up a finger. They might spin their wheels and argue for the rest of eternity. She didn't have that kind of time.

Asiku and Usuku turned to face her. Asiku craned an eyebrow once more. "What would you have us do?"

"Well, first off, you both agree that humanity really has nothing to do with this. You've been trying to hurt each other due to mutual disrespect. In return, you both disrespected the very people who worship you." Kouji tried not to squirm. Who was she to advise the leaders of the gods?

"The humans had less to do with this than we had with needling each other," Asiku agreed.

"It was unfair of us to drag humans into it," Usuku admitted.

"It's also unfair to plague them with Nightmares and steal the sun from a whole city," Kouji said.

"I can't undo the Nightmares. They exist now, just as humans exist, and they have their purposes just as humans do," Usuku replied. "But again, there are tools to combat them." He glanced between Kouji and her mother. "The most I can do is get them to refocus their energy from attempting to hunt you down and destroy you."

"I guess that's fair." Kouji shrugged. "What if you both agree to accept whatever penance the other offers?"

The gods looked at each other. They had to understand this was the only way out of a loop they'd been trapped in for over ten thousand years. They both complained of things that had bothered them forever.

"No other person would dare suggest this to us, you know that?" Usuku said.

Kouji tilted her head. "Why not?"

"No one would dare suggest we were both at fault. Are we not King and Queen of the Gods? Are we not the Day and the Night? Are we not perfect?" Asiku countered. That last one was up for debate, but they didn't need that argument.

Kouji shrugged. "I understand all that, but something has to put this stalemate to rest. You've been at this for so long. What have the other gods suggested? I'm sure they know better than I do."

"They would not dare." Usuku sounded amused.

"And none of the higher beings have offered?" Kouji asked.

Asiku waved her off. "They would never be bothered. Our progenitors find our dealings beneath them."

"Oh, like the gods and humans."

Usuku frowned. "Nothing so simple, but whatever." He turned to his queen and stared her down. "Has this gone on too long?"

"It has," she concurred.

"And we would never dare apologize to each other over this," Usuku said.

Asiku nodded. "Never."

"Then, what is there to be done?" Kouji asked.

Asiku's eyes cut to Usuku. "Will you agree to mutual penance? Then, we can put this whole business behind us."

Usuku folded his arms across his chest. "It seems like it'll be the only way to settle the matter. What are your terms?"

The gods sized each other up. They spoke privately. In the end, they agreed that their punishments wouldn't be forever and they'd share the same fate. They'd live as average humans, giving them both a chance to take in how the other was hurt or humiliated. It'd also give them a chance to experience how they'd hurt humanity. They'd become mortal as soon as they left the Other World.

They made the deal as if Kouji wasn't even present. They sealed everything with a handshake. It seemed so simple. Their will be done.

Samar was showing Alvin and Mechi how to meditate, to help focus them when fighting Nightmares. They had done all right fighting Nightmares the many times she had taken them out, but she didn't trust them on their own yet. The other day, Mechi went out of his way to fight a Nightmare and was almost swallowed into the Nightmare's gaping maw.

"Samar, do you have the Holy Book?" Evinia was scanning Samar's bookshelves once more.

"You have, like, four copies," Samar replied.

"Not in Jinoi," Evinia said.

Samar made a face. "You don't read Jinoi."

"You're going to teach me eventually." Evinia smiled at her.

Samar blew out a breath. "Okay, you're probably right about that. Might have to teach them as well." She pointed to each male at her shoulder.

"I'm gifted at languages." Mechi's grin meant he was joking.

"I won't entertain you," Samar replied. He leaned into that big brother thing more and more each day. It wasn't as annoying as it used to be.

Mechi sucked his teeth. "You're no fun."

"And you're meant to be meditating. Now, focus," Samar ordered.

She checked on Mechi and Alvin to make sure their postures and positions were correct. They were good and dutiful students. Things went well until Evinia gasped. The three warriors tensed.

"What?" all three said in unison, on their feet and ready for war.

"Did Nightmares break in?" Alvin asked.

"No." Evinia stepped closer to the window. She blinked, almost like she was confused.

It hit Samar almost immediately. "Is that the sun coming out?"

"Yeah. The clouds broke." Evinia pointed out the window.

"What do you think that's about?" Mechi asked with raised eyebrows.

Samar's heart thumped. "Kouji." She turned to the door. "I should...I should..." She pointed to the door, unable to form words.

"You think she's awake?" Evinia asked.

She started to leave, forgetting to put on shoes. She was about to open the door when there was a knock. Samar jumped, and everyone behind her dropped into fighting stances.

"Nightmares?" Alvin guessed.

Samar snorted. "Not likely. They've never come knocking on my door, and I've never seen my protections fail." The incident at Moonless Night Security was an exception. Nothing like that had happened before or since.

"Then, who the hell is that? No offense, but everybody you know enough to have at your house is already in your house," Mechi pointed out.

Not everyone. Samar's heart hammered in her chest as she turned back to the door. Could it actually be? She yanked open the door and gasped.

Kouji stood before her with Goddess Asiku behind her. Kouji was dressed as usual and the goddess had on the typical elegant clothing

Samar had become accustomed to seeing her in. Something was off, but it didn't matter.

"Kouji," Samar breathed, happiness overwhelming her entire being to the point where she was momentarily paralyzed.

"Samar!" Kouji rushed her, stepping inside and grabbing Samar into a crushing embrace. Samar's arms went around Kouji's waist without a thought. She held Kouji as close as possible.

Kouji's scent flooded her and calmed her in ways she'd never be able to explain. Her soul took root again. She buried her face in Kouji's neck and inhaled. Kouji laughed.

"May we come in?" Goddess Asiku asked.

Samar pulled away just enough to smile at her. "Of course! Come in! This is Kouji's home as well, after all."

Kouji sniffled. "I'm still welcome?"

"Of course! Are we not engaged?" Samar grinned.

A tear slid down Kouji's cheek. "Even though…even though I fell back to sleep?"

Samar gave Kouji a soft kiss on the cheek. She wasn't sure if Kouji would welcome a kiss on the lips right now. Perhaps that'd be too fast. They had been separated for almost a month, after all.

"Come in and we can all talk over tea." Samar waved both Kouji and Asiku in, then closed the door behind them.

Kouji and Asiku stood before Samar's family. They all stared at each other as if they had never seen one another before. Samar didn't want to process that just yet. She went into the kitchen to prep the tea. She grabbed her best cups, which didn't say much. Still, she couldn't serve a goddess tea in any old thing.

Once everything was on or out, she rejoined the group. Evinia had fetched the dining mat and was in the process of laying it out. Everyone else waited without a word. They all sat down as soon as the mat was flush on the floor.

"No idea if I have anything to serve with the tea," Samar said with an apology in her tone.

Evinia tilted her head. "Didn't we buy cookies at the market?"

Samar brightened. "Oh, right." She looked around. "Are cookies okay? I'm not sure there's enough for anything more."

"It's fine." Kouji reached out and patted her hand.

Everyone waited quietly, as Samar returned to the kitchen. She fixed the tea, poured it into the cups, and put the cups on a tray to serve. Once everyone had a cup of tea in front of them, the silence roared between them.

"So the sun's out," Samar stated the obvious. This should be enough to start some conversation. Why was the sun out? Why was Kouji awake?

"Yes, yes, it is." Asiku nodded. "If you would like me to explain…"

"Please, do," Samar said.

Asiku sipped her tea and winced. "Ow!"

"I'm sorry. I didn't think it was hot." Samar noticed her siblings sipping their tea. They seemed fine.

Kouji patted Samar's knee. "Mother's getting used to being human. Give her some time. Sensation apparently is very different. She thought the sunlight would blind her."

"It beams!" Asiku scowled and pointed out the window.

Samar blinked as she took in what Kouji said. "What do you mean, human?"

Asiku smiled. "I'm currently as human as you and your family." She motioned to them all with a delicate hand.

"Excuse me?" Somehow, this was the most bizarre thing Samar had ever heard in her life. How could a goddess, the very Night, be human?

"Okay, let me start from the beginning," Asiku said. "Kouji's been distraught ever since going back to sleep. She was troubled over not hearing from you."

"I'm sorry," Samar said. "I visited, but I never knew what to say. I didn't want to seem happy, but I also didn't want to seem miserable. You were trying to protect me, but you had wanted and deserved your own life. I wasn't sure how to approach you, so I remained silent."

Kouji sighed, but took Samar's hand. "I would've been happy to hear your voice. I missed you so damn much."

"I missed you too." Samar brought Kouji's hand to her lips and kissed her knuckles. "But that doesn't explain why your mother is human or why you're here?"

Asiku tried her tea again and winced. "I offered to talk to Usuku. We should've had this conversation a long time ago, but it always devolved into an argument about who was at fault. Kouji was restless and wanted to confront him. She convinced me to take her, and her presence made a difference. We had our usual problems, but Kouji said something no god would dare say to us. She suggested a solution."

Evinia arched an eyebrow. "And the solution is for you to be human?"

"Me and Usuku. We're atoning toward each other. Kouji suggested we just punish each other to make up for the sins we committed against each other. It's a task easier said than done."

"But you are human." Evinia's tone was both curious and confused.

Asiku nodded. "I am. As is Usuku."

Samar couldn't fathom this. "How would that even work? You have duties as gods."

"We have others filling in for our duties, while we have to live normal human lives. It took more time than expected. We had to construct lives as humans before donning our new forms," Asiku replied.

"So you have a job?" Alvin asked.

Asiku shook her head. "No, we didn't get to construct that. But we have some knowledge of how your world works. We were given some of the basics, like bank accounts with enough money to keep us alive until we can get jobs."

"Wait, Usuku is out there by himself?" Evinia asked with horror in her eyes.

"Shit." Samar squeaked and turned quickly to Asiku. "Forgive me!"

Asiku waved that off. "Don't worry over that, my dear. I've heard swearing before. And to answer your very good question, no, Usuku is not out there by himself. One of our sons volunteered to come to this plane with him. He's more knowledgeable with everyday human matters. He should keep Usuku safe."

"What happens after you live human lives?" Samar asked.

"The punishment is fulfilled and we return to our divine forms. But we have to really try. Should Usuku go out tomorrow and walk into the ocean, the punishment won't be done, and he'll just reincarnate back into his human form. At the end of our lives, when we die as mortals, we shed these skins and return to our divine selves."

"Do you have a home? What are the basics?" Mechi asked. Good question.

Asiku held up a purse. She pulled out a wallet and a phone. "Um...will these help? I think I have a home. An apartment in the Kalang district."

Mechi's eyes went wide. "Oh, nice."

"May I?" Evinia motioned to the purse.

"Please. I'm sure you all can explain all of this to me." Asiku handed the purse to Evinia. "Well, to us." She pointed to Kouji. "Just as I get to live my life, Kouji now gets to live hers. Nightmares will, unfortunately, continue to roam the planet. But they won't be hunting Kouji like before. They will still be tempting humans. The sun is now allowed here in Oganja. The day has returned."

Kouji turned to Samar. "And I'd like to return if you'll have me."

"Of course." Samar latched onto Kouji, not caring that she spilled her tea. She held Kouji tight. "We're still engaged."

Kouji let loose a happy sob. "Yes! Please!"

Evinia smiled. "I think we should celebrate. We can make a huge dinner and get to know each other." She turned to Asiku. "I can help you navigate whatever basics you have for your life."

"Yes, thank you." Asiku smiled.

"So, meal first," Evinia said.

Samar nodded, loving that idea. After they finished their tea, Evinia and Asiku went to the kitchen. Mechi and Alvin offered to go out for snacks in a very unsubtle way of leaving Samar and Kouji alone. They moved closer to each other.

"We can be together, if you want," Kouji said.

Samar's brow wrinkled. "Of course I want that. I'm sorry for leaving you to think otherwise. I really just couldn't bring myself to say anything to you. It all seemed wrong. You being gone seemed wrong."

"It felt wrong to not be here."

"So everything will be okay?" Samar's heart raced, fearful of an answer she was certain wouldn't come.

Kouji shrugged. "As far as I know. Are you still planning to hunt Nightmares?"

"It's a family business now," Samar said. "We're working on getting Vinny to see at least impressions of them."

"Room for one more?" Kouji asked.

"If that's what you want. This is your life now. You get to live it the way you want to."

Kouji kissed Samar's knuckles. "Then, yes. I like fighting Nightmares with you. Besides, unlike Mother, I still have my divine powers."

Samar sighed, contentment washing over her. She rested her head on Kouji's shoulder, and Kouji kissed the top of her head. They sat just like that until Evinia and Asiku served dinner. Mechi and Alvin had returned at some point with special drinks for this special occasion. They had a great meal around the dining mat, and Evinia toasted the return of Kouji, Samar's betrothed. Everyone else raised a glass. Things would be all right.

The End.

Other Books by S.L. Kassidy

Warrior Class
Sky Cutter
Taming the Wind
Blood Rain

Please Baby

Scarred Series
Scarred for Life - Book 1
New Cuts, Old Wounds – Book 2
Bandages – Book 3
First Degree Burns - Book 4
Learning to Walk Again – Book 5

Nature of the Beast

About S. L. Kassidy

What is there to know about me? Not much. I was born, bred, and raised in New York, and I have no desire to live anywhere else. One day, I would like to travel to a few places, but for now I am content where I am.

I started out writing poetry in junior high and continued to do so for ten years. I wrote short stories, usually fantasy and romance stories, for my own entertainment throughout high school and college. Back then, I wrote strictly for me and those stories remain locked in the back of my closet in little notebooks, written in my almost unreadable, tiny handwriting. In between writing those stories and poetry, I managed to get a college degree in history.

After graduating college, I had a semester off before graduate school, and I didn't really have anything to do with my time. So I took a chance and wrote a fanfic and dared to upload it to the Internet. I was surprised that other people enjoyed my work, and I've been posting ever since. I had quite a bit of fun with fan fiction and eventually decided to try my hand in original fiction. I suppose it was sort of like coming back around to what I had been doing in high school and college, except this time the stories were for whoever wanted to read them. After I uploaded my first original story, I didn't looked back. I plan to continue writing as long as I continue getting ideas for stories and it continues to be fun.

Connect with Shea
Email: slkassidy@gmail.com
Facebook: S.L. Kassidy

Note to Readers

Thank you for reading a book from Desert Palm Press. We appreciate you as a reader and want to ensure you enjoy the reading process. We would like you to consider posting a review on your preferred media sites and/or your blog or website.

For more information on upcoming releases, author interviews, contests, giveaways and more, please sign up for our newsletter and visit us at Desert Palm Press: www.desertpalmpress.com and "Like" us on Facebook: Desert Palm Press.

Bright Blessings

www.ingramcontent.com/pod-product-compliance
Lightning Source LLC
LaVergne TN
LVHW040041080526
838202LV00045B/3427